A Royal
Abduction

ETT IMPRINT & www.arthurupfield.com
PO Box R1906
Royal Exchange NSW 1225
Australia

First published by Hutchinson & Company 1932.

First electronic edition published by ETT Imprint 2015.
Published in paperback by ETT Imprint 2015, reprinted 2020 with the help of Upfield scholar Kees De Hoog.

ISBN 9781922698612 (pbk)
ISBN 9780994309648 (ebk)

A Royal

Abduction

Arthur W. Upfield

ETT Imprint
Exile Bay

CONTENTS

A ROYAL ABDUCTION

PART I

THE ABDUCTION

CHAPTER I

EARLE LAWRENCE

IT can be stated that the abduction of Her Royal Highness the Princess Natalie of Rolandia was an indirect effect of the Great War on the mentality of Earle Lawrence. The war broadened his mind, opened it as sunlight opens the bud of a flower.

He was in his twentieth year when the war broke out and he hastened to enlist – riding some two hundred miles from his father's station in the far west of South Australia to reach the nearest recruiting depot. At that time he was quite an unexceptionable young man, possessing no more than ordinary faults of character, and many virtues which endeared him to his people, and made him popular with his father's stockmen.

It is said that Australia either makes or breaks the man who emigrates there. With equal truth it can be said that the furnace of the war melted character and remoulded it, the finished product seldom being precisely what might have been expected. Young Lawrence went to the war carrying a heart aflame with ideals of patriotism and chivalry. The trenches stripped from him the first of these ideals, but not the second. Whilst he retained his consideration for weak men, women, and children, he came thoroughly to believe that rich men, singly or in combination, were fair game to be plundered by those capable of plundering.

The war moulded him, physically and mentally, for the five terrific years he spent in America as a member of the most efficient and ruthless gang of bootleggers, dope merchants, and smugglers of Asiatics with which that country ever was cursed. Not for him to be reshackled by Peace with the chains of Restraint and Convention. Receiving his discharge from the Australian Imperial Forces in London after over five years of army life, he bitterly grieved his father and mother by going west to Canada, thence passing to America, where he met a man who introduced him to the "Ace" of the B., D. and C. Pack, which being interpreted means the nameless head of the Booze, Drugs and Chinamen Gang.

At the end of the first year of his association with these people he had risen to the position of "King" of the B., D. and C. Pack, responsible to the "Ace" for an army of some two thousand men and women. It is not impossible that he would have dethroned the "Ace" himself, had he not fallen in love with a woman who declined his advances.

So serious was this rejection that Earle Lawrence decided to quit America and to return home, there to settle down and try to make up to his people for the heartache he had caused them. But he had gone too far. The years of danger and of constant mental excitement were too many to permit calm, placid, cow-like days to be lived contentedly again. He conceived the astonishing plan of abducting at one and the same time a Princess and his former superior, the Ace of the B., D. and C. Pack.

On the morning of December 2nd, 1927, he stood on a wharf of Fremantle Harbour watching the 17,000-ton luxury liner *S.S. Rajah* swing in between the horns of the breakwater and creep slowly up the fairway. Conspicuously he stood, among many hundreds of welcoming spectators, watching the marine mammoth without a thrill at sight of her copper-coloured hull, blue-topped funnels, and the beautiful lines of her cruiser-stern; for he was thinking of 45-knot motor-boats and howling blizzards roaring across the Great Lakes, and of the man who financed and directed the vast trade in contraband from Chicago.

What a man was the Ace! Invariably icily calm, clever to the point of devilishness, and perfectly ruthless in action; an enigma, an unknown, to all save the King, the Queen, and the twenty Jacks. Never a mistake made in the planning of a *coup*, the part of each unit clearly defined in perfect co-ordination with the whole. A man who met failure among the rank and file with dismissal, and a man who ordained death, sure and swift, for treachery on the part of his officers.

It was the Queen whom Earle Lawrence had grown to love, the woman who had held equal authority with himself, and she was the daughter of the Ace; a woman of beauty and brains, fired by a not uncommon yet unworthy ambition.

She with her father stood among the hundreds of passengers lining the deck-rails of the approaching vessel. Lawrence sought for her vividly-remembered face long before it was possible for those on the quay to distinguish features. His heart ached for the sight of her, and because of his desire for her a daring and complex plan was ripening to execution in his mind.

As a pelican slowly gliding along a quiet lagoon the great ship moved up the harbour with hardly a ripple at her bow. She certainly was the last word in floating luxury, and all her passengers were wealthy, the majority of them dollar millionaires. They were seeing the world in comfort on this especially chartered ship, which had taken them to Europe, showed them Asia, was making her last port of call in Australia, and would take them on to Africa and South America. There was on that floating castle nothing wanting that money could buy. It was a pleasure yacht hired by a party of millionaires who temporarily made of the world a playground. A constellation of four hundred Midases. Money! Money! Money! Millions upon millions of American dollars flowed hither and thither at the will of these Gods of the Heaven of Money.

"A little bird whispered that you wanted me."

So softly were the words spoken that Lawrence did not hear them until they were repeated. They came from his left, and, slowly turning, he gazed a little vacantly into a face that was long and thin, with a receding chin and probably a receding forehead, too, had not the old felt hat concealed it. It was a weak face, in odd contrast with the widely-spaced blue eyes, clear and steady. The whisperer was shorter than Lawrence, or seemed so, and his clothes were rough and soiled.

"I remember your face, although I don't remember your name," Lawrence said in his pleasing drawl. "Why should I want you?"

"Dunno, 'zactly. Blue Everett kind of hinted you was looking for me. I'm Knight. You remember Sir Knight, and–Amiens?"

"Ah!"

Lawrence breathed the exclamation. Amiens! When he and this man and hundreds of others walked through Amiens in small parties, keeping in the middle of the streets to avoid the falling glass from the buildings that rocked from the explosions of aerial bombs. The roar of the explosions, the tinkling of breaking glass, the hum of the raiders' engines. They had been forbidden to enter the abandoned buildings, and camped that night in the central square. But before dawn, when the German 'planes returned with fresh loads of bombs, he and this man, "Sir" Knight, had looted seven jewellers' shops and carefully selected gems that eventually netted them many hundreds of pounds.

Money! He had had sufficient money for his needs, but he had not been satiated with excitement even by the war, but needs must go on looting, risking detection and death. Yes, he wanted this man standing before him.

With a jerk of his head he invited Sir Knight to follow him out of the surrounding press of humanity. He sauntered to the corner of the adjacent wharf shed, and not immediately Knight followed. When he did join Lawrence the latter questioned him rapidly.

"What are you doing now?"

"Wharf lumping," Knight answered.

"Have you been in gaol?"

"No –" with a grim laugh.

"You are not known officially to the police?"

"No."

For several seconds Earle Lawrence studied the weak yet alert face of Sir Knight. In years Knight was about forty-five; in ripeness of experience he was about a hundred and forty-five. Born in Rio de Janeiro, of Irish parents, he had spent his first twenty-five years on the pampas plains of South America. Lawrence had seen him first in the desert of Egypt, giving an exhibition of revolver shooting in the approved style of Deadwood Dick. The man's quickness and accuracy were astounding. Lawrence spoke very softly.

He said: "I want a man able to shoot, willing to shoot how I want him to shoot, a man willing to obey orders without question, for about three months. For his three months' service I am prepared to pay handsomely. For three months' service I am prepared to pay you one thousand pounds."

"When do I start?" Knight asked anxiously.

"At the moment I cannot quite tell you that. I shall know for certain to-morrow afternoon. At six o'clock to-morrow evening you will call at the Savoy and ask for me."

"All right. That'll do me."

"Very well. Do you happen to know where Warrant-Officer Bussey now is?"

"Yes. A bloke told me only last week that he was wheat-lumping at Burracoppin."

"That is on the goldfields line, is it not?"

"Yes. About two hundred miles east of here."

"What time does the Kalgoorlie express leave to-morrow night?"

"About half-past eight."

"Well then, as you may have to go to Burracoppin on that train, you had better be dressed for the journey when you come to the Savoy Hotel."

"You're not wanting me to shoot up the old man, are you?"

Lawrence laughed. "Rather not," he replied good-humouredly. "If I undertake the stunt for which I want you, I want him to be my second officer, if he is willing. Anyway, Sir Knight, to-morrow at the Savoy at six."

When Earle Lawrence edged himself once more into the crowd the liner was being warped into the quay. The crowd was cheering, and the cheers were answered by those on the ship. On the cruiser-stern the ship's band was playing the latest jazz hit from Broadway and the ship's complement, dressed in white uniforms, were throwing into the air little multi-coloured balloons that rose swiftly to the cloudless sky. The brilliantly coloured scene was typical of an Australian harbour in midsummer. Yet it was not the air or the scene which excited the heart of Earle Lawrence; it was the serene face of one woman of the many who leaned on the ship's deck-rail.

CHAPTER II

THE VAN HORTONS

MR. VAN HORTON leaned against the rail guarding the top promenade deck of the s.s. *Rajah* and gazed down at the crowd swarming on the wharf. He was not thinking of the vast underworld organisation of which he was the head, nor of the fearless man who at one time had been his brilliant first officer. He was thinking that, after all, the United States of America was not the world, although it might be the world's centre.

The tour had been a revelation. Europe he had found of absorbing interest. Egypt had laid on him the spell of a mighty past. India had given him understanding of the British genius for government. Japan and China mystified him, whilst the islands of the Pacific and of Malaysia revealed to him an undreamt-of world. It was the vast continent of Australia, seen through its cities, short journeys into the country, and glimpses of its coastline, which stirred his imagination and gave to his mind the clarity of the visionary.

He saw distinctly that no longer were the Americas the New World. Their newness was gone, worn away by the gigantic influx of European immigration. They were modern, no longer new. Time had shifted the New World to Australia, and, when this southern world supported a full-grown nation, America would be fighting for a place in the sun.

It admits of no doubt that these thoughts running in the mind of Mr. Van Horton were the fruit of knowledge that the United States was rapidly becoming too small for Mr. Van Horton. He had made twenty-seven million dollars out of spirits, drugs, and prohibited immigrants, but the very nature of his business had compelled him to hide his light under a bushel. The tour had brought the position acutely home to him, for he had been obliged to swallow the unpalatable fact that he "cut no ice" with great world personalities. This, as well as other impressions of the tour, tended to diminish his importance and dignity in his own esteem.

Like all exceptionally clever men, Mr. Van Horton was vain. It may be justifiably assumed that had he returned to America the impressions of his world tour would rapidly have become blunted, and he might well have appeased his vanity by passing from the world of illicit trading to that of politics without his business acumen or his morals receiving any jar.

To observe his stocky figure, to examine his dead-white face, was to receive the impression that he was a tenth-rate stockbroker. It was not until Van Horton's steel-grey eyes bored into one that his dynamic personality was revealed. Here was a man small of body but big of brain; insignificant in physical appearance, great in mentality. No one seemed ever to have known Mrs. Van Horton, yet her mating with this man must have been an attraction of opposites. The offspring of that union was Helen, a woman with her father's mind and her mother's physical perfection.

She stood beside Van Horton, her elbows resting on the broad teak rail. Slightly above the average height of women, Helen Van Horton was of the true Saxon type and beauty which invariably arrest the attention of men of all creeds and races. Her eyes of greyish-green had her father's trick of steady penetration, which she sought always to veil under languorous drooping lids. That was the only thing in common she held with him, save the gift of attracting or repelling other people with remarkable ease. Not yet thirty years of age, her pose was sure and regal. A woman – a very lovely woman indeed to look at – a woman whose voice matched her looks: slow, soft, and made the more fascinating by a slight Virginian accent.

"If that is not Earle Lawrence, then it must be his ghost," she said.

"Er – what's that?" demanded Van Horton, startled out of his day-dreaming.

"Really, Pops, isn't this voyage enough of a bore without my having to repeat what you distinctly heard?"

Once more his alert self, her father inquired blandly: "You said something about Earle Lawrence?"

"You'll see him standing at the corner of that wharf shed. Please do not make me point."

Van Horton's brilliant eyes carefully searched each feature of his daughter's face as though he would see there the cause of her boredom. "You seem peeved this morning, my dear," he said, in his habitual expressionless tone of voice. Then, turning his gaze shoreward, for several seconds he stared at the well-built figure dressed in white duck, white shoes, and white sun-helmet. He noted with approval how spotless was that raiment. It was the kind of rig the immaculate Lawrence would wear, and if further proof were needed it was to be seen in the long black cheroot held at the angle of a howitzer-gun by the firm lips. "Thought he was in China," the millionaire murmured.

"It is all the same," Helen drawled.

Van Horton shrugged as he had seen Frenchmen shrug. "Well,

anyway, he'll be better than a Cook's guide," he said.

"I believe he will be. He can be very interesting if only he wouldn't keep looking at me with soppy eyes."

"It is better, my girl, to be regarded with what you term soppy eyes than with eyes of indifference or loathing," Van Horton said significantly. "I liked Lawrence because I found him an exceptionally clever man, a reliable man, and a man of determination. His faults are few in our profession, but would be virtues in a minister. He would have made an excellent bishop. Come along! Let's meet him."

Already many of the American visitors had disembarked and were making their way through the crowd to the river steamer that was to take them to Perth. On this steamer a band was playing, as though in opposition to the ship's band, music far more sedate, music that held a lilting marching strain, played by quite young men and youths in the uniform of the Young Australia League.

Van Horton's vanity was fed from a rare dish. The music, the welcoming crowd, the sirens of the shipping, the brilliant day and the sparkling colours flattered his self-importance. Such welcomes had been extended by the cities of Sydney, Melbourne, and Adelaide. All through Europe their presence had been officially ignored, but here was a people who recognised wealth and worldly success, and willingly paid unstinted homage to him and his fellow Midases. Without doubt these Australians were a warm-hearted, worthy, discriminating people.

When his daughter and he reached the wharf Van Horton subconsciously altered the angle of his panama hat and patted his blue tie. He was unconscious of throwing back his shoulders when the crowd made way for them. People stared. He thought they stared at him, whereas all eyes were centred on the fair-complexioned Helen, arrayed in a frock of forget-me-not chiffon she had purchased in Paris. Through the crowd they saw Earle Lawrence walking as though he were a battleship and the people a huddle of fishing-boats.

"Good day-ee, Van!" he said in his distinct way. "Day-ee, Helen! It's good to see you again."

They were shaking hands. It was two years since Helen had seen this man, who so often had borne her company in fierce adventures and breath-taking situations. He was the one man she never could subdue with a look or snub into confusion. Whilst he stood before her with bared head she discovered that the years had made no difference to him. It was as though the icy winds and scorching suns had fortified his skin with some time-defying balm. His hair was still a glinting brown, with riotous waves. His clean-shaven face bore then, as always it had done, an expression of amused tolerance of the moods and foibles of humanity in the mass. His eyes, invariably half hidden behind lowered lids, now as in the past revealed in their grey depths the spirit that *would* be free.

"It is a surprise to meet you here, Mr. Lawrence," Helen said, emphasizing the "Mr." a point.

"Yes, Lawrence, it is a surprise. Surely you're not here to meet us especially?"

"I am," the Australian told them. "I have been kept informed of your progress through Australia by the newspapers, and decided to do my little bit in cementing the universally-desired friendship between America and Australia. With our countries united in brotherly affection, neither need fear the Asiatic."

"Hear, hear!" cried a listening bystander with enthusiasm.

"Piff!" murmured Van Horton, failing to understand that the welcome was not extended because of the financial standing of the visitors. He said loudly, however: "I agree – I agree, my dear Lawrence. The great Saxon peoples must unite to face the growing Yellow Peril. However, we are going to Perth. Your city offers us its hospitality. Come along with us, and point out the places of interest."

So with Van Horton on her right and Earle Lawrence on her left, Helen Van Horton was escorted to the waiting river steamer *Zephyr*.

They found standing room aft; and, when the usual questions regarding their various healths in the immediate past and the present had been asked and answered, they fell momentarily into silence.

Earle Lawrence knew that the short voyage up the river Swan to the city of Perth would reveal more to the visitors than he possibly could. The sunlit air, as clear as crystal, brought the river banks and the tiers of houses on the low hills beyond them to within hands reach. He was proud of his superb country; he knew his pride had solid foundation.

Van Horton, whilst gazing at the slow-moving panorama, was not a little astonished by it. His ideas regarding Australia had been vague, and he saw here as he had seen elsewhere proofs that this vast country was not inhabited by naked savages and a few wild-whiskered men in big hats and top-boots brandishing stockwhips. The panorama was endless and entrancing. All the way to Perth, some twelve miles from Fremantle, houses were dotted over the low hills, houses that stood in their own grounds, shaded by ornamental trees, cool and inviting.

Whilst they swung round Woodman's Point, with the great sweep of high ground on their left over which later in the day they were to motor through King's Park, the Van Hortons silently looked ahead to where the City of Perth flowed up from its esplanades, over the crest of the high ground, in great buildings, pointed here and there with church towers and factory chimneys.

"I believe," Van Horton said slowly, "I believe this is the loveliest city I have seen, excepting perhaps Sydney."

"Well, you have now seen all the cities. What do you say to allowing me to show you the real Australia?" Lawrence murmured. "Next month the Princess Natalie of Rolandia visits Australia. Why not join me in kidnapping her? She is good for a million-dollar ransom."

CHAPTER III

PLANS AND PLANS

FROM the moment the Van Hortons and their fellow globetrotters landed at the Barrack Street jetty at Perth there occurred no further opportunity for Earle Lawrence to enlarge on his astounding proposition. Van Horton himself forgot about it. For the fourth time in his life he found himself to be an Important Personage.

This day much incense was offered to the vanity of Van Horton. On the jetty the visitors were received by the Lord Mayor of Perth, attended by the chief dignitaries of the city. After the civic reception the visitors were taken through the streets in motor-cars. They were entertained at lunch in several hotels, and during the afternoon many of them were motored through the Darling Ranges, east of the city. They were the guests that evening of members of the Rotary Club, the Australian Natives Association (whose members, strangely enough, are white folk), or the Chamber of Commerce. The Americans were made to feel that their visit was an historical event, a national honour, and the hospitality extended to these amassers of the dollar was lavish in the extreme.

The following day the Van Hortons were the guests of Earle Lawrence. Calling for them at their hotel, he motored them to his house built among the hills a little distance from Kalamunda. It was not a large house, nor was it expensively furnished, but from its wide-shaded veranda there was to be had an uninterrupted view of the Swan River lying like a silver snake on a mosaic flooring which was Perth, with Fremantle on the further edge bathed by the blue ribbon of the Indian Ocean.

After lunch they three lounged on the veranda, Van Horton lying back in his chair, his head supported by clasped hands, and Helen gazing at the wonderful view through powerful binoculars.

"You know, there is a definite peculiarity about your cities which I have found nowhere else in the world," she said, suddenly lowering the glasses and gazing straight at Lawrence, who was seated on the low veranda wall, idly swinging one flannelled leg and smoking a cigarette.

"What is that?" he asked.

"It is a little difficult to explain," she replied slowly, once more using the binoculars. "Your cities appear to be free, living things. Other cities look as if chained down; yours flow out into the infinite as though impatient of restraint. Look there! Perth appears to be a great metropolis twice as large as New York – a metropolis of garden suburbs. Yesterday you said something about the coming visit of Natalie of Rolandia. What precisely did you mean?"

The abrupt change of subject caused Van Horton to sit up and search for his cigar-case.

"Ah! I had forgotten that little statement-cum-suggestion, Lawrence," he said, after opening the case. "If my memory is correct you said something about kidnapping the Heiress Apparent to the Rolandian throne. You are flying high, my boy; but spill it."

Lawrence found the other's eyes boring into him. The stare he returned, smiling. "You are really interested?"

"Interested in anything and everything; even such a fool idea as abducting a princess."

"May I explain?" Lawrence asked of Helen.

Once more she lowered the glasses to look at him from beneath drooping lids. The look fired him and she knew it. She liked him well enough to torment him. "Anything about a real princess will interest me," she told him with unwonted emphasis.

Slipping from the rail, he took the vacant chair between them and lit the cheroot he produced from the box lying on the small mahogany table. "The idea occurred to me two weeks ago as I read the official programme of her visit to Australia," he said in preamble. "Since then I have read up the history of the country and its politics.

"The House of Pravoff has ruled Rolandia for nearly six centuries. It has ruled with an iron hand, whether hidden or not in a velvet glove. Even the Great War and its effects on emperors and kings failed to shake the power of the Pravoffs. You may remember that the old king, Charles, who died during the last year of the war, had two sons: Boris the elder and Peter the younger.

"Boris, the Crown Prince, was a dud. Had he been a common person he would have been hanged. Of that his acts leave no doubt. Peter was the old man's favourite, and the favourite of both Court and country. He was popular and a real sportsman. King Charles brought pressure to bear on the incorrigible Boris to step down in favour of his brother; but Boris wasn't having any, and no pottage was good enough to tempt him to sell his birthright.

"So the old man called a secret Cabinet meeting where it was decided that on his death Peter should be proclaimed king, and if Boris kicked he was to be banished out of the country. That was a week prior to the old king's sudden illness and death.

"There appears no doubt that the illness was genuine enough, and that his death was not unduly accelerated. The same cannot be said of the death of Peter. He died very suddenly from an assassin's bullet, and it was rumoured that the killer was hired by Boris. It was significant that the probable assassin, whom no one dared to accuse in public, was eventually promoted to the rank of general in the army. And the army is quite an efficient machine, too.

"Now Peter had one child, the Princess Natalie. She is the next in succession, because whilst Boris was Crown Prince he fell in love with a blacksmith's daughter, who would be satisfied with nothing less than marriage. Even in half-civilised Rolandia the methods of seventeenth century aristocrats with women are not regarded with favour; so Boris, who was keen, married her.

"His love for this woman is the only decent thing known of him. He has consistently refused to marry a woman of royal blood, and has consistently demanded that his legal wife be made Queen. This no section of public opinion will permit, and last year Natalie was legally made the Heiress Apparent.

"I met a man only last week who had travelled much in Rolandia, and he told me that since the death of King Charles extraordinary precautions have been taken for the safety of the Princess Natalie. You see, influential Rolandians had Boris' measurements to the inch; and, whilst they put up with him on the basis of grin and bear it, they were not taking any chances of losing the last of the House of Pravoff and being obliged to recognise the eldest son of the blacksmith's daughter as the coming King.

"Natalie I have never seen. She is, as you may know, a very pretty girl, a dark beauty of twenty-three years. It is universally agreed that she is the most popular Princess in Europe, her popularity being based on two foundation pillars of great strength. In the first place she treats Boris with open contempt and ignores the possible danger of hired assassins, causing her retinue constant worry. She interests herself in any movement that aims to better the conditions of the people. That endears her to the Rolandians. When, after listening to the persuasions of the diplomats, she resolutely refused to marry the Crown Prince of Lohenmarke and publicly stated that she would marry when she liked and where she liked or loved, the gentleman's father said many nasty things, and it was only by great luck that the League of Nations prevented a brawl. A Princess who demands love in marriage and has the pluck to say so quite logically enraptures our modern democracies.

"The fact that several of the Big Powers have been engaged in a diplomatic battle concerning certain important alliances and trade concessions is generally known. Boris flatly declines to favour any country, not because he fears the others, but because he thinks that as Rolandia has done well in her isolation for many years, she can continue to do well as she is. And Boris is one of those grimly obstinate cusses.

"Coming to the Princess herself, she decided some time ago to broaden her mind by undertaking a world tour. She seems tremendously keen to fit herself for the task of queenship. Several of the Big Powers, to further their individual claims, and believing that Natalie will be more amenable to reason than King Boris, have done everything of an official nature to organise the welcome of their peoples. Great Britain has loaned her a battle-cruiser, and everywhere in the Empire she has been accorded great ovations.

"When she comes to Australia she will be surprised at the warmth and affection with which she will be greeted. We have had much practice in the art of welcoming the world's elite. We spend money lavishly, but as it is borrowed money no one seems to mind."

Lawrence was smiling cynically. His hearers certainly were keenly interested.

Van Horton was impatient. "Well," he urged, "get right down to it."

"According to the official programme," Lawrence went on, "the Princess is due to reach Sydney on the morning of December 26th. She will arrive at Melbourne January 1st. Before reaching Adelaide, where she is due January 10th, she will stay with Sir Henry and Lady Lund at Mount Lofty for three days. After two days spent in Adelaide she will leave for Port Augusta, where she will travel over the Great Western line to Western Australia, arriving at Perth January – but there, we trust she will not arrive at Perth.

"Now, from the time she reaches Sydney until she arrives at Port Augusta, any attempt at abduction would inevitably fail. Whilst it would be possible to hold up her train and take her from it, it would be wholly impossible to keep her. The eastern and southeastern seaboards are too thickly populated. The opportunity occurs during her crossing the great Nullarbor Plain of South Australia – a plain practically empty of people, save a few blacks.

"Foreseeing that during the crossing of the plain no more danger from lunatics and assassins could be expected than if she were crossing the South Pole, we may assume that her guard will be composed only of a few policemen. One second, please!"

Lawrence entered the house through one of the open French windows, to return almost instantly with a large-scale map. This he spread out over the table, and the Van Hortons rose to stand beside him. His voice betrayed unwonted excitement.

"See! Here is Eucla, on the Great Australian Bight. Till recently it was the most important telegraph transmission station, linking the west and east of the continent. When the Great Western Railway was built, the instruments and staff were transferred to Cook, which, as you see, is five hundred and thirteen miles from Port Augusta, and roughly seventy miles from Eucla.

"To-day there is not a soul living at Eucla. Here, twenty miles east of Eucla, are vast underground caves which are known only to me and one other bushman. Please keep in mind Caves, Eucla, and Cook. They are the key points.

"It is morally certain that the Commonwealth Government will place a special train at the service of the Princess Natalie. When it reaches Cook, we take her from the train, rush her by car to Eucla, abandon the car at Eucla, and use camels to take her to the underground caves. Once there, the possibility of rescue is extremely remote."

"Why not take her off the train at Deakin?" Van Horton interjected. "It is much nearer to Eucla."

"Because from Eucla to Cook there is a road, and from Eucla to Deakin and Hughes there is no road," Lawrence replied. "There are three contingencies to be guarded against. One, is to make sure that on the day of the abduction no overland motorist reaches Eucla from either east or west; two, that we are not pursued from Cook until after at least four hours; and three, that for several days before and after the abduction there are no aboriginals, not one, within the triangle represented by Forrest, Fisher, and Eucla. These three points I can deal with successfully."

"How would the blacks interfere?" inquired Helen languidly on reseating herself.

"After the hold-up the authorities will most certainly gather up the nigs and use them as trackers," Lawrence explained. "I can deal with them in a way that will ensure their not being within the triangle I have mentioned. Were they not so dealt with, it would be difficult to avoid being seen somewhere between Eucla and the caves. Although they are hardly likely to number more than sixty, yet the danger of observation would exist. After we leave Eucla, we have to cover our tracks so thoroughly that the most expert of them will not see which way we passed."

"We would want men," Van Horton put forward tentatively. "I have at command twenty excellent men."

"They would have to be-excellent."

"They equal the best in the B., D. and C. Pack."

"Have you worked out the costs?"

"Yes. The whole scheme could be put through for forty thousand pounds."

"Dollars?"

"Rather less than two hundred thousand."

"Have you fixed the ransom money?"

"Yes. We could get a million dollars."

"We couldn't get *one*."

"Eh!"

"I said we couldn't get a dollar."

Van Horton was leaning back in his chair, his pudgy fingers meeting in the form of an arch on which his chin rested. His white face was expressionless, but his eyes were almost glaring.

"We cannot use our American methods here because we have not our American organisation. Neither No. 1 nor No. 2 abduction plan could be used. There isn't the time to organise channels through which we could reach the proper people in Rolandia. I doubt if there could be any method evolved by which we could secure the money in safety. Time certainly is against us. The demand for money must follow immediately after the abduction, because every minute which passes after an abduction increases the risk of discovery. No. It won't do. Your plan may be foolproof. I should be better able to judge after hearing the details and going over the ground. But ransom – you won't get it."

"I agree. You wouldn't get a cent," Helen said in her slow way.

"Humph!" Earle Lawrence, who had been standing by the map-covered table, began to pace the veranda in silence. He possessed what colloquially is known as a "poker face". In his heart he was satisfied, because he had foreseen that the point when next he spoke. He was bluffing with what is known in poker as a routine flush, and his name for a routine flush at the moment was – vanity.

He was fully cognizant of Van Horton's greatest failing. He was aware, too, of Helen Van Horton's ambition to rise high in society, an ambition that had barred him from her desired embraces. Her rejection of him had not embittered him in the slightest. It merely spurred his determination to win. And he was fashioning weapons to bring him victory.

"I thought it probable you would raise that objection," he said blandly. "Therefore I have a second suggestion to make. Please understand right now that I have no very keen wish to make much money, for I have quite sufficient for my needs. What I want is excitement, and this abduction would provide it. It would be the greatest, the most famous *coup* in all history. A nation entertains a royal lady who some day will be a Queen, and we simply pluck her from the welcoming arms of that nation, and, in effect, say: 'What about it?'"

And Lawrence laughed infectiously.

"Let us have your alternative proposition," Van Horton prompted, his pulses suddenly quickened.

"Well, let us suppose the Princess is successfully abducted. She is taken by Earle Lawrence, Australia's premier bandit, to the underground caves east of Eucla. There she meets fellow-prisoners in distress in the forms of Mr. and Miss Van Horton, who are forcibly abducted whilst on a motor trip into these hills. The situation would compel mutual sympathy. Almost certainly it would compel warm friendship between the Princess and Miss Van Horton.

"Eventually, by trickery, Mr. Van Horton prevails over the terrible Earle Lawrence and his gang, and is instrumental in restoring the Princess to freedom and her position in life. It is quite possible that the Princess would wish to show some mark of appreciation of the services rendered her. Knowing that the Van Hortons are millionaires and therefore people of consequence in the States, she could make them no material presents. What better could she do than press upon them an invitation to visit Rolandia, there to become her guests and temporary members of her Court?

"Think!" Lawrence urged, "Think!"

Van Horton's eyes were gleaming whilst his brain raced. Lawrence could not look into Helen's eyes. She was using the binoculars again, and at the farther end she saw, not Perth, but a Throne Room, a Queen seated, and Helen Van Horton standing near as the Queen's friend.

"You would become world-famous," drawled the tempter. "Every newspaper in the world would be printing your names. Millions of people would know of the Van Hortons. You could give up the B., D. and C. Pack and enter politics. Your nomination for the Governorship would be assured, your ultimate victory certain."

"But what of you? What would you get out of it? What would you want?" were sudden questions fired by Van Horton.

Lawrence yawned. The pose of indifference was perfect. With a movement of his hand he indicated the house. When he spoke there was impatience in his voice.

"Can't you understand?" he said. "I lived four epic years of war. They were followed by five fierce years in the Pack. And now – what?

Nothing. I am like a man deprived of cocaine. I am suffering the after-effects of prolonged mental excitement. I am so bored with life as it now is that sometimes I could cut my own throat. Let us go more fully into the scheme. It is perfect, you will agree. And then, for the love of Mike, let us have some action."

"I'll promise nothing," was Van Horton's wary assent.

CHAPTER IV

NATALIE

WELL-NIGH everyone of us is at heart a royalist. Furthermore, nearly everyone of us is a snob. There is not a man or woman who is not conscious of superiority to someone else and, at the same time, of inferiority to some other someone else. From the time men started living together in communities these hereditary characteristics have been gathering force, so that to-day the more democratic a people may seem to be, the more enthusiastic is that people's welcome to visiting Royalties or other outstanding individuals.

The Heiress Apparent to the throne of Rolandia was well accustomed to cheering crowds. From earliest memory she had been used to men bowing and women curtseying, and to both in mass waving and roaring welcome. During her tour countless thousands had paid her homage, primarily because she was of Royal blood, and secondarily because her dark vivacious beauty was stamped by millions of pictures on the hearts of millions of men. She had caught and held the admiration of the world by her stubborn refusal to marry where policy dictated but heart demurred.

Accustomed though she was to adulation throughout her twenty-three years, Natalie was overwhelmed by the welcome accorded her by the people of Sydney. There was that in the spontaneous enthusiasm which met her when she landed and accompanied her all the way to Government House which astonished and startled her. Other crowds, other phenomena. There had been times when she had heard hisses beneath the cheering, times when she had sensed hatred barely cloaked by the universal roar. But here, at the first Australian city to be visited, there was nothing in the tremendous welcome but pure joy. To her it was a revelation, this homage from a people to whom her country was unknown.

"I am – what you call it? – embarrassed?" she said to His Excellency the Governor of New South Wales, who sat at her side in the open car that pushed slowly through the masses of people, among whom police and troops had difficulty in keeping a clear way.

"Your Highness has now for three years been a romantic figure to most of the world," explained His Excellency.

"But why?"

"All men are lovers," he said gently, in his bluff quarterdeck fashion. For several minutes the tumult made speaking an impossibility. Then, when the chance occurred and he found her looking at him, he added: "We British people have very democratic views, Highness. We are democratic as to the institution of marriage. We believe that princesses no less than common people should marry for – love."

"Oh! So that is it. As though *I* would marry Carl with his so pimply face and green eyes, and his chin – what is it? – so near his neck. His Majesty was in a rage. He said shooking – no, shocking – things."

"Dear me!" murmured the Governor politely.

"Yes, and I said – well, perhaps you can give the guess what I – I, Natalie – said to him."

His Excellency saw a pair of violet-blue eyes laughing at him as his daughter's eyes had done when she was quite young. It came to him that this young lady, dressed neatly but superbly in one of the latest Paris confections, was years younger than her real age. He was charmed. He liked the little determined chin, in whose centre was a definite dimple; and, quite suddenly the worry of his official duties slipped away and he found himself as light-hearted as anyone of the humming crowd.

Natalie captured the hearts of all who heard her speak in her quaint broken English. Her voice had that clear musical intonation indicative of the highest culture – for Royalty must set a standard in speech as in much else – whilst her ever-ready smile was unaffectedly gay.

"I like your so beautiful harbour," she told a prominent Sydney citizen. "But why, oh so why, do you hide your city with coloured – what you say? – strings and bunting? We have the streamers and the bunting in Naagrade, but not your so magnificent buildings."

That speech swept Australia. Her journey south to Melbourne – Canberra, the sink of the nation's wealth, was not ready to be visited – was almost equally a triumph. Her special train sped on its long journey through hamlet and town, and when Natalie had a fleeting glimpse of a small battalion of school-children formed up on a station platform at which the train did not stop, she said to her chief equerry, and a representative of the Governor-General:

"Why was I not informed about those so little children? At once ascertain if waiting children are ahead. If so, you will order the train to go slow through stations where children there are to greet me, and me you will conduct to the coach and platform where I can stand and greet them."

"Highness, such a proceeding would cause the train to arrive late in Melbourne," protested the equerry.

"Then tell the man-engineer-driver to drive faster between stations. Go! I greet the children."

The gentleman in waiting departed to hold conference with other officials. He repeated verbatim what the Princess had said, and was unaware that hidden among the officials were two very-much alive newspaper men.

Several hours before her arrival in Melbourne the incident of the school-children's welcome was in the minds of tens of thousands of readers. Her welcome to Sydney was surpassed by her welcome to Melbourne, which in forty-eight hours had been divested of its gaudy decorations, permitting her to see the city as it really is. And by no means was Natalie disappointed.

There were times, however, when she was bored to death, and occasions when even her young strength threatened to fail. Towards the end of her stay in Melbourne fatigue began to show in her eyes, and she was indeed very thankful on her arrival at the home of Sir Henry and Lady Lund, situated near Mount Lofty, south-east of Adelaide, where she was to stay for three days with absolutely no public duties to perform.

She found old Sir Henry and his lady kindly and sincere, and felt at once the entire absence of stiffness. The Australian authorities had made no mistake when they selected Sir Henry as the host of Natalie for her three precious rest days. Her suite housed two miles away, attended only by her favourite maid, the Princess found herself able to do just whatever she liked.

To Lady Lund she said, a little wistfully, on her arrival late in the afternoon: "Please – please forget that I am a poor little princess. I am not really. Just now so tired am I a great big girl."

And white-haired Lady Lund, seeing the expression in Natalie's eyes, held out her hands, forgetting as she was requested to forget, and with her arm round the Royal waist herself escorted her guest to her suite of rooms.

"Trust an old woman, my dear," she whispered. "We always dine at seven, but would you rather not dine with us, but have a little meal brought you when you put on a *négligé* wrap and are at your ease?"

"Oh, that so lovely would be!" Natalie exclaimed, the old sparkle in her eyes. "But you make my so sad excuses to your husband and come and eat with me. I want to talk – oh! – of silly things, things which come just into my mind, and not from someone else's."

Thus it was that Natalie, Princess of Rolandia, dined *tête-à-tête* with a British knight's wife, a little woman of seventy who for forty years had worked with her husband in the Australian bush, and was too old to put on the airs and graces of new aristocracy.

Lady Lund's genuine simplicity charmed the world-weary girl. Clad in a silk wrap, curled up on a divan placed before the open French windows, Natalie said all her "silly things", and her hostess aided and abetted her in her longing to forget for three days. At nine o'clock Lady Lund insisted on her guest going to bed, and left her in the hands of her maid.

Natalie was not awakened the next morning. She woke herself at about eleven, and the first person she saw was little Lady Lund seated before an electric coffee-urn, patiently waiting.

"Slip into a gown, dear, and come and sit by me and take coffee and buttered rolls, as all good Parisians do at this hour of the day," invited Lady Lund.

"That will so nice be," Natalie sighed blissfully. "My maid, please, will you call?"

"Your maid also is having a rest cure. I insisted on it. The poor woman is on the verge of a breakdown." Lady Lund smiled in her bewitching way. "Come, put on that kimono. You are not a princess just now, you know."

For the fraction of a second Natalie's deep blue-violet eyes gleamed resentment. Then the gleam vanished and they were filled with a joyous sparkle. Probably for the first time in her life she put on the kimono without expert aid, and then, with her feet thrust into a pair of velvet slippers, she slipped to the back of Lady Lund's chair, and, throwing her arms about the little woman, kissed her behind the ear, saying, with unwonted seriousness:

"Thank you much for so kind as to tell me now no longer am I princess. So we forget. Completely! Princess – to the devil! Now, now, my so dear foster-mother! Do you not remember about the Princess Natalie; but beware, beware I say, of the girl Natalie. You know what I so like to do?"

"What would you like to do?"

"Engage – yes, that is right – engage in a pillow-fight."

Natalie burst into unrestrained laughter when there dawned on Lady Lund's face a look of horror. "Not with my pillows, dear. They are stuffed with feathers which my dear mother plucked from the breasts of geese ninety-five years ago."

"Then tennis it shall be, till lunch-time. Have you a court? Can you find someone to play with me? Someone like yourself who will remember that the – no, I mention not her rank, she to the devil is – that the visitor from Rolandia is just a girl, Natalie by name – Mademoiselle

Natalie or Miss Natalie? Is there?"

The old woman's eyes were bright. Natalie noted the pride and the affection in her voice when she said: "There is my son. He will be only too pleased to play tennis with you. Raymond is his name."

An hour later Natalie walked with Lady Lund through the Italian garden which was the pride of old Sir Henry. The courts were situated beyond the period garden, and when they emerged from it they saw a flannelled figure actually running to and fro across a court trailing a heavy iron roller. Watching him was a man, his back turned to them, who seemed all shoulders and arms.

Hearing their voices, this man turned. Seeing them, he removed his battered felt hat. Natalie's eyes widened with interest, for here was the most astoundingly powerful and the most ugly man she had ever seen. There was about his face more than a hint of a gorilla. His nose was squat and his nostrils open and turned outward. His forehead, half hidden by thin dark brown hair, was narrow and low. But his mouth was straight, his lips were fine, and his jaws were square. His body was almost cubic in its proportions, and the hand that did not hold the hat hung down almost to his left knee.

"Good morning, Snell!" Lady Lund greeted.

"Good morning, Marm," the man replied, surprising Natalie with the soft and musical quality of his voice. He regarded both Natalie and her hostess with steady brown eyes, and the girl noted with curiosity that he did not bend his rigid back in respectful obeisance. Lady Lund's orders had been given.

"Raymond!" called the white-haired old lady.

The flannelled figure rushing about the court with the heavy roller halted with surprising suddenness, looked in their direction, waved his hand, ran the roller off the green, and came towards them as a man gone mad. Between him and them was a wire-netted fence ten feet high. Natalie saw him leap upward, saw him grasp the top of a fence-post, pull himself up, and vault the fence without touching it with his body. He dropped on his feet before them.

"My dear Raymond, you will hurt yourself one of these days. When will you understand that you're grown up?"

"Not for a few years yet, mother." Then, with a boyish grin: "I've only just turned thirty."

For two seconds Natalie was guilty of staring. Her eyes examined this most energetic person with interest. She regarded a man standing six feet high in his tennis shoes, broad-shouldered, slim-hipped. He was not a handsome man, yet on his face was unmistakably the stamp of clean-living youth. His wide-spaced grey eyes gazed down at her with impish joy. His wide mouth was stretched, not by a mere smile but by a positive grin.

"Heard you wanted to play a set, Miss Natalie, so I had to do some rolling in quick time. My name's Raymond. At your service as a playmate – while you are our guest."

The qualification was significant. It told the girl that when she was no longer the guest of these people this man would not presume to forget that she was the daughter of a king.

Natalie looked at her hostess. Lady Lund was smiling softly. She knew without doubt then that this Raymond had made no attempt to be coarsely familiar. Like his mother, he wanted her to forget for just a little while what she was.

"I must leave you now for an hour, as I have things to attend to," the old woman said in her sweet way. "Raymond, on no account are you to tire our visitor. Remember that she is here to rest."

"If she does exactly as she wishes that will be resting, mother mine." Then to Natalie: "Will it not?"

"It will, my so dear Mistaire Lund," replied this astonishing Princess. "I'd like to run about and help you pull the roller thing. You know, you did so absurd look. I absurd want to be also."

"Come along, then. Let's hit the balls. Sweet William has stretched the net."

"Sweet William!"

"Yes. Look at him! My companion-valet-punching-partner-mechanic."

CHAPTER V

THE REST CURE

HER stay with the Lunds was the only perfect holiday the Princess Natalie had ever enjoyed. It was that because for the first time in her life she experienced the pleasure of living wholly as a woman free of the iron chains of Royalty. Her half earnestly expressed wish to Lady Lund to be wholly free for three days had been accepted literally – not a little to her surprise, for she had thought people could never forget, and certainly to her delight.

She was charmed by the patriarchal Sir Henry, the maternal sweetness of his wife, and with the youthful vigour and transparent boyishness of Raymond Lund. Even "Sweet William" Snell she had grown to regard as an invaluable adjunct to this wonderful holiday.

Yet, as with all splendid holidays, the days were compressed into hours and the hours into minutes. Natalie played tennis, she played the piano for her host and hostess, she sang to them and laughed with them. The lassitude and the fatigue slipped from her. Her broken English was heard everywhere, in the house, the gardens, and even in the *chef's* pantry one midnight when, led by Raymond, they raided it. She herself fed the two tame kangaroos with sweet piecrusts and, during the afternoon of the third day, was permitted by Raymond to drive his eight-cylinder, eighty horse-power Southern Cross car for ten miles through the hills.

A stolen ride that was, for it was tacitly understood between the Princess' advisers and Sir Henry and Lady Lund that she was not to leave the grounds without an escort. When they returned to the garage Natalie seemed loth to leave the wheel. With her fingers playing idly about its rim she turned on her companion a radiantly flushed face, saying: "Oh, what a so beautiful car!"

Then quite suddenly her eyes clouded and she added: "If only I were always Natalie, and could own and drive a car like this where I wished, when I wished! It has so lovely been. And to-morrow! To the devil with to-morrow! You say what? There remains a few tiny hours of freedom. What shall we do, my so wonderful Mistaire Lund?"

"Well, you've driven a straight-eight Southern Cross, so what do you say to trying your hands with a Henry?" Lund inquired with humorously raised eyebrows.

"A Henry?"

"Yes. A product of Mr. Henry Ford. A 'tin Lizzie', you know."

"I not quite understand."

"Then I'll show you a Henry. Wait there. I'll run her out of the garage."

Raymond Lund vanished within the double doors of the garage. Natalie heard a succession of squeaks, several loud reports, and then a bursting roar. The roar increased and into view came a side-boarded vehicle on wheels, its rear half with the body of a truck, its front half as that of a pre-war car. In place of tyres the wheels were fitted with two rims, one outside the other, and between these rims was a series of semi-elliptical springs held in place by ordinary shackles. The engine roared and spluttered, and the car-truck shot forward, swept round in an arc, and came to a halt close beside the gleaming Southern Cross – the ancient and modern in close proximity. Lund brought down the throttle lever and the roar subsided.

"What do you think of her?" he asked unabashed. "Nineteen-fourteen model, can do forty miles an hour at twenty to the gallon, and can be guaranteed to be more reliable, more accessible, than the car you sit in. Moreover, she'll go anywhere, even if she only sparks on one cylinder, cut a track through sand-drifts, pull herself out of bogs, and then lose that fifteen-hundred pounds, nineteen-twenty-seven product. This Henry is a hum-dinger, believe me."

"I'm afraid so hard it is to believe," Natalie said laughing.

"Well, you have my word for it. I've taken Henry from Adelaide to Darwin, and from Melbourne to Perth, and from Sydney all round Australia to Sydney. See these patent non-puncturable tyres? Sweet William and I invented 'em. They've done fifty-seven thousand miles and are hardly worn yet. Now, do you know what is the most wonderful thing about a Lizzie?"

"I afraid am I know nothing," Natalie admitted.

"Well, Lizzie is human," Lund told her seriously, but with a hint of laughter in his eyes. "You know, they say that every seven years the human body completely changes. So does Lizzie. There is not a part in her that was in her seven years ago, excepting the steering column. Tell you what! I'll leave Adelaide in this dear old Lizzie the same minute you leave in your special express, and I'll wager you a pair of gloves to a silk necktie that I arrive in Perth before you do."

"But it is a long way. And my trains go night and day."

"It is nearly seventeen hundred miles from Adelaide to Perth both by rail and by road, but I'm game to bet."

"I take you. My gloves are size three, and I prefer grey suede." She and Lund both laughed.

He said: "All right. But please remember I like my ties dark blue with a light blue stripe." And then suddenly the laughter fled from his face and he became serious. "I was forgetting," he said after a little silence.

"What you forget?" asked Natalie softly.

"I was forgetting that when you arrive in Perth you will not be just Natalie."

"No." Natalie's mouth was an O. "No," she repeated.

"Anyway, we've still time to tryout the Henry."

That made her look at him, to discover that he was his usual boyish self, and she suddenly recognised that she liked this youngish man who refused to permit a shadow to rest on her till her three days of freedom was over. Yet –

"Still, the wager is as you said," she cried. "Think now! If you to Perth arrive first, you will wave me good-bye with a blue flag. I will look for it. Then I will send the necktie with the stripes you so desire. If I not see the blue flag and you are in Perth, write to me at Naagrade. If you are not in Perth when I reach that city, you will send the number three suede gloves to me at the Palace, Naagrade. Is it understood?"

"Yes, quite."

"And, Mistaire Lund, win or lose, you will write me one long letter, explaining your so wonderful race, eh?"

"Yes, I will write you one letter," he assented, with emphasis on the "one", since she had emphasised that word.

It cannot be said that Lizzie charmed Natalie. She spoke her mind freely and laughed delightedly when Lund told her that the ancient Ford was a he-man's car; in which, by the way, he was entirely accurate, because a 1914 Ford requires quite a lot of manhandling on a cold morning.

Her last evening there was as the others had been, quiet and happy, and absolutely restful. Outside the small family circle she saw no one other than the doctor, who called and chatted for half an hour, and in his heart blessed these Australian gentlefolk for their understanding and firmness.

For three days the Lunds' home had been practically a fortress. To assure the Princess freedom from annoyance in any shape or form Raymond and his mechanic-valet had enlisted a hundred unemployed returned soldiers to co-operate with officialdom in securing privacy. No unauthorised person could approach Sir Henry's residence. The Princess' doctor aided and abetted his Royal mistress' wishes. He refused permission for even her own courtiers to allow themselves to be seen by her, so that by the evening of the third day all danger of the threatened nervous breakdown was banished.

To the last minute the Lunds maintained the pretence that she was an ordinary woman. Never once did they remind her of the inevitable moment when again she would become a world-popular Princess.

The evening fled. At eleven o'clock Lady Lund rose. "My dear," she said in her gentle but firm way. "My dear, just look at the time."

Natalie suppressed a sigh. How delightful it had all been! How lovely it was to see someone stand up before she did, and hear a suggestion, half a command, half a pleading!

Crossing over to Sir Henry, she held out her hands to him, and, looking up into his placid hazel eyes beneath the white brows, said simply: "Thank you, Sir Henry! It has been a wonderful holiday. Oh! I so hope you will come to Naagrade quickly soon, so that I can acknowledge so my debt. Good night!"

"Good night, my dear! A dreamless sleep, I hope," was his reply, accompanied by a smile of genuine affection.

Raymond waited, holding open the door for his mother and their guest. When he held Natalie's hands precisely as his father had done a moment before, he caught his breath, for the girl's eyes were misty and she looked more lovely than before.

"Good night, my so wonderful playfellow!" she said, almost whispering. "I shall look for the blue flag. So disappointed shall I be if not I see it waving at Perth. I shall remember always the so absurd man who runs here and there with a roller garden so big. Good-bye!"

He saw her with his mother crossing the hall before he softly closed the door. Turning, he found his father watching him, and, joining the old man, said calmly but with a strangely white face: "I think, Dad, that the cure has been successful."

"I agree. We have indeed been honoured in being permitted to extend hospitality to Natalie and *the Heiress Apparent to the Rolandian Throne.*"

Raymond nodded, and, walking to the open window, passed out on the veranda, where the kindly darkness of night closed in all about him. "Natalie and –" Yes, the second half of the hyphenated personality was real, so hatefully real.

Natalie's farewell to her sweet old hostess was of longer duration. She wept tears of gratitude whilst she clasped the frail figure in her strong young arms, and, when the final good nights had been exchanged, and her room door had closed behind Lady Lund, she realised that the fairy had gone, and in the morning would come her "armourer" in the person of her favourite maid.

She awoke at dawn, mentally alert, refreshed, and, slipping into a wrap, crossed to the open French windows before which she sank into a Chesterfield. A mile beyond the house was another whale-backed hill, separated from her by a deep valley still hidden in the darkness of night. Above the sharply silhouetted summit of the hill the sky was tinged with pink and pearl grey, tints that deepened every second.

Natalie wondered if, after all, the preceding days and nights had been but a dream. If so, it had been a beautiful dream, where she had been a caged bird suddenly freed. Ah yes, free! Memory of it was vivid. Now the awakening had come, and no longer was she free.

That period of freedom from the chains of Royalty had been to the Princess a revelation. From the cradle she had grown up to a life circumscribed by Court etiquette and governed by rigid rules and taboos, rules and etiquette so strict and unbreakable that mere custom had kept her figuratively in a strait-jacket. To her it had been her life because she had known no other. Whilst she had had ideas of the freedom enjoyed by the common people, she had had but small idea what the freedom of common people really is.

For three days she had been able to live without iron restraint. She had been able to speak as she really wanted to speak, talk spontaneously and not with an ever-guarded tongue. She had been able to move about, to play tennis with Raymond Lund and croquet with Lady Lund, and enjoy the inexpressible delight of playing and moving without being watched.

Whilst she lay crouched up on the Chesterfield and saw the sun appear from behind the hill with the whale-back, Natalie for the first time in her life desired mightily to rebel against her destiny. For one mad moment she cogitated the idea of hastily dressing, slipping out of the house, and running away – away across that beautiful sunlit country of hill and dale, never to be recaptured and rechained to the service of a people. Yet she stirred not from the couch, remaining passive, though her eyes were misty and her lips trembled a little, a very lovely woman and yet a wistful child.

She was still there when at eight o'clock the door opened to admit the Baroness Schulz, her chief lady-in-waiting.

"Why, awake already, Highness!" the lady said in her stolid, cheerful way. "Why, you look splendid this morning. The rest cure has been of wonderful benefit. The Baron asked me to say that Your Royal Highness will leave punctually at ten o'clock."

Natalie stood up. The Baroness curtsied.

In the Rolandian tongue the Princess said coldly: "Very well, Baroness. I am ready."

It was a simple statement, quietly uttered, spoken as a man might speak who has lived for three weeks in the condemned cell and says to the hangman: "I am ready."

"Where do I breakfast, please?"

"Your Royal Highness breakfast's at nine o'clock with Sir Henry and Lady Lund, Doctor Jowski, the Baron and myself. Do you consent to Marie bringing you coffee and rolls before dressing?"

Natalie inclined her head. She saw that the Baroness' frigidity was caused by her own coldness, and, forcing a smile, said in English: "I must tell you of my so wonderful holiday some day, Baroness. You will then me forgive for being the devil this morning is."

"Oh, Princess! Natalie – my Natalie!"

There were tears in the girl's eyes. Her voice quavered, but her voice came clearly: "Send to me Marie. Adelaide awaits me."

CHAPTER VI

THE RACE

"THERE ain't nothing more that can be done to her," William Snell informed Raymond on his return from watching the Princess Natalie's drive through Adelaide to Government House. "I've given her a set of new pistons, ground in the valves, gone over the ignition, and cleaned out the petrol system from tank to inlets."

"Sweet William" Snell regarded his employer solemnly across the bonnet of the pre-war Ford. His overalls were stiff with grease and oil, his dank hair hung low over his forehead, obliterating it, giving the impression that he possessed no forehead whatever.

"Spark her up!"

Snell "sparked her up" with such vigour that the crank-handle appeared likely to be put out of shape. There came two loud reports and then an ever-soaring hum. Both men listened with the intentness of doctors trying to arrive at a decision from a patient's breathing.

"She'll do!" Lund shouted, whereupon Snell switched off the engine. "We'll have to push her hard to get to Perth before Her Royal Highness," he said. "According to the official schedule the Princess' special trains will get her there in ninety-seven hours, which will permit her to spend one night at Port Augusta and twenty-four hours at Kalgoorlie so that she can be shown the Golden Mile. We ought to do it. The spare parts will be delivered in the morning. We'll give Henry a trial spin in the afternoon and load up. We'll have to leave at seven sharp the morning after, so that we get an even break with the Princess' train."

"No doubt we'll leave Adelaide on time, but we won't hit Perth before the Princess," Snell announced gloomily. "This 'ere antique is past her prime. The chassis will fall apart if she's pushed so as to get her out of breath."

"Then she mustn't be put out of breath. We have *got* to get to Perth before the Princess."

"Kind of important?" Snell inquired.

"Yes. It's the most important thing that has ever happened to me," Lund told him with sudden grimness.

The ugly face of the other was immobile whilst the small black eyes examined the youthful countenance. Then: "There ain't nothing wrong with the Southern Cross."

"Agreed. Yet I promised the Princess I would be in Perth to wave good-bye as she left Australia. I said this concern would beat her special trains. There was a little bet, Snell, between us, you understand."

"Humph! I think I'm beginning to," Snell said dryly. "Well, if that's the way the hen cackles, we'll have to do our best. One thing, we know the road. We'll have to keep to race conditions. What was the stakes?"

"A pair of gloves to a blue striped tie."

"Ho! Gloves, eh? A tie! An' we got to keep going for more'n four days to win a tie! Why, I seen a hundred quid won and lost on a fly race up a window-pane. Go like blazes, day and night, without a decent sleep for four days to win a tie. Lumme! But perhaps there'll be a diamond-studded pin to go with the tie?"

"Snell, cut it out! You are treading on my feet."

"No offence, no offence! If you wants to get to Perth, that's good enough for me."

Between these two men existed a friendship heated and welded into unbreakable strength by the fire of the Great War. Snell, prior to 1914, had been a warder in a South Australian prison. Possessed of tremendous strength, and a ju-jitsu expert, he had by 1917 become the champion wrestler of the Second Division of the Australian Army Corps.

Unfortunately, William Snell succumbed to the lure of the A.I.F.'s favourite game, two-up. As a gamble there is no game of chance more fair, provided the tosser does not substitute double-headed pennies for the orthodox coin.

In early 1918 both Snell and Captain Lund were in camp at Warminster, both recently recovered from wounds, both expecting to be redrafted back to France. At a two-up school one afternoon, at which Snell was present, double-headed pennies were introduced. Years of prison life and contact with criminals had given to the ex-warder an eagle eye for possible roguery. Discerning the trick, Snell punched. In his wrath he punched too hard, with the result that he was court-martialled on the charge of murder.

It was a serious charge. The game was an illegal game. One can bet on a horse against tremendously unfair odds in the shape of owners, jockeys, and bookmakers. Gentlemen bet on horses, but not at two-up. Hence two-up was officially frowned on even in the A.I.F., where official frowns were regarded with contempt. Snell found himself in a tight corner, and knew it.

Now the youthful Captain Lund regarded soldiering as a serious business. It was not all influence which had gained him rapid promotion in the space of fifteen months. Having a wide knowledge of the King's

Rules and Regulations, he offered to become Prisoner's Friend, and was so accepted by William Snell. During his conversations with Snell prior to the court-martial, Captain Lund came to understand the almost brutal nature of the man, held in leash only by a fine sense of what is right and what is wrong. A lamb and a lion both inhabited the soul of Snell.

After his acquittal he became Captain Lund's batman, and during the epic months in France which followed never an officer was served with greater devotion than Raymond Lund. Forager, cook, adviser, and human mule in one, William Snell became his officer's shadow.

The war over, he might have gone back to the prison service. Lund asked him to tea one afternoon and introduced him to Sir Henry and his mother. There was at the end of the war no conceit in the remoulded character of the old young man. Lady Lund was too fine a woman to think of the ethics of stupid society. The man with the gorilla-like face had stared at death with her boy time and again. He had ignored danger to assure for her boy a little comfort when there was none to be obtained by others.

So Snell had his tea with the "toffs". Of the war he would say nothing, but of anecdotes of prison life his store was full and his tongue was glib.

"Well, Snell, I'll see Mr. Ivanhoe, the Chief Secretary, and get you reinstated," Sir Henry had said.

To which Snell had replied: "Thank you, Sir Henry! But I was thinking the Captain might be wanting a man-servant – vallies, they call 'em. You see, we got to kind of understand each other."

Thus it came about that Snell continued to be Raymond Lund's shadow. As a body-servant he was a lamentable failure, which made little difference to his master, since Lund was too much of a man not to be capable of putting on his own trousers. Where he was of immense value was with his rapidly assimilated knowledge of motor-engineering, which he obtained in Lund's experimental workshop and garage. He became as keen on the job of evolving a non-puncturable motor-tyre as Lund himself, and his part in the final construction of the tyre with which the Ford was fitted was not by any means small.

Thus the friendship cemented by war was continued into the peace. Between them there was no exhibition of servility on the one part or of lofty superiority on the other. Snell knew his place and never desired to step out of it. He was Raymond Lund's man to the last ditch, and he knew Lund knew it.

A friend of Lund's once said: "Your man, Snell, is devilish familiar, old top."

"Do you think so?" Raymond asked quietly. "I hadn't noticed it. Anyway, I don't pay Snell to call me 'sir', and bow and scrape, and figuratively wipe the floor with his waistcoat. I like a man to stand square on his feet – which Snell does."

They worked together in perfect harmony, the older man finding in Lund an object of affection denied him by woman on account of his ugliness. On the other hand, Lund, who was an idealist and one of those lucky men able to retain through life many youthful illusions, greatly admired Snell for his prowess as a wrestler, his uncanny knowledge of men, and his affection which at rare moments was revealed.

They became absorbed by the problem of the unpuncturable motor-tyre. Many were the ingenious devices evolved and tested in such record speed runs as between Adelaide and Sydney, and Adelaide to Perth. Once they held the Adelaide-Darwin speed record, winning it with the identical car, with its somewhat unsightly double-rimmed wheels, with which now they set out to beat the trains of the Princess Natalie.

With muffled exhaust they rolled along the Prospect Road, their ears well-nigh deafened by the roars of the crowd farewelling the Princess. The day was fine and hot, as it can be hot and fine in South Australia in January, and, when once clear of Adelaide, the exhaust silencer was shifted by a lever, and the engine broke into a staccato roar. With no silencer on the exhaust, thereby assuring a cooler engine and lower petrol consumption, lacking mudguards, windscreen and hood, the vehicle appeared to be a cross between a buggy and a racing car.

Petrol, oil and water supplies had been worked out for a previous trip, so now were a matter of routine. No difficulty as to these essentials would be experienced between Adelaide and Port Augusta, roughly a distance of two hundred and sixty miles. From Port Augusta to Ceduna, in the far northwest corner of Eyre's Peninsula, they would have to take reasonable precautions in carrying supplies. Then came the run over the stretch of country between Ceduna, S.A., and Norseman in Western Australia, a distance of some seven hundred and sixty miles across the Nullarbor Plain and the Hampton Tableland, which was barren of townships with their petrol and oil depots. There were some half-dozen station homesteads, where petrol might be obtained or might not.

"O.K.?" Lund asked.

"Ar!" answered Snell, who was driving.

They were passing through general farming country, then looking dry and baked. By the clock on the dashboard they took shifts of two hours at the wheel. Beyond Gawler, beyond Peterborough, the last of the poor wheat harvest was being stripped. Drought had come, and farmers were anxious or despairing, according to their temperaments. After crossing the Flinders Range at Horrock's Pass, the road became rough and the strain on the semi-elliptical springs between the double rims was severe. Above the roar of the engine Snell heard a faint squeak. He was not then driving, but his hearing was super-acute, and for finding faults in mechanism by sound he had few equals.

"Pull up!" he ordered.

"Anything wrong?" asked Lund, obeying.

"Wheel springs want oiling. Test nuts."

Without further speech they got down, one on each side, snatched up oil-cans and spanners, and oiled every shackle and tested every nut.

The work occupied barely three minutes. Then on again, dropping ever lower from the range to the flats bordering Spencer's Gulf, at the head of which lies the town of Port Augusta. That town they reached forty-five minutes after Princess Natalie. Whilst she slept in her special car in the station marking the eastern terminus of the Great Western Railway, Raymond Lund and the iron Snell kept the old Ford roaring westward toward Ceduna.

Already they were feeling the cramping fatigue of constant motor-travelling, although as yet the driving strain was not acute. Their only halts, other than for the purpose of taking on petrol and oil supplies, occurred for half an hour at sunrise, sunset, and midnight, to boil the billy for tea. The midday meal was eaten whilst travelling, and was accompanied by wine much diluted with water.

At Ceduna, a small settlement town, then apathetic in the grip of drought, they took on six eight-gallon cases of petrol and one case of oil. They purchased also a week's supply of rations in case of breakdown, for there was a stretch of two hundred and twenty miles between station homesteads. For water they had the rain-sheds erected originally for the use of the linesmen patrolling the old overland telegraph line and spaced from twenty to thirty miles apart.

People at the homestead of Callona – the first of the six sheep stations – wondered why they did not stop. For the succeeding forty miles their average speed across undulating country with rough rock-strewn sandy summits was a bare ten miles to the hour. Near White Wells Station the track improved, and at Nullarbor Station homestead, where there were a surprising number of aboriginals, they arrived at the edge of the vast Nullarbor Plain, with no habitations between them and Mundrabilla Station in Western Australia save buildings of the abandoned telegraphic transmission station at Eucla.

They had bitten deep into the Nullarbor Plain when the Princess' train reached Ooldea, eighty or ninety miles to the north of the east-west track, the natural surface of which was in excellent condition.

"If Lizzie could do it, Bill, this road would allow her to speed up to a hundred miles an hour," Lund said, whilst pouring water into the radiator at the time of the change of driving shifts.

"If rats 'ad wings they'd fly," grunted Snell, lighting an enormous and most evil-smelling pipe.

"You don't say!" came from the water-pourer, the light of enthusiasm still in his heavy-lidded eyes.

"Well, what have we been doing while I've bin asleep?"

"She touched forty-three."

"Well, she's your 'bus, Captain, but the time's gonna come when at forty miles per the guts is going to drop right out of her," growled Sweet William. "We got spare pistons and big ends and a crankshaft, but if she comes to pieces in atoms we come to a full and everlasting stop. Slow but sure is this old gal's motter. Take 'er gently and she'll love you for years; treat 'er rough, and she blows to bits."

Lund climbed in beside his servant, then behind the wheel. "Well, for heaven's sake keep her moving," he exclaimed feverishly. "If you don't the Princess will be half-way to Durban when we reach Perth."

"If I do she'll be at Durban before we wake up – if ever we do when Lizzie bucks. Take a snore orf. I'm driving, and I'll darn well drive how I like."

"Oh, all right!" Lund sleepily told him good-naturedly. "But if we miss the Princess at Perth, I'll lick the hide off you."

"You wouldn't have a dog's chance. But don't worry. Get a sleep. There ain't a blasted train in Australia wot can beat this Henry at a level start."

Lund slouched down in the hard seat, arranged a pillow against the specially built seat-back, and was asleep the instant his head rested against the pillow. Bill Snell, chewing the stem of his pipe, drove on, his eyes red with want of proper sleep, yet the body of him as iron against the attack of cramp. All the time his ears were attuned to the roar of the engine, ever expectant, ever waiting to catch the tell-tale knock of a big end, a worn gudgeon-pin, or a dry shackle on a wheel.

The song of an engine was the only music Bill Snell appreciated. Stand him outside a motor shop, start up a car within the shop, and Snell would tell you the make of the engine by its running sound. Ask him to listen to an engine knock, and he would tell you precisely where was the seat of trouble.

He was dozing his off shift when a wheel-shackle pinioning two semi-elliptical springs to the patent tyre began to complain faintly for the want of oil. That tiny squeak awoke him, and, calling Lund's attention to the shackle, the car was brought to a stop, and both men descended to locate the dry shackle.

Raymond Lund was kneeling beside a rear wheel when a sharp stabbing pain shot into his left knee. At first he thought it was an ant-bite. Standing up suddenly, he looked down and saw hanging by the cloth a dun-painted globe as large as a walnut from which, at various angles, two-inch needle-pointed spines thrust outward.

Pulling it out of his trouser-leg, he examined it more closely. It was quite heavy. "What do you make of this, Bill?" he asked, frowning.

"Dunno," replied Sweet William. "Why, here's another!"

CHAPTER VII

ZERO HOUR

MR. VAN HORTON had made his millions in the illicit trading of alcohol, drugs, and prohibited immigrants by applying to this nefarious business common horse sense, plus brilliant organising ability, plus his gift to see further into the future than the average man. His talents at the disposal of any lawful business would have gained him as much money in the same period of time. Why he chose the course he did appears inexplicable, unless we attribute to him the mental kink exemplified by the Irishman who, on landing at Sydney, asked if there were a Government, and, on being told there was, announced that he was "agin" it.

Or the attraction may have been the mental excitement obtained by playing a most dangerous game. "Game" is the word. When a man pits his mind against the mind of another man or men, whether in crime versus the law, or in business versus business, he plays a game every whit as much as if he is playing poker or cricket. To some men, and Van Horton was one of them, the greater the odds against them, the greater the spice of the game.

Modern business knows but one law, and that is to keep within the law. Crime is governed by no law at all, but by the instinct of self-preservation. To become a successful criminal a man or a woman must be prepared to commit every crime in the calendar – which, fortunately, is the reason why there are exceptionally few successful criminals. Because Van Horton was prepared to commit every crime in the calendar, and had actually committed most of them, for that reason he was America's Napoleon of Crime.

A psycho-analyst considering Earle Lawrence would have noted several outstanding points that for ever would prevent his occupying the position enjoyed by Van Horton. Together they had worked in harmony, as two interacting cogs in a piece of efficient machinery; but, whereas Van Horton could stand alone and had done so, the Australian could never be successful acting on his own initiative.

The fatal bar to a career of crime for Earle Lawrence was his unwillingness to commit every crime in the calendar. He could visualise a magnificent plan, yet be quite unable to work out the tiny details so that they fitted together so precisely as to make the plan sound from foundation to apex. Many of our statesmen are like Lawrence, but compared with them Lawrence was a genius in that he recognised his failings or limitations.

Without the leadership of Van Horton the plan to abduct the Princess Natalie would have remained a pleasing dream in the brain of Lawrence. The abduction would not have been attempted. But when Van Horton agreed to become Commander-in-Chief, Earle Lawrence was wholly satisfied to act as Chief of Staff.

In a high-powered car he had taken Van Horton over the country that was to stage their operations. The millionaire had seen for himself the vital points of attack and retreat, asking pertinent questions, deciding for this and against that. And these decisions satisfied Lawrence, because he saw that they were accurate.

Van Horton had come to see the practicability of the scheme. He saw that the abduction could be carried out if based on accurate groundwork; and he saw, too, that what had seemed at first the most difficult part, that of holding the Princess secure after the abduction, was also practicable – in fact, this latter presented less difficulty than the abduction itself. After a conference with Helen, he agreed to act, agreed with perfect confidence that the scheme could be put into execution.

Lawrence had taken the Van Hortons to the underground caverns, which had astonished them with their vastness and beauty. He had proved to them that this series of caverns had but one accessible entrance, that they were clean and healthy, and could be made entirely comfortable. Situated twenty miles east of Eucla, and approximately halfway between the transcontinental road and the sea, they were ideal in that they were sufficiently distant from Eucla, which most certainly would become a hive of investigators, and yet a bare seven miles from the overland road.

Between the caves and the road, a few years before, an optimist had sunk a trial bore for oil. The shack near the bore-head still stood. A geologist, a drink-sodden wreck of a man, had been established on this site, for it was necessary to provide adequate reason for bringing from Perth and Adelaide six motor-trucks loaded with supplies to permit at least a dozen people to live in comfort in the caverns for three months. Those trucks had to traverse a road seldom used. The people at the few station homesteads, people starved for news and human society, would certainly be sufficiently curious to want to know what the trucks were carrying. Therefore it might reasonably be expected that the truck consignments would attract inquiry after the abduction, and a subsidiary reason was necessary to account for them.

The oil-bore provided the subsidiary reason. The shack was made habitable. New boring plant was bought and erected. The geologist was installed. Afterwards a camel team in charge of an Afghan made its appearance, and in two nights transported from the oil-site to the caverns supplies, furniture, cooking-stoves, electric-light plant, books, a gramophone, and a harmonium for the especial pleasure of Mr. Van Horton.

It was the evening prior to the day that was to witness the greatest *coup* of Van Horton's career. He and Earle Lawrence were seated at a table within the hut at the spurious oil-site. On the table lay pinned a large-scale map of the locality. It was nine o'clock.

The wireless receiving set at the further end of the hut had enabled them to follow the triumphal progress of the Princess from capital city to capital city. They had been informed by the Adelaide broadcasting station of the precise minute the royal visitor's special train had pulled out of Port Augusta. Through the same medium of communication they knew that the British battle-cruiser, *Iron Duke*, the ship loaned to Her Royal Highness for her tour, was then nearing Albany in Western Australia on her way to Perth, where Natalie would go on board and be conveyed to Durban.

That evening's weather forecasts from both Perth and Adelaide predicted fine, calm weather for the succeeding forty-eight hours. A wedge-shaped anti-cyclonic high was based along the Great Australian Bight, its apex a little north of Darwin.

These weather forecasts were of supreme importance. On them depended the choice of one of two plans, both plans perfected to the minutest detail. They were known as the "calm" and the "rough" plans; and, since the plan adapted to calm weather was chosen, we need not be concerned with the alternative plan. After quite a long silence Van Horton spoke, in the sharp crisp tones he invariably used in business.

"I am glad the weather is to remain fine and the sea calm," he said. "It permits us to execute the simpler plan of the two, and simple plans are always the best. The most important roles will be played by Bussey and the half-caste woman. Bussey impressed me favourably; the woman less so. You are confident that they are both letter-perfect?"

"Yes. The woman is exceptionally intelligent for her class."

"And the beach clues have been dropped at the proper time?"

"Yes. They were put into the sea at the second."

For perhaps the hundredth time Van Horton studied the map. Lawrence smoked a cheroot without a sign on his imperturbable face of the steadily growing excitement within him. Seated near the fire, for the evening was cool, was the Australian geologist, Dr. Woolworth. Without looking up, the American again spoke.

"There are two weak spots we must guard against," he said, as though these weaknesses had just been presented to his mind. "The first of them is our friend, Doctor Woolworth. He is a man mentally weakened by alcohol, and if he should be tested, which is probable, he may not survive the test."

The man by the fire moved uneasily, but did not speak. The firelight was kind to his haggard features, softening the stencil marks of physical abuse. Ordinarily he appeared sixty years of age. Now he looked forty, which was his real age. His hair was greying, what there was of it, and his hazel eyes were blurred; the fire of youth burned out with brandy.

"Woolworth will be all right. You can leave him to me," Lawrence said significantly. "Who is the other weak spot?"

"You," replied Van Horton.

"I?"

"Exactly. Yourself."

"In what way do you think I'll fail?"

"In being squeamish." Abruptly Van Horton turned sideways and looked at his lieutenant with his soul-piercing eyes. "It is your one fault," he went on coldly. "You are clever, but you are not ruthless. You take absurd chances in preference to decisive action. You would prefer to knock an enemy down with your fists rather than kill him, even when you know if you don't kill him the odds are in favour of his killing you. It is a pity I cannot conduct the business in person. As I cannot do so, the leadership falls on you, and I would point out that soft measures in this affair will endanger not only yourself, but everyone of your men. When the time comes, you have to remember to the exclusion of all else that your objective is twofold. First you have to get possession of the person of the Princess, and secondly you have to get her away from Cook. You must allow nothing and no one to stand in your way."

"I shall not allow anything to stand in my way," Lawrence affirmed, in a tone of voice which caused Van Horton to look at him as though he saw him for the first time.

Silence once more, Van Horton going over in his mind the details of a perfect plan, Earle Lawrence thinking of Helen Van Horton, then with her maid and a cook in residence in the caverns, three miles away. She was the greatest prize Lawrence ever had wanted to win, and to himself he silently swore that to possess her he would conquer his distaste for taking human life.

From the still night without came the sudden bellow of a camel.

Neither had heard its soft-footed approach, although it was expected. The animal was sent to its knees and a half-caste alighted and entered the hut.

"The train will reach Cook at half-past three to-morrow afternoon," he said in soft drawling English.

"Very good, Fred," Lawrence said. Then to Van Horton: "Well, do we send word?"

The American nodded.

To the half-caste Lawrence said: "Go back to Eucla. Tell Bussey to dispatch the cars east and west, and to destroy the telegraph line east and west of Eucla. The east car will pick me up at the junction in the morning."

"Orl right," the dark-faced rider murmured, and vanished into the night. They heard the camel complaining when it was urged to its feet, but they did not hear it depart.

"I think I'll go back to camp," Van Horton decided, getting to his feet and stretching his arms. "There is nothing I can do now. Everything depends on you."

"I shall not fail."

They placed over their shoes slip-over boots made from sheepskins with the wool on the outside. With these pads of wool between the soles of their shoes and the ground, no trace of their passing would be found even by the sharp eyes of native trackers. Lawrence escorted the American across the starlit plain to the hole in the ground giving entry to the caverns. He then returned to the hut, found the doctor asleep on his camp-stretcher, carefully set two alarm clocks to awake him at three, and slept on a rug before the dying fire.

With the break of day a car was driven rapidly towards Eucla, containing two men, from a point forty miles west of the empty telegraph station. The tonneau of the car was loaded with two hundredweights of the spiky globes similar to that on which Raymond Lund had knelt. One of these men, using a short-handled, sharp-pointed iron fork, was throwing over the back of the car quantities of these rubber-tyre destroyers, leaving a trail over which no car with pneumatic tyres would proceed for more than half a mile at the maximum. A second car, occupied by two men and loaded with the same material, left a point on the overland track forty miles east of Eucla, and travelled rapidly towards the telegraph station. Whilst the western car was to lay a spiked trail all the way to Eucla, the eastern car was to lay its trail only to the junction of the Cook-Eucla road, three miles north of Eucla and at the edge of the Nullarbor plateau.

At Mundrabilla Station, sixty-seven miles west of Eucla, a corroboree that had started two days previously was still going on. About sixty aboriginals lay that dawn drunk with stupor and full stomachs. At White Wells Station, far to the east, another hundred natives were enjoying themselves in like manner. At a native water-hole, thirty miles north of Ooldea, there was a precisely similar gathering. In the vicinity of the transcontinental railway, between the stations of Ooldea and Forrest, and throughout all that area of country between those places and the sea, there was not a single Australian aboriginal to be found. All had been withdrawn to the places named at the behest of various chiefs bribed with vast quantities of food and diluted drink. Earle Lawrence had made sure that, south of the railway, there should be no living soul, other than the members of his gang, on an area of nearly nine thousand square miles.

The telegraph line had been erected in 1877, and taken over by the Commonwealth in 1900. On completion of the Great Western Railway a new line was erected beside the railway, the transmission station removed from the old line to the new, and the old line rented to the pastoralists. It was, however, still a force to be reckoned with, which was why Lawrence ordered its destruction. Had it been really all-important, he would have arranged for the active lines along the railway to be cut at half a dozen places, but the complete isolation of Eucla was necessary only for six hours at most following the kidnapping of the Princess.

The organising genius of Van Horton had made the two plans as nearly perfect as the human mind could conceive. He had brought into full blossom the bud that had grown in the brain of Earle Lawrence. Lawrence's ideas rested on the likelihood of fine, calm weather at that time of the year. Van Horton was too big a man to trust to the vagaries of the weather. Immediately he had gone over the ground, studied the multiple conditions, and had sorted out those difficulties to be elaborately met, and those to be dealt with in a simple practical manner, he saw that Earle Lawrence's ideas were excellent if the weather were fine. If it chanced, however, to be rough at sea, the Australian's house of cards would fall, so that he created an alternative plan to be adopted if the weather forecast favoured stormy conditions. Both plans were as far-reaching as human ingenuity could make them.

The calm weather plan proved suitable. Van Horton went to sleep; Earle Lawrence smoked an after-breakfast cigar whilst the dawn was paling the sky, and at intervals looked at his watch. He spoke after an unusually long silence.

"Looking at my watch invariably reminds me of the trenches on Gallipoli and in Flanders," he said, gently smiling at the grey-faced doctor, who was smoking a cigarette beyond the small table. "Especially am I reminded of a particular hop-over when we lay just east of Corbie.

Zero hour was set for 5.25 a.m. I was a platoon sergeant, and our platoon officer was a young Melbourne buck, a mere new-chum at soldiering, yet set to lord it over veterans. The only virtue we veterans demanded in an officer was courage. His morals did not interest us, his conscious superiority made no impression. We knew that he was, like everyone of ourselves, a mere cog in the machine.

"As I said, all we demanded of an officer was courage – not the stupid brainless courage which sacrifices men's lives, but the passionless calculating courage which conserves lives. The officer of my platoon at Corbie lacked either kind of courage. He stood with us in the trench as dawn flickered in the east. In his hand was this watch. The look of him told me that he would fail. To-day I pity him with all my heart as he stood there deep in the hell which many of us had looked upon but had never fallen into.

"Zero hour struck. The barrage fell. Above the roar we could hear the platoon leaders on both our flanks blow their whistles. Our officer stood, the hand which held his whistle powerless. The colour of his face was more terrible than if he had been a three days' corpse. I was standing beside him.

"'Sir!' I said.

"He made no answer. No sound issued from his lips. I knew he read my purpose, for I saw it in his eyes, saw in them a look which ... I ... shall ... never ... forget."

Earle Lawrence sighed. Dr. Woolworth's eyes were wide. He had not served with the army. He was, however, cursed with an uncontrolled imagination. Horribly, whilst he sat there, was he pictured to himself as that pitiful officer?

Lawrence continued: "Thirty seconds had passed and my platoon had not gone over. I made no feint, nor did I hurry in taking from his holster his service revolver. His eyelids fluttered not once, not even when I shot him dead. Even as he lay at my feet his wide-open eyes held in them that terrible expression.

"In fair fight I have killed quite a lot of men, Doctor. That poor runt was the only man I have killed in cold blood. I never wish to see in the eyes of another man what I saw in the eyes of that man. It disturbs my sleep. But, Doctor, if you have one little drink to-day I'll see that terrible look in your eyes a second ... two seconds ... before you die."

The faded blue eyes of Dr. Woolworth were almost bulging. The tip of his tongue flicked his dry lips. He made an effort to speak and failed. Lawrence smiled in his cold, unmirthful way, and, donning his white helmet, nodded and went out, leaving the doctor still licking his lips with the tip of his tongue.

As has been said, the site of Dr. Woolworth's spurious boring for oil was situated between the Ceduna-Eucla road and the underground caverns. Earle Lawrence walked along the rough track from the shed to the road, and he wore over his boots the slip-overs made of rough sheepskin with the wool outside. The ground he walked over was hard, gritty limestone, but here and there were small patches of sand. Even on these sand patches his sheepskins left no track, merely the faintest tiny circles and curves which a breath of wind would wipe out.

Gaining the main and single road from east to west, he found awaiting him Sir Knight, seated at the driving-wheel of a car, and Blue Everett seated on the back of the tonneau, his feet resting on boards that lay on a mass of the metal globes armed with spines.

Earle Lawrence nodded. No one of them spoke. Sir Knight drove on to Eucla, and Blue Everett went on forking up the spined globes and tossing them out over the track behind them.

Here the plain was covered with low scrub, six to ten feet in height. The track wound in and out, and quite suddenly they came to the edge of the plain, where it drops for several hundred feet to the low coast country. A branching track on their right revealed the way to Cook. The car swept round a bluff in what ages ago must have been the actual coast. There flashed into sight the western edge of the plateau. The car rounded a bend to the south, and there, across three miles of flat, stunted, bush-covered country, hundreds of feet below, lay the red-roofed buildings of Eucla, a miniature deserted town.

Eucla lay against humped sand-hills of dazzling whiteness, hills of sand rearing up behind it, cutting it off from the ocean as their summits cut and curved into the indigo blue of the sea.

The track descended the face of the bluff in a long slant. On the plain below the car sped towards the deserted township, leaving a lengthening trail of white dust, which rushed upward, and then hung in mid-air like smoke from a steamer's funnel.

The substantial stone buildings of the one-time hive of telegraphic activity slid towards them, reached them. The car braked to a halt close to an iron telegraph pole, and Earle Lawrence, looking up, saw that there were now no wires attached to its cups. Bussey came in, and with him Slim Jim. Five minutes later Ted Norton arrived with another man. The half-caste and his half-caste wife stood outside what probably had been the chief official's residence. Including Earle Lawrence, there were there twelve men and one woman, and everyone of them wore over their boots or shoes rough sheepskin slip-overs having the wool outside.

CHAPTER VIII

THE REHEARSAL

IN the largest room of the largest building at Eucla were assembled more than a dozen men, a half-caste woman, an Afghan in Australian clothes but wearing the turban of his country, and Earle Lawrence. It was ten o'clock in the morning, and Lawrence had called them together after a late breakfast.

The buildings of this small township or village were constructed of stone blocks with corrugated iron red-painted roofs. Eucla might have been a small garden city on the outskirts of London if one turned one's back on the towering white sand-hills between it and the ever restless sea. For years that room had known the click-clacking of innumerable telegraphic machines. Now, save for a rough deal table at one end, it was void of furniture or fittings.

On the table stood a clockwork train. It was drawn up at a miniature station, about which were small pieces of limestone representing buildings. Beyond the table stood Earle Lawrence, dressed as usual in spotless white duck. Behind him, suspended against the wall, was a roughly drawn large-scale map. Before speaking the tall Australian cleared his throat.

"To start with, I want reports from some of you," he said in his pleasant drawling voice. "Blue Everett, have you closed the east road?"

"Sir Knight and I laid a trail with the spiny burrs for thirty-nine miles to the junction of the Cook-Eucla road," a well-built, sandy-haired man of forty replied in a distinctly cultured English voice.

With red crayon Lawrence drew a mark on the map representing Blue Everett's operations that morning.

Lawrence inquired then of a short, black-moustached man of uncertain age: "Did you close the west road, Larsen, as instructed?"

"Yes, boss. Me closed de road wid de spines from here to tirty-tree mile," replied Larsen in a German accent.

Again Lawrence used the red crayon.

"Bussey!" he called.

"I destroyed the telegraph wires for a quarter of a mile each way by cutting them each side of every standard," reported a stocky man of great physical strength. His voice was loud and harsh, trained on a drill-ground. His moustache was full and the ends were waxed. A typical drill sergeant out of the British Army, he went on with clipped sentences. "Later I overhauled the gear. Saw to each pair of sheepskin boots. Oiled, tested, and loaded the automatics. Examined the masks and found same in order. Accompanied Smithson in tuning the car engines. Made certain each car carried fifty per cent. more petrol and oil than is normally required. Saw to it that each car was provided with spare tyre on rim pumped to regulation pressure."

"Good! Ah Khan?"

In perfect English the Afghan spoke: "My camels are a little south of the junction of the three roads, that is, between Eucla, Ceduna, and Cook. They are in charge of my Australian son, Robert. The pack-saddles are in order. The padded cases are also in order."

The next man called was Peter Cuff, the half-caste, a tall, slim young man with a reddish-black complexion. "Yesterday I was at Mundrabilla Station," he said in soft, velvety tones. "I found there a large number of natives engaged in a corroboree. I left with Lattee, the chief, a case of whisky. This morning those people will be very sick. At Cook I received word from a friend at Ooldea that at that place there is not one native. I am sure there is not a single aboriginal anywhere near Cook, or Eucla."

"Very well," Lawrence said. "That completes our isolation. You all see that to-day up till midnight at the very earliest no motorist can reach this place. We are assured, too, that there are no aboriginals in all this central southern country to observe us and possibly report our actions later.

"Everything has been done to preclude failure. We have at our head the cleverest man in the – ah – underworld of America, and, I venture to say, the world. Not one single point has been left to chance. I have drilled you in your parts till you have been sick and tired of it. That drilling, however, has been necessary; because, if one cog fails or breaks, the whole machine, carefully oiled as it is, will break down.

"We are not a rabble attempting the impossible. We are a disciplined intelligent force about to carry out a plan so drawn up as to be perfectly effective, yet simple. If you each and all do your parts within the next twenty-four hours, we shall have executed the most wonderful *coup* ever conceived. For the last time we will rehearse. As I call out your names you will state to which car crew you belong."

In answer to their names every man other than the half-caste and the Afghan spoke a number – one, two, or three.

"Now, as I call you, please step up to this table and repeat what your actions will be when the Princess' train stops at Cook. Number One car crew first. Sir Knight!"

In turn the men walked to the table whereon were set out the miniature model of Cook and the standing train. Bussey was to board the special car. Sir Knight was to attend to the engine crew. Three others were to hold up the people gathered at the place where the Princess would alight. The remainder indicated the precise positions they would occupy during action. Every man knew his particular job, and because of the model on the table there would be no confusion, no waste of time, no misunderstanding. At last this strange rehearsal was over.

"You are letter-perfect," Lawrence complimented them. He was as pleased as a play-producer before the opening night who is sure of his cast. "Now I'll hear Bussey and Lily tell me what they will see at Eucla late this afternoon, and will tell the detectives who certainly will arrive before tomorrow morning. Lily, go outside, please."

When the half-caste woman had withdrawn, Bussey described how he was several miles south along the coast examining dog-traps. He saw a ship put in at Eucla. He described the ship. He saw it steam away. When finished, he went outside and sent in the woman. She stated how she had heard several cars arrive, and saw a party of men and a lady walk over the sand-hills towards the jetty. She followed, and from the summit of the most seaward hill of sand saw the party transferred by a small boat to a ship. Her description of the ship corresponded exactly with that given by Bussey.

"Excellent! That, I think, will be all. We will leave here punctually at one o'clock. Ah Khan, you go back to your camels. Have them saddled and loaded and waiting at half-past four. A last word to all of you! You will be issued with the automatics with which you have practised so frequently. Remember this! You will shoot only when absolutely necessary. After to-day, you will spend a month to two months in enforced idleness. Then a ship will call here and take you to Shanghai, or some other Eastern port, where you will be paid off at the agreed price of one thousand pounds per man. From a port like Shanghai it is comparatively easy to travel to any country you wish."

"Party – 'Shun!" barked the ex-drill instructor. His small eyes were gleaming; the points of his moustache were trembling. "Three cheers for Mr. Lawrence!"

He led the cheering. Lawrence flushed slightly whilst watching their excited faces. He glowed with pride at having brought them together – ten men who had gone through the Great War with him, had suffered disappointments and hardships as he had done, and had discovered that the placidity of peace was akin to the slavery of the rowers' bench.

He was thinking of them when the three powerful cars climbed the cliff face that marked the southern edge of the vast Nullarbor Plain. There was first and foremost the indefatigable ex-Warrant-Officer Bussey, whom first he had seen and heard at Blackboy Camp in 1914. At first he had hated Bussey. It being against the Australian Army Regulations to swear on a parade ground, Bussey quickly became a super-expert in the art of insulting sarcasm. Trained in the British Army, Bussey was first and last a soldier. He knew his job far better than any one of the officers. On parade he was a devil; off it he was the friend of every man in trouble.

Coming next was the quiet Sir Knight of retiring disposition. Inoffensive save when in action. When Sir Knight went over the top he invariably left behind his rifle. But in each hand he carried a heavy Colt revolver, which he used with unerring skill.

Then there was Blue Everett, sometimes called Gentleman Blue, the man who had had the distinction of being promoted to commissioned rank three times, under three different names, and three times being cashiered for insulting language to commanding officers. When Blue Everett met a fool, at a time when discretion had been slightly dulled by rum, he simply had to describe the fool to the fool's face.

And what a fighter was Larsen! Jack Larsen, born in a German settlement on the Murray, in Victoria, of German parents. He had gone to a German school. In that place in Victoria he had seldom heard the English tongue. When at the age of twenty he ran away from home, he had to learn to speak English. But what a fighter! What a temper he had shown when he had thrown away his bayonetted rifle and set to work with his two hands, his boots, and his teeth! There was no artistry in Larsen's fighting; and the fact that he killed Germans did not lessen his joy therein.

Yes, they were good men, all of them. Even Peter Cuff. He, too, had gone to France. He was a queer cuss, to be sure. The shelling made a coward of him, but bullets had no effect on his courage. His *métier* was scouting in No Man's Land. There he stole about as a black shadow and as soundlessly. And the trophies he brought back! Memory caused Lawrence to shudder. The trophies were hearts, German hearts, skewered on a piece of wire.

The others, if of less distinction, were all good men. Fred Bennett, once a Major of Artillery, and until recently a confidence trickster and a blackmailer. Morgan, just plain thug, whose army *bête noire* was military policemen. Morgan always carried a knife. Sometimes he showed the knife to the interested and pointed out the eight notches, each notch representing the life of a military policeman. It was an experience when

Morgan could be persuaded to give a demonstration of stabbing. Robinson, too – but there! they were all men proved by the war to have no nerves, no mercy, and no scruples. Lawrence was satisfied that they would do.

Having gained the great flat tableland, the cars sped roughly north-east. For the first few miles the low bush hemmed in the track, so that Blue Everett and the Major, who knew England, thought they recognised South of England lanes bordered with rhododendrons. Presently the scrub thinned, fell away, vanished, and they were speeding across the plain proper, so vast, so open, that the slight undulations were invisible, giving the impression that it was one mighty billiard-table covered with a grey-green felt.

It was three o'clock when they first saw Cook, and the leading car pulled up. They then were about ten miles from the railway. At that distance all that could be seen was the great corrugated iron structure used as a locomotive shed, and two small black squares hovering about the earth in the heat haze. The black squares were water-tanks set on pile staging. Close to the ground, so low that they seemed part of the horizon-line, were the whitewashed roofs of the railway-men's houses, whilst the sun was reflected, as from silver, by the unpainted iron roofs of the telegraph buildings.

Of those in the cars, Lawrence and Bussey and the half-caste only had visited Cook before. The leader looked at his watch, saying: "It is now five minutes past three, Bussey."

Looking at his own watch, Bussey replied: "Checked and correct."

"Good. You and the others will remain here for fifteen minutes, when you will come on, and the Major with the third car will follow after a lapse of five minutes. When within one mile of Cook you will stop, get down, and pretend to change a tyre. The Major will catch up and appear to be helping. You will not come on further until the train is about three miles from the station. Then proceed according to orders."

"Right, sir." Bussey almost saluted.

Lawrence drove on. With him were Blue Everett and Sir Knight.

Their part was the most ticklish of any. It was foreseen by both Van Horton and Lawrence that the psychological moment for action was immediately the Princess' special train stopped. Within a minute after it stopped, armed detectives, who would travel in the fore part of the train, would be surrounding the Special Car No. 1, containing the Princess.

It was Bussey's work to board that special car. The *chef*, who was heavily bribed, would perform certain services. Cook being a locomotive depot, the engine that had brought the train from Tarcoola would normally be uncoupled and run into the shed, and a waiting engine would be coupled up and take the train on to Rawlinna. Since it was inadvisable to delay action until the Tarcoola engine was uncoupled, the crew of that engine must be prevented from taking on the train at the first sign of attack.

The train was to be pulled up directly opposite the telegraph buildings. Lawrence drove the car to the eastern end of them and stopped. The three men got down, but did not move away from the car. Practically the whole of the population other than railwaymen on duty were gathered close to the line, each and everyone of them gazing eastward along the twin ribbons of steel which met into one far along the rule-straight permanent way.

The day was brilliant, hot, and dead calm. A thin wisp of smoke rose straight from the chimney of a near-by wooden hut. A row of these huts stretched away parallel with the railway. They looked, on that dead flat surface, like dolls' houses floating on a placid calm ocean that bore never a ripple, never a swell.

"Here she comes! Here she comes!" shouted a man who stood on a water-tank staging. Lawrence glanced at Everett, who nodded. Sir Knight smiled and produced his crape mask.

CHAPTER IX

THE NULLARBOR PLAIN

IT is said of the Great Western Railway of Australia that its trains are the finest in the world. That is an overstatement of the two facts that it is certainly the finest railway in Australia and that its rolling stock is of the best – facts duly appreciated by the Perth-bound traveller who, at Kalgoorlie, must needs change into the state railway train of Western Australia. The difference is analogous to that between Raymond Lund's straight-eight Southern Cross car and the dilapidated Ford car-cum-truck.

The Princess Natalie's special train which conveyed her across the continent was composed of a first-class sleeper coach, a first-class lounge car, a dining car, a brake van, and the Special Car No. 1, being drawn in that order by a powerful engine. Her retinue, and the Australian officials who accompanied her, occupied the sleeper coach and used the lounge and dining cars. With the Baroness Schulz, the Countess Merlwitz, and three maids, the Princess exclusively occupied Special Car No. 1, which was wholly self-contained. She slept in one of the luxuriously appointed bedrooms, her ladies-in-waiting occupied the second, whilst the maids used the several three-berth compartments. Since the maids waited on the ladies and took their meals in the dining car, there was during the daytime only one man on that car at all times, and he was the *chef*.

Whilst Van Horton and Lawrence were perfectly well aware of these conditions, governed by the maidenhood of Natalie, they foresaw the probability that during the daytime the representative of the Commonwealth Government and members of nobility in the Princess' train would spend some of the time in that special car. They foresaw also that the only persons likely to carry firearms would be the small staff of detectives who, whilst they most certainly would parade the entire train during the halts, between stops would remain in the lounge or the first-class sleeper coach.

The position of the special car, coming as it did after the brake van at the very end of the train, favoured the abductors. This position was dictated by one of its attractions to tourists. At its very rear was a spacious observation platform, from which it was possible to gain uninterrupted views on both sides of the line and rearward over all that country through which the train had just passed.

The wide view that this platform gave to the observer charmed the Princess. Her journey occurred at the very worst time of the year, when the sun is a furnace, the earth an oven, and the wind raised by the train laden with dust. Nevertheless, the Royal visitor preferred the dusty observation platform to the heated interior of the coach, and there spent many hours marvelling at and appreciating this "so wonderful" railway journey.

The "Lake Country" east of Tarcoola, South Australia, presented to her the first striking picture in a landscape composed of red sandy soil and thick scrub with dark green foliage. The lakes were dry and their flat surfaces were covered with salt, which sparkled in the sunlight as fresh-fallen snow. The miniature volcano standing in the centre of Island Lagoon, surrounded by a snow-white sheet, peculiarly enough reminded her of Raymond Lund, and she found herself wishing that she was there on the shore of the lagoon alone with him, when they could race across the brilliant carpet and explore that "volcano".

The next morning, when she passed out to the observation platform, the entire scenic world had changed. The train was speeding across the Nullarbor Plain, which extends from east to west for 450 miles. The horizon to the north, east, and south, which the platform permitted Natalie to view, was as far-flung as the horizon of the ocean, and far more clear-cut in that atmosphere. Covered with blue-bush and salt-bush, its slight depressions hidden by its vastness, the plain fascinated Natalie as no previous part of her tour had fascinated her.

Sometimes she lost herself in the illusion that the train was a ship tearing across a weed-filled ocean in a dead calm. She wondered what it would be like were she to fall from the train and be left there in the midst of that immensity, alone, imagining herself as a lone castaway in a cockle-shell boat out of sight of land.

The estimated area of the Nullarbor Plain is 100,000 square miles. So generally flat, so entirely free from hills and watercourses is this plain, that the railway line is permitted to run in a straight line for 330 miles. Natalie and those with her began to sense the enormous land mass of the Island Continent...

"Wonderful! Wonderful!" Natalie breathed.

"There is nothing, Princess, I venture to say, quite like it in the world," the Government's special representative, General Hatters-Smith, told her. He was an iron-grey man who, in uniform, looked less like a general than would the fat boy in Pickwick. His equatorial thickness was enormous, indicating that in peace-time at least generals know how to feed.

Turning to him, Natalie laughed gaily, and, because she was afraid he would guess she was laughing at him, she exclaimed: "The plain, so like is it, I am reminded of a tennis-court made by the Gods of Olympus. Tell me, my so wonderful General, of it."

General Hatters-Smith, who had "swotted up" the railway guide pamphlet for this very purpose, described its area and geological formation; adding descriptions, too, of the blowholes and the known underground caverns with such loquacity as to create the belief that he was a hard-bitten explorer. He was beginning thoroughly to enjoy his own eloquence when the train began to slow up, and, seeing the look of inquiry in Natalie's face, he said, with an undiplomatic expression of annoyance: "Cook, Your Royal Highness! This is an unimportant wayside station, called Cook."

The door behind Natalie opened, and there appeared Baron Schulz, carrying a sheaf of papers. Bowing low, he advanced. "Highness, we stop here for nearly an hour. The programme is thus: Your Royal Highness will be pleased to speak a few words to the school-children, after which several of the leading officials will be presented. One of the important telegraphic transmission stations being situated here, if it please Your Royal Highness, you shall be conducted over the chief building and shown the instruments, which promise to be of interest."

"I concur, Baron. How many children are there expected to be?"

"About forty, Highness."

"*Mon Dieu!* – and they live here surrounded by this great openness. Certainly will I speak with them. I will have presented to me the heroic teacher."

The train was slowing to a stop with grinding brakes. A maid appeared with hat and gloves. She held a mirror whilst Natalie put on her own hat, an extraordinary custom she had adopted since leaving Adelaide. Then Natalie possessed herself of the mirror, and reached out her hand for the powder-puff. The train was almost stopped, when the ladies-in-waiting, the Baron, the General, and the maid visibly jumped at the sharp report of a pistol.

Into Natalie's blue eyes flashed a glint. She said: "Marie, the puff, quick! Then fetch me my automatic."

A fusillade of pistol-shots rang out. The Princess calmly powdered her face, holding the mirror before her. The Baron paled. The General had never before been so near exploding guns, and looked it. An audible gasp escaped the lips of the Countess Merlwitz

"Princess!" exclaimed Baroness Schulz, "within the coach it will be safer. Please, please, Highness, come."

"Marie is a creature so slow," Natalie said calmly.

Then she was rudely brushed aside by a man who sprang to the communicating door, slammed it, and faced them. Holding an automatic pistol in each hand, his features blotted out by a roughly-made hood-mask of black crape allowing only his gleaming eyes to be seen, his wavering pistols appeared to cover them all at the same time.

A motor engine roared. The Baron sprang towards the man in the black hood. His left-hand pistol roared with an ear-splitting report, and Baron Schulz, fighting with his hands for air, sagged slowly at the knees and collapsed.

For two full seconds there was not a single sound. Those two seconds seemed to those on the observation platform of Special Car No. 1 to be a two minutes' silence, following the passing of a very gallant gentleman. The silence was ended abruptly by a cacophonous uproar. The Baroness moaningly fell on the body of her husband. The Countess screamed. A shot was fired, followed by others in rapid succession. There came a tinkle of broken glass. Car-engines hummed. And during this noise the blazing blue eyes of the Princess Natalie met and held those glittering orbs behind the mask. She saw them move to the General. She saw when she looked at him his face bedewed with perspiration, his eyes wide and awful with horror. And then she felt a hand grasp her arm above the elbow and heard a cool, drawling voice say: "Princess, will you kindly come this way?"

Half turning, she looked round, wrathful indignation surging into her face. A tall and big man was towering above her, a man whose head also was enveloped in a black crape hood. The light in her eyes was as a living blue flame.

"Come!"

The word was accompanied by inexorable pressure on her arm. She knew then the impossibility of resistance; realised, too, that to resist would result in an exhibition of foolishness. She permitted the man to help her to the ground. Only three steps did she take before she was forced to climb into the tonneau of a closed car, but during that short space a swift glance up along the train showed her a small crowd of people held motionless by the automatics of three men. Three bodies lay on the ground between her and them.

In the car, seated beside the big man who had taken her from the train, she said icily: "I shall make special command to be present at your so delightful hanging."

CHAPTER X

THE MEETING AT EUCLA

SITTING bolt upright, her gaze centred through the windscreen on the track winding ahead across the plain, her eyes like stars, her pulses throbbing with excitement, the Princess Natalie was rushed towards Eucla at fifty miles an hour in a superb car. Earle Lawrence, sitting beside her, glanced at her, expecting to see signs of fear on her face, but saw instead an expression of outraged dignity. The man in him marvelled at her courage and was pleased.

With a quick movement he took off the concealing hood. "I trust, Princess, that the experiences in store for you will prove a delightful change from the tedious official routine of a royal tour," he said in his pleasant drawl.

The Princess not deigning any reply, Earle Lawrence went on:

"Forgive me, Highness, if sometimes it will be necessary to force my society upon you. I am a bad, loathsome brigand, but I have always respected the conventions and clung to the ideals of a gentleman, although at no time have I been recognised as one. You see, my grandfather was a governor of a convict establishment, my father was a gold-miner, and I have always been an adventurer."

"Why do you do this?"

The Australian found himself being examined by blazing eyes. His own eyes were actually dancing with pride of achievement, of triumph. "Why do I do this? Why, for money, of course. I have no possible doubt that your country will pay me a good round sum for the safe return of Your Royal Highness."

"So you think you will hold me for ransom?"

"Emphatically, I do think so."

"Fool!"

"Pardon?"

"I said you were a fool, a so damn fool."

"Somehow, Princess, I cannot agree with you."

"It is – what you say? – immaterial."

"I agree there, Highness," said Earle Lawrence, with an astounding chuckle. "We will not argue over such a trifle. What do you think of the great Nullarbor Plain?"

To this somewhat irrelevant question she made no answer, but continued to look straight ahead, past the driver's black hood. The car rocked when it made the wide curves, bumped alarmingly now and then in flashing over the shallow, empty water-gutters. The wind it made felt cool against her heated face, but failed to cool the flaming anger fed by memory of the dastardly murder of old Baron Schulz. Her anger could give place to no other feeling or emotion just then.

The minutes slipped by with the miles. Lawrence offered no further remark. Before her he laid an open silver cigarette-case filled with cigarettes, but she did not give it a second glance. She did not see the shrug he gave, but did hear the match struck which lighted his cheroot. With this at the corner of his mouth, at an angle of forty-five degrees, he settled himself back comfortably and went over in his mind the incidents of the hold-up.

It had been accomplished without a hitch, precisely as he and Van Horton had planned it. In no other part of the world could it have been carried out successfully with so small a number of men at his disposal. The plan had been brilliantly conceived, brilliantly executed. The men had worked as the components of a machine, without individual hesitation or haste. In one respect it was a pity. Slim Jim Jackson and Ted Nolan had been killed in the short skirmish. There was a third man – Robinson, he thought – badly wounded. It would make Bussey short-handed, but then Bussey was as full of initiative as a bran-tub of bran. Sir Knight had done splendidly; his shooting had been a marvel of accuracy. There remained only the get-away of the survivors. The process of laying the red herring past Eucla would be comparatively simple.

Yes, it had been a most daring *coup*. The whole world would ring with it. The plan had been made fool-proof by the genius of Van Horton, and for the life of him he could not see how it could fail. And behind that fool-proof plan lay waiting his own super-plan, which only time would put into execution.

The mind of Lawrence went back to those days when he was a colonel, as it were, in Van Horton's mighty organisation, directed from Chicago. As a unit of that organisation, he realised his mental inferiority compared with the supreme intelligence and power of Van Horton. Aye, the gentle-spoken, bland Van Horton, whose house and offices were guarded by a squad of gunmen, and who walked abroad guarded by his gunmen more efficiently than ever any European monarch was guarded by soldiers or police!

In those days Van Horton was "The Chief". It was "The Chief" who decided the "removal" of any unit suspected of lukewarmness or disloyalty, and it was one of his famous "Two Hundred", a band of pitiless thugs, who carried out the "removal". It had been a wonderful human machine employed to extract vast wealth from the sins, the weaknesses, and the vices of millions – a machine which often cast from itself a clogging clinker in the shape of a corpse.

Never at any time during his association with Van Horton in America had Earle Lawrence felt entirely safe, not even when he had become one of Van Horton's ten chief executives. There had been Timms, one of Van Horton's admired supermen. Timms had been about to descend the steps of his hotel on Forty-Seventh Street when one of the Two Hundred had shot him, and then had leisurely escaped in a waiting car. And all Timms had been known to do was to address and post a letter to a rival gangster who was rapidly attaining to power.

But here was Van Horton, not so very far from Eucla, but thousands of miles from Chicago and the units of his organisation. The shoe now was on the other foot with a vengeance, a permutation that Van Horton did not seem to appreciate. The conditions that reigned in Chicago in nineteen-twenty-four now obtained ascendency at Eucla in nineteen-twenty-eight, with the difference that the positions of Van Horton and Earle Lawrence were reversed. And Lawrence thought of the proud beauty of Helen Van Horton with a hard smile of triumph.

For more than an hour the silence between the Princess and Lawrence was maintained. He was too much absorbed in memory and reflection to force speech, yet never for an instant did he relax his vigilance to prevent any attempt, suicidal though it would have been, of his prisoner to leap from the fast-running car.

What a *coup* it was! The most audacious, the most perfectly carried out *coup* in all history. Even then from Cook the astounding news would be radiating east and west to the eastern cities and Perth, thence to all points of the inhabited globe. He and Van Horton had succeeded in placing Cook on the map. In twenty-four hours millions of men and women who had never heard of the little township would know precisely where it was and the whole of its short history. Somehow he must contrive to get the subsequent issues of important newspapers. And then there was the series of documents which on certain dates would be posted in various parts of the world – documents addressed to confederates in other cities where they would be re-addressed and posted to the editors of newspapers.

The low salt-bush had given place to the dense-growing, eight-foot scrub. They were nearing the junction of the three roads where Ah Khan was waiting with his camel train. The car swerved round several sharp bends. For a fleeting second they saw on their right a deep gully. Then almost directly ahead the blue water of the Great Australian Bight sparkled as a long flat turquoise. The next second it was gone. The engine hum died down. Brakes were applied, and quite suddenly they pulled up just in time to avoid knocking down the gesticulating Ah Khan.

"What's wrong?" demanded Lawrence, fearing that some unforeseen hitch had occurred. The Afghan pointed east.

"You hear? Car coming," he said shrilly.

"Car coming! Impossible! Those tyre-prickers would stop anything."

"You hear!" Ah Khan almost commanded.

"Take my place!" Lawrence snapped, hearing now the roaring hum of a motor-engine unsilenced by an exhaust-chamber. "Blue, come with me."

He stepped out. Ah Khan climbed into the car. The Princess did not move. Only her eyes were gleaming. She saw that the Afghan was wearing strange woollen boots. She observed, too, that the driver and her abductor were both wearing similar boots. She wondered why this extraordinary footwear.

Lawrence and Everett walked along the track leading to Ceduna. They walked fifty paces, and stopped.

Round a corner of dense scrub appeared a unique object on four wheels, which roared and rattled as an alarm-clock within a steel ball. Natalie saw the tall Australian raise his arms and wave. The oncoming contraption slowed, finally stopped.

"Good day-ee!" drawled Lawrence.

"How do?" responded Raymond Lund, who was driving. "What's up? Broken down?"

"Yes, a slight mishap," Lawrence replied, deciding that the best thing to do was to bail up these two most inconveniently arrived travellers until Bussey and the others joined him. To gain time, he went on: "Your car has most peculiar tyres. A new patent, I guess?"

"Yes. It is fortunate we possess such tyres. Otherwise the metal burrs some fool has laid along this track would have torn ordinary rubber tyres off the rims. That is your trouble, probably?"

"Well, no. So far my tyres are all right. You refer to metal burrs. What are they like?"

"Fish one out of the box, Bill," Lund ordered grimly.

Sweet William produced a specimen and handed it to Lawrence, who examined it as though he had never seen one before. "Rather extraordinary," he said.

"If I lay me hands on the bloke wot dropped it, he'll think his day's work is over," Snell growled deeply.

"Well, we must move – unless we can be of any assistance. We are due in Perth Friday morning," Lund told the tall man. "Be advised. Go back. You'll never reach Ceduna with the track covered with those spiny things."

Lawrence frowned with assumed perplexity. Lund became obviously impatient. Precious minutes were passing.

Sweet William searched his pockets for tobacco, and, finding none, stood up to reach back over the load for a fresh tin. When he stood up, the Princess saw his ugly face, and knew beyond all doubt who was the driver of the machine she felt sure she recognised. She attempted to rise, but the Afghan pushed her back with one arm.

"Mistaire Lund! Mistaire Lund! Go –"

Both Lund and his henchman heard the frantic cry. For two seconds Lund was paralysed with sheer astonishment. The Princess! Natalie! Here! On the Eucla trail in that car ahead?

"What the devil – !" he cried, still mastered by surprise. He made to get out, and found himself looking down the black muzzle of a squat automatic. He heard Snell draw in his breath, and, since Snell made no volcanic movement, deduced that the second man had Snell covered.

"Please keep your seats," Lawrence ordered in a calm voice containing hidden menace.

"You dog!" Lund almost snarled in his impotent rage. Apprehension, surprise, anger battled within his brain. A hundred questions fought to be asked. "You dog! What's your game, eh?"

The "eh" was barked as a man will bark when speaking to a recalcitrant hound. The timbre of it spoke of habitual mastership; the authoritative air of an officer addressing an unruly subordinate. The blood crept up into the bronzed cheeks of Earle Lawrence, yet his gun hand never wavered, nor did his voice hold any indication of the sting he suffered. He said, still cool outwardly:

"The game, as you call it, does not really concern you. Reaching this place at this particular time is most unfortunate. Common sense dictates your elimination by contracting the forefinger of this my right hand. Common sense only awaits temptation, I assure you. From where have you come?"

"Adelaide. My name is Lund, as you heard that lady cry out."

"Lund! It is not a common name. As the lady in my car knows your name, it requires no Sherlock Holmes to infer that you are the son of Sir Henry Lund, with whom recently she stayed for a few days. Am I right?"

"You are."

"In that case, I am relieved at not acting according to the rules of common sense. However, do not tempt me. Please remain as you are. I hear my friends coming."

The still sunlit air, oppressive in its very stillness, vibrated with the hum of engines. Lund moved his gaze from the pale grey eyes above the automatic, and, glancing at the halted car containing, he was certain, the Princess Natalie of Rolandia, saw two other cars slow up and stop beyond it. A party of men wearing black hoods and ungainly woollen boots hurried towards them.

CHAPTER XI

GUN FIRE

THE officer responsible for the safety of the Princess Natalie during her sojourn in Australia was known, both to his colleagues and the members of the underworld, as Knobbs. His real name is not material to this history of the abduction. An experienced officer, with twenty-four years of service to his credit, he had drawn on this experience, as well as on the experience of his European prototypes, in compiling one set of regulations to be carried out by his subordinates when the Royal train stopped at any country station, either to permit the Princess to meet the people, or for the engine to take on water.

These regulations differed entirely from those that prevailed when Natalie left the train at a city, where his guards were invariably reinforced by men of the city or state police. During train journeys, when a halt was approached and the train was slowing down, the man on guard at either end of the special saloon or coach was joined by yet another man. Immediately the train stopped there alighted from both ends of it four men, two to each side, and these converged rapidly on the special coach, situated somewhere near the centre of the train.

The situation of the No. 1 Special Car of the transcontinental train was, as already has been noted, at the rear end, with a brake van between it and the dining-saloon. This necessitated a slight alteration in the position of the guards on duty at all times. The fact, also, that the passenger was a woman, and that she was surrounded by her women, also counted against the forethought of Knobbs. Had the person to be guarded been a Prince, a King, or a Duke, one or more detectives could have been stationed in the car itself.

The procedure at the halts between Port Augusta and Kalgoorlie, however, required only slight modification. The two detectives on duty at the brake van end of the Special Car alighted from the fore platform immediately the train stopped, and hurried along to take up positions one on each side of the near observation platform, whilst two others occupied similar positions at the front end of the car.

This arrangement was considered adequate to forestall any mentally unbalanced person bent on making a disturbance. That actual danger would threaten the Princess whilst in a capital city was considered unlikely, since her country's Government was far more monarchal than that of the British Empire. But, and it is a perfectly reasonable supposition, danger of physical violence was considered to be almost negligible while she travelled on the Great Western Railway, across a stretch of country hardly more populous than the South Pole.

The first hint of the outrage at Cook received by Knobbs was when he saw Bussey board the train before it stopped by jumping on the rear platform of the Special Car. The crime of lese-majesty shocked his trained official mind. On the instant he recalled just what he must do to a lunatic obsessed with the idea of shaking hands with a Princess. Reaching up, he pulled a communication-cord, which rang a bell in the brake van, ordering his two assistants to rush through the Special Car and deal with the situation that had compelled the signal.

The men were already standing on the fore-platform of the Special Car. Hearing the bell ring in the brake van, they sprang to the door of the Special Car. It was locked.

Before the train stopped they were on the ground. So was Knobbs. So were four other detectives. The crack of a pistol shattered the still air. It shattered, also, the illusion of a harmless ass bent on shaking hands with a Princess. A woman among the small crowd outside the station building screamed hysterically.

Knobbs saw three men with black hoods over their heads appear near the crowd, threatening it with pistols. He did not see Sir Knight one minute earlier climb into the cab of the engine from the further side. Neither did the train crew, until after he had gained the footplates.

With a revolver now in his hand, knowing where his first duty lay, Knobbs raced along to the Special Car, at the heels of one of the men whose duty it was to take up a position at the rear. A car with two hooded men in it rushed to the rear platform, and from it one man sprang to the platform steps when Knobbs and his colleagues were four yards off. The driver of the car opened fire the instant after a report came from the rear of the Special Car.

Poor Knobbs died in the execution of his duty. Possibly he would have had it so, for subsequent events would have "broken" him. Blue Everett turned his gun on the second man, and with icy coolness shot him in the thighs. Nearer the crowd at the station buildings the man called Ted Nolan fired once into a coach and then collapsed. Slim Jim Jackson on the further side of the train was killed by the detective racing to the rear, and this man was shot by Bussey at the instant the Princess Natalie sank into the rear seat of the car which flashed off on its way to Eucla.

The fact that the Princess was standing on the rear platform of the

Special Car whilst the train slowed to a stop most certainly aided the abductors. It obliterated that margin of time which was the only ghost of a flaw in a perfect plan. From the time Bussey boarded the train until he left it to whistle his men to retreat to the cars, the stopwatch record could have been no more than one hundred seconds.

At the retreat whistle Sir Knight sprang from the engine. It was the first time anyone there, other than the engine crew, realised he had been on the footplates. The three men who had held up the crowd joined him when he passed, ranging themselves one on either side, and one behind, and the four of them walked at an easy pace some ninety yards to a waiting car. Sir Knight held a six-chambered Colt revolver in each hand. He had refused Earle Lawrence's proffered automatics, preferring the weapons he had learned to use with amazing accuracy in South America. His guns belched flame and smoke, and above the uproar a man screamed beyond a window of one of the sleeper cars. A detective who fired from the steps of the dining-saloon slid down those steps to the ground, and although wounded again fired. Sir Knight shot him through the right forearm and walked on, urging forward his two companions, who climbed into one of the two remaining cars, which roared away towards Eucla. It was then that Sir Knight ran to the wounded man, Robinson, and half carried, half dragged him to the third car, behind the wheel of which sat Bussey covering the retreat and rescue.

The senior of the four remaining unwounded detectives was a sergeant. For five to ten seconds he gazed with a blank mind at two cars speeding across the southern plain, and at the rising dust that hid the third car a mile further on.

Then, with startling abruptness, he was galvanized into furious action. To the foremost male members of the Government staffs at Cook, who hastened forward, he barked: "The chief telegraphist! I want him." To one of them who acknowledged the position, he added: "Anyone here own a motorcar?"

"Yes. There are two here," was the reply.

"I own one," volunteered a bystander. "Do you want it?"

"You bet! Trot it along, quick. Office?"

The chief telegraphist raced towards a building with the sergeant at his heels.

Within, the detective seized pad and pencil and wrote furiously on four sheets. "Have 'em sent off at once. Now! Where does that road lead to those cars took?"

"Eucla."

"What's there?"

"Nothing. Place deserted."

"Any crossroads?"

"Yes. The track from Ceduna to Norseman meets it three miles this side of Eucla, and leaves it at Eucla."

Again the sergeant's pencil flew over several sheets. "Get these off," he snapped, then mopped his face with a large blue handkerchief. "Hell! There is going to be hell over this. But they can't get away. Send out and hunt up some trackers. We may want 'em."

The telegraphist shook his head. "There is not a nigger in the place," he said with a frown. "They disappeared three days ago, and as long as I've been here that has never happened before. There are always one or two at least hanging about for tucker and tobacco. The gins give our women a hand washing-day."

"Ah! Strange, doocid strange! You know there were no niggers at Ooldea, and that is a recognised camp where trans. passengers are met by niggers who do stunts for tucker and tobacco. By gad! Do you think this kidnapping gang's got anything to do with that?"

"It seems possible." The Cook man was looking keenly at the detective. He went on: "Do you know that at Eucla there is a jetty? Steamers used to call there before the telegraph staff was moved."

"The devil! A jetty! Still, they won't be much safer at sea than on land." The sergeant was thinking as he had never thought in his life, and whilst he was weighing this sea versus land problem in his mind he saw a clock on the wall which registered a quarter to four, and realised that there were but four hours or so between then and darkness. Without another word he ran outside, there to find an almost new car waiting in charge of its owner-driver. Seated with him was a man with a camera, a special representative of the Australian News Service.

The policeman's jaw opened to speak, but no speech came. He waved his hands above his head and resigned himself to fate and the smiling newspaper man, who had taken and left in a subordinate's charge for dispatch a string of pictures which was to set the world alight.

With two colleagues beside him and the third on the floor, the sergeant almost yelled: "Eucla! And don't get under sixty miles an hour!"

CHAPTER XII

MR. BUSSEY EXPLAINS

"UNDERSTAND! I've commandeered this car," shouted the sergeant, whose name was Brown, after watching the speedometer soar to forty miles an hour and remain steadily at that figure.

The driver nodded.

"Understand, it belongs to the Commonwealth of Australia, which will make good all damages. Let her out, d'you hear?"

The driver did let her out. At the end of the first mile the pointer of the speedometer registered fifty-four miles per hour. It was steadily moving towards the sixties when, suddenly, the car swerved off the road, bumped alarmingly over the irregularities of the virgin plain, and was rapidly brought to a stop. The driver said succinctly: "Punctured!"

He climbed down from the car. The sergeant clambered across the knees of a colleague in his haste, and, without troubling to open the door, slid over the side. The near rear-wheel was the first he saw. It was partly deflated, and he could hear the air seeping from the inner-tube, a sound that intensified the savage expression on his large red face.

"Come on! Get a move on!" he roared, exasperated to the point of apoplexy.

"I'm jackin' her up. Can't you see?" growled the driver, hidden by the bonnet.

The senior officer could not see. He walked to the front of the car, where he halted to gasp with rage so fierce as to be soundless. The offside front tyre was entirely flat.

"Look!"

One of the detectives held in the palm of his hand a dun sphere as large as a walnut, from which protruded four two-inch spines of toughened steel. The others closed round to see the cause of their trouble. One whistled. The sergeant swore. The driver pointed to the nearside front wheel. Stunned to silence by a growing sense of impotence, the little crowd of men gazed on the tyre, which was visibly deflating.

"One of us must go back and borrow some tubes," a man said, and then laughed with a note of harshness.

The driver was stooping over the ground in front of the car and picking up several of the spheres. "What's the use of tubes and tyres, anyway? The darned track is covered with the things."

"Then we must carry on with flattened tyres," the purple-faced sergeant snapped. "Come on, come on! Don't gape. Get a move on."

"But the tyres will come off," expostulated the driver, heartily wishing he had not volunteered his services and the use of his beloved car.

"What's the odds?" The sergeant was now on the verge of madness. He saw the vision of himself as an inspector becoming blurred with the passing of every precious second.

Then he fancied he saw the light, and at once his anger and impatience subsided and he became again the cool, efficient police-officer. "Push her off the road. Then all hands on to the tyres. Get 'em mended. Once mended, we can travel over the plain parallel with the road."

It took them three-quarters of an hour to patch eighteen punctures. Afterwards for an hour they drove over the virgin plain with, however, a maximum speed of twenty-nine miles an hour only. And when they reached a point fourteen miles from Cook a belt of broken stone-covered country compelled a return to the track.

"It ought to be clear now," was the sergeant's doubtfully expressed opinion.

But Sir Knight had done his work quite thoroughly in obedience to the orders of Earle Lawrence. The detectives' car had not proceeded a hundred yards when the treachery of the bush track was telegraphed to them straight from a wheel-rim.

A vast sigh of resignation escaped the sergeant. "Go on!" he cried with forced calmness. "Go on! Drive like the blazes till she cracks up."

It was four o'clock in the morning before the car's headlights revealed the cluster of buildings which was Eucla. Not a shred of a tyre remained on any wheel. Nor was there any sign of an inner-tube other than a red fringe of rubber round the battered ends of the valves.

"Now then, lads! We'll go through these buildings," came the soft voice of the sergeant before anyone of them alighted. "Remember! Any funny business – shoot! We're up against a crowd of thugs."

The night was clear and quiet. They could hear the roar of the surf coming to them through the salt-laden air. From landward came the tinkle of two bells. No light or sound issued from the buildings close by.

The first building they examined was the main edifice that had housed the innumerable telegraph instruments. The place was empty. The evidence of tourists' fires lay in the hearths. Littering the floors were pieces of wood cases, an empty meat-tin, beer bottles and bottle straws. Many of the large window-panes were broken by the stones among the litter, revealing the fact that modern motor vandals had come, stayed a night, and had departed as unreasoning vicious beasts, leaving an unmistakable spoor.

The next building in the row proved equally barren of occupation. This building appeared to indicate that once it had been an hotel or boarding-house: it was long and rambling, and at its rear were great underground cement water-tanks, roofed for protection against sun and birds. No indications of human presence were found in the next house. The building that had been used as a billiard-room was securely locked, but a torch thrust through a broken window revealed the table – and nothing else.

It was in the house which doubtless had been the chief official's residence that the police came upon the half-caste and his wife in one room, and Bussey in another. At their sudden entry the woman, who awoke first, uttered a scream of fear when the several torch-lights fell on her. The husband, apparently not fully awake, sprang up from the bedding laid out on the floor, and before he was thoroughly awake he was handcuffed. Bussey saw the handcuffs glitter, and, having twice been handcuffed before, he knew precisely how to hold his wrists so that the snapping bracelets would not hurt.

"Had 'em on before, my man, eh?" growled a detective. "Now then! Who are you and what are you?"

"Name of Bussey. Dogging 'ere," growled the man of cubic proportions, adding: "Who are you and what are you?"

"That you will soon find out," the sergeant snapped from the doorway. "Bring 'em into this room, and we'll look 'em all over."

In what appeared to have been a dining-room the three prisoners were ranged against a wall, Bussey actually grinning, the half-caste immobile, his facial expression one of vacuousness, whilst the woman, with flashing, indignant eyes, held round her the blanket one of the raiders had hastily snatched up and handed to her.

Before them, notebook in hand, stood the sergeant. Beside him one of his men held a hurricane-lamp so that the light fell on his book as well as on the faces of the suspects. To Bussey he said: "What's your name?"

"Bussey. I'm dogging 'ere. An' there ain't no law to stop me, and you ain't got no right to bail us up –"

"How long have you been dogging?" cut in the sergeant.

"'Bout two months. Done well, too. We got thirty-seven dogs."

"And you – who are you?" This to the half-caste.

"I am Peter Cuff. She's my wife. We're giving Mister Bussey a hand."

"Oh!" For a second or two the sergeant was busy with his notebook.

Then, to Bussey: "Where are the men who drove the cars here that are now out on the road?"

"Out on the briny."

"How did they get there?"

"Don't know. Never seen 'em go. Peter's missis says they boarded a boat."

"How was it you never saw them?"

"Mister Bussey and me was out on our trap-lines," interposed Peter Cuff. "We didn't –"

"I'm not talking to you. Now, Bussey, where were you when the cars arrived?"

"Somewhere about four miles south of here close to the beach – that is, if Lily is right an' they got here about half-past six."

"And you?"

"Two or three miles along the Mundrabilla road. I was on my way home," stated the half-caste easily.

"Now, Lily! Where were you?"

"I was here, cooking, when I heard the cars coming, and I ran out in time to see four cars pass and pull up at the edge of the sand. Several men got out, and a woman. They took no notice of me, and went on across the sand-hills towards the jetty. It looked very funny because they were in a hurry. When they were no longer in sight I ran after them, and over the last hill I saw them get into a small boat and watched the boat go out to a little steamer. Then the steamer went off. I watched it go round the west point, where the old beacon is. That's all."

"Humph! Take Bussey outside – out of hearing," commanded the sergeant. And, when they had gone: "Now then, describe the ship."

The woman hesitated.

"Come! Describe the ship."

"It was a little ship. Just a little ship." The woman was evidently perplexed. What an actress!

"Well, what colour was it?" asked the sergeant more gently, seeing that his brusqueness was unnerving her.

"Colour? Oh! It was white, all white."

"How many funnels?"

"One. Only one. And two tall masts."

"You couldn't see any name written on her?"

"Oh no! It was too far away."

Again the sergeant wrote in his book. He said when he snapped it shut across a finger that marked the page: "I'll be back in a minute."

Of Bussey, whom he confronted on the road outside just when day was breaking, he demanded to know: "You say you were along the coast when the ship came in?"

"I didn't say anythink of the sort," Bussey returned blandly. "I said I was four miles along the coast, south, when the cars must have arrived."

"Well, did you see a ship off the jetty, here?"

"Yes, I did."

"What sort of a ship was it?"

"She looked like a gent's yacht to me," Bussey said readily. "A white-painted boat with one funnel and two tall masts."

For ten seconds the sergeant looked hard at "Mister" Bussey with steady eyes. "Mister" Bussey did not flinch. Almost a hundred times had he and the woman, Lily, answered exactly the same questions put to them by Earle Lawrence in all degrees of official bluffness or blandness.

"Have you been down to the jetty since that ship called?"

"Have I wot?" rejoined Bussey. "Do you think I'm likely to go gallivantin' over orl that sand after I bin out for fifteen hours over a trap-line? Wot do you take me for? A bloomin' camel?"

For the first time the sergeant smiled. "By the way, I heard bells. Are those horses yours?"

"They ain't horses. They're camels. They belong to Peter Cuff."

"All right. I am inclined to think you people have nothing to do with these goings-on. Go and give the woman a hand to cook a feed for us all. Latham, see that they cook it and play no tricks. Take the bracelets off him and the half-caste."

The fourth detective, whose name was Cameron, had been stationed for many years in the far west of New South Wales, and the sergeant was aware that Cameron was an expert bushman. Sighing for the want of black trackers, he yet was forced to accept the services of a mere white man possessing the white man's defective vision. With Cameron he examined the abandoned cars. The two saw the sets of tracks going straight to the jetty, and to one side of them the tracks made by Mrs. Cuff. Every track, save those made by Mrs. Cuff on her return, pointed to the jetty. There were the tracks made by at least a dozen men and one woman. Even the sergeant could see that.

The two men, accompanied by the Press photographer, carefully avoiding the ribbon of disturbed sand, disturbed by the many feet of the abducting party and their captive, yet followed it past the old store building now nearly buried by the mounting sand. They crossed the two sand-ridges and noted with interest how in the gully beyond them the truck-line between store and jetty lay revealed still for ten or twelve yards. Beyond that place, right to the base of the jetty, hundreds of tons of sand had been blown across the line, burying it deep.

Arrived at the rough wooden jetty, the detectives saw that the single-arm stationary crane at the seaward end had recently been used. The wire rope hung over the jetty and fell down to the water. When they got to it they turned the windlass and wound up the rope, and at the end of it there came out of the sea a chair like that used by painters. They found also a light scarf of blue silk, caught on a splinter of wood beside the steps that led down to a broken landing-stage.

"That belongs to the Princess," declared the sergeant.

"It does. She wore it when she was taken off the train," Cameron agreed. "Gosh! It is a calm day, yet it must have been a ticklish business to bring a small boat alongside in this swell. No wonder they used the crane to lower themselves down into the boat. Had they used these steps the boat would have been in danger of being smashed against the piles."

"Too right. I'm beginning to understand that this abduction was very well planned. Ah! Look!"

The tide was setting strongly to the west, and it was bringing towards them an oar. Without comment the two men watched it. In a few minutes it was brought close, and they could see that it was a full-sized oar in use with a lifeboat. It was almost new, and Cameron said: "It hasn't been in the water very long. See! Nearly half its thickness is out of the water. We may discover other evidence on the beach itself."

The sergeant, recognising the probability, fell in with this suggestion, and for an hour they scoured the sandy beach east and west of the jetty. They found, flung up by the last high tide, a fruit-case in which sodden wrapping-paper was still held fast by gum to the sides. They found, too, an apple, half-eaten, potato peelings, and a copy of a Perth newspaper dated January 8th.

"If Bussey or his mate have had no papers this month, Cameron, then we'll know someone on that ship was in Perth on January 8th. The ship itself may have been in Fremantle or Albany about that date. It's a clue, anyway."

Decidedly that paper was a clue. It had been tossed into the sea from the jetty by Earle Lawrence, who had carefully watched the mysterious tides and currents. He had thrown it into the sea at the instigation of Mr. Van Horton. It was Van Horton who had thought of the oar, the half-eaten apple, and the fruit-case. The scarf was another careful clue.

CHAPTER XIII

THE "RED HERRINGS"

HIS usually clear, buoyant mind clouded by a mixture of emotions, including dismay, astonishment, and anger, Raymond Lund realised one definite danger by which both Snell and himself were faced. In the big Australian of easy speech he recognised unmasked menace. Admitting the obvious, a man who had abducted H.R.H. the Princess of Rolandia from a transcontinental train in broad daylight was not the sort of man who would hesitate to carry out a threat he had made. Lund knew that if he did not obey he would be shot. To disobey would not be courageous; it would be sheer stupidity.

The arrival of Lund and his servant-companion had made for Earle Lawrence a new problem. The most important part of the great plan was the drawing of the "red herring" at Eucla which the genius of Van Horton had created. It had become the vital component part, to be put into execution without delay. Every minute of time was precious; for, although the precautionary measures taken against instant pursuit had been eminently efficient, it was impossible to guard against every chance that might aid the detective force. The greatest danger to Lawrence and his men, a danger that no precautionary measures could eliminate, was the inopportune arrival at Cook of an aeroplane. Plans for a transcontinental aerial service were then well advanced, and the completion of landing grounds between Adelaide and Perth was all that was necessary for the service to become active. Already several 'planes had made the journey without any landing conveniences whatever.

Speed at this juncture, therefore, was vital. Lawrence sent three men to one of the cars. There on the back seat two of them removed their ungainly sheepskin boots, the third man returning with them. Lund and Snell were ordered to stand up in their car-cum-truck. Their hands were then tied behind them and their arms lashed to their sides with the turbans worn by the Afghan and his son. Still menaced with automatic pistols, the two pairs of sheepskin boots were placed over their own and securely fastened. They then were ordered to get out.

Lund could not but notice that these operations were carried out unaccompanied by anything resembling mental excitability. Not a man spoke other than the leader. Those men not actually engaged stood quietly aside, and, since they were not wearing the big enveloping head-masks, Lund was enabled to glance at each, seeing in the faces of some evidence of lives of rascality, and in the features of others the unmistakable stamp of culture. Undoubtedly a well-disciplined party.

The leader again gave an order, and Ah Khan got out of the nearest car, whereupon he gallantly assisted to alight a lady whom both the male prisoners recognised as Australia's Royal guest. With her Afghan escort, his nationality now submerged in his Australian clothes and minus his distinguishing turban, the Princess walked towards Lund, wearing sheepskin boots. He expected her to reveal anger, or show genuine and pardonably outraged dignity. In her eyes was neither one nor the other. They were actually alive with a dancing light of impishness.

"Oh, Mistaire Lund, is this not – what you say? – a lark?" she said. "Joost – no, just – fancy being kidnapped in this way by this man so conceited is he thinks to be Napoleon."

"The situation is intolerable," Lund fumed with impotent anger. "I look forward to the day, you, when I'll thrash you into insensibility with a stockwhip."

"Had I not been pressed for time and my mind occupied by important matters, I could be amused by your infantile threats," Lawrence drawled, icily cool. "However, there will presently be plenty of time to bandy pleasantries." Turning to the amused gang, he added: "Bennett, you will conduct Her Royal Highness to the waiting camels. Larsen, you will assist Ah Khan and his son to escort the male prisoners. Stand no nonsense, but no killing except as a last resource. Bussey, go with them for at least five hundred yards, when Ah Khan and his son will remove their sheepskin boots. You bring the boots back to the two sitting in the car, so that we can proceed."

Ten minutes later, Bussey returned with the desired boots, which were put on by those men who had given up theirs for the use of Lund and Snell. The entire operations at the junction of the roads had been carried out without a single person treading on the ground with ordinary boots or shoes, which would have left tell-tale tracks to be seen by a possible black tracker. In the eventuality of one coming across the tracks of the Afghan and his son five hundred yards from the junction, it would lead him and the accompanying detectives to the camel camp, and by then following the camel-pad they would arrive at an oil-bore where camels and Afghans would be camped, having but recently delivered to the geologist stores and machine parts.

Having dispatched the prisoners, Lawrence then directed a man to crank the engine of Lund's Ford car and lead the way to Eucla. He and the others in their three cars followed after. During the next half-hour there were made several changes of footwear. When the men got out of the cars they wore brand new boots one size larger than their proper fit. They each carried a second pair of boots of peculiar construction, but of the same size as those then being worn. The sheepskin boots were left in the cars. The half-caste woman, who had climbed into one of the cars, got out, wearing the shoes recently belonging to the Princess. Lawrence had apologetically borrowed these when equipping her with a special pair of sheepskins.

From another car the body of Robinson, shot in the fight at Cook and dying during the furious drive south, was taken by Bussey, who, carrying it across his broad shoulders, accompanied the others over the maze of sand-hills to the jetty. They walked in such a manner that it was impossible to observe by the distinct tracks they made how many men had passed but here and there the imprint of the Princess' shoes was plainly to be seen.

At the seaward end of the jetty the painter's chair at the end of the crane rope was lowered into the sea. The Princess' lace scarf was securely attached to a splinter on one of the wooden crossbeams, whilst the body was expertly weighted with handy pig-iron and dropped into the water.

The party then took off their boots and donned those they had carried. These had the position of the toes and heels reversed, and their design and manufacture had been carried out roughly but effectively by Bussey. They were most uncomfortable to wear, but the distance back to the cars was not more than a quarter of a mile. The woman, Bussey carried on his back. She had taken off the Princess' shoes, much too small for her, with a sigh of relief, and Lawrence had taken charge of them for their rightful owner.

Once again in the cars, the second relay of boots gave place to the sheepskins, each man then having slung round his neck two pairs of boots a size larger than his fit. Across the white, wind-ribbed hummocks of sand there could be distinctly seen the boot tracks of twelve to fifteen men and one woman. Every track pointed to the jetty, none from it.

"We'll get on," Lawrence said, impatient of time. "Bussey and you, Peter, get out on your trap-lines as planned. Lily – ah! I see you have on your own shoes again already – just go indoors till we've moved off, then come out and walk directly over the dunes to the ridge nearest the sea, where you will lie down and look at the water for two minutes. Afterwards come back and examine each of these cars for ten minutes or so. Then you can go indoors and cook your husband and Mr. Bussey a well-earned meal. And don't forget the white ship with one funnel and two tall masts."

She smiled at him with gleaming teeth. Lawrence smiled back, and knew she was his slave. Then he, with still further depleted retinue, walked back to the junction of the roads, keeping well off the track, so as not to obliterate in any degree the wheel-marks of the cars.

So was laid the red herring at Eucla which proved wholly successful in its purpose. The world was forced to believe that the Princess was taken on board a small steamer, which the navies of three nations failed to find in the vast southern ocean.

One hour and a quarter were occupied by the abductors in walking the three miles back to the tableland and Ah Khan's camels. The train was made up in two sections, each comprising eleven camels, one of which, the leading animal, carried the long iron riding saddle used in Australia. The majority of the pack animals were strong seven-year-olds able to carry up to 800 pounds. These carried, slung on each side, large packing cases of sufficient capacity to hold comfortably a harmonium.

There were ten of these cases in all, loaded on five camels. They were empty save for a flooring of thick padding which extended half-way up the four sides. The remaining animals carried genuine loads of stores and machine parts. The purpose of the empty cases was identical with that of the giant jars in the treasure cave of the Forty Thieves. Each case was fitted with a cunningly concealed door that could be opened and shut whilst still slung from the camels' backs. They were provided as hiding places for the Princess and the members of the gang, other than the Afghan camel-men, in the possible if improbable event of meeting with strangers or aboriginals whilst journeying from the road junction to the bore-site and the caverns beyond.

No conceivable precaution was omitted by the genius of Van Horton, assisted by the astute brain of the Australian bushman. The death of three members of the gang made it possible for Lawrence to provide these peculiar "bolt holes" for his two unwanted prisoners. He ordered that Raymond Lund and Snell be each shut up in a case carried by the same camel.

Without useless protest the travellers to Perth climbed into their prisons. The doors were shut on them, whereupon, not uncomfortably seated in the dark interiors, they both saw the several auger-holes that admitted air. The Princess was invited to swing into one of the riding saddles, the animal being then permitted to get to its feet. Whilst several of the remaining camels were roped down, the other members of the gang climbed to the top of the pack-loads, which they rode as best they could.

On the second riding camel, which led the long string single file, rode

Earle Lawrence. He as well as several others began continually to search earth and sky for human observers with the aid of powerful glasses, prepared at an instant's notice to drop to the ground and vanish inside the empty cases.

Ah Khan led the string towards the bore-site. The Princess began to enjoy the thoroughly novel experience. The impressions her mind received were so rapid and so various that only with the lapse of time did they become sorted and labelled. The vast plain, so deceitful in its vista of space, so like a dead calm sea covered with blue-grey seaweed, became as a picture indelibly painted on her mind. She had wondered, when on the observation platform of the train, how it would feel to be left behind alone; and here, within the space of three hours, she was riding a camel alone, save for several bandits, and two brave men held prisoners within packing-cases.

The next minute the metamorphosis was temporarily forgotten, and her interest was caught and held first by the long shadows cast by camel and rider, and then, when the sun met the illimitable horizon, by the rapidly changing colours of the earth.

She was reminded of the Throne Room of the palace at Naagrade the very first time she had been in it when quite a small girl. Then it had been empty. The setting sun shining through the windows that stretched from floor to ceiling had shed its warm light on the magnificent tapestry hanging on the wall behind the two thrones, whereon later she was to see her grandparents seated. And, as the light of the sun waned and vanished, so the purple tints of the tapestry had changed from scarlet and orange to brown and white, and then to deep grey and black.

So it was now with the Nullarbor Plain. For a short space of time it was aflame, a veritable sheet of blood. Anon it was purple, with millions of tiny points of glinting silver; then dark green, darkening yet into one tremendous unbroken circle of black, whereon was never a reflection of the stars blazing above.

It became a world undreamed of save by the occasional traveller in it seated beside a lone camp-fire. Space in that night appeared to have been enlarged a million-fold. Natalie came to understand a little the meaning of the words "universe" and "eternity"; here was space without limit, without beginning or end, in which the stars seemed confined to easily measurable human standards.

Space! The silence of space was there. It hemmed her in so that she found comfort in the slight creaking of a camel-load. No man spoke. The rubber-footed animals made no slightest noise. It was an invisible world of emptiness, of silence; far away, millions of miles away from the nearest world that was alive with human movement, human tumult. She formed a wish that she was nearer to that world wherein was sound, and it was long after, it seemed hours afterwards, before she knew that the far-distant sound was caused by the waves rolling upon the coast rocks miles to the south.

CHAPTER XIV

THE REST CAMP

QUITE suddenly the camel train stopped. How far and how long she had been riding the Princess had no idea. It seemed that she had been riding the leading camel for many hours and many miles; whereas in actual fact she had ridden for exactly four hours, and the speed of the camels had been a steady two and a half miles an hour.

Without warning, her mount suddenly fell on its knees, almost throwing her out of the saddle; and an instant later its hindquarters sank down too, so that once again the saddle was horizontal, but so near to the ground that she could touch it with her wool-booted feet.

Someone spoke. It was Earle Lawrence. "I hope you were not jarred, Princess. Some camels lie down directly they are stopped, and begin to chew. My own mount was not so prompt in that respect as yours."

"Are we arrived?" she asked coldly.

"No. We have only covered half the distance," he explained, ignoring her coldness. "We are in a slight hollow, and Ah Khan is about to light a fire, at which we shall make tea, eat a little, and rest for an hour."

"You will, of course, humane be, and allow Mistaire Lund and Sweet William forth to come from those boxes?"

"Most certainly. Shutting them up was unavoidable. For the rest of our way they may stop in the open air – if they promise to be good."

"Go! Release them."

Disdaining his proffered assistance, she slipped off the camel and made her way towards the growing flame of the newly-lit camp fire. Quickly the fire burned up, its ruddy glow revealing to her a scene unique and, had it not been for the known character of the men, not without much charm.

She saw twenty-two kneeling camels placidly chewing the cud. Several men were engaged removing the loads from their backs by easing the ropes, so that the heavy weights rested on the ground on either side of the recumbent beasts. A young man, swarthy and hatless, filled several large billy-cans from metal water-drums. He brought them to the fire and then stared with unconscious directness at the Princess. She thought him good-looking in his dark way. A moment later Lund and Snell, still bound, were conducted to the fire. At Lund she smiled, whereupon the scowl on Lund's face vanished and he smiled back at her.

"Cramped?" inquired Earle Lawrence politely.

"Gone beyond cramp."

"You must be uncomfortable, nevertheless. If you are agreeable to give me your parole and guarantee the parole of your friend, say for an hour, I will have you set free for that time."

"Surely you do not intend to keep us in this condition for weeks or months, unless I give you our parole?"

"Oh no!" Lawrence answered with a grim laugh. "As I have already explained to Her Royal Highness, this is our half-way rest halt. At our destination it will not be necessary to bind you. Now, your parole or not?"

Lund nodded. "Snell will make no move," he said, "nor will I."

Without further delay their freedom was accomplished. In the mind of Earle Lawrence there was no doubt that when Lund's word once had been passed it would be kept. As has been stated before, he was a good character-reader.

At first neither Lund nor his man could move an arm. Sweet William grunted with the pain of returning circulation. Tiny beads of perspiration broke out on Raymond's forehead, and seeing them Natalie understood what he was passing through, and unhesitatingly began gently to rub his arms.

"Thank you ever so much!" he said to her after he could move his arms freely. "A packing-case is less comfortable to ride inside than outside. Yet what Sweet William and I have gone through must be a trifle compared to what you have been made to suffer."

"Oh! but it was nothing, Mistaire Lund – nothing to me. Poor dear Baron Schulz they shot. Others, too, they killed. It was a pity so great, Marie, my maid, was so slow."

"Indeed! How did your maid's slowness affect the situation?"

"Her – no, she – I sent for my so beautiful automatic. If only she had returned quickly, happiness would have been with me."

"Pray be seated, Princess," Lawrence invited. He carried a camp-chair and placed it for her near the fire, for the light sea wind had become chill. "Here, Lund, is a case for you and your silent friend. Rest up. Ah Khan will have the tea made in two ticks. See, we have asparagus sandwiches and goodly slabs of cake, to say nothing of cigars and cigarettes."

"You are certainly a hospitable blackguard," Lund said, a little less frostily – for which, since he was ravenously hungry, he could hardly be blamed.

"You will find me really affable," returned Lawrence, smiling with his lips though his eyes were cold, "if you can remember that there are gentlemen who fought in the war as privates equally as well as the officers."

"I was not thinking of the war. I was thinking of the abduction of this lady and the murder of an old man," Lund said quietly.

"Well, well!" And Earle Lawrence laughed easily. "Throughout history abduction has been peculiarly the activity of kings and aristocrats, acclaimed by the world as gentlemen. The majority of these romantic affairs were extremely unpleasant for the women. Of course I am only a common person, and, being such, can claim no credit for regarding all women with respect.

"You need have no uneasiness regarding Her Royal Highness. In my underground castle there already are two – er – involuntary guests in the persons of Mr. Van Horton and Miss Van Horton. Van Horton is a millionaire, and I am hoping he will pay quite generously for the unique experience he is enjoying. Miss Van Horton is accompanied by her maid, so that, Princess, you will not be entirely without service."

"Am I to understand that you hold in captivity an American millionaire and his daughter, with her maid?" demanded Lund.

"Most certainly. Otherwise I should have been obliged to bring from the train at Cook one of the ladies or a maid who accompanied the Princess that far. One must observe convention even on the Nullarbor Plain."

"You so kind are, Mistaire What-they-call-you," Natalie said, actually smiling. Just then the flickering flame died down and they did not see the expression revealed in her violet-blue eyes. "Had you not had killed the Baron Schulz, there are things which some day I might have regarded with forgive – forgiveness."

"That is a point I should like cleared up," Lawrence said. "By the way, my name is Lawrence – Earle Lawrence. Not that I am a lord, but my mother's maiden name was Earle. Here, Everett! What were my orders regarding shooting?"

"We were told not to shoot unless forced by circumstances, and then only to wound."

"You see," Lawrence said in his easy way, "I am almost as much upset by the death of the Baron Schulz as you must be, Princess. Believe me, it was my hope that no one's death would result."

"But you shot him." Lund's statement was really a question.

"Princess, defend me, please," Lawrence had the audacity to urge.

"I saw the Baron killed, not by you. But you accomplice are. Yet, nevaire mind now. Give me cigarette, I crave you, Mistaire Lund. What, permit me to ask, is the amount my ransom to be?"

"Having regard to the finances of your country, I thought of fixing it at about two hundred thousand English pounds, Highness."

"Beeg amount of money – so beeg! You grow wings on your back – you fly through the sky before you get it. His Majesty to the devil will see you."

"Possibly His Majesty King Boris, will do as you suggest," Lawrence said, chuckling.

"And Mistaire Lund, too, I presume you ransom want?"

"Decidedly. Let us place it at ten thousand pounds."

"You should come out of all this quite independent," Lund observed.

"That is just the idea, Lund. Try a cigar. No? A cigarette, then. Well, whether I make a fortune or not at this sort of hotel-keeping, there appears to be no reason why we cannot arrange to live amicably together whilst you are my guests. You will see presently that my castle is well guarded, and that chances of escape are nonexistent. Once there, we may just as well play poker to fill in the time as bicker and quarrel. For my part, I am prepared to be friendly."

"Poker! Ah! But no money have I," and both Lund and Lawrence were astonished by the regret in her voice.

"Money!" echoed Lawrence in return. "None of us have any money. We will play for matches. I will give you each a gross of matches to gamble with."

Half an hour later they were again moving across the plain. Lawrence had given his male prisoners the option of renewing their parole until noon the following day, or being again trussed and forced into the padded cases. Understanding that resistance was useless, that violence would assuredly be met by vastly superior violence, and having had one experience of cords, turbans, and packing-cases, Raymond Lund gave his parole and that, too, of Snell.

He saw – what man of common sense would not? – that in the circumstances violence at that stage would not extricate the Princess from her situation, even if violence won freedom for himself and Snell. Neither knew their destination, nor did they know what actually had happened at Cook. So it came about that he and Snell each rode on some soft material placed on a camel's hump between the tops of swaying empty cases slung a little higher than their precarious seats. It was rough riding, but infinitely better than the interior of a packing-case.

To Lund the position was amazing. Even then there were moments when he was inclined to doubt the evidence of his ears and eyes. To abduct a Royal princess, surrounded by members of her suite and a guard of detectives, from a special train, was a stupendous feat. Why, for sheer incredibility a cinema picture producer would hesitate to use so fantastic a story.

But, by gad, what an epic affair! In the Australian cities at that moment there would be excitement equal to that which thrilled the people at the outbreak of war. The hue and cry would be tremendous. They would pour troops and police and trackers on the Nullarbor Plain as a child would empty sugar grains from a basin into a saucer. It would be but a matter of time before this Lawrence man and his gang would be surrounded and forced to surrender.

"Ah! But before the surrender what would happen?" Lund felt cold all over. To save themselves, might not these modern brigands kill the Princess and those Van Hortons, and, most certainly, Snell and himself? For the first time since meeting Lawrence at the junction of the road Raymond Lund began to feel a little gladness that he also had been taken prisoner. At least he would be near the woman known more intimately as Miss Natalie. Events might so shape themselves as to provide him with the opportunity to escape with her. There did not appear to be so great a number of the gang that no chance ever would be offered.

Within his heart something stirred. It was as a subtle fragrance spurring memory, battling to create again a forgotten incident, a forgotten life perhaps in a former incarnation. For some minutes he wondered about it. A rabbit thumped a warning at the soft pad-padding of the approaching camels. The ground-thumping rabbit set in motion a train of thought. A rabbit – a horse – a kangaroo – Flashlight, the hunting horse. How Flashlight did tremble when he saw a kangaroo! How eager did he always become to give chase, a-thrill equally with his rider!

Lund had been his rider. Lund thrilled strangely now. The thrill stirred his heart. And his heart had thrilled, thrilled so much that it felt like stopping, when he sped across No Man's Land, following the flashing, smoking curtain of the barrage. War! Yes, that was why his heart stirred in riding a pack-camel across the Nullarbor Plain. War! Action! The enemy this gang of abductors and murderers. Nine years had passed in security and peace since he had experienced that heart-thrill.

He began to think of William Snell – Sweet William, the taciturn, loyal, lovable Snell. Had he searched the wide world for a better companion in this affair than Snell he would have been met with failure. Snell the wrestler, Snell the ju-jitsu expert, Snell the Hercules. What a man in a fight! A man – nay, a dozen men!

And not a single word had Snell uttered since he and Lund had looked at the O-end of an automatic pistol muzzle. Not a word had come from him during the rest hour by the camp fire. Of what had he been thinking? Of what was he thinking, seated on the camel behind him? Lund was glad he had intimated to this gang of ruffians that Snell was his friend. Of course Snell was his friend. Their friendship had been made a real living thing by the Great War. If Sweet William had been his valet, and his mechanic, what of it? None knew better than Lund himself that Snell had adopted those rôles because of that war-made friendship. Well, when he had called Snell his friend, he had been perfectly truthful.

Time passed without conscious measurement, so much possessed was Lund by his thoughts. It had been an evening and a night filled with many enigmas, and the greatest enigma of all was the Princess Natalie herself. She had so utterly shattered his conception of Royalty. True, during her stay at his father's house she had revealed herself as a very womanly woman. She had successfully dropped the mantle of hauteur which he had always thought members of reigning families invariably wore. But now, during the last few momentous hours, she had revealed a quite new facet of her sparkling personality. If the simile may be forgiven, she had formerly been as a purring cat, whilst now separated and fleeting moments had seemed to indicate that she had not been a purring cat, but a purring tigress, disguising incredible swiftness of action and implacable fierceness.

So engrossed was he in these reflections that he was quite startled when the camel-string stopped near a spidery-looking structure outlined against the indigo sky. It stood on his left side. On his right side, twenty yards distant, he could discern the outlines of a hut with the glow of an interior light coming from an open doorway. Surely this was not the palace of which the chief brigand had spoken?

"Hang on!" ordered a man on the ground whose features were indistinguishable in the darkness. Then his camel was "hooshed" to its knees, and he slipped off his perch to stretch his cramped limbs. "This way," he then was ordered.

He found himself with the Princess and Snell and several other men. Earle Lawrence joined the group after a whispered conversation with three men. Flashing an electric torch, he carefully examined the sheepskin boots of everyone there. To the Princess he restored her own shoes, politely removing her sheepskins to allow her to put them on, and then replacing the sheepskins over her shoes.

"We have to walk now for nearly three miles," he said. "Forgive me, Princess, for imposing this new hardship on you. We hope to minimize it as much as possible. Directly you begin to feel tired, please tell me, when you may use the rough sedan chair two of us will be carrying. Now, please, all of you, forward!"

When they had proceeded a dozen paces, he halted and hailed Ah Khan: "In the morning you will not forget to back-track to the rest camp, and secure any dropped clues our prisoners may have laid," he said. "See that there are no cigarette or cigar ends littered about the rest camp. Robert, you will track us to the cavern and search likewise for dropped evidence of our passing." He paused to hear their assent.

To Raymond Lund, he explained: "We really have to be careful, you know."

A ROYAL ABDUCTION

PART II

THE HOUSE OF JEWELS

CHAPTER XV

MATCHES

H.R.H. NATALIE OF ROLANDIA slept the sleep of sheer exhaustion on a plain iron bedstead that supported luxurious bedding and costly linen. She slept for twelve hours, and then opened and closed her eyes against the glare of twin electric bulbs blazing above her head.

For several moments her surroundings perplexed her. The room was strange and utterly unlike any room in which she ever had slept. The walls were irregular and of many angles. Suspended from them were blue velvet hangings that caught and reflected the light as the surface of a mountain lake reflects a clear evening sky.

From a swift survey of the room itself her gaze fell on and examined in turn a well-furnished dressing-table supporting a large, oval, bevelled mirror; a wardrobe of Queensland oak; a washstand of the same wood, marble-topped, on which were dainty ewer and basin; a small bookcase with a glass front revealing shelves filled with books; two cane-bottomed chairs, and an inviting Chesterfield. In shape, a most irregularly built room; in furnishing, plain but replete with solid comfort. Natalie did not know it then, but the furnishing of that room was an indirect compliment to her rank offered by the three greatest crooks of America and Australia in combination.

The occupant sat up in bed, and, throwing wide her shapely arms, yawned without restraint. She was recalling now the incidents of the day and the night before that day, for surely she had slept through the day just passed? How long had she really slept? Hours and hours, and by then the whole of the civilised world would be in an uproar. They would know of her abduction at Naagrade. The excitement of the people would be intense. His Majesty King Boris would by now be dreaming dreams. His niece had been taken from a train by a gang of thugs, whose only apparent motive was ransom. Well, he would evade paying it. If they killed Natalie it would be regrettable, but it would strengthen his hands. He would have his adored wife made Queen. His eldest boy, becoming the Heir Apparent, would follow closely in his father's footsteps, and for yet another half-century the war-creating international financiers would be kept out of Rolandia.

Natalie knew her uncle Boris so well as to be sure that this would be his train of reasoning at that moment. Always he had been jealous of her;

always had she hated him. In a moment of fierce anger, when the mystery of her father's assassination continually balked her efforts to unravel it, she had exclaimed to old Baron Schulz: "He's a low, cunning, evil, scheming beast!"

This sentence quite accurately summed up the ruler of Rolandia. How sick and tired she had been of Court life at Naagrade, where the evil influence of King Boris pulled her one way, memory of a beloved father drew her another, and the desires and intrigues of financiers acting through the Governments of several big Powers were always exerting magnetic force from sundry other directions. Seated there on her bed, a prisoner of a most unusual bandit, Natalie felt no anger in her heart against her fate. On the contrary, she was beginning to enjoy herself in a similar delightful way to that experienced when she was the guest of Sir Henry and Lady Lund. It was certainly an adventure which appealed to her very complex nature. She swung her legs over the edge of the bed, then heard a distant "click" and, somewhere beyond the room, the ringing of a bell.

Seated there on the edge of the bed, Natalie listened to the ringing bell. It sounded quite a long way off, and after about ten seconds suddenly stopped. Save for a soft humming sound everything was very still, and she wondered where Lund and all the men were who had entered that underground place with her. The last she had seen of Raymond Lund and Snell had been when they disappeared round the angle of a passage conducted by three of the bandits.

The man calling himself Lawrence had brought her to that amazing room, explaining that it was her chamber, and that in a minute he would bring her some refreshment. As good as his word, he had brought her coffee, a dish of *pâté de foie gras*, and some buttered scones. Without speaking, he had set down the tray on the dressing-table and withdrawn with a bow in which she suspected a hint of mockery.

She remembered how tired she had felt whilst she ate and drank. She remembered discovering the silk nightwear laid out on the bed, and how she had quietly undressed and slipped between the sheets. She ought, she thought, to have switched off the lights, but had fallen asleep before that idea had occurred. And now she was awake and wondering at the silence.

It was then that Julia appeared. She entered suddenly from behind one of the blue velvet hangings. She was dressed in black, but above her wrists were white linen cuffs, and set on her raven black hair was a tiny linen cap. She carried a silver tray. Of all the astonishing things that had happened to the Princess within the last twenty-four hours, the appearance of this chic, obviously French, maid was the greatest.

"Who are you?" Natalie inquired calmly.

The girl, who was about twenty-five and very pretty in her dark vivacious way, curtsied with the grace of long practice. In her native tongue she replied: "I am Julia, lady's maid to Miss Van Horton, madam. Miss Van Horton desires me to convey to Your Royal Highness her respectful salutations and this note."

"So!" That was all.

The Princess slipped beneath the clothes, whereupon the maid swiftly set down the tray on a chair and flew to arrange the pillows to permit Natalie to sit up comfortably. Then, with a cup of steaming black coffee in one hand, the opened letter in the other, and Julia standing at the foot of the bed, Natalie read:

> *The House of Jewels,*
> *Saturday.*
>
> *It was with regret that I found myself deprived of the honour of greeting Your Royal Highness last night. The Chief Brigand of this underground castle had not troubled to inform me that you were expected. I learned of your arrival hours later, and, peeping in on you, found you fast asleep.*
>
> *The bell announces that you are awake, and I am taking the liberty of dispatching to you coffee and rolls by my maid, Julia. Will you be pleased to share her with me? She is the greatest jewel here. And if you will permit me to follow her, I'd love to tell you of this place and these awful people.*
>
> *Helen Van Horton.*

This missive Natalie perused twice. Its tone was respectfully friendly, if not couched in the language of Courts. Certainly the offer of Julia's services was generous. To the girl she said in French, which she spoke fluently: "What is the time?"

On hearing her own language, Julia's eyes sparkled. "It is half-past four, Madame."

"Morning or afternoon?"]

"But the afternoon, Madame."

Again the Princess read Helen Van Horton's note. She was tempted to question the girl, but refrained. "Ask Mlle Van Horton to come to me," she said in the dignified yet kindly tone her class uses when speaking to household servants.

Curtsying again, Julia vanished.

A minute later, Helen Van Horton appeared. Her first meeting with the Princess Natalie of Rolandia made a vivid impression on this American woman. She saw a dainty form propped with billowy pillows, attired in silk nightwear, sipping coffee from a fragile china cup. The dark brown hair fell forward over each shoulder in long, gleaming plaits. She saw herself examined by wide violet-blue eyes which appeared never previously to have seen a woman. The face was small, the features regular, the skin beautifully coloured with youth and health. Helen Van Horton knew she herself was a beautiful woman. She recognised the dark beauty of this Royal Slav with unfeigned admiration. Suddenly the exploring blue eyes changed in expression. There flashed into them warmth and friendliness, and Helen felt both gratified and attracted.

"You are Miss Van Horton?" queried Natalie.

"Yes, Princess. I felt I ought to pay my respects at the earliest possible moment in these most extraordinary circumstances. You see, we are both hostages or prisoners of this man calling himself Earle Lawrence."

"He mentioned your name to me as we ate the camp fire near – no, no, as we ate near the camp fire. Do you speak French? This English language so hard it is to learn."

"I always thought I could speak French until recently, when my father and I visited France," the American said, laughing

Natalie sighed regretfully, saying: "Well, my English I must practice. Sit here, please, on this so nice bed, and tell me how you were abducted. But first will you please give to me a cigarette? There, you see, lies a box – and matches."

"We may accuse our chief brigand of every atrocity, but we cannot accuse him of starving us, either of food or cigarettes," Helen Van Horton said, holding a light to Natalie's cigarette. "In many ways he is most likeable and, thank heaven, a thorough gentleman."

"There are two kinds of the gentleman," Natalie instantly pointed out.

Again the other laughed softly, and her laughter was pleasing. "Yes, I know, Princess. But the man Earle Lawrence is a gentleman in the right way. He even apologised when he chloroformed me."

"Chloroformed you – a gentleman in the right way!"

"He did so. I must tell you. You see, Pops – that's my pet name for father – and I met him in Perth, where we were staying for some days on our tour round the world. He invited us to his house among the hills not far from the city. After dinner he offered us a glass of special Australian wine, saying he was sure we would agree that it was superior to anything France could produce.

"It was lovely wine to drink, but it was drugged. I awoke in a large closed car as it was passing through a town. Pops, I saw, was still unconscious. Beside me sat this Earle Lawrence. I tried to scream, to attract attention. He saw what I was about, so he drew my head down on his shoulder and held a cotton pad to my nose. And he said, he actually said: 'Please accept my apologies, sincerely made.'"

Helen Van Horton paused in her colourful narrative. Her eyes were centred, not on the Princess, but on a spot on one of the velvet hangings. She felt a sense of pride, the pride of the creative artist.

"Go on! Proceed! To it hop!" urged Natalie, as impatient as a youngster hearing a tale from the *Arabian Nights* which had been interrupted.

"Oh, the days and days of travelling in that car!" Helen went on. "It seemed almost a year. Actually it was four days till we reached this place. We have been here now a month. Mr. Lawrence has been in communication with friends of ours in Chicago, to whom he forwarded a letter written by Pops saying they must see that a large sum of money is lodged in a Cape Town bank. Already Pops has paid him a large sum – a first instalment, as it were. I don't understand all of it, but Pops says it will be all right in the end. He is fearfully angry at being made to pay so much money."

"But suppose refuses he to pay more?"

"I don't know what would then happen. Pops won't tell me," Helen explained. "Anyway, that is how we come to be here. But tell me, Princess, please, how come you to be here? I was never more surprised in my life when I heard."

So in her vivid, broken phraseology Natalie described the hold-up of her special car, the fight which followed, her meeting with Raymond Lund, and her journey across the Nullarbor Plain. She was saying how she was so much fatigued that she had omitted to switch off the lights, when the maid, Julia, brought in a parcel wrapped in brown paper.

"A present for Her Royal Highness," she said. "Monsieur Lawrence sends it with his compliments."

Natalie took the parcel and poised it in her hand, as if judging its weight. She found it not heavy. Helen brought a pair of small scissors and cut the string. The paper was removed, and there was revealed a large package wrapped in green paper, bearing on one side an enlarged label of a famous brand of matches. The green wrapping was removed. Within were twelve smaller packets each containing twelve boxes of matches.

CHAPTER XVI

A MIXED GATHERING

A gong was struck. Precisely how distant it was impossible even to guess. The tone was deep, and the sound made up of a short burst of rapid notes followed by three distinct bell-like clangs. Then came the echoes, seeming to rebound from the walls of Natalie's chamber. She looked inquiringly at Helen Van Horton.

"That is the dinner gong," Helen explained.

Both she and the Princess were dressed for the evening. Helen wore a frock of Air-Force blue georgette, whilst the gown in which the Princess was arrayed had belonged to the American and had been altered by the expert Julia to fit Natalie's shorter and more delicate frame. This dress was of similar material to Helen's.

"If we may, let us go," proposed Natalie, jumping up from the Chesterfield. "I so hungry am, and to my nostrils come many savoury flavours."

"I, too, am glad to hear the gong, Princess. Let us go now, but be prepared for surprises."

Helen Van Horton held aside the blue velvet hanging. Natalie's sharp eyes observed that it disguised an entrance to the apartment unfitted by door or frame. Electric light bulbs were fixed in profusion everywhere. They revealed a large cavern, almost fifty yards across and roughly circular. The floor was level and covered with fine sand. The roof was vaulted: it rose to a central peak or arch forty feet above, and suspended from the rough ceiling was a cluster of lights.

"The Sword of Damocles!" murmured Helen.

It hung from the cavern roof half-way to the floor, a glittering needle-pointed stalactite, reflecting the electric light in every tint and shade of the spectrum. It was as a peacock preening its feathers, for once oblivious of the hen birds as represented in duller colours by crystallised lumps of rock set in the limestone walls that sent back gleams of brown and slate blue from their irregular polished surfaces.

"Isn't it lovely?" and in the voice of Helen Van Horton was genuine enthusiasm.

"So beautiful!" murmured the Princess. "You say the Sword of Damocles, mademoiselle. The Cavern of the Sword, this. I wonder! I wonder so much if it will some day fall. Perhaps it will fall on the head of him who shot old Baron Schulz. Shall we hope it does?"

"Oh, Princess!"

The exclamation was forced from Helen Van Horton. She had been looking again at the stalactite when Natalie had expressed her definite wish, and when its meaning penetrated to her understanding Helen's eyes fell to the virile little figure. Natalie's eyes now were almost black. In them was an expression that shocked the elder woman. It shocked her because it surprised her, and her guard was down.

"Why not?" Natalie asked quietly, but after the habitual interest-in-all-things of the innocent expression had returned. "Poor Baron! A nice man so was he. Almost was he my foster-father. But I must not grieve, must I?"

"We cannot help grieving for those we love, Princess," and the American's voice trembled, recalling her own sorrow. "It was a shame – a vile thing to do. But we must go on. They will wonder what has become of us. My father! Will you permit him to be presented?"

"But certainly."

Before they left the Cavern of the Sword, Natalie noted three passages running from it, one passage slanting downward, the two others level yet rough with uneven slabs of rock. All three were lighted. Helen conducted her a little to the left of her own room, where round a great jutting abutment of rock was disclosed to them a fourth passage, at least seven feet wide and eight feet high. They followed this passage in several curves for fifty yards, coming suddenly round a corner into another huge cavern, at whose further end electric stoves and ovens gleamed darkly behind a man dressed in the white uniform of a *chef*. Two other men were seated at a near table.

That was all the Princess then saw of the "thieves' kitchen". Helen piloted her through an opening in the rock into yet another great domed room, in which was set up a long and wide table bearing spotless linen and brilliant glassware. Standing in two groups were several men. From one of these groups Earle Lawrence came to them.

"Having already introduced myself, will Your Royal Highness permit me to present your fellow-guests?" he asked in his easy manner.

Natalie gravely bowed her head in assent. Experienced though she was in the great world of people outside Court circles, the character of this man baffled her. Standing before her with just the right degree of deference, dressed in plain black trousers and dinner-jacket, correct starched shirt, collar and white tie, in appearance he was exactly the same as the thousands of men she had met and forgotten. His voice was cultured, his manner easy and assured. Turning, he indicated the amasser of millions, also in dining clothes.

"This is Mr. Van Horton, of Chicago," he said. "He and Miss Van Horton are welcome but involuntary guests. Mr. Van Horton, Her Royal Highness the Princess Natalie of Rolandia."

The American bowed. The Princess extended her hand. Helen noted with satisfaction that her father took the tips only of the strong little fingers, and bowed again over them. No doubt he had been busy with the book on etiquette she had procured for him.

"I wish that the circumstances of this meeting had been happier, Princess," he said in his unaccented, clipped tones. "However, my daughter and I have found our imprisonment not so irksome as it could well be."

"I am sure father and I will try to make it as pleasant as possible," interjected Helen, and then realised she had made a slip, and hoped the Princess would not observe it.

To Mr. Van Horton, Natalie said: "It all rests – what you say? – on the knees of the gods, Mistaire Van Horton. I my decisions have made. The foolishness of this abduction would delightful be, had good men not died in cause of it. There I see yet another prisoner, Mistaire Lund."

"I am glad you can take it so calmly, Princess," Raymond said, stepping forward. "Your Royal Highness may be assured of our efforts, added to those of Mr. and Miss Van Horton, to make life here a little interesting. In turn, may I present my friend, Mr. William Snell?"

Lund stood a little in front of the others. She noted that he wore a well-cut lounge suit of navy blue, and intuitively understood that it was the only suit he had brought from Adelaide on his strange motor-car. Looking up into his face, she was astounded to see him close his left eye in a vulgar wink. She felt the blood begin to mount into her cheeks before realising that the wink was significant. She remembered Snell perfectly. He was the faithful servant, the privileged companion, but not the equal of the Lunds. Yet here was Raymond Lund presenting Snell as an equal, an action surely dictated by some mysterious purpose!

Dressed in dark grey, the ungainly figure reached Raymond's side. She noted that, in spite of his ungainliness, the man she had so often heard called "Sweet William" moved with the light, silent tread of a cat. When he stood before her, his big head thrust forward, his long arms limp, she thought she never had seen a man more ugly. But afterwards she thought how strange it was that, when she looked into the small brown eyes, her uneasiness as to the future vanished, for she knew in her woman's heart that in William Snell was a mighty protective force. She smiled. Snell, master of himself, bowed awkwardly.

"I am made happy to meet you, Mistaire Snell," she said simply.

Snell bowed awkwardly again. His expression was blank of any thought. She reflected now how stupid he looked: just a big, devoted, faithful dog!

"Your Highness – honours me," he said with gruff difficulty, and ventured to step aside. His place was taken by Van Horton, who was smiling. He offered his arm, which she accepted, and led her to a seat at the far end of the table.

Lund, who had met Helen Van Horton two hours before, escorted her to a seat and seated himself. At the head of the table Natalie found on her right Mr. Van Horton, Helen Van Horton, Lund and two other men. Seated on her left was Earle Lawrence, then William Snell, with, beyond him, a big sandy-haired man, two others still further away, and Julia, the maid. A man dressed in the white coat of a ship's steward entered with the soup, and from the signs made to him Lund gathered that he was deaf. Natalie was much less of a snob than many of her inferiors, but she wondered if it was the custom in certain circles in Australia for maid-servants and obviously rough men to sit at table with ladies and gentlemen.

The thought passed. Every minute this strange adventure became more fantastic. Conversation appeared difficult to start. A man at the bottom end of the table, a man with a big black moustache, took his soup with much noise. The maid, Julia, glared at him. The black-moustached man leered at the maid.

Natalie wanted to laugh. Instead, she said: "Are we in the earth deep?"

"No, Princess, a mere fifty feet or so," Lawrence informed her. "There are passages, however, which lead down to caverns at least a hundred and fifty feet below the surface. They are well worth exploring. Some time we must go on a tour. There are the blow-holes and a river, whilst in one of the caverns there is a perfect skeleton of some beast or fish – I don't know which – that must have lived thousands of years ago. I questioned Doctor Woolworth at the oil-bore, but could get nothing out of him. His interest is in minerals, not fossils."

"How did these caverns come to be discovered?" Lund asked. "I take it they are not widely known."

The deaf steward or mess-waiter was placing before them salted snoop, and whilst waiting for him to offer dishes of vegetables Lawrence talked secret history.

"I own a cattle station a good many miles north-east of this locality. It belonged to my father before me, and his name was not Lawrence. In the year nineteen-eleven or nineteen-twelve I took a trip through the southern portion of the Nullarbor Plain in the hope of locating sufficient suitable country for another station.

"I had with me a black boy born at Eucla. One day this aboriginal refused to go further, saying, in effect, that this spot was taboo. He was prepared to circle it, but not to go right through. Seeing no reason why I should travel twenty miles or so in a half-circle when, by going straight, I could make it ten, I came on, and the blackfellow rode west and met me later.

"It was quite by accident that I discovered the hole in the ground you will remember to have come down via the steps. Then there were, of course, no steps. No means of getting down. Not until a second visit did I manage to do so with ropes."

"Then the blacks know of it?" Lund questioned.

"I think not. It has been taboo for so many generations that the fact of its existence has become lost in legend. No" – and Lawrence spoke with conviction – "I am positive that I am the only person who knew, till recently, the exact location of these caverns. The blacks will not come here, not even if they manage to track us, which they will never do now. Every precaution was taken against being tracked, and fate has made this doubly sure by the widespread thunderstorms that have raged during the afternoon."

"But surely you cannot hope to keep Her Royal Highness hidden here long enough to collect a ransom," objected Lund with conviction. "Every foot of the plain, huge though it is, will be minutely examined."

"On the contrary, I honestly believe the plain will not be examined at all," Lawrence stated. "Be logical, Lund! The fact that Her Royal Highness honours us this evening certainly proves that her abduction from the transcontinental train was carried out successfully. It was an undertaking, you will agree, demanding *finesse* in planning and courage, plus rigid discipline, in execution. If not now, you will later appreciate the brilliance of the *coup*. In order that we may all be interested in what happened after the abduction I have installed in the next cavern or apartment a good wireless receiving set."

"I take it that your object in carrying out these abductions is money?"

Earle Lawrence laughed pleasantly. "Of course," he assented. "I have every hope of collecting from Mr. Van Horton the further sum of twenty thousand pounds. Rolandia, not being exactly rolling in wealth, I am disposed to ask only two hundred thousand for the safe return of its Crown Princess."

"And how much do you expect from me?"

For several poignant seconds the two men stared at each other.

"I have not decided what amount of ransom to fix in your case and that of Mr. Snell. Ten thousand was a rough guess. Obtaining ransom money presents concrete difficulties. With regard to Mr. Van Horton and his daughter, I have representatives in his home city, Chicago; likewise in the case of Princess Natalie I have representatives in Naagrade working through other representatives in Paris. Positive representation in significant quarters is more important to success than the actual abduction. No, I have not decided what to do with Mr. Snell and yourself."

During this conversation Natalie had elected to remain silent but observant. The Van Hortons appeared much interested in what Lawrence was saying. She was consciously comparing the two Australians. In several physical respects they were much alike. Both were an inch or two above six feet in height; Lawrence was a shade the heavier. Both spoke with culture; both voices held the slow, distinct drawl, unaffected, musical.

There the resemblance ceased. Lund's features were regular and finely moulded. Lawrence's face was larger, his forehead was wide, and the hair growing high and back from the frontal bone gave to his face a look of great mental strength. In the eyes of these two men lay the greatest difference. Lund's eyes were granite-grey, steady and calm; Lawrence's eyes were large and light-grey. They seemed always to radiate great enthusiasm, giving the impression that here was a confirmed optimist. Obviously, Lawrence was extremely temperamental. He did not appear capable of carrying out an astounding abduction which required cold and close calculation to back up brilliance of conception. Yes, he baffled Natalie entirely.

As for Mr. Van Horton, inexperienced Natalie could not "place" him at all. Helen appeared transparent enough. The Princess thought she liked Helen Van Horton, as much for her downright views of life as for her beauty. She was sure the Van Hortons would improve on acquaintance.

Snell put a pertinent question. Natalie, looking at his square face then, decided that, although he possessed undoubted physical strength, he was not mentally very much alert. "If the money for the ransom of Her Royal Highness does not come to light, what will happen?" he asked in his low gruff voice.

"It is a contingency which at this stage I decline to consider, Mr. Snell," Lawrence answered, still smiling.

"It's water in your petrol-tank, anyway. If it reaches your carburettor your engine will kind of miss-fire. I'm thinking your engine is going to miss-fire in any case, money or no money. You can't get away with a stunt like this, because it is too big."

"I cannot agree with you, Mr. Snell," Lawrence said calmly.

"It makes no difference to me if you agree or not." Snell, who sat with his chin held up by his cupped hand, one elbow resting on the table, suddenly swung sideways and pointed a forefinger straight at his host. "I've seen men with faces like yours beyond the little bars set high in cell doors. Men with the colour of your eyes are born to be hanged as sure as the sun rises and sets."

This statement produced a profound silence. Natalie emphatically felt the sudden tension. Beyond the room, beyond the silence, came the sound of tin and iron dishes being bumped about in the kitchen. The *chef* was humming a tune that reminded the hearers of the musical accompaniment of a familiar hymn.

Van Horton coughed. "Obviously, Mr. Snell, you are a character-reader," he said.

"I am," Snell admitted. "For seven years I was a student of criminals; for the last three of them being chief warder of a South Australian gaol. I got that way that when a bird was taken out of the cage I could tell him straight how many years he would serve the next time. Yes, I'm a character-reader all right."

Another period of silence followed. Natalie was about to break it with a reference to the killer of Baron Schulz, when the *chef* in his kitchen burst into doleful song to the tune of the hymn, "Now the day is ended." To the diners the words came distinctly:

"Death is all around Us –
with his Hempen Ropes.
Soon will all our necks stretch,
so good-bye to our Hopes."

CHAPTER XVII

A PLEASANT EVENING

THE effect of the *chef's* gruesome song was reflected variously on the faces of the diners. Natalie was not quite sure of its import, and it was obvious to Lund that she was waiting expectantly for another verse. Instead of it there came a resounding crash, as though the autocrat of the kitchen had thrown from one end to the other a heavy tin baking-dish. Came then a deep masculine voice: "Wot's narked you, Pessy?"

An answer came in sulphuric tones: "Blessed are the Dead!"

Whereupon a second baking-dish followed the aerial flight of the first.

In the dining-room the first to break the silence was the lady's maid, who laughed in high falsetto.

"Julia!" exclaimed Helen Van Horton severely.

Julia flushed scarlet and hung her head.

Earle Lawrence sighed loudly and long. "Pessy is our *chef*," he explained. "His real name is Alfred Tuttman. The word 'Pessy' is short for Pessimist, which friend Tuttman certainly is." He was smiling again now, but Sweet William, who had been watching him expertly but not obviously, had seen actual fear for a fleeting instant. "Princess, may I suggest we go into the drawing-room with you ladies for our coffee and cigarettes?"

"But certainly, Mistaire Lawrence," she said, rising. "Tomorrow the dear Mistaire Tuttman must be presented. His so wonderful song he must sing to me again."

She and Helen Van Horton led the way to an adjoining cavern. Smiling at the perplexed Lawrence, Van Horton went in with Lund. The sandy-haired man, Snell, and Lawrence followed. Julia and the others passed out into the kitchen.

Now, whilst the "dining-room" had been furnished simply, and no efforts made to conceal its rough rock walls and irregular roof, the inner cavern was decorated with taste and furnished luxuriously, beautified by Nature itself. It was roughly egg-shaped, and possibly sixty feet in length. Three great stalagmites formed glittering pillars, tapering near the floor. A dozen stalactites hung for several feet from the roof and immediately below their needle-like extremities short, thin pillars were being built up from the floor by the ceaseless dripping of lime-saturated water. At one side an irregular opening in the wall of the cavern gave view of a smaller cave or natural alcove, in which was placed a harmonium revealed by lights set above the summit of the opening.

Electric bulbs, set apparently haphazard in the roof, made the suspended stalactites and pillars blaze with multiple colours. The electric glow was reflected also by slow-seeping water creeping in runnels down the walls, as though the walls were daubed with bright yellow and soft brown. Elsewhere blue velvet hangings hid the uglier harsh limestone. Scattered about were divans and lounge chairs upholstered in blue silk, small mahogany and Queensland-oak folding tables, with boxes of cigarettes and cigars displayed thereon. The scene was bizarre, Oriental in its meretricious richness.

"Mistaire Lund, to you I would talk," Natalie said deliberately when she joined him. "On that couch we will sit, and you shall light my cigarette and tell me how you came to leave Adelaide."

"I shall be delighted, Princess," he said, with obvious eagerness.

"And I will play to you," Van Horton announced, with an old-fashioned bow that caused his daughter to wonder how or from whom he had learned it.

"May I join you?" Helen asked Natalie.

"But certainly."

Julia brought in a tray loaded with coffee utensils. Her face was flushed, her dark eyes glittering with restrained excitement. Helen Van Horton wondered, and decided to ask the girl later what had happened.

"You know life has suddenly become fantastic," Lund observed when Van Horton began to play on the harmonium the tune to "Now the day is ended, Night is drawing nigh". "That was a remarkable verse the excellent *chef* sang, was it not?"

"Most apt, indeed," Helen Van Horton murmured.

"If you remember, tell it me," Natalie urged Lund with mischievous eyes. "At the English not yet am I quick."

Lund repeated the verse slowly and accurately, and the Princess laughed out with delight.

"What a man!" she said. "What – what you say? – what wit! Well, Mr. Lund, how came you riding over the so wonderful Nullarbor Plain in that so funny automobile?"

Realising that the race that originated in a bet between the Princess and him was to be kept secret, he explained the invention of the patented spring tyres, and gave the reason of the journey as being for the purpose of testing them under severe conditions. He told the ladies, Rolandian and American, how glad he then was that he and Snell had taken the journey because of its results.

"I cannot but feel that the situation here is utterly amazing," he went on. "To observe you and the other people here almost obliterates the fact that we are hostages of a daring gang of crooks. Observe the man Lawrence. Few men look less like a scoundrel than he does. Then there is that other man with light red hair and deep blue eyes. Blue Everett, they call him. His war career was remarkable. In appearance he is aristocratic. When you hear him speak it is to know that his education was of the very best."

"They certainly do not conform to the conventional type of bad man," the American drawled in her alluring voice with its soft Virginian accent.

"I agree, though one bad man only I know. His Majesty, my uncle! Ah! There you see the beast on his countenance. A bad man, a – what you say? – an expert bad man. No, that not it. Profesh – professional. Yes, he is professional bad man, allied with the devil."

"Then your experience of the bad man must now be enlarged," Lund said, unable to suppress a smile at what he saw in the violet-blue eyes set in the vivid face. "No. I find it hard to remember that quite recently those two men pointed automatic pistols at us and threatened to blow our heads off if we made any movement.

"When we arrived here we were both placed in a tiny cave and handcuffed to a length of chain securely fastened to a stalactite. The chain allowed us perfect freedom to the extent of some ten feet. Snell and I were so tired, for we had had a hard three days, that we fell asleep instantly on the mattresses laid on the floor. And then came Lawrence to inquire how we had slept, and hoping he awoke us refreshed. He said how sorry he was to treat us like dangerous homicides, but from then on we were free of the place so long as we behaved ourselves. Escape was impossible, for the only entrance would in future be well guarded, night and day."

"Practically the same conditions are imposed on my dear, mild-tempered father," said Helen Van Horton, adding: "Princess, you must really explore this wonderful place with me."

"That I shall do," Natalie responded gravely.

"Julia has perfect freedom underground, too," went on Helen. "She is a wonderful maid and so brave. Nevertheless, it did not at first seem right that she should eat with us. The men, too, are obviously of a lower social order, no matter what their morals are. Yet when I complained to Mr. Lawrence, he merely laughed, and said a little practical socialism would do us plutocrats a vast amount of good."

"Life has certainly become socialistic."

"It has. It adds to what you said about life in general. It makes it fantastic. There is Julia sitting talking with your friend Mr. Snell; here is Her Royal Highness of Rolandia; there sits the chief brigand dreaming dreams, helped no doubt by the music of a harmonium played by a dear old thing of a Chicago millionaire. I have never even read of such a complex social gathering."

"It will be something to talk about for years after we escape," murmured Lund.

"When we do!" Helen Van Horton exclaimed. "Why, to escape would be impossible. There is only one way out, and that is guarded night and day by armed men."

"Well, for all the guard, we'll find a way."

"Do you think so?"

"I am sure of it. Snell and I have been in heaps of tighter corners."

"It would so lovely be to outwit Mistaire so clever Lawrence," Natalie cried softly. "I want him in prison. He killed my so kind friend through an accomplice. I told him I my commands would give to be present at his so delightful hanging."

"Oh, Princess!"

"I mean it, my so dear Miss Van Horton. We of the House of Pravoff never forget. Just, we are. Justice and revenge – your English words to us alike are in meaning. Mistaire Lawrence shall hang. I shall see him hanged. It is my wish."

Helen Van Horton recorded later in her extraordinary diary her impressions of the early part of that evening. It proved to be one of the few occasions since she had relinquished her active part in the B., D. and C. Pack that she was roused from the state of boredom which fresh places and people had served so far only to deepen.

The imperfect English of the Princess Natalie gave piquancy to her emphatic views. Helen felt that housed within the small body was a very powerful personality, wonderful in a girl brought up in the rigid seclusion of a Royal Court. This Princess was beyond all her preconceived ideas, for she could not understand that modern Rolandia was still almost medieval in its conditions, and the House of Pravoff autocratic indeed.

As for Raymond Lund, she liked him immensely. She liked the way his calm, honest, steady eyes sometimes twinkled. She liked the musical inflections in his voice, as well as his unselfconscious, well-bred manner. As Natalie had earlier compared him with Earle Lawrence, so now did Helen Van Horton. In each the result was the same. The personality of

Lawrence failed to surmount this severe test.

The harmonium player closed the instrument and came sauntering down the room. Pausing at a table near Lawrence, he selected a cheroot, and, having bitten off the end, looked down on the Australian with penetrating eyes, saying: "It is half-past seven. I would suggest the wireless."

Having lit his cheroot, Van Horton joined the Princess' group. His pale face was void of expression, his eyes veiled with half-closed lids. "I have been thinking of Australia," he said. "When I am playing I can always think rapidly. I have been dreaming of Australia as it will be fifty years hence."

"I like listening to dreams," Natalie murmured.

Van Horton smiled at that and became seated. "Since we are both visitors to this country, our impressions of it may be much the same, Princess. I have been through a lot of the land near the coast, where the white man's civilisation is located. Yet only by studying a map can it be thoroughly realised that the white man is settled on a narrow outer ribbon of an enormous landmass. Do you know, Lund, I am inclined to believe that your national policy of a White Australia will at some not far distant date cost you your inheritance?"

"Why?"

"You are too slow in populating your empty spaces."

"Because most of the map of Australia is blank, you think we are at fault. Well, our present population is a little over six millions. What number of people do you think the country could support?"

"Any number from eighty to one hundred millions."

"I was told by the so wonderful Prime Minister that ninety millions of people here could live," stated Natalie.

"I remember someone telling me that the entire British Empire could live comfortably in Australia, if necessary – some four hundred and fifty million," contributed Helen.

Lund sighed, and said very seriously: "It is such estimates evolved in the addled brains of publicity-hunting politicians which may cost us dear – not our empty spaces. Overseas people, including the Asiatics, having no other sources of information, believe the figures you have quoted, and, believing, cast envious eyes on Australia. The vast interior of Australia will for ever remain empty until some genius can alter climatic conditions. A great part of Australia is desert country, and from desert country, or even pastoral country, you cannot obtain the products of close settlement. People who have to win a living from such country consider that Australia cannot support more than double the present population."

"I do not quite understand," Van Horton ventured.

"Just so. It is difficult even for a city-born city-dweller of Australia to understand," Lund went on quickly. "But in the bush you are soon up against the impossibility of making a silk purse out of a sow's ear. You cannot make things grow without rain. In the interior of Australia the rain may fall twice or thrice in a year. When our population reaches twelve millions, Australia will be full. It is the stupid emphasis always placed on our empty spaces – which, as in Arabia and North Africa, never will support people – that creates envy in the hearts of foreign statesmen. If they realised the truth, the absurdity of thoughts of annexation, of invasion even, would be quite evident to them."

"You surprise me," Van Horton said.

"Lawrence will confirm my views, I feel sure."

At that they looked across at Lawrence seated before the wireless set. From the loud-speaker suddenly blared a man's voice drowned by cackling static. "The thunderstorms have made things difficult with atmospherics," announced the operator. "Those storms which passed us to-day must now be between us and Adelaide. Conditions may be better later, but I doubt it."

"I so disappointed am," Natalie cried softly.

"I am, too," joined in Helen Van Horton. "The cities must be excited by your abduction, Princess. It is such a pity. But we may hear clearly to-morrow, if Mr. Lawrence permits the use of the instrument."

"I had it installed especially for my guests," Lawrence said, adding under his breath: "Curse that cook!"

For from the kitchen came the doleful voice of the *chef*, raised in song:

> "Another day has ended
> Deep down in this cave;
> We grow ever nearer
> To the peaceful grave."

CHAPTER XVIII

SNELL THE IMPERTURBABLE

THE Princess awoke, and, feeling no desire to sleep again, switched on her lights and looked at her tiny jewelled watch. It was half-past seven, and she knew that above ground the sun already would be burning hot. There in her bizarre chamber the air was cool and surprisingly fresh, wanting only the perfume of flowers to make it as sweet as the gardens of the palace at Naagrade.

Before leaving her the previous evening, Helen Van Horton had said that Julia would bring her coffee and rolls at half-past eight, and that breakfast, as usual, would be served at nine. Sixty minutes, however, is a long time to wait when one is not drowsy with sleep, and especially when one has smoked really too many cigarettes the night before. Steaming coffee and a fresh buttered roll recalled to her mind the quaint songster of the kitchen, and the idea was born in her brain to dress and go along to the culinary department, there to ask for a cup of coffee of this "so witty *chef*". With Natalie impulse was generally followed by action.

It is a peculiarity of the human brain that scents, scenes, and sometimes little tasks, revive memory of half-forgotten incidents. That morning, when dressing without expert aid, she remembered old Lady Lund, who had been the first to prove to her that a maid was not an absolute necessity to existence. Of all the hostesses Natalie had met during her world tour, in fact during her life, little Lady Lund was the most understanding. What would she be then thinking? Wondering, perhaps, where she was, if she was alive; unhappy, possibly, because of the curtain of concealment which had dropped between a Miss Natalie and the world.

Then the purpose of her dressing so early that morning revived memory of that thrilling adventure with Raymond Lund, when they had crept along to the cook's pantry at midnight, there to find and eat a most delectable and unusual supper.

How long ago that now seemed to be! Years ago: an incident of another life when she was neither Crown Princess nor the hostage of an abductor; when she had been just Natalie, gay, unfettered, happy. It was real, of course, for with her in those strange caverns was her then playmate, and the faithful, grim, unfathomable Sweet William. And when she stepped from her chamber it was to find Sweet William admiring the Sword of Damocles. "Good morning, Mistaire Snell."

Snell turned, surveyed the ravishing picture she made for an appreciable space of time, bowed awkwardly and said: "Good morning, Your Royal Highness!"

A few steps brought her close to this primeval man. "Mistaire Snell, are you astray – no, lost?"

Snell permitted himself to smile. His eyes became still smaller, and his lips drew outward at the extremities. "No, Marm, I'm not lost," he said softly. "I know now the general lay-out of this joint. I've been rambling around for an hour."

"This joint! I not understand."

"Joint?" Snell repeated with a puzzled expression, his eyebrows almost meeting the black low-growing hair. "Joint means a house or a gaol or a place, Marm."

"Oh! I afraid am I am not acquainted yet with your Australian language," Natalie sighed. "You speak English in Australia, yet so strange English. But have you discovered important things during your so early wanderings?"

"Cute" was the word Snell then was thinking, but did not voice. He liked this flower of a woman more and more. She had a brain in constant use, for although she might deviate in conversation she returned to the point always.

"Well, I have located the main caverns," he said in his slow, distinct way, as though what he was saying was a well-learned lesson. "There is this one, out of which lead your room, Miss Van Horton's room, and Julia's room. There is that one in use as a kitchen, and the two together, like one of them hour-glasses, where we eat and listen to the piano thing. There is two fellows on guard at the biggest cavern of the lot, the kind of outer one, where the steps are to the surface."

"Ah! That is guarded by two guards? Well, Mistaire Snell, could you not rush, overpower them, escape?"

"I could rush 'em all right, Marm, but they would stop me with a stream of nickel-plated bullets before I reached either one. If I had a gun I'd stand a chance."

"Well, you may have a gun one day. Take me, please, to the kitchen. I would talk with the singing *chef*."

"This is the passage, Marm."

"What else you find this morning, Mistaire Snell?" she asked whilst he piloted her along the winding passage through the limestone.

"I've found out where the man with the gallows eyes sleeps," Snell informed her quietly. "I know just where the remainder of the gang hangs out. The only man I haven't located is Van Horton."

"What you think of Mistaire Van Horton?"

Her question brought Snell to a halt. He glanced swiftly up and down the passage. "Marm, he's a bad man," he said.

"Oh! But –?"

"When I first seen him my back hair sort of stood out."

Snell went on, looking at her seriously. "I know nothing about him, nothing against him. I only know about this hair here," and he rubbed the nape of his neck. "It stood out when I first saw him. It always stands out when I meet a bad man. You see, Marm, I'm closer to the monkeys than most. I kind of feel what I can't know or understand."

"You may be right, Mistaire Snell. I have had – what you say? – intuitions. Well, let it now pass. I my coffee wish to take. But with you I do not agree when you say close to the monkey are you."

"Well, Marm, my arms are overlong, and my legs too short. And I can smell blood two miles away, and can see in the dark."

They walked on a few paces. Then it was she who paused, and, placing her fingers on one iron-hard forearm, said softly: "Mistaire Lund, he is my so dear friend. Mistaire Lund claims you as his friend. To me you shall be my friend, too."

Snell smiled wistfully. At that moment she did not think him ugly. Again she thrilled at the might of him, receiving confidence, as warmth from a fire, that no danger would overtake her whilst he was near. The strength of him made him indestructible.

"Thank you, Marm!" was all he said then, and moved on.

The kitchen, when they approached it, seemed very quiet in comparison with the evening before. They had traversed the whole passage and had come to where it entered the great cavern used as kitchen and main living-room of the men. Tuttman was standing with his back to the electric cooking-stoves. In his deep solemn voice he was saying plaintively: "Let the girl alone, or you'll hit trouble head on."

Natalie and her escort stopped at the scene being enacted between them and Tuttman. Almost in the centre of the floor the black-moustached Australian-German held imprisoned in his arms Helen Van Horton's maid. Larsen was trying to kiss Julia and exerting all his strength to force down an arm that was held against his throat. Larsen's back was turned to Natalie, but Julia saw her and Snell. So hysterical was she that she cried out in French: "Release me from this beast, please – please!"

The he-man obviously saw reflected in her face the advent of others, for suddenly he let go and swung round – to find Sweet William standing a couple of yards behind him. The Princess drew close whilst yet these two looked at each other as fighting cockerels before engaging. Larsen's face was white with rage and frustration. Snell's expression was one of calm, curious surprise.

"Mistaire Snell, thrash me that man!" commanded Natalie of Rolandia.

"Certainly, Marm," replied Sweet William, as though she had asked him to pass the salt at table. He took precisely two steps towards Larsen when Larsen sprang off the ground, and Larsen's heavily booted right foot flashed upwards to Snell's face. The action was so swift as almost to deceive the eye. The boot came to within an inch of Snell's face before Snell's hand closed over the ankle and held it in that, to Larsen, most uncomfortable angle.

Larsen began to dance on one foot in an effort to regain equilibrium. He tried valiantly to withdraw his imprisoned foot, with about as much success as a rat caught in a dog-trap. "Let go!"

"Why? You wanted me to inspect the sole of your boot, didn't you?" inquired Snell mildly. "Well, I'm doing so. You'll soon have to get it mended or buy a new pair. Don't wriggle. You're not a worm on a hook."

"Haw, haw, haw!" A bellow of laughter came from Tuttman. "Wot are yous trying to do, Larsen? That ain't the way to dance the Black Bottom."

Ridicule banished discipline and memory of orders from Larsen's mind. Sanity tottered to a fall. His right hand streaked to a hip-pocket. Snell waited for one fraction of a second longer, waited until the man's hand closed on the butt of the automatic, when it was momentarily imprisoned by the cloth.

Then the gallant was sent spinning. He spun like a top on his one foot, swayed dizzily and crashed against a table. Natalie saw Snell appear to hesitate, to be unable to decide precisely what to do next. The significance of Larsen's hand in his hip-pocket was not unmeasured by her. Snell appeared so stupid, his face blank even of any indication of temper.

Yet Larsen had not regained his balance before Sweet William was on him. It seemed that he moved very slowly. Certainly his actions were not those of a man engaged in a rough and tumble death or victory combat. He would not have shown less perturbation had he been punching dough in a bakehouse.

Larsen, however, did not appear to notice that Snell's movements were slow. A huge, hard, hairy-backed hand clouted him a terrific blow on his right ear, and before his bullet-shaped head had stopped jerking to the left, the left ear met Snell's other huge iron-hard hand. The Australian-German forgot all about the automatic pistol. Red, flaming, illimitable rage consumed his brain. His hands were taloned as eagle's claws, and as claws they reached for Snell.

After that the very earth was erupted into cosmic chaos. To the onlookers two masculine bodies became one with four legs, and sometimes an arm, or two arms, waving frantically. Natalie saw Larsen's face for an instant. Larsen's eyes were closed. He looked a dead man. Snell turned her way, and his expression was that of a much bored baker giving his dough an extra punching. Natalie was bereft of feeling, unconscious that she breathed. It was the most wonderful thrill she had ever felt, and she did not begin to appreciate it till later.

No one saw Earle Lawrence enter the kitchen. No one saw him take half a dozen paces towards the scene of combat with his right hand in the pocket of his spotless white drill coat. For two seconds he stood undecided what to do, unobserved by anyone, and still not noticed he left in search of Blue Everett.

Julia's eyes were as black pools of ink. Natalie's right hand fingers were being severely bitten by small ivory teeth. Tuttman was slowly and methodically sharpening a butcher's killing-knife on a large steel. His actions were purely automatic, for not once did he look at what he was doing. As a somnambulist he sharpened his knife without cutting his hand. He breathed heavily, far more heavily than did Snell. Larsen did not appear to be breathing at all, and Natalie began to think once more. She thought how silly it was for Snell to go on pounding a man when he was dead.

And then Larsen was sent across the floor like a grass-cutting boomerang. Snell rose to his feet and dusted his clothes with his great hands, saying calmly, without any tremor in his voice: "He's thrashed, Marm."

Natalie wanted to run to him and hug him.

"What is the reason of this violence?" inquired Blue Everett politely from behind her.

Natalie looked at him coolly; Snell as a butcher will look at a beast for slaughtering in guessing its dead weight.

Tuttman broke in. He seemed quite cheerful. "Larsen tried to kiss the tart," he said. "The lady ordered the bloke to thrash Larsen. Larsen is kind of thrashed by the looks of him. Ah me!

"The morning bright and early,
Another day has come.
Sixteen men on a dead man's chest,
Yo ha! And a bottle of rum."

"Please give me a cup of coffee, and then repeat that verse slowly," almost whispered Natalie.

CHAPTER XIX

ERIC LACEY TALKS

TUTTMAN was one of those long, thin, cadaverous men whose complexion is invariably a sickly white heightened by black hair and a wispy, black, drooping moustache. Pessimist was writ large in lines about the lantern jaws and the never-smiling bulging eyes.

"Be seated, Marm," he said in the tone of an undertaker ushering a mourner into a cab.

The Princess accepted the plain wicker-bottomed chair Tuttman placed for her at one end of the spotless deal table. The horrified Julia watched him spread a newspaper before the Royal prisoner, and on this paper swiftly place a cup and saucer and a basin of sugar. From a brilliantly polished stove he snatched the coffee-pot and filled the cup.

"When the Prince of Wales was in Adelaide I made coffee for him, Marm," he said. "Before I went to France as a six-bob-a-day tourist, the Frogs knew how to make coffee. When I left France they knew how to make it better."

"It lovely is," Natalie complimented him, sipping.

"Yes, Marm, it is," Tuttman agreed. "Of course any fool can make coffee with fresh cow's milk. To make it like a liquor with condensed milk is where the art comes in. Take a cup, Mister Snell?"

Snell nodded, received a cup, and drank it whilst standing behind Natalie.

Julia vanished.

Natalie regarded the *chef* as a small child will look at a passing king. She said: "A poet you are, eh, Mistaire Tuttman? I have heard you sing."

"Yes, Marm. I am a kind of poet," Tuttman admitted. "Leastways, where I come from I'm called a song-writer. I writes the songs and other blokes sings 'em. Ole Billy Williams sang two of my songs with great success. One of 'em was called 'A poor little bride in 'er coffin'."

"It must have been – what you say? – the weeps."

"The weeps, Marm! Why, when Billy Williams sang it in London the house used to rock with laughter. He says to me: 'Alfred, your song's a winner; write another, and I'll gamble it gets a place.' So I wrote my 'Ode to the Future'. But before it reached Billy Williams he was dead. Then I sent it to Caruso."

"Ah! the great Caruso. I heard him sing so lovely at Milan."

"Yes, Marm. He could hoo-la-la orl right in Eye-talerno language wot no one could understand," Tuttman went on with withering contempt in his voice. "He wasn't a patch on Billy Williams – not a patch. You could understand wot Billy *was* singing about."

"Have you got your 'Ode to the Future'?" asked the Princess, who understood only half what the *chef* was telling her with so much unctuous enthusiasm.

"Yes, Marm; I'll get it." With astonishing swiftness he strode to a small off-cave, wherein he slept, to return with a roll of foolscap. This he unrolled, sweeping aside the half-emptied cup of coffee, the artist in him knowing little of social distinctions, or, if knowing, temporarily forgetful. "Here we are, Marm. 'An Ode to the Future, written by Alfred Tuttman, Esquire, music taken from Moody and Sankey'. Forty-two verses in all." He stood back and upright, a poetical genius awaiting the applause he was positive would come.

Earle Lawrence came in, obviously impatient for breakfast. The mess-room waiter stood by, a large electroplated tray under his arm.

Natalie, who could not read English handwriting quickly, pretended to read the neatly-written stanzas. Then: "Beautiful! Most beautiful!" Tuttman found himself being regarded with wide, solemn eyes. "Permit me, Mistaire Tuttman, to lend – no, borrow – this manuscript for one, two days. Let me copy, yes, translate it into Rolandian!"

"I would be proud, Your Royal Highness," Tuttman endeavoured to say calmly.

"It shall be done. In Naagrade I will command it to be sung at the Kursaal."

Rising to her feet, she glanced round, saw Lawrence and the waiter, and Larsen staggering away through the entrance to a cave she had not entered. "Good morning, Mistaire Lawrence! A little while ago your accomplice with the black whiskers, *au* Kaiser, assaulted the so *chic* Julia. It was necessary he should be beaten. I commanded such to be."

"The incident was very regrettable, Princess. I do not think it will be repeated."

"Not for a little while, certainly. Well, *au revoir*, Mistaire Tuttman. I will speak with you again. Mistaire Snell, accompany me."

Natalie could be very regal. She possessed the trained gift of walking, and when she passed through the small group, among which was the chagrined Lawrence, her poise was one of haughty contempt; but, once in the long winding passage leading to the living-caverns, the iciness of her bearing melted, and to Snell she said softly: "Later you shall read to me this Ode. Now take you heed what I say: Cultivate the so wonderful *chef*. Become his friend. With care we will make of him an ally."

"Very good, Marm. He could be useful if he liked."

"How, think you?"

"Well, if we could lay our hands on some strychnine, he could poison all the gang," suggested the unsmiling Snell.

Natalie sighed. "My so dear friend, you and I both live three hundred years too late."

"Yes, Marm," agreed Snell, although he did not understand to what he agreed.

At table they occupied the places of the previous evening. Larsen's place was vacant, and the incident from which the vacancy resulted was not brought up for discussion.

"I am afraid you all retired too early last night," Lawrence said casually. "At about eleven wireless conditions greatly improved. I tuned in on Perth, and heard it announced that Eric Lacey will give a résumé of the Great Abduction Case at half-past twelve to-day."

"Do you refer to the famous novelist-criminologist?" inquired Van Horton.

"The same. He reached Perth yesterday by the *Orvieto* on a short tour of Australia. They've got him to speak on the wireless, and what better subject could Australia offer him?"

"But what can he know about it?" Lund asked.

"He will know all there is to know, Mr. Lund, by noon to-day. He is to be placed in possession of all the facts and supposed facts, and from those data will form his opinion."

"I like his novels," observed Helen. "They are so thrilling. If his plots are taken from real life, there must be some dreadful people in the world."

Earle Lawrence laughed. "Present company excepted?" he inquired.

"Just then I was not thinking of you," Helen retorted coolly.

The topic of the famous visitor and his many novels, with their offspring of plays and cinema films, sufficed throughout the meal.

At noon all the company gathered in the "drawing-room" save Larsen, Tuttman, and the guards on duty. At the wireless set Earle Lawrence tuned in to the Perth Broadcasting Station. There was exceedingly little static and the announcer's voice came clearly, giving the market reports, the acceptances for the races the following day, and the overseas news items. Then Mr. Eric Lacey was called on to speak to the people of Australia. After several seconds of utter silence a thin, hesitant voice came through:

"Greetings, everybody! I am told that the atmospheric conditions in

Perth this morning are excellent, and I do hope the same clear conditions exist over all Australia, so that those residing in the great open spaces" – Van Horton looked at Lund, who smiled – "as well as the city-dwellers, will hear how much I appreciate the welcome extended to me by this great country. What I have seen of Australia much appeals to me. I think Perth a wonderful city and the people so free and nice" – Lund now smiled at Earle Lawrence. So often had they heard this strain before. The mob, however, seemed never tired of hearing it.

Evidently Mr. Eric Lacey paused to let his complimentary phrases sink in. Or it may be that he absent-mindedly for the moment waited for applause to reach him in that soundproof room.

Then: "I come to find Australia involved in the most amazing occurrence in criminal annals I ever heard of. Since the dawn of civilisation, since the time of Cain, crime has walked hand in hand with virtue. We have had criminal nations as well as criminal individuals, and although the march of civilisation tends ever to lessen national crime, individual crime appears to be spreading at an alarming rate. Representatives of law and order are engaged in an eternal battle with law-breakers. Every new invention is seized upon and used by both sides. Very clever men occupy the positions of the opposing generals, as it were. Not only do both sides use every weapon science has made available, but both sides plan and maintain intricate organisations. Recent criminal activity in America, in Chicago especially, proves that both sides are so cleverly led and cleverly organised that the peace of the people in general is always gravely disturbed.

"You in Australia appear to have been remarkably free from organised crime. I wish to stress the words 'have been'. Two days ago the first and most complete evidence of organised crime in Australia was revealed in the astounding abduction of Her Royal Highness the Princess Natalie of Rolandia, whilst journeying from Adelaide to Perth. It is obvious even to the meanest intellect that the achievement of abducting a Royal Princess from a train, on which were a crowd of people and armed detectives, was based upon wonderful criminal organisation.

"The actual abduction was not unaccompanied by loss of life. The abductors acted with the ruthlessness of Mexican or Chinese bandits. With modern automatic pistols they shot their way to their objective, which was the person of Her Royal Highness. With her they escaped southward from Cook in high-powered automobiles, leaving two of their dead and taking with them one seriously-wounded comrade. Two of the detectives were killed, two others wounded, and that gallant courtier, the Baron Schulz, was cold-bloodedly shot down because, unarmed, he ventured to protect his future Queen.

"In this year of grace a hold-up of such magnitude is an amazing thing. It would seem to be a case utterly impossible to happen in Australia or in any law-abiding civilised country. Attempted assassinations of Royalties by unbalanced fanatics are in a way understandable. Abductors of ordinary people are not uncommon. But the abduction of a Royal Lady in the circumstances noted, abduction whilst she was the guest of a nation, and, so far, wholly successful abduction, is a matter of very grave import to all of us, in the British Empire especially.

"Available evidence to date points to the fact that the Princess was taken to Eucla, on the Great Australian Bight, where she and the gang – it is reported that the gang numbered at least fourteen – boarded an ocean-going yacht. At the moment the British battleship *Iron Duke*, two Australian destroyers, and the *Java*, a cruiser of the Netherlands Navy which was at Melbourne, are scouring the Southern Ocean; whilst the French cruiser *Babette* is rushing southward from Singapore, and other ships belonging to the navies of Britain and Japan are ordered to steam to the South Pacific and southern Indian Ocean. To date no news of the yacht is to hand, although besides the warships named there are in the Bight no less than thirteen mercantile ships fitted with wireless and now manned with extra look-outs. It seems impossible for the yacht to get away, and at any moment we may have news of its capture.

"We all know how the roads to Eucla were effectively blocked to motor traffic by their being covered with small metal spheres from which protrude two-inch steel spines. That operation carried out by the abductors was an extraordinarily clever move. It has prevented the rapid transportation of representatives of the law to Eucla. It also prevented black trackers being rushed to Cook and Eucla, and it is now reported via the repaired telephone lines that thunderstorms have passed over all the plain, washing out any tracks that may possibly have been left. The laying of those metal spines was a veritable masterpiece.

"A representative of the firm of Norwood and Blaye, Newcastle, New South Wales, has reported that a rough model was shown them three weeks ago, and an order received to manufacture fifty thousand. Messrs. Norwood and Blaye are makers of wire-netting and barbed wire. They completed the order in the specified ten days, delivering for cash to a man who stated he wanted these peculiar objects to lay a trail round a field – you call it a paddock, I believe – in which were many valuable prize rams in danger of being attacked by wild dogs. He said the laying of these spines would be cheaper than erecting an eight-foot wire-netted fence.

"Being a novelist, I have kept till the end the most surprising development. Yesterday afternoon there was delivered by messenger at the offices of an important Sydney newspaper a letter signed by one Earle Lawrence. The paper in question brought out a special evening edition featuring a photographic reproduction of the letter. It reads:

> *To the Editor, The Daily Tribune.*
>
> *Sir, – You will now be in possession of the main facts concerning the abduction of Her Royal Highness the Princess Natalie of Rolandia. You will know, too, that she is my guest at sea, in an exceptionally fast ship which was disguised as an ocean-going pleasure yacht.*
>
> *In order to allay any public anxiety, I wish to make it known through your paper that she will be treated with all the consideration and respect due to her rank, until such time as the sum of two hundred thousand pounds is paid over to my representative in Paris, who will act according to instructions. I may add that the ransom has been fixed at the low figure stated to suit the financial situation of the country, and that it is the minimum figure.*
>
> *Yours, etc.,*
> *Earle Lawrence.*

"That is the crowning impudence of a most daring and atrocious crime," went on Mr. Eric Lacey. "News from Eucla is slow in coming through. The position on the Nullarbor Plain is a little mystifying. An old Ford car with wheels fitted with peculiar double-rimmed steel tyres instead of rubber was found standing with the other abandoned cars, and it is believed that it was recently driven by a well-known and respected Adelaide gentleman.

"This is the situation up to the moment. I have been asked to talk to you again at eleven o'clock to-night, and I hope that by then I shall be able to tell you that this marvelously organised gang of abductors has been apprehended and that Her Royal Highness is safely restored to the protection of our Empire. *Au revoir*, everybody!"

Earle Lawrence switched off and rose to his feet. His eyes were aflame with a strange light. He said, calmly enough: "It's a great game!"

CHAPTER XX

A PRIMEVAL RELIC

TOWARDS the end of lunch, Helen Van Horton suggested that the prisoners should undertake a tour of exploration. "You cannot possibly object, Mr. Lawrence," she told the Australian a little pettishly, Van Horton adding: "No, Lawrence, you can raise no objection to our going. You have made escape impossible. Besides, we really must have exercise."

"I have not the slightest objection in the world," Lawrence said, smiling with his mouth only. "As a matter of fact, I must attend to some important business this afternoon. On that account, could we not put off the exploring trip till tomorrow?"

Helen yawned politely. "Surely your lieutenant, Mr. Everett, would be an efficient guide? He could take one or two other men as guards if you think us really dangerous."

"How about it, Everett?"

"I should be delighted to act as guide," Blue Everett assented in his cultured drawl. "As for guards, we will dispense with them. I am sure both Mr. Lund and Mr. Snell appreciate the impossibility of escape, even if they became so unkind as to hit me over the head when my back was turned."

"I shall attempt nothing so dramatic to-day. Snell and I are not fully recovered from the fatigue of our interrupted effort at record-breaking. About a week from to-day we may become dangerous."

"What are your wishes, Princess?" Lawrence asked.

"To walk I desire, Mistaire Lawrence. I also am yet fatigued.

Like Mistaire Lund, dangerous I shall be one week further on."

"I shall remember the date," Lawrence said gravely.

"Possibly it well would be," she told him with unsmiling face.

He saw her dislike of him in her blue eyes, and that hurt his vanity, for the man was proud of his physique and his good looks. He had thought that with polite deference in addition to his address he would by then have worn away her dislike, so natural at the time of the abduction. Lawrence was coming to understand a little the iron strength of mind housed in so pretty a head; and, as he had been compared with one other by these two women, so he then compared them: Natalie being a quick, active tigress; Helen a purring, sleepy panther. He had never seen Helen aroused, nor had he seen Natalie in her playful moments.

Half an hour later the party assembled in that cavern from which opened Natalie's bed-chamber.

Blue Everett joined them, carrying half a dozen electric torches, which he distributed. "We shall want them at various points," he explained, "where our system of lighting does not extend. I am, of course, no geologist, but the little I do know of the Nullarbor Plain and its formation may be of interest. In my role of guide I will explain as we proceed."

He took them along a passage lighted by an electric bulb at every dozen yards. The walls, roof, and floor were roughly uneven, and, in that light, of a dark putty colour. Here and there water trickled down a wall, causing gleams of black and brown. Sometimes from the roof water dropping at long intervals was forming stalagmites of all sizes and ages.

"Ages and ages ago all this limestone through which we are walking was deep in the ocean-bed," Everett told them. "At that time, doubtless, Australia was only a few islands or chains of islands separated by hundreds of miles of water. Then probably came a great upheaval. Thousands of square miles of ocean floor became dry land, and other great areas sank still further beneath the water. I understand that at no great distance from the shore of the Bight the depth of water is more than three thousand fathoms.

"Even here, at this depth of what now is dry land after all these countless years, there are to be found shells, fish shells, made by fish when the brontosaurus roamed through the carboniferous forests. See! here is one held fast in the rock." Snell prised it out with his knife, and when it lay on the palm of his thick, stub-fingered hand, they saw that it was exactly the same sort of shell that the sea-slugs carry on their backs to-day. With them evolution seems never to have been.

The passage suddenly dipped steeply. Now and then they passed heaps of rock rubbish, denoting that the gang had cleared up the rock litter to ease the going. They came to where two streams of limpid water spouted out of the wall less than a yard apart, falling with a blue diamond glitter into a deep rock-basin from which it overflowed and ran in a sharply-cut gutter down along the centre of the passage, till it met a crevice into which it fell. The right-hand stream was perfectly fresh; that on the left was saltier than the sea.

Farther on they came to a roughly circular hole in the floor of the passage having a diameter of almost five feet. The members of the party were obliged to hug one of the walls to pass by.

"A blow-hole," Everett explained. He struck a match, and the current of air sucking downward extinguished it. "I have come across and examined a number of natural blowholes," he went on, "and they act in different ways, no two exactly alike. In some the air is always sucked downward; in others the air is always rushing upward so strongly that it is impossible to drop your hat into it. Yet other holes alternately suck and expel air, some near the sea in accordance with the rise and fall of the tides. This particular hole sucks and expels air with extraordinary regularity, alternating precisely every sixty minutes. I have timed it, and find it to be as accurate as an hour-glass."

"Is it deep in?" asked Natalie, able to follow with ease Everett's clearly-spoken, precise English.

"Listen, Highness," he said, and dropped in a piece of rock. They heard it ring from side to side at intervals of seconds. The sounds grew faint and yet more faint whilst time passed with apparent slowness. Then came silence, and Natalie would have spoken had not Everett continued listening. Finally came up from the blow-hole an extraordinarily deep vibrating booming, like distant thunder, or ocean breakers crashing against a rocky shore heard miles away on a still night.

"I don't know the rate at which an object drops through the air," Everett said. "But that piece of rock must have dropped a tremendous depth. I think, from repeated experiments, that the air-shaft is probably a thousand feet deep. You will remember the long interval of silence between the last tinkle made by rock striking rock and that booming sound. It raises the theory that the air-shaft sinks to a huge cavern in which is a great lake. The rock we dropped struck the water, and the soft sound of its splash was amplified by the walls of the cavern and sent up the air-shaft, cavern and shaft forming a sort of gigantic ear-trumpet."

"Extraordinary!" muttered Van Horton, genuinely interested.

"A feller wouldn't have much chance of getting up if he fell in," said Snell, regarding Everett as he had that morning regarded Larsen. "Or," he added passionlessly, "was pushed in."

"Don't!" Helen Van Horton almost whispered, with a shudder. "Come, let us go on. That hole fascinates me horribly. How dreadful if one fell in and was not killed in falling!"

The passage appeared interminable, and the first break in it came when they reached a small cavern, so thickly pillared with stalagmites that they were forced to proceed through them in single file. The lighted passage continued to the right; to the left was the dark, gaping orifice of another passage. The place was filled with a continuous humming sound as though from a gigantic top, and, since the cable that was laid along the passage they had just traversed continued through the lighted passage before them, Lund and Snell surmised that at some point down it was situated the dynamo that gave light and heat. Everett's next words proved their surmise to be correct.

"Further along is the hydro-dynamo, which we will visit presently. But first I would like to show you the skeleton of the fish or beast which I am sure would excite the scientific world if made known. Shall I go first?"

Leading them into the dark passage, it was made visible by their torches. They followed its tortuous windings down a sharp rock-strewn declivity for nearly two hundred yards, when they entered the largest cavern in the whole underground system. It was so immense that the combined power of their torches failed to penetrate to its farther side.

The guide halted. "The extent of this cavern is exactly nine hundred and eleven paces," he said. "As you see, the floor is covered with deep sand, and I am inclined to think that when the land was under water the sand was washed down to this cavern. How high the roof is we have not yet been able to ascertain."

The beam of his torch flashed upwards. Other beams of light, as though trying to assist his, failed to reveal the roof. Their voices were so vociferously echoed that to carry on a conversation was difficult. Lund thought that the acoustic properties were probably unique in the world.

With Natalie at his side and the others following in close order, Blue Everett led the way along the broken right wall. From out of the darkness beyond the range of their torches a thousand coloured points of light blazed, winked, and vanished, as though they were the ever-changing irises of a thousand great cats. The stalagmites, built up from the sandy floor to varying heights, became columns of scintillating masses of precious stones, blue, green, yellow, and white. It was as though they walked through the cave of the Forty Thieves, or had wandered into a jeweller's super-showroom.

"The House of Jewels!" murmured Helen Van Horton to Raymond Lund.

"It is a wonderful place indeed," he agreed softly, trying also to defeat the echo.

But it would not be outwitted. It whispered back: "The House of Jewels – The House of Jewels – The House of Jewels!" as the mocking chorus of a community of hobgoblins. And, again, "A wonderful place! – A wonderful place!" was taken up in like manner and endlessly repeated.

Out of the darkness loomed what appeared to be an intricate maze of white-painted scaffolding, yet in all the structure, as in Nature, there was not one straight line. Drawing near and coming to stand beside it, they saw that the scaffolding was built of gigantic bones bleached to the whiteness of chalk by time, rising to thirty feet in places, and extending from the wall into the far blackness of the cavern.

"What is it – fish, fowl, or mammal?" Everett asked.

"Extraordinary!" ejaculated Van Horton. "Why, it is far larger than the reconstructed brontosaurus and the ichthyosauria in the museums of New York and Berlin."

"How did it get in here?" asked Snell.

"Probably when all this rock was mud," suggested Everett. "When the mud was solidified into rock, this creature was embedded like a mastodon in an iceberg, and when the rock was honeycombed with caves the skeleton, being harder than the rock, was left as we see it now."

"It would take some killing, anyway," said Snell.

"Yes," replied Everett. "It does not look as if it died by violence. It may have been drowned in a tidal wave, or poisoned by the fumes of a submarine volcano."

The others regarded the monstrous remains in silence.

The Princess was thinking that Everett was the most remarkable member of the gang, and determined to cultivate his acquaintance at some future time.

He spoke again: "They are so old, those bones, that even the vibrations we set up here with our voices tend to destroy them. Look!" He threw the beam of his torch on a bone almost four feet thick and motioned them to draw near.

Then he said: "Look at the dust – look at the dust!" And they saw falling from the curved surface of the bone tiny particles of matter, as fine as dust in sunlight.

"It looks massive enough, does it not?" Everett went on. "Yet it is so old and so fragile that you could blow it away with a pair of hand-bellows."

"Well, he would have made a bonzer house-dog," surmised Snell. "Pity his feet are gone."

Torch-beams flashed downward to explore for the thing's feet, and then one became steady, held at a point where, distinctly outlined on the sand, was the imprint of a naked foot. Other beams flashed over the ground, revealing lines of imprints.

Everett bent over them. The reflected light revealed his face, and they saw the expression of wonder change to one of perplexity. With his torch he followed up the tracks, saw how the man had trodden on a great bone with the effect of severing it as though it had been but the froth of whipped cream.

The silence was broken by Lund. "No man made those impressions," he said.

"Neither did that skeleton," added the American.

"Then what made the so strange marks?" Natalie pertinently inquired of Blue Everett.

Everett looked first into the faces of Van Horton and Lund before replying: "I cannot say, Princess."

"But whatever it is, and in shape it is a man's foot which made the marks, it has been moving around this skeleton recently," was Van Horton's opinion.

"The date is difficult to fix, Van Horton," objected Lund. "Tracks made on the sand here might well last an eternity, for there is neither wind nor rain to obliterate them."

"True! But they look fresh to me," said Everett.

"They can't be. There is not a man alive with that shaped foot. Why, those tracks must have been made by a monstrous gorilla. Look at the outline of the prehistoric toes."

"Let us get away. I am feeling nervous," Helen whispered.

It was as though each in turn was touched on the shoulder by Fear. Everett led the way back to the lighted passage. Other than Snell, no one liked the idea of being last. Natalie was thankful that Snell was last.

CHAPTER XXI

THE IRON YOUTH

BLUE EVERETT had taken the exploring party to the cavern in which was installed the hydro-dynamo, and there they had watched the great ceaseless flood of water pour out of a horizontal cleft in the solid limestone and tumble into a seemingly bottomless pit. In his quiet direct way Everett explained how the big water-wheel was geared to set the 220-volt dynamo humming at a terrific speed.

Yet the zest of the tour had been effectually damped by the sight of the extraordinary tracks on the sand near the skeleton of the great beast. Raymond Lund's theory that they, too, had been made ages before did not hold water. No one troubled to dispute it. Everett knew, although he then said nothing about it, that those tracks were not there when last he had visited the deepest and greatest cavern; and both Van Horton and Snell knew, too, that Everett had previously been there and would have noted the tracks had they then existed.

Whilst returning to the inhabited part of the underground palace the explorers spoke but little. Each one of them knew that somewhere in the bowels of the earth there lurked a monster whose footprints were far larger than any man's. What sort of a thing it was in aspect even imagination failed to visualise. There were the tracks, imprints of a foot with four long toes and one huge main toe longer than the others and widely separated from them. Both Natalie and Helen Van Horton remembered that there were no doors to their sleeping chambers to be locked and barred.

It was the surprising behaviour of Earle Lawrence which for the time banished from their minds the uneasiness created by the mysterious footprints. He, with Sir Knight and a man named Fred Bennett, awaited them in the Cavern of the Sword, and, without any preamble, Lund, Snell, and Van Horton suddenly found themselves looking down the barrels of automatic pistols.

"What the deuce!" ejaculated Everett.

"Search them for firearms, Everett," commanded Lawrence in steely tones. "The slightest move, gentlemen, means finis."

The unexpectedness of the situation enhanced the melodrama.

Helen Van Horton stood with clasped hands and wide eyes.

Natalie looked on the hold-up with narrowed eyes and grim little mouth. "Is it that you practise for the cinema?" she asked with velvet voice. "Or are you short of the cash so hard, Mistaire Lawrence?"

"Neither, Princess. I am looking for an automatic pistol which Larsen lost during his fight with Mr. Snell."

"So! But there you use wrong word. Mr. Snell he thrash the bad Larsen. Of fight there was none. I commanded a thrashing, not a fight. A thrashing it was."

"Excuse me, Highness! Everett, is there a gun on anyone of them?"

"No."

"Now then, Snell, what did you do with that gun?"

"Tell the tale and I'll report," Snell said, his eyelids so low that his eyes were almost invisible. He stood with his bullet head thrust forward from hunched shoulders, so that he seemed to have no neck, whilst his hands were opened and the fingers wide apart.

"Larsen says that the instant you sprang on him the fingers of his right hand were touching the pistol in his pocket, groping for the butt. When he recovered consciousness the pistol was not in his pocket. During the scuffle you must have taken it out. What have you done with it?"

"Are you a dead man, or are you a live man?" inquired Snell with a horrible leer.

"Alive, of course – very much alive."

Snell's voice in reply was as the growl of a sleepy bear. "If I had had Larsen's pistol you would have been very dead – believe me."

"Yet the pistol you must have had," Lawrence persisted. "No one, other than Mr. Lund or Mr. Van Horton, would have taken and kept it. The other men all possess one. The kitchen, the dining- and sitting-rooms, and all the bedrooms, have been thoroughly searched, without result. The pistol is missing. You had the opportunity of taking it. I myself witnessed the way you man-handled Larsen."

"The man Larsen, of course, hates Mistaire Snell," Natalie cut in. "He commits these lies hoping to put Mistaire Snell to disadvantage. I was watching Mistaire Snell thrash the so obnoxious Larsen. Never saw I the pistol change pockets. Mistaire Tuttman, he of the so great 'Ode to the Future', also watched. Did he see the pistol change pockets? Did you, Mistaire Lawrence? Bah! Again, Bah! Child you are in hands of this Larsen man. He plays – what you say? – on your stupidity. The great joke, eh?"

She laughed up at Earle Lawrence, and Lawrence's conviction weakened. "Well, it's got to be found," he said to all of them. "In this community we can have no unauthorised person carrying concealed weapons. I am prepared to treat you, gentlemen, with every courtesy, but at the first move you make of a hostile nature my men and I shoot to kill. Understand that!" And, turning abruptly on his heel, Lawrence strode away.

Helen Van Horton laughed mockingly, but the Australian never turned. "Princess, let us go to my room, where Julia can bring us afternoon tea. Shall we?"

"We will. Tired am I with walking. *Au revoir,* Mistaire Lund and Mistaire Van Horton! Perhaps, Mistaire Snell, some time I will have Larsen once again thrashed."

Inclining her head to each of them in turn, she sauntered to the cave set aside for the use of Helen Van Horton, with that lady following her closely. Julia was sent to the kitchen for afternoon tea, and Helen herself did all a hostess could do to make Natalie comfortable.

"Do you think, Princess, that Mr. Snell really got the pistol from Larsen?" she purred, arranging cushions for Natalie's back.

"That I think impossible, my so dear Helen."

Helen sighed. "If only he had taken it! You know, I feel so helpless. I do wish I had a pistol."

"I, too," Natalie said grimly.

"Can you – but can you use a pistol?"

"Oh yes! A pistol I can use with – with – with accuracy. Practice I used to do after the time I rode with my father through the streets of Naagrade in an open carriage. A man threw a bomb. He ran past the guards and threw it."

"Yes – go on," urged Helen with parted lips.

"He missed. The bomb the horses killed. A soldier slew the man. It was a pity. My father loved those horses. So did I. They screamed in agony as they lay kicking in the dust. Yes, as I said, it was a pity the soldier slew the bomb-thrower. My father was always a kind man, but just."

"He would have punished him?"

"Of a certainty. The man's end would – what you say? – be prolonged."

"Not tortured!" Helen gasped.

"Oh no!"

"Well"

"Let us discuss the great thing which makes the so funny tracks."

Natalie was lying back in a deep easy-chair, which Helen Van Horton had just put there, looking like a big fragile doll. The small vivid face was stern, the violet-blue eyes inscrutable, the lips thinned into a straight line.

To Helen, seated on a large floor cushion, she looked like a picture of one of the ancient Chinese empresses who held unlimited power over millions.

"They are peculiar, aren't they?"

"So peculiar! I wonder if, as Mistaire Lund said, long ago they were made," Natalie remarked tentatively, adding: "Or is the thing making the tracks with us here in these so wonderful caverns?"

"Oh! I hope not, Princess. There are no doors," Helen burst out, truly alarmed. "I must get father to persuade Mr. Lawrence to have every nook and cranny searched. I shall never sleep until it is done."

"I wish I had a pistol," Natalie said, sighing.

"So do I, Princess. I should feel safer."

The hours slipped by in idle discussion. Natalie liked Helen Van Horton. She was so sympathetic to her every want, and her conversation, too, was always interesting when she talked of people and places. The sound of the dinner-gong took them unawares.

The well-cooked dinner was eaten almost in silence. At the head of the table the Princess made no effort to force conversation, contenting herself with studying the others. It might be assumed that she was acutely conscious of the indignities being thrust on her, that she might excusably feel resentment against her abductors as well as at the veiled insult of compelling her to eat with a lady's maid and men of Larsen's stamp. As she confessed later, however, the situation was so strange that she accepted the circumstances as though she had been used to them. Both her companions and the members of the gang interested her much, because they were people whom she never had previously met, or represented classes with whom she had come in contact only at public functions.

Still, she was able to winnow the wheat from the chaff, and classify both into their various grades. Her first impressions were being replaced by the results of considered judgment. Raymond Lund, of course, she had got to know intimately. He was so emphatically allied with an exquisite period of happiness when she forgot everything but that she was a young woman. Van Horton mystified her. He was so unruffled for a man forced to pay away a large sum of money. To this his daughter also appeared indifferent, but the Princess reflected that perhaps they possessed so much money that its real value was not appreciated.

Still more mystifying than Van Horton was the red-haired man, Blue Everett. Both in appearance and speech he was a cultured English gentleman. So, too, was the thin dark man, Fred Bennett. They both seemed so out of place in company with the man addressed as Sir Knight and the Australian-German, Larsen. She noticed that when dinner was over and they retired to the drawing-room Everett and Bennett followed with Earle Lawrence, whereas the others of the gang drifted out to the kitchen and their own quarters. The time being a little early for the wireless news, she motioned Lawrence to be seated beside her.

"I would have you tell me how you came to assemble men so mixed," she said, autocracy in her voice.

"You mean my comrades, Princess?"

"Precisely."

Leaning back in his chair, a long cheroot at the angle of a howitzer gun clenched between his strong teeth, he surveyed Everett and the dark man for some seconds before speaking.

Then: "I suppose it is the logical result of the Great War," he said in his pleasant drawl. "We are the remnants of the Iron Youth so laudated by the Germans. In 1914 we were clean living, transparently decent, sport-loving young men. We stood at the threshold of life, at the milestone on the road where we should have selected our walk in life.

"The machine of militarism claimed us. We had hardly left school when we were thrust into a world unforeseen by parents and schoolmasters, a world of terror, of death, of filth. Those of us who lived, learned to regard legalised murder as we had learned to regard football. We were sunk into the jungle from which our prehistoric ancestors had emerged. It is now a hard thing to say, Highness, but fortune favoured not the survivors but the dead and the dying.

"From school direct to war; from war direct to peace to which we were become strangers. We were the Iron Youth all right, but when the peace came we were Iron Robots, without a guiding intelligence to direct us, cast aside. Gone was our youth. Vanished were our chances of youth to make good in a world of peace. The dead were at peace in their graves; we who survived were left stranded, stunned, lost, contemptuously ignored. As though we had fallen on the earth from Mars, we were regarded by the stay-at-homes as curious insects worthy of notice for a little while, but soon to be forgotten."

The dreamer was dreaming, and when he paused, Natalie, strangely thrilled, urged him to go on with the dream.

"I don't know very much either of Everett or Bennett," Lawrence resumed. "That is, very little of their pre-war history. They belong to the class who rarely speak of their people and their youth. I've no doubt they were loved by good women, mothers and sisters and friends. Doubtless, too, they were clean, hard sportsmen, keen on the careers they were starting to follow.

"I know dozens like them. And the war fouled them and soaked their souls in beastliness. Yet for all that they could never forget what they had been. They were honest enough to know that what they had been they could never be again. It is not for you, Princess, nor for any woman, to know just what we all went through. We did things in that war which we had never thought about even in our wildest nightmares. Do you know that when the peace came I knew that never again could I look into the eyes of my mother? How could I, when I had shot men, had stabbed men, and in horrible blood frenzy had even cut men's throats? No, I could not let the pure woman who bore me see on me the indelible mark of the beast.

"I rather fancy Blue Everett and Bennett thought as I did. The war made us plain unvarnished crooks. To-day, nine years afterwards, we would not hesitate to kill if menaced or obstructed in any desperate undertaking we planned to carry out. When peace came we were banished from decent civilian life, and strangely enough we didn't care a jot. It is extraordinary how case-hardened a human being can become."

For a little while Natalie pondered on the dreamer's strange dreams. When she spoke it was quite softly. "Yet Mistaire Lund and Mistaire Snell, they knocked the door and allowed were to enter good civilian life."

"Agreed. I am not daring to state, Princess, that the war made every soldier a crook. Far from it. Nevertheless, it did make crooks of some of us, and it was not very difficult to gather into a band a number living in this country. There are some here who were criminals before the Army claimed them. Larsen is one. Sir Knight is just plain adventurer. Bussey – you have not seen him yet – is a soldier, simply nothing else. Morgan most of his life has been a sandbagger, pickpocket, and downright thug. Tuttman, the chef, I knew before the war. He was a pastry-cook, a Sunday-school teacher, struggling to educate himself with classical poetry and prose. I have seen Tuttman scalp a man more neatly than any Red Indian could do.

"Here, Princess, we are back in our element," Lawrence went on. "Bussey is our sergeant-major and maintains good discipline, to which no one objects. You would think that if there was one thing of which the war sickened us it was discipline. We did get sick of it, to be sure. Now we like it. I believe sometimes that if we were put back into the hell of No Man's Land we would be happy. We shall get a million dollars for your person. We shall all retire rich men. But we shall not be happy; not so happy as we are now."

"It is all very sad, Mistaire Lawrence," Natalie told him, unable not to feel sympathy.

"You are quite right. It is sad. It is a most terrible tragedy. When the peace came every allied nation had at its disposal a vast human machine. The governments smashed those machines when they could have used them to clean up the mess of war, to purify the rotten public life, to organise the people, to get back to the prosperity and sanity of pre-war days. But no! Each efficient war machine was broken up, so that politicians and profiteers might hold securely the places and wealth they had filched from the nation during its agony. Yes, Princess, you behold the Iron Youth. The iron is in us and will remain.

"Let us try and get Perth."

CHAPTER XXII

WAR – AND THINGS

RAYMOND LUND, having sought permission to take Earle Lawrence's vacated seat, sank into the chair beside Natalie. There below the surface of the Nullarbor Plain, in a rock-room of bizarre aspect, the gathering was precisely like any similar gathering of well-bred people. Mr. Van Horton was smoking a cigar whilst reading absorbedly a red-covered novel. His daughter was conversing with William Snell whilst they sat at opposite ends of a Chesterfield, and it was observed by Natalie that Miss Van Horton was doing most of the talking, Snell proving to be a most excellent listener. Julia, the maid, was laughing at something Blue Everett was saying, whilst near the entrance the tall dark man called Fred Bennett was gazing fixedly at the vaulted roof as though wrestling with a difficult problem. Sir Knight, entering, seated himself beside Bennett, whereupon Bennett's tilted face became normally perpendicular and he obviously asked a question.

"How are your first impressions wearing, Princess?" Lund inquired with a smile.

"In parts they wear, Mr. Lund. They have become – what you say? – patchwork. The man Lawrence my calculations has upset. He spoke of the Great War and of its effects even more great. He told to me his heart. He said when it was done, afraid was he to meet his mother. Did you in the war kill men by the cutting of their throats?"

"I do not remember having done so," replied the astonished Lund.

"Well, did you scalp men like the so artistic Red Indian?"

"Heavens, no!"

"How, then, did you kill men?"

Natalie was very earnest, and Lund wondered just what Lawrence had been telling her. Seeing his diffidence in replying, she repeated her question with the steely impatience of her house.

"It is not a pleasant subject, Princess," he said at last. "War is a very dreadful thing. Modern war is so horrible that when man meets man with pistol, bayonet, and bomb, after confinement to a trench where he has suffered tremendous nervous shocks from exploding shells, it is a fight not between reasoning men lifted high by mental excitement, but rather between somnambulists possessed by devils. A man's mind is dominated by one idea, to kill or be killed. There is no other thought; no room for anything but the one idea. Since you press the question, I will say that I have killed men with bombs, with the bayonet, and with a revolver. I have also clubbed men with the butt end of a rifle. But shall we talk about something else? What do you think of my friend Sweet William?"

"When you came back, was it afraid you were to look your mother in the eyes?" went on the inexorable Natalie.

"No!"

It seemed to both that for a very long time their eyes met and held in a soul-searching look. Natalie's were the first to break away, and whilst regarding the points of her shoes with downcast face she wondered at the acceleration of her heart, even whilst she knew that Lund's "No!" was his final word on how he had seen men die in the Great War. For the first time in her life she had come against the rock of masculine decision.

"Your friend, Mistaire Snell, I like much," she said softly. "He is – what is it? – the human ice-block. As hard as ice and as cold as ice. I say, and he do – I mean I command, and he obey. What is the word? Ah, I know! An automaton is he. Wonderful! He is my friend, Mistaire Lund."

"He is mine, too," Lund told her quietly. "When I presented him to you as my friend I made open acknowledgment of the fact. Yet I believe there is due to you a slight explanation. I introduced him as a social equal when you knew that he was my servant. I did so simply because, as my equal friend, I felt we would be permitted to remain together; whereas had I stated he was my valet or my mechanic he might have been kept in separate quarters. It was really a case of 'united we stand, divided we fall'!"

"Of course. You revealed wisdom, Mr. Lund. Our mutual friend is a horse of a darkness. What he thinks, knows no one. At one time he looks as a big stupid dog, at another like the scientist man regarding with calmness the rushings about of a rabbit. Dear, dear! When I tell Mistaire Snell to open war on these brigands I myself will enjoy. He goes! Was ever a man so mighty?"

Sweet William was sauntering to the entrance of the drawing-room cavern with the ungainliness of a gigantic crab, yet with the sure-footedness of a prowling tiger. They watched him cross the outer cavern used as a dining-room and pass out into the short passage leading to the kitchen.

Natalie sighed. Then: "Yes, Mistaire Lawrence is of the strange mix-up. He makes to me a mystery. Also the so rich Mistaire Van Horton."

"Van Horton is a silent man," Lund observed.

"Deeply run water so still."

"Probably he is worrying about having to pay a second instalment of a huge ransom, Princess. He told me this afternoon that already he had paid twenty thousand pounds, and will have to pay a further twenty thousand, together with a verbal bond of silence, before he and Miss Van Horton will be released."

"But what says he of the alternative?"

"He doesn't know what will happen if he refuses to pay further. Earle Lawrence as yet refuses to state the alternative. However, the time must come when we shall know. Lawrence cannot keep us here for ever. Ah! Now we may have interesting news."

"Good evening, everybody!" This was Mr. Eric Lacey's greeting from a sound-proof chamber more than eight hundred miles distant. "As I promised earlier to-day, I will now give you the latest developments of what the newspapers are calling 'The Royal Abduction'.

"Allow me to tell you at once," went on the thin voice with its careful enunciation, "that there is no tidings of the yacht upon which is Her Royal Highness the Crown Princess of Rolandia. The Defence Department, at Melbourne, issued a bulletin at ten o'clock this evening, Eastern States time, announcing that all ships engaged in the search had reported no sight of the yacht which called at Eucla and took on board abducted and abductors. In total there are nine warships and twenty-seven merchantmen within a radius of fifteen hundred miles of Eucla.

"Somewhere in the vast Southern Ocean there is a white-painted steam-yacht. It should be remembered that that yacht cannot go indefinitely without coal. It must call at some port, if it does escape the network of shipping all about it, to re-fuel. Alternatively, it must meet at a predetermined rendezvous a collier ship, and undoubtedly all such ships at sea will be closely examined by the searching war-vessels.

"There now has been established excellent telephonic communication with Eucla. During the afternoon three aeroplanes have effected a landing on the difficult bush country in the vicinity of the deserted telegraph station. They unloaded important passengers in the persons of Major-General Sir Thomas Quod, of the Defence Department; Chief Inspector Smith, of the South Australian Police Force; Mr. Archibald Devine of the Australian News Service, and two renowned aboriginal trackers.

"Unfortunately, the delay caused by the abductors' tyre-destroyers covering all road approaches to Eucla have been aided by widespread thunderstorms over practically all the southern areas of the Nullarbor Plain, from which falls of rain up to 150 points have been reported. It is estimated by Police-Sergeant Brown, who was the first to reach Eucla from Cook, that a little over half an inch fell there, wholly obliterating the tracks made by the abductors and Her Royal Highness on the sand-dunes between the buildings and the jetty.

"However, General Quod, who is in supreme command at Eucla, states that the trackers will examine the ground around the station and all the country bordering the roads leading from it. He is sending tomorrow two 'planes on scouting expeditions, whilst the third will transport petrol, oil, and food supplies from Forrest, where a landing-ground already has been surveyed and now is being rapidly prepared.

"From all this we may gather that it is thought possible by those on the spot that after the Princess reached Eucla she may have been taken to a land destination by aeroplane or other means of transportation, and not taken aboard a yacht, as was reported to Sergeant Brown by the dingo-trappers living at Eucla. If this is so, there must be, to us, an unaccountable change of front since the arrival of General Quod, because Sergeant Brown has reported that he is wholly satisfied with the statements of the trappers, supported by the evidence found along the beach of the recent proximity of a ship.

"It will be recalled that the wife of one of the trappers, a half-caste, was cooking in one of the buildings when the abductors' several cars arrived. She saw a dozen or more men, with a lady, walk across the sand-hills towards the jetty, and, following on after, witnessed their embarkation into a small boat which took them out to a white-painted yacht having one funnel and two tall masts.

"Her evidence is corroborated by one of the dingo-trappers, who saw the yacht hove to and watched it steam away from a point on the sand-hills several miles south of Eucla. This man is highly intelligent. At the outbreak of war he was a sergeant-major on the Instructional Staff of the Defence Department, having served eighteen years prior to his appointment in a crack British regiment. During the war he served with distinction, being discharged as a warrant-officer, first class. His record is excellent, and nothing is known against him. His evidence, therefore, is of value.

"Perhaps the employment of trackers and aeroplanes is a gesture to the world that Australia is doing everything possible to recover the person of its august guest. Decidedly no loophole should be left unexamined, and every effort must be and is being made towards this nationally desired frustration of an atrocious crime. Relations between Great Britain, Italy, and France remain calm, but Italian unofficial opinion is tinged with deep indignation at the supposedly poor protection afforded to Her Royal Highness whilst passing through

Australia. From Rolandia there is no news: the censorship is complete. Yet rumours of a disquieting nature are circulating through Europe.

"A strange case has come to light which may or may not prove that the Princess Natalie is not the only prisoner on board the yacht. It will be remembered that a few weeks ago the *S.S. Rajah*, chartered by a New York travel agency, called at all Australian ports. Her passenger list bore names well known in the United States as of people very well blessed with this world's goods. In fact, the passengers were millionaires and the liner was often referred to as a 'luxury ship'.

"When she was due to sail from Perth two of her passengers failed to go on board. They were a Mr. and Miss Van Horton, of Chicago. The boat, at great cost, was detained eight hours from sailing whilst urgent inquiries were made for them in Perth and Fremantle. Finally the *Rajah* sailed without them.

"To-day the evening papers publish a cablegram from a Mr. John A. May, an attorney of Chicago, stating that he has received a cablegram dispatched from Adelaide on January 2nd, purporting to be signed by Mr. Van Horton, and instructing him, Mr. May, to transfer the sum of twenty thousand pounds to the Bank of Australian Industry in Adelaide. Mr. May also states in his cable that on December 9th, five days after the *Rajah* sailed from Perth, he was instructed to transfer to the same bank a similar sum, and had done so.

"It appears that Mr. John A. May became uneasy at the second demand for so large an amount. He cabled the manager of the bank inquiring how the first twenty thousand had been drawn upon. The manager replied that over one week before Mr. Van Horton had issued open cheques for the whole amount made payable to Earle Lawrence. The money had been paid on demand in untraceable currency. It was then that Mr. May discovered that Mr. and Miss Van Horton had missed their boat at Fremantle, and the coincidence of the name on the cheques written by Mr. Van Horton and the signature on the letter published by the Sydney newspaper, which states that the Princess is the hostage of Earle Lawrence, gains tremendous significance.

"If we assume that Mr. and Miss Van Horton are also prisoners on Earle Lawrence's elusive yacht, and that already twenty thousand pounds have been paid to Lawrence, there is cause to wonder how much ransom money is being demanded of Mr. Van Horton.

"Additional facts seem to indicate that this Earle Lawrence is a wholesaler in the abduction trade. This morning I told you that among the cars abandoned by the gang was an old Ford car with peculiar double-rimmed steel tyres. It is now proved that this vehicle belongs to

Mr. Raymond Lund, the son of Sir Henry and Lady Lund, of South Australia, with whom the Princess stayed for several days before she reached the city of Adelaide.

"Sir Henry Lund states that his son, with a companion, left Adelaide at the same time as the Princess Natalie to race her special trains to Perth, in order to put to the most severe test the fully-patented steel-spring-rimmed tyres with which the car was shod. The test was decided upon on the spur of the moment.

"This morning it was thought that Mr. Raymond Lund had had some part in the abduction, but late news from Eucla states that he arrived there after the roads had been covered with the tyre-destroyers. This fact, in conjunction with the information received from Ceduna that he purchased sufficient petrol and oil to get through to Norseman, disposes of the theory that his destination was Eucla.

"Then again Mr. Raymond Lund possesses an irreproachable reputation. He is widely known all over South Australia, and his university and Army records are brilliant. It appears that what actually happened was that, his car-wheels being unpuncturable, he and his companion reached Eucla at the same time as the gang with their Royal prisoner. The logical result of that meeting was that Mr. Lund and his companion were forced to accompany the gang to the yacht. Just where the meeting did occur it is impossible to state exactly, as no one witnessed the actual arrival of the cars at Eucla; the wife of the dingo-trapper, you will remember, being at the moment engaged in cooking. When she first saw the cars they were already stopped outside."

Mr. Eric Lacey coughed. He ceased speaking, and his hundreds of listeners scattered through the great bush-lands could easily picture him rearranging his notes. He coughed again, a cough nervously high-pitched in tone, as might be given by a small nondescript man, frightened by being dragged into the light at a middle-class party.

Then: "There has been found on the beach at Eucla an oar from a ship's lifeboat, a fresh apple, half-eaten, and a fruit-case to which wrapping-paper still adheres. This flotsam of the tides certainly proves that a ship was at Eucla very recently. Additional proof of a very important nature has been found in the form of a newspaper sheet printed in Perth and dated January 8th.

"Bussey and his companions state that no newspapers have reached them save an Adelaide paper dated December 27th, left there by a motorist passing through January 3rd. The paper picked up on the beach evidently came from the ship, and proves that if not the ship itself then someone on board was at a West Australian port on or after the 8th

January. Inquiries are being pushed at the ports of Fremantle, Albany, and Bunbury regarding the arrivals and departures of shipping since the beginning of the year.

"The story grows, ladies and gentlemen. Piece is being fitted to piece, and the dénouement, when it comes, is bound to prove both dramatic and romantic. I hope to talk to you again to-morrow at one o'clock. In the evening I am leaving by express to Adelaide, where I trust I shall be permitted to get into touch with you again over the air. Good night, everybody!"

For almost a minute no one in the cavern spoke. Natalie saw plainly that Earle Lawrence was nervous. Mr. Van Horton smiled at his daughter, as though to encourage her to believe that their imprisonment would not last much longer.

"The house of cards you erected at Eucla appears about to tumble to the ground," he said to Lawrence.

Lawrence rose from the chair beside the wireless set and stifled a yawn. His eyes were brilliant. "The foundations were made very strong," he drawled. "There was no crack or weakness in them. I always lay solid foundations before I begin to build."

"Still, the roof may blow off," Helen Van Horton said, laughing sleepily. "Well, I'm for bed. Will Your Royal Highness accompany me?"

"But certainly," Natalie agreed, jumping up. "I feel so tired that not even the monster man awake will keep me."

That caused Helen's eyes to round. "I had quite forgotten," she said.

"You need not be nervous, Miss Van Horton," Lawrence assured her. "I have placed a man on guard in the passage which leads to the dynamo chamber and the other in which is the skeleton. To-morrow we will carry out a minute search of every crack and corner of the place. We cannot have things like the maker of those tracks disturbing our peace of mind."

The two girls withdrew, and, after seeing Natalie to her room, Helen went on to her own. Julia undressed the Princess and left her in a négligé smoking a cigarette. For half an hour Natalie pondered, not on the skill with which Lawrence had covered his operations at Cook and Eucla, not on the worst aspects of war, but on what she had seen in the depths of a pair of steady dark-grey eyes.

Slipping into bed, she switched off the light and nestled down beneath the clothes. Yet she knew no comfort. A hard lump just below where her hip sank into the mattress created annoying discomfort. The bed was too narrow to permit of her lying on either side of the place in the apparently unshaken mattress. She switched the light on again. Then she got out of bed and with her hands tried to soften the lump by pulling at it. It was, she found, quite a hard, compact lump. Mystified, although drowsy, Natalie slipped her hand beneath the blanket and sheet laid over the mattress. Her groping fingers sought and found the object, hard as steel – an object with a squat, ugly barrel and comforting hand-grip. A piece of paper was wrapped about the pistol stock, and when her hand was withdrawn her fingers held the paper.

Natalie's eyes were blazing as black opals, and the lines about her mouth made it a picture of fierce grimness. With the paper crumpled into a ball in the palm of her hand, she slipped to the cavern entrance and looked out. There was no one in sight. Near the bed once more, directly under the twin electric bulbs, she smoothed out the paper and read, printed in block letters:

GUN LOADED. TELL NO ONE.

The second of the two abbreviated sentences was heavily underlined. The first, after a little puzzling, she understood. The word "TELL" in the following sentence baffled her. What was the meaning of that small word?

Once again she switched off the light. Then, with eager impetuosity, she snatched the automatic pistol from its concealment, felt for and made sure the safety-catch was down, and sprang into bed, there to hug the grim weapon as a smaller girl would hug a doll.

"T-E-L-L"! The letters kept repeating through her mind. What did they mean? "No ONE"? Yes, "no one" meant, not anyone. T-E-L-L – T-E-L-L"? Ah! It came in a flash – the meaning of the word. She was to let no one know she had the pistol, and the heavy lines beneath the words meant that it was most important that she should "tell no one".

She thrust the pistol into hiding beneath her pillow. Snell – Mistaire Snell! Her mind thrilled. Ah, what a pity it was Mistaire Snell and she had not lived three hundred years ago!

CHAPTER XXIII

TRANSLATIONS

THE following morning every man other than Morgan and Larsen engaged in a well-organised search for the thing that had left its footprints about the skeleton in the great cavern at the lowest point of the system. Van Horton, Lund, and Snell were no less industrious than Lawrence and his men. They worked for three hours, but, when they returned for a well-earned lunch, their labours had been without result.

Only on the sandy floor of the great cavern, which had been temporarily flooded with electric light, an extension having been made from the main cable by a man named Little, had the tracks been seen. In every passage patches of sand lay thick where the rock had been worn lower than the general level, sand lay in the Cavern of the Sword, it lay in parts of the kitchen; yet only in the deepest cavern of all were the monstrous footmarks imprinted.

Since Tuttman also had joined in the search, they were perforce obliged to wait half an hour for lunch to be served; and, after washing away the grime and dust from face and hands, Lund and Snell found the two ladies in the drawing-room cavern, and Mr. Van Horton in the tiny alcove playing the harmonium.

"Pops said you found nothing," Helen burst out, her usual calmness visibly disturbed. "Do you still think that whatever made the marks is really alive?"

Raymond Lund, finding himself directly questioned, replied lightly: "The footmarks certainly are mysterious, but whatever made them is not now in the caverns, I am positive, because every crevice and hole has been minutely examined. There is, I believe, nothing of which to be nervous."

"We lowered a bunch of torches down the blow-hole," added Snell. "Smooth as a drain-pipe, and gets wider as it goes down. No cat-burglar could tackle it."

"Still, I do wish that our rooms were protected with doors." Helen's usually drawling voice was now a little petulant. "I could hardly sleep last night, I felt so frightened."

"You do not give me the impression that you are a nervous woman, Miss Van Horton. But even supposing the thing did come into your room, a cry would bring a dozen men to your assistance, most of them well armed."

"All the same, I am not going to sleep alone to-night." Helen Van Horton glanced at Natalie with genuine appeal. She was not acting just then.

The Princess understood the look, and her expression hardened. "Fear is the great enemy," she said, with a sudden whimsical smile. "Unless beaten at the first it becomes big in strength. I shall continue to sleep alone in my bed so deep. Afraid I am not of fear."

"But I am. I'll get Julia to bring her bed into my room. Whatever made the tracks must be like a huge monkey, and of that animal I am terrified. When I was a little girl, a friend of ours kept a tame monkey, and one day it dropped out of a garden on my head. I'll never forget the fright it gave me. Nor the smell of it."

Bennett and Sir Knight were absent from lunch, and their places were taken by the thick-set, beetle-browed ruffian addressed as Morgan, and a second man of quite ordinary appearance in a low way.

After lunch, Helen Van Horton complained of a headache and went to her room to lie down, and the idea occurred to Natalie to command Sweet William's company to help her translate Tuttman's 'Ode to the Future'. Armed with the carefully tied roll of foolscap, ink, a fountain-pen, and a writing-pad, these representatives of diametrically opposed social orders retired into the drawing-room, leaving Lund and Van Horton discussing the probable effects of the transference of the world's gold to America on international trade.

The first stanza of the 'Ode to the Future' already has been quoted in this history. It concerned death and hempen ropes, and a parting from hope of every kind. Natalie made her scribe read slowly each line, explaining abstruse words, but her efforts to find Rolandian words to rhyme she found very tiring at the end of the third line of the opening stanza. Whilst pretending to write, she said softly: "Did you place in my room the pistol so beautiful?"

"Yes, Marm," Snell replied without looking up from Tuttman's masterpiece.

"Where obtained you that pistol?"

"Took it off friend Larsen, Marm."

Natalie sighed. She repeated the last line of the stanza three times in her quaint English before she said: "Why gave you me that pistol, Mistaire Snell?"

"Well, I thought Your Highness might find it handy," Snell told her seriously. He was coming to be more confident in his speech with this Royal lady, who was so regal yet so friendly, so aloof and commanding, yet at times so delightfully human. "You see, Marm, if it comes to a brawl, me and Mr. Lund can use ourselves to some order. Both of us is kind of strong. A pistol might help you out of a tight corner, and, if you'll forgive me for saying so, I kind of think you wouldn't scream instead of pulling the trigger."

"Surprise you me so loquacious are you," murmured Natalie.

"Beg pardon, Marm! I don't get you."

"Ah! I forgot. You know not Rolandian. Now I ask you this: Did you write on the paper round the pistol?"

"Yes, Marm."

"Why say you: 'Tell no one'?"

"We thought it best if no one knew you had the gun. As I told you, my back hair stands out when I look at Mr. Van Horton, also it kind of moves a bit when Miss Horton speaks to me."

"Explain!" commanded Natalie, the translation temporarily forgotten.

"Well, Marm, it's like this: I'm like a dog when he meets an enemy. He seems to know an enemy, either dog or man, before it is proved. When I was a warder I came close to many proper bad men. Mr. Van Horton and his daughter may be all right now, they may be millionaires; still, my back hair stands out when I'm near them. In consequence, I don't trust either of 'em."

Snell found himself examined by deep violet-blue eyes in a peculiarly inquisitive stare, as though Natalie saw him for the first time, and marvelled at his plain features.

"Just now you said 'we'. Does Mistaire Lund know of the pistol?"

"Yes, Marm. He told me to plant it in your bed."

"Hum! Where was the pistol when search was made by Mistaire Everett?"

"In Mr. Everett's left-hand pocket, Marm. When I saw Lawrence and Fish-eye, him they call Sir Knight, waiting for us, I knew something was up. I had to get rid of the pistol, and Blue Everett's pocket was as good a place as any. Of course, when the show-down was over, I took it back again."

"You are the – what is it? – the magician."

"I've been shown how to pick people's pockets by gents who could take a man's glass eye out of his face and sell it to him back," Snell said modestly.

It was then that Natalie sat back in her chair and laughed without restraint. Her laughter fled into the outer chamber where Lund and Van Horton, now joined by Earle Lawrence, were talking. It was infectious, delightful. It made even Van Horton smile. But Snell's face remained pensive. He wondered why the Princess was laughing, unless she was laughing at him.

"Her Highness evidently has found something amusing in Tuttman's poetry," Earle Lawrence remarked, lighting his second after-lunch cheroot.

"She is an amazing little woman," Van Horton gave as his opinion. "One moment she is supremely cold, the next delightfully feminine. However, Mr. Lund just put to you a pertinent question, the answer to which would be interesting."

"Oh yes! You said, Lund, that General Quod's trackers are bound to come across Ah Khan and his camels' tracks somewhere, which will lead them to the spurious oil-bore. As a matter of fact, by now Quod will know all about Ah Khan and all about Doctor Woolworth's effort to find oil on the Nullarbor Plain."

"How?" Lund asked shortly.

"Well, you see, I anticipated that every person known to be on the plain would interest the inevitable investigators at Eucla. Accordingly, as it is my policy always to run to meet danger and not to await its coming, I dispatched Ah Khan and his son with the camels to Norseman, where they will pick up loading for my station in the northeast. Doubtless they arrived at Eucla very early this morning. On being questioned, Ah Khan will say that he has just delivered stores and machinery to Doctor Woolworth. He will describe the location of the oil-bore. Some time this evening General Quod or the chief police officer will certainly reach Doctor Woolworth's shack. Whoever comes will find Dr. Woolworth, well known in Western Australia as an authority on minerals and mining, superintending three men sinking a bore in the expectation of finding oil. Doctor Woolworth will be discovered very drunk; but his foreman, Sir Knight, will be able to answer all questions relating to the work."

"I take it that Woolworth is in your pay?" Lund asked.

"Yes, he is. It was necessary to account for the loads of goods brought from east and west by motor truck: stores, furniture, the dynamo, the harmonium, everything. The old oil-boring site was a fortunate chance. I employed Woolworth not because of his knowledge or his character, but because of his reputation as a geologist. As a matter of fact he is without character, good or bad. He is the one weak link in my armour, which is why I have sent Sir Knight to act as his foreman, and to see that he is too drunk to answer questions."

"So to-night the land investigators will be three miles from here?"

"Precisely. And the guard at the outer entrance will be doubled," Lawrence drawled significantly. The insinuation brought a smile from both Lund and Van Horton.

"It is probable that the trackers will work further in than the oil-bore," suggested the American.

"No," Lawrence said definitively. "The taboo will keep them away from the place. They will find all manner of excuses not to approach from the oil-site. That taboo is worth a thousand machine-guns."

For a little while the men were silent, all three of them smoking reflectively. At last Lund asked a further question: "Assuming we are not rescued, how long do you propose to keep us here?"

"At the longest, three months."

"In that case, don't you think it would be acting in common decency to allow us to write to our people, saying we were well and suffering no hardship? In the circumstances there could be no objection to your censoring the letters. My mother and my father both will be greatly worried at my disappearance, whilst I am sure Mr. Van Horton's friends would be relieved by news of him."

"It would be impossible to grant that request, Lund. You see, we are all supposed to be far out in the Southern Ocean. You must wait for the three months to expire. By then the Princess' and Mr. Van Horton's ransoms will have been arranged. Possibly your own as well. I see no objection to ten thousand pounds in your case.

"At the end of three months Eucla will certainly once more be deserted. A ship commanded by a friend of mine will then actually call at Eucla, and actually take us all off. From Eucla we shall proceed to a foreign port where arrangements will be made to release you all in a manner which will not hinder the future actions of my men and myself. But for three months, remember, we are at sea."

"Sometimes, Lawrence, I am inclined to think you are the devil," Van Horton said calmly.

CHAPTER XXIV

NATALIE'S ANCESTORS

IT must be, said on behalf of the Van Hortons and Earle Lawrence, that they spared no effort to make the following two weeks as little tedious as possible to their Royal captive. In spite of the malaise of boredom from which Helen Van Horton suffered, she invariably appeared interested in everyone and everything, and was unremitting in her attentions to the Princess.

To her father one afternoon whilst they talked in the former's room she said: "You know, Pops, I honestly think she is rather nice. I never imagined that a real Princess was like what she is. I suppose we get our ideas of Royalty from the *Prisoner of Zenda* school of novels; lovely women, regal yet gracious, warm yet innocent."

"I fear it is so," Van Horton told her dryly, adding: "With regard to this Princess, I am beginning to believe we have captured a very clever as well as lovely little woman. She has the makings of a very powerful Queen. Do you think she will wish to know us when she is a Queen?"

The daughter looked at her father for several searching seconds before replying. "I cannot tell you," she said slowly. "As a matter of fact, although I have tried, I cannot quite understand her. It is like seeing her at the end of a garden path, and when one walks towards her there is certain to be some place, not always the same place, where she will raise a hand and command one to stop. I seem never actually to have reached her. And then sometimes I think that that horrible Snell person has been permitted to reach her."

"Snell! Ah yes, Snell," Van Horton murmured with half-closed eyes. "As you are with the Princess, so am I with Mr. William Snell. I can't place him, and that annoys me, because I have prided myself on the ease with which I can place men."

Had Mr. Van Horton succeeded in exactly "placing" Sweet William, it is doubtful if he would have refrained from the act of murder. Equally, had Helen Van Horton really understood Natalie, she would have been shocked by the revelation that Miss Helen Van Horton was not as consummately clever as she thoroughly believed.

Whilst the millionaire acknowledged that Natalie was a psychological mystery, he did not then realise precisely what he had undertaken when he agreed to finance her abductors. His study of psychology doubtless had been undertaken under very favourable conditions. Where his education was deficient was in the history of Rolandia, and especially of its Royal House, whilst a knowledge of the Mendelian laws of heredity would have proved of service to him.

When he conjointly planned to kidnap the Princess Natalie, he kidnapped with her Europe's most notorious brigands, murderers, saints, inquisitors, heroes, and lovers. He should figuratively have climbed the genealogical tree from Natalie's branch. He would have found her father a gentle, studious, peace-loving man, her grandfather a man of iron who believed in floggings for the common people and duels for the aristocrats. Then there was great-grandfather Paul, who evidently thought much of King Solomon's sire – sufficient, anyway, to emulate that scriptural character's penchant for other men's wives, the unwanted husbands falling before his paid duellists or assassins. There was a Prince Karl, who might have used his undoubted talents to better advantage than in the somewhat uninteresting study of men dying from the then little-known poisons; and a Queen Olga, who wooed all sorts and conditions of men in rapid succession, afterwards, when they began to bore her, signing their death warrants as coolly as a millionaire signs cheques for his household bills.

Van Horton would have met the Duke John of Tourliss, the finest soldier of his century; the Prince Joachim who composed operas that have become classics; and the Lady Mignon, who insisted on remaining in Naagrade in the early sixteenth century, devotedly nursing a groom when Naagrade was rotten with the plague.

And when finally his downward climb had brought him to the root of this family tree, then and there, on the veranda of Earle Lawrence's house near Perth, he would most emphatically have declined to have anything to do with kidnapping a woman in whose small person the ghosts of those formidable ancestors dwelt. As it was, his estimate of the Princess was wholly wide of the truth. He failed to gauge her potentialities for danger to himself because, with the vast majority of Royalty-governed men, he regarded a Princess as a being higher than an ordinary mortal, a being who always had been jealously guarded from the common touch and reared in an atmosphere of cotton-wool and chest-protectors. He failed to understand that, contrary to popular belief, the blood of a Royal Princess is red, that she is own sister to every other woman, feeling the same sensations, pains, and desires common to the sex of Mother Eve, possessing all the virtues and vices that are the common heritage of women.

Thus, in his dream of false security, he lived almost

somnambulistically from placid day to placid day, reading many novels, and spending hours in writing his autobiography, which he hoped to publish anonymously, and which he thought he knew how to make a "best seller". Unlike others of the dwellers in the caverns, he did not suffer from the want of exercise, whilst the continuous absence of sunlight on his face seemed not to make any difference to its pallor.

Everyone was kept conversant by wireless of the progress of the search made on the high seas for Lawrence's imaginary yacht, as well as of the investigations carried on at Eucla. The public interest was kept alive far longer than the proverbial nine days, and tens of thousands of people in Australia were as avid for news of Natalie and her fellow-prisoners as were the members of the small community on the Nullarbor Plain for news of any kind from the outside world. Mr. Eric Lacey and others gave prognostications of the end of the search, much as several well-known writers foretold the end of the war in 1914, with much argument, many maps, and endless statistics.

The official party at Eucla was baffled. Ten days elapsed before General Quod admitted it, when numberless notebooks had been filled with his observations, his questions to Bussey, the half-caste and his wife, and later to Sir Knight as foreman at the oil-bore, and the poor drink-sodden Dr. Woolworth together with their replies, their life records, their descriptions, and the names and standing of all their relatives. The black trackers, as predicted by Lawrence, had found excuses for not entering the tabooed area.

And now Quod, with his policemen, had flown away back to Adelaide, leaving the utterly weary Mr. Bussey, the well-fed half-caste, and the now rich woman – she had been well paid to cook for the investigators – to their peaceful occupation of dog-trapping. And, with the continued absence of the cats, the mice were permitted to play – that is, when the absence of the cats had been definitely established.

At breakfast one morning Earle Lawrence said that his sergeant-major had sent an "all clear", and that after a further week he and his companions would transfer to the caverns. In the meantime he had made arrangements for everyone who wished to take the air and exercise on the surface during the early morning and late evening. He reminded them that throughout the day the sun was uncomfortably hot on the plain in February. He suggested that, since they had for so long lived underground, it would be as well if they did not essay their first emergence into daylight until after the sun had set.

"There is now no need for us to live below here without change," he went on pleasantly, adding, after looking directly at Van Horton, Lund, and Snell: "But, nevertheless, I should perhaps dispel any idea you may have of escaping by informing you that half an hour before we go up several of my men will occupy concealed positions on the plain, where they will earnestly protest against escape with high-powered rifles. Of course we shall all have to return before it gets quite dark."

"May we walk about?" inquired Natalie with utter demureness.

"Of course, Highness."

"A pity to me it seems you cannot set your men working a tennis-court to make," she said.

"It would be a good idea, Lawrence, if we could make a court," Lund put in. "I, for one, am becoming horribly flabby from all this inactivity. I suppose you didn't think of purchasing racquets and balls with the furniture?"

"Alas, my mind was full of other matters."

"I can quite believe it," Helen drawled. "Anyway, you cannot be expected to think of everything."

"At the time, Miss Van Horton, I was not planning a garden-party," Lawrence told her with unruffled calmness of voice, but with eyes that gleamed wickedly.

These little passages-at-arms mystified Natalie. They revealed on the part of Helen a feeling that could hardly be caused by her temporary imprisonment. Helen might hate the man on account of her position, for which he was obviously responsible, but her attitude towards him did not seem to emanate from genuine hatred. There seemed to be something more impersonal in her attitude, for which there was no adequate explanation. There was, too, a difference in Lawrence's behaviour towards Helen from what it was to her, and even towards Julia. There were moments, very few, apparently unguarded moments, when she caught Lawrence looking at the American in a kind of calculating and examining manner; and, whilst she sat at the head of the table with Helen Van Horton on her right facing Earle Lawrence, the astonishing thought occurred that perhaps Lawrence was in love with Helen, had declared his love, and had been contemptuously rejected.

For the rest of the meal she spoke but seldom, these thoughts and mental questions fully occupying her mind. At that time Natalie was beginning to think more seriously of Sweet William's instinct that Van Horton and his daughter were not the moral people they certainly appeared to be. She had to admit that Helen Van Horton was most thoughtful of her comfort, was well-bred, well-educated, and both interesting and amusing at a time when her friendship was an emphatic boon. Yet for all that, Natalie admitted to herself at long last that there was something in the other's personality which kept her at bay. Was Sweet William right after all in his seemingly absurd suspicions?

She decided to watch and wait. It would give her a fresh interest, and that interest should be served some time that day by a conversation with William Snell in which they would compare notes.

The many conversations she already had had with this dour, grim man had created in her a profound admiration for him. She had discovered in Snell many views identical with her own. In him she found a force that only a very thin veneer of civilisation held in restraint, a force that was diametrically opposed to convention, contemptuous of laws made by weaker men for their protection. Not only was he tremendously strong physically, he was strong mentally in that he suffered no emotion ever to be revealed on his ugly face. He was of that type of man, brainful, conscious of native power, which goes forward and upward to the heights of worldly success with the smashing imperturbability of a steam-roller.

The bond between him and Raymond indicated the attraction of opposites. Natalie's quick perception told her that Lund was transparently clean and honest, a gentleman in the very widest sense of the word, one so clean as to find it difficult to believe mental uncleanness in others, one so honest as to take everyone to be straightforward till they proved themselves otherwise. The fundamental difference between them was that whilst Lund held everyone innocent until proved guilty, William Snell believed everyone to be guilty till proved innocent. And in their respective ways she liked both enormously.

She liked Raymond Lund the better for his quiet refusal to describe to her the deeper horrors of war, for she still retained her girlish illusions of the chivalrous days of knighthood. Even so she delighted in drawing out Sweet William, the esquire to her knight, when in his unconsciously humorous way he entertained her by describing, in gruesome detail, but in racy Australian, what he had been obliged to witness at the hanging of several murderers.

There was a good deal of original sin in Natalie's make-up. When Earle Lawrence abducted her from the special train at Cook, the world lost its chance to observe the emergence of a very great personality.

A ROYAL ABDUCTION

PART III

THE TERROR

CHAPTER XXV

OBJECTIVE DISCIPLINE

IF Raymond had kept himself in the background, as it were, it was not because he was naturally without initiative, or because he found the situation below the surface of the Nullarbor Plain too difficult to make any attempt to end the now irksome confinement.

The gang of which Earle Lawrence was the head was preeminently efficient by reason of the surprising discipline maintained at a very high level. It was not the kind of blind obedience actuated by fear of the leader, nor was it the grudging obedience to orders based on recognition of necessity. Duties were carried out with invariable cheerfulness and with machine-like regularity. Every day at noon Blue Everett posted up in the kitchen a roster of duties for every man for the ensuing twenty-four hours, and not once did Lund see any discontent or hear any grumbling.

It was the absence of grumbling and discontent in this band of ex-soldiers which astonished him, because the prototype of those men had grumbled and complained for four years, even whilst they ignored hardship and carried on. Some time later, during a conversation with Blue Everett, he came to understand the matter more clearly. They each had been offered a thousand pounds, plus a varying bonus, for three months' service, provided they accepted the regime of discipline which they were shown was utterly necessary to achieve success. Of the Australian soldiers it has been said that they were the most undisciplined mob ever sent to France. Doubtless there was some justification for this statement, yet the fact emphatically exists that when zero-hour arrived in their trenches there was no lack of discipline. They were casual in saluting and slovenly in shouldering their arms, because there was not a man living in the world possessed of sufficient eloquence to convince them that saluting and going through musical comedy drilling had the slightest chance of winning the war. Which was the reason why they saluted – when they had to – as though their arms were tortured with neuritis, and their rifles on parade appeared as heavy as howitzers. As actors for the cinema they were crass duds.

On the other hand, when it was understood that discipline was necessary, there was no finer body of men. At critical times discipline always prevailed, as witness the incident related to Dr. Woolworth wherein Lawrence shot his platoon officer for nerve-failure. Here, every man under Lawrence appreciated the desperate audacity required of them and the discipline necessary to carry the objective with success and final enrichment. The discipline among this gang was the visible result of every member of it being himself a stern disciplinarian.

Including Lawrence and the harmless mess-waiter, there were nine men in the caverns, with Bussey and the half-caste, Peter Cuff, at Eucla, and Dr. Woolworth and another man at the oil-bore – a gang of thirteen all told. However, until the arrival of the Eucla garrison, Raymond Lund was concerned with no more than eight well armed, superbly disciplined, determined men. Excepting Lawrence and Tuttman, all were quartered in that cavern from which exit to the surface was possible, and throughout the whole twenty-four hours two of them were mounted on guard, one at the foot of the steps, the other at the entrance of the passage that led to the kitchen and the series of caverns beyond.

The effectiveness of this guard was trebled by the fact that the passage from the men's quarters and the kitchen was some fourteen yards in length, quite straight, and with smooth walls and floor. It was impossible to enter the passage from the kitchen without being observed by the first guard at the farther end. And Lund had proved to his entire satisfaction that the sentries never dozed, never indulged in reading. They carried out their monotonous duty as though expecting attack at any instant.

Any hope of "rushing" the guard was doomed to absolute failure. There was no other point of egress from the caverns, a fact of which both he and Snell had made sure during their tours and throughout the search for the nebulous thing that left surprising tracks about the prehistoric skeleton. Even the temporary possession of Larsen's automatic pistol brought no tangible advantage. Success might be achieved if other weapons could be secured, and they two, with Van Horton, being armed, carried out a well-timed hold-up. Three desperate men might win freedom; but they had always to think of three women, equally precious with themselves.

There was difficulty, too, in retaining any weapons once in their possession. It never could be foretold when they would be searched again, possibly when the flash of opportunity would not happen to enable Snell to act as he had done with Larsen's pistol. In any case it seemed now too late; for, acting on his suggestion, Snell at various times, with his extraordinary dexterity, had picked the pockets of several of the gang, only to find that every man carried his automatic in a holster slung beneath the armpit. It was a position that bunkered even a man of his expertness.

The next problem Raymond tried to solve was how to escape alone and make his way to Eucla – whilst General Quod and his staff were there – and afterwards to Cook. Upon no other could devolve such an attempt, because Van Horton, when sounded, admitted he would not know which way to go when he got free; and Snell was too poor a bushman to make his way to Eucla, twenty-five miles south of west, or Cook, a possible seventy-five to eighty miles north, across trackless bush country. Such an attempt would be accompanied by so great a risk of failure and death as almost to put it out of court save as a last gambler's throw. For the only opportunity occurred during the early morning and the evening, when they were permitted to take the air within a radius of one hundred yards of the camouflaged entrance But then the guards, numbering five, were always out first, occupying concealed positions and armed with rifles. One did not know where they were, a position far worse than seeing them occupying definite stations. A sudden dash in any direction might take him straight up to one of these guards, who would assuredly be waiting with cynical nonchalance to shoot him down.

In the comparative seclusion of their cave he and Snell talked for hours discussing the problem of escape. There seemed to be no solution. The natural fortress in which they were confined, the rigid system of guards, and the absence of any outside assistance, presented a blank wall over or through which it was impossible to penetrate.

Life to Lund at that time was by no means unpleasant. He found the Van Hortons resigned to apparent fate with the cheerfulness of confirmed stoics. Being cultured people, he discovered many tastes in common. Of Natalie he never tired. She had become the one woman, who yet was a star he could never possess. With passion that sometimes caught him by the throat he listened to her quaint English, spoken so musically, giving him a delight both exquisite and agonizing. He danced with her during the gramophone dances organised by Blue Everett, he won and lost countless matches from and to her at poker, of which she became a slave as soon as she had mastered the rudiments of this king of card games. Yet never, he was sure, did he permit his secret to show in his voice or within his eyes.

Yes, matches! Everyone had been presented with a gross of boxes of matches with which to gamble. Was ever a party of men better disciplined who, without complaint, consented to gamble with matches? And was there ever a band of men, willing to confine themselves for three months within limits equalling those of a yacht, perform punctiliously routine duties, and put out of their minds any thought or desire for alcohol, of which not a drop was purchased since the scheme of abduction was planned?

Assuredly, as Lawrence had said to Natalie, they were of the Iron Youth, iron in purpose, made pure iron in the furnace of war: morally defective, certainly, but still terrible in their outlook on life; of iron, too, which the mellowing conditions of almost ten years of peace had failed to rust.

Lund got to know them all: the brilliant Lawrence; the quiet, reserved Everett; the morose Bennett; the uncouth Morgan; the excitable Larsen; the casual, indifferent Sir Knight; the bitter man named Little; and the disillusioned dreamer, Alfred Tuttman. Perhaps Little expressed the secret views of all when he said to Lund one evening after dinner:

"Peace – hell! We was fighting to end war. We ended a war all right, and after the war what happened? Peace? I don't think! Slavery! The old, old slavery. Our bayonets were beaten into ploughshares all right, but we pulled the plough and masters got paid for the wheat. Wages! The basic wage! Work! Yes, for us work. We won the war, but millions died in doing it. What happened then? I ask you. Back to slavery, the slavery we knew before the war. The world was no better for those millions dying; no better because I used to scream in hospital every morning and evening when they opened my wound to wash it out. Not a bit. Work – or starve. Our ancestors in the days of Rome, and Greece, and Babylon, were better off than we are. Then, the slaves had to be fed and clothed, and they went to the arena to watch the fights, and afterwards slept under a roof in a house. Now they give us wages, because they can't be bothered buying our clothes and food, and finding house accommodation, and writing us tickets for the pictures. We're supposed to be much better off. I don't think! 'Work or starve', they say. 'We are much obliged to you for winning the war and saving our wealth from the Germans. But now you must work or starve.' Me, I learned a lot in the war. I got a full education, and now I won't work, nor will I starve; for there ain't no work in breaking into a toff's house and helping myself. The war showed me what freedom was, and may I be damned if I go back to slavery!"

They were doing it – men like Everett and Bennett, no less than Morgan and Little, who had been an employee of an electrical supply company and had installed the electrical equipment – for one thousand pounds apiece, plus a bonus and a passage to freedom in some foreign port. This sum, when compared with the huge amounts hoped for from ransom, seemed inadequate for men accepting equal risks and conditions with Earle Lawrence. It would have been more equitable had they engaged to receive nothing from failure and a proportionate amount from success. The matter engaged Lund's mind very much, but he failed to see the light until the time when many things were made clear.

That was a time now not far distant, for the terror was beginning which gripped every man, made chaos of order, nervous wrecks of brave men, revealed and defeated evil: such evil as to make angels of men like Peter Cuff, who collected Germans' hearts on a piece of wire in No Man's Land, and Tuttman, who scalped his enemies Red Indian fashion.

Lund was washing in a plain enamelled basin prior to dressing for dinner – for he had borrowed a dinner-jacket from Earle Lawrence – and Snell was brushing his hair, having of late become quite fastidious in his appearance – when Lawrence suddenly entered their room, his face very pale, his eyes unnaturally wide. "Come with me, you two. Something has happened which concerns you equally with everyone here."

"What's gone wrong?" Snell demanded, his brown eyes appearing mere points of blackness.

"You'll soon see."

Hurriedly throwing on his lounge jacket, Lund followed Snell along the short passage to the Cavern of the Sword. There were grouped Everett, Van Horton, Morgan, and Larsen, whilst Helen Van Horton and Natalie stood together outside the latter's chamber.

"What is it, Mr. Lawrence?" asked Helen with rounded eyes. "What has happened?"

Lawrence looked at Van Horton. Van Horton laid a hand on her arm and pushed both her and Natalie back into the room. They heard him say quietly, but in steely tones: "It is nothing of much consequence, my dear. You will keep Her Royal Highness company whilst we look into a slightly troublesome matter."

Now with an automatic in his right hand, Lawrence rapidly led the way along the passage, past the twin miniature waterfalls and the sinister blow-hole, through the small chamber called the Junction, from which the dark passage led to the Cavern of the Skeleton, and along the passage that brought them finally to the cavern where the great falling stream of water worked the wheel and the dynamo.

Beside the dynamo lay the ex-electrician, Little. He had been choked to death. There were blue marks on his throat. And, on a patch of sand near the body, quite clear and distinct, were the imprints of a great naked foot.

CHAPTER XXVI

A CHEF'S ANGER

IN shape the cavern in which tragedy had occurred was roughly circular, its roof some twenty feet above the floor. At a height of sixteen feet there flowed out from the rock a powerful stream of water which fell into a seemingly bottomless pit, the orifice of which was many times that of the waterfall. At one side of the pit was set a 220-volt dynamo driven by a large wheel fitted with cup-shaped paddles that under the weight of the falling water slowly turned. Geared cogwheels drove the dynamo at the requisite number of revolutions per minute, and a clutch bar fitted on the main spindle between them and the water-wheel made it possible to free the dynamo, whereupon the water-wheel spun round at a much faster rate. Behind the dynamo were the storage batteries and switchboard, from which a cable was laid throughout the passages to the Cavern of the Sword, where the power was distributed through lighter wires fixed to walls and roofs.

Such was the power-house in the House of Jewels, a simple enough proposition to a practical electrician of Little's calibre.

For so great a volume of water the sound of its fall was very light. When Lawrence threw the dynamo out of gear the lights began slowly to wane and the noise of water falling on the wheel further diminished. On switching over to the storage batteries the lights leapt to their former brilliancy. The wheel now offering almost no resistance, the water fell silently into the pit, and from the tremendous depth there arose a sound no louder than that made by the dynamo when in action.

The body lay on its back. The face was swollen and discoloured; both hands were clenched. The wide, staring eyes reflected a horror which even death could not dim, and on the throat were the marks of four fingers and a thumb. In life Little had been a man of only average strength; and whilst Raymond Lund looked down on the corpse of the bitter and disillusioned burglar, there entered into his mind, ridiculously enough, the hackneyed saying: "A storm in a teacup". To Little, life had become no more than a storm in a teacup, merely a freshening storm blowing for a short time through his material body. Lund wondered at that moment if the world had benefited by the agony that formed clay had given the soul of Joseph Little, once a decent man fighting for the welfare of his country.

"As you know, Little was in charge of the power system," Lawrence began, his voice calm, but his pale grey eyes gleaming with sinister light. "He was due for duty at seven o'clock in the guard-room. Not having reported to Blue Everett at seven, I came along to hunt him up, and found him as you now see him. He was quite dead."

"He'll never be no deader," growled Morgan, thick-set, almost neck-less, bullet-headed.

"You will observe that the man, or whatever it was that killed him, strangled him with one hand," Van Horton barked, so suddenly that Lund started. "The average strangler uses both hands, one on the throat, the other at the back of the victim's neck. It makes the best purchase. The strangler in this case was so abnormally strong that only one hand was necessary. I think we may assume that no one here possesses such strength."

"I dunno," objected Snell evenly. "I reckon I could do it with one hand if I had the chance."

"Then I hope you will never take the chance with me," Everett said in his cultured tones.

"Hear, hear!" Larsen growled. The black-moustached gentleman stretched his neck significantly. "Ug! I 'ope I do not die dat way."

"Wot are we goin' ter do with him?" demanded Morgan pugnaciously, as though habitually used to meeting opposition.

"Well, now that you are acquainted with the fact that Little is dead, and the manner of his death, the easiest way to dispose of his body is to toss it into the pit there."

"Save shovelling, anyway," Morgan agreed. For a second he looked at his leader, then, swiftly stooping, he caught the feet of the corpse, dragged it to the edge of the pit, and "slewed" it over the edge without very much effort. Turning then to Lawrence, he asked: "Wot 'appens to 'is thousand quid?"

"It will not be divided among the others, Morgan."

"Then 'oo gets it?"

"His sister, who lives at Northam."

"So you see, my dear man, that assuming the axiom that the weak go to the wall, the strong will not inherit their possessions. It is a thought very comforting to the weak."

"Orl right, Blue! Cut it out," Morgan growled, to relapse then into sullen silence.

This callous disposal of one of their comrades and the equally callous discussion concerning the dead man's pay did not shock Lund so much as might have been expected. It was the kind of action and talk fairly prevalent among first-line soldiers hardened to steel by war. It surprised him, however, after this long lapse of time, to understand that there were men whom the peace had failed to mellow.

Everyone examined the tracks. Here and there over the floor, like pools of water left by the tide, slight depressions were filled with white sand. On two of these sand patches did the fresh, clear-cut outlines of a monstrous naked foot resemble that of a man. In size and shape they were identical with those discovered by the exploring party near the great skeleton.

The several men gathered about them looked up and at one another, their eyes veiled by low-hung lids, their tongues silent. The question hammering at each brain was: What kind of a thing made those tracks and killed Little with one hand? And then, after a while, when even imagination failed to supply an answer, a second question flashed into their minds. Where hid this Thing?

As sharply as recently he had spoken, Mr. Van Horton pointed to the tracks and said to Lawrence: "If you intend to keep us here one hour longer, we have got to find the thing which made those footprints. Not one of us is safe from it."

"We searched pretty well the other day," growled Morgan.

"We'll search again," said Lawrence with unusual crispness. "We'll begin at the guard-room, and work back to the cavern where is the giant stalactite. When that part of the system is cleared we'll have a man stationed at this side entrance day and night, until we find and destroy the monster. It's here somewhere; and, as Mr. Van Horton just said, we have got to find it."

"What about rigging up an alarm in every passage?" suggested Sweet William. "There are sand patches almost everywhere. In each passage there could be buried a couple of contact plates which when trodden on would ring a bell or gong or something."

"Do you know anything about constructing such alarms?" Lawrence asked, pleased with the suggestion.

"Not much, but enough. I used to be good cobbers with a bloke who was one time switch operator in the execution chamber at Sing-Sing. He explained to me how they corpsed 'em in America. It's all a matter of electrodes and contacts."

"You're a nice bloke to be living with, I don't think," Morgan said with a wicked look.

Raymond, smiling grimly, looking Lawrence full in the face, said: "My friend is sometimes a little blunt-spoken. But he could manage those alarms all right. If I may make a suggestion, I would point out that if the proposed guard was placed just within the cavern instead of in the passage, he would be able in a way to guard the entrances to the caves occupied by the ladies. It would, I am sure, reduce their inevitable nervousness. "

"Yes, yes. An excellent suggestion," applauded the millionaire. "But, still, it may not be necessary, beyond one night anyway. We shall find the brute. We must hunt until we do. Or," turning directly to Lawrence, "we must be allowed to go."

"The guard will ensure our safety, Mr. Van Horton. Come, let us return. The ladies will be anxious and Tuttman annoyed by our keeping dinner waiting."

Again back in the Cavern of the Sword, Lund and Snell passed on to their own cave at the further end of a short passage leading from the larger one, leaving Van Horton and Lawrence to explain the gruesome tragedy in what way they wished. Whilst changing his coat the tall Australian asked Snell what he thought of the murder and the horrific tracks made by the killer. But Snell apparently had no opinion to give. Instead, he said softly:

"I'm glad the Princess has that gun. If she sees the thing she won't scream and throw a seven. She'll shoot. She's the shooting sort, be-lie-eve me. There's one thing, though."

"That being – ?"

"Better warn her not to shoot unless it attacks her," Sweet William replied. "When she starts pulling the trigger a lot of people will know she's got the pistol. And then she won't have it long."

"I'll tell her." Lund completed his dressing by putting on his feet ordinary walking shoes in lieu of pumps, which he had left at home. Still, he felt thankful for the borrowed dinner-jacket, because it at least gave him a feeling of equality with the handsome Lawrence and the dapper millionaire. Then: "What do you make of those tracks, Bill?"

"Nothing, Captain, nothing. All I hopes is that whatever makes 'em don't try to get into bed with me. Cripes! A man wouldn't be thinking of his honeymoon, would he?"

"There are times when you are positively humorous. Do try and smile sometimes."

"Can't. The thought of going to bed with that prowling gent gives me no reason to smile. Hadn't we better go along?"

"I'm ready. Come on!"

In the chamber where hung the great stalactite they found the Princess awaiting them. She had on a gown of forget-me-not muslin cunningly and artistically made, she told Lund later in the evening, by the "so sweet" Julia. Obviously, Julia was as great a dressmaker as she was a maid. Without speaking, Natalie turned to the passage leading to the dining-room via the kitchen, and with her hands commanded Lund and Snell to walk one on each side of her. Half way along the passage she paused, saying in her clear tones: "Helen! The lovely Helen now lives in hell."

"Pardon, Princess!" exclaimed Lund, whom an intimate acquaintance of several weeks failed quite to render incapable of being surprised by this amazing woman.

"What killed her, Marm?" Snell ventured diffidently.

For three seconds Natalie looked at her escorts alternately, noting the surprise in Lund's grey eyes, the flash of interest in Snell's small brown orbs. Then she began to laugh, and her laughter thrilled them both. Realising the ambiguity of her statement, she felt the fun of Snell's calm interest in Helen Van Horton's fate and Raymond's well-bred astonishment.

"My friends! Oh, my friends! You are so droll. Or may it be my English grammar so like a cocktail is, all of a mixedness?"

Slowly they walked on. "No, the so lovely Helen not yet is dead. She is fearful. The monster in the depths afraid makes her. So – so peculiar."

"She imagines the thing to be a huge monkey, Princess. You will remember she told us that once a little monkey fell on her head, badly pulling her hair and scratching her face. Doubtless that most unpleasant incident is the cause of her present unreasonable fear. But are you yourself not nervous?"

"*Non, monsieur*. I have the thing of wonderfulness which protects its little gaoler – no, keeper," Natalie said, looking up at him with eyes that held no fear. "But listen! The so poetical Tuttman sings his ode."

That evening Alfred Tuttman became an active volcano. All *chefs* are volcanoes, as Australian station owners and hotel managers will testify. Some erupt more than others, and the volcanic fire almost invariably is stoked into fearful energy when the dinner they have carefully created is slowly spoiled by delayed service.

On this evening Tuttman's dinner of five courses was by this time nearly an hour later in being taken in. The spoiling of his efforts was a crime Tuttman, as any other *chef*, did not suffer gladly. The story of Little's passing, told vividly by Sir Knight, offered no mitigation, and at the entry of the Princess with her escort he had reached the point of mental perturbation when obviously the only course to be adopted to avert total insanity was the soothing action of sharpening his largest carving-knife on his largest steel. And, whilst thus engaged, he sang to the well-known evening hymn-tune:

"Another day has ended
And the hangman weeps a tear
Poor old Little's busted,
And none can raise a cheer."

Then came Larsen's shrill voice: "You shut up dat. Little, heem my friendt."

The *chef* stood behind his service table, the huge knife glittering about the steel as though it were the wings of a butterfly. At the further side of the table Larsen danced with most un-German excitability. Tuttman's dark eyes were gleaming, his drooping moustache quivering, the points like the nervous tentacles of an octopus.

Sir Knight seemed greatly amused. Again Tuttman sang melodiously, unsmilingly:

"Larsen was a clever bloke,
He tried to kiss a tart;
But Cupid left his bow at home
And couldn't shoot a dart."

It seemed that Larsen very suddenly froze. The nervous twitching of his limbs ceased, whilst the pallor of his face became so accentuated that the vast bristling moustache looked as though an ink-bottle had been spilled over a sheet of paper. The smile on the face of Sir Knight became a fixture, a smile painted on a carnival mask.

To the watchers at the other end of the kitchen the frozen tableau suddenly burst into terrific life. Larsen's right hand flew up under his coat towards his left armpit, and coincidently the butterfly about the steel became a pointed shaft of silver lying along Tuttman's open palm held on a level with his right ear.

So quickly did Sir Knight act that there was no apparent difference in the time. All three seemed to move at the precise split second. The easy-going, slouching Sir Knight stood in a crouching attitude on the table between the combatants, much in the manner of a terrier snarling at two tom-cats. Life, breathing, palpitating life, again was stilled to a tableau, remained so for seconds, ended when Morgan came in from the guard-room.

Sir Knight saw him crossing the cavern and then jumped, his arms wide. He landed in front of Larsen when that little fury dragged from its soft leather holster his second issued pistol. Sir Knight's long arms became wrapped around the little German, his body never moving from its position between Larsen and Tuttman, although what Larsen lacked in height he made up for amply in strength and agility.

Doubtless the odds were even and the battle would have lasted for several minutes had not the bullet-headed Morgan intervened. He slid a great knotted forearm across Larsen's throat, and his right knee flew upwards and became jammed into the small of Larsen's back. And, whilst Larsen gurgled and his face became purple, Morgan growled as a wounded bear at the extremity of its lair: "Drop yer gat, or I'll flatten yer neck like a bit of cardboard. Better be quick."

Sir Knight caught the automatic just before it fell from Larsen's stiffening fingers. Tuttman began another verse.

CHAPTER XXVII

POKER – AND LOVE

VAN HORTON and his daughter delayed dinner by yet another twenty minutes, and when they reached the dining-room it was to find the others waiting with varying degrees of impatience in the inner cavern set out as a drawing-room.

"Princess, will you be pleased to accept our apologies?" Van Horton asked when he stood bowing before Natalie. "Helen, I am afraid, has been upset by the occurrence this evening, and only after much persuasion has been induced to dine at all."

Helen stood a little behind her father. Gowned superbly, the paleness of her complexion, to hide which no cosmetics had been applied, enhanced her somewhat Grecian beauty, whilst the perturbation of her mind caused her eyes to widen more than their wont. Lund decided that she had never appeared more beautiful.

"It understandable is," Natalie said gravely. Then, going to the American, she impulsively slipped an arm around Helen's waist and drew her close to herself. "Be not afraid, my so dear Helen. Of the hobgoblin let us forget. Remember only that the so wonderful Mistaire Tuttman, he of the 'Ode to the Future', has prepared dinner to-night *à l'Australie*. Also presently I relate to you his new poem. Mistaire Lawrence, describe to me – a tart,"

"A tart, Princess, is pastry on which jam is laid," Lawrence answered, puzzled, because he had not been present at the fracas in the kitchen.

Natalie frowned delightfully. Turning to Lund, she questioned him: "Why, then, should Mistaire Tuttman refer to pastry having overlaid it with jam?"

"Mr. Lawrence's definition of the word 'tart' is English, Your Highness. Tuttman used it in the Australian sense, which is girl, or sweetheart – sweet-heart – sweet tart – tart."

Natalie broke into a gurgle of laughter, laughter that certainly raised the spirits of Helen Van Horton no less than the others. Still laughing, the company became seated, after the Princess had taken her usual seat at the head of the table. The mess-waiter, a nondescript person who was deaf and dumb and was consequently called "Deedee", served the soup. It was kangaroo-tail soup, the kill having been made by Sir Knight the evening before, near the oil-bore. Following the soup came minced kangaroo steak and bacon, with potatoes and haricot beans, in turn followed by braised rabbit. The sweets consisted of real jam tart and Australian peaches – out of tins.

From that meal Blue Everett, Larsen, and Sir Knight were absent. At its close Julia and Morgan immediately withdrew. The tall dark man, Fred Bennett, and Earle Lawrence, took coffee with the others in the drawing-room, Bennett later joining Lund, Snell, Van Horton, and Natalie in a game of poker. Begging to be excused, Helen drifted towards the harmonium. Lawrence fitted ear-phones to his head and became attentive to the wireless set.

At this juncture Snell was well to the good, his "winnings" amounting to some thirty-one full boxes of matches. Natalie was down seventeen boxes, Lund fifteen, Van Horton stood about even, Bennett had six boxes in hand. Both Lawrence and Helen Van Horton were heavy losers.

Lund shuffled the cards and asked Natalie to cut. He then dealt, and, since Natalie required time to arrange her hand and decide what cards to throw away, Raymond had always the opportunity to take a covert look at the others. Invariably Bennett, Snell and Van Horton acted in precisely the same manner. There sat three born poker-players. Lund noticed that immediately Snell, Van Horton, and Bennett touched cards their faces lost all expression, becoming negative masks. The fact that they were playing for matches, with bets limited to four matches, did not lessen their keenness one iota. Those three knew, as did Lund, that Natalie did not hold even a pair. As far as Lund could tell from their faces they each might hold a hand as poor, or had picked up a Royal Flush.

With a delicious *moué* Natalie threw in four cards, and bought four from the dealer. Bennett discarded one and bought one. Snell and Lund each bought three. In the pot the matches were accumulating. From Natalie's face the gentlemen knew that the four cards dealt her made her hand passably good. She started the betting with two matches. After some hesitation Bennett raised the bet. Van Horton drew out. He was followed by Snell. Lund raised the betting.

It was now Natalie's turn to raise the bet or pay to see the hands of Bennett and Lund. She remembered that the dark man had held four cards and bought one. Obviously, he had held two pairs. The one he bought was unlikely to give him a full hand. Again she raised the betting. Bennett, hesitating again for the fraction of a second, raised it still further. Lund threw in his hand and, leaning back in his chair, lit a cigarette and fell to watching the duel between the Princess and Bennett.

By no means ill-looking in his dark way, Frederick Bennett, ex-Major of Artillery in the Imperial Forces, bearing the indelible Oxford and Sandhurst stamp, bet once more. His head was slightly bent forward over the table, and what could be seen of his face revealed the vacuity of a sleep-walker. Natalie flashed a look at her opponent and betted again. With as much expression as a robot Bennett raised the bet.

The pot was almost full of matches. Natalie felt a slight coldness run up her spine, for the man seemed to lose all his humanity, to take on the icy habiliments of fate. It was uncanny.

"I'll see you, Mistaire Bennett," she cried, with just a hint of desperation in her voice, and passed towards the pot the requisite number of matches.

Bennett turned over his cards. They comprised a three of spades, an ace, and three kings. Natalie bit her lip, and, turning up her cards, the others saw that she held a six high straight.

"Only one card you bought?"

"Only one, Highness," Bennett replied in his cultured, somewhat high-pitched voice.

"Well – well I" Natalie was nonplussed. "I thought when you bought only one card that two pairs only you held. You held three kings?"

"Precisely, Princess. With poker one should always vary one's routine. Please accept my condolences. You held an excellent betting hand, which you were not afraid to back." He shuffled the cards for her. "Your deal, madam."

So the game went on. Fortune favoured Natalie often, but although she tried she could not control the light in her violet-blue eyes. Lund played with less enthusiasm that evening, his thoughts being on the situation which had further developed with the killing of Little. He wondered, should the monster not be discovered, how Lawrence would deal with it. The thing simply had to be found and, if not human, destroyed. How would these men who, adopting a discipline under which there was no gambling for money and total abstinence from intoxicating liquor, behave if the threat continued? From the card-table his eyes lifted to the alcove. Helen had ceased playing, although she still sat before the instrument. Lawrence was leaning on one end of it, talking earnestly. He seemed to be pleading.

He was pleading. He was saying: "To me it seems at least a century ago that I proposed to you and you refused. In actual time it is only three years, and the seeming hundred years proves how empty my life has been throughout the three years.

"You will, of course, remember what to you may have been a mere incident, but which to me was the greatest crisis of my life. You were very beautiful then, Helen, and I loved you with all my soul. Tonight you are more beautiful still, and even still more do I love you."

Helen Van Horton was conscious only of the man's brilliant eyes, aflame with a hard, cadmium-tinged light. He was so tremendously in earnest that she felt a slight sensation of pity, and for perhaps two seconds his success in winning her hung in the balance. Through her mind flashed a succession of pictures of him, beginning when first she had seen him on his elevation to the position of king in the vast gang of which her father was ace and master. The mental pictures showed her seated beside him whilst he drove a great car through the streets of Chicago during a successful get-away one midnight, with several pursuing police cars roaring behind him. It was his nonchalant calmness in situations like that which undoubtedly attracted her.

Then there had been that adventure one freezing cold afternoon when she was a passenger on a forty-knot motorboat running before a north-westerly gale. On board were two tons of drugs – opium, heroin, and cocaine. And then out of the misty spray ahead dashed five long shapes to intercept them. At the cry of the look-out in the bows Earle Lawrence, captain of the boat, had pushed away the helmsman and spun the tiny glittering wheel this way and then that, sending his craft straight for one of the United States revenue cutters until a collision seemed so imminent that she cried out. But at the very last second he had twisted the bow to port, missing the other boat by a margin of only three feet, then bore away to starboard in a zigzag, as the centre forward of a football team will dribble a ball through all opposition.

She had never forgotten the man's face as she had seen it straining forward over the shining steering-wheel. Calm to the point of death, only the eyes moving, gleaming with the identical light that now they held. A man of action in supreme moments, yet at others dominant in discussion when he had evolved some brilliant plan.

Yes! Helen Van Horton, when forced to admit the dictates of her heart, which was seldom, realised that she liked Earle Lawrence. She liked his unfailingly sure poise, his evident breeding never betrayed by lack of manners, his good looks. Yet she did not love him. She knew that after several searching, analytical, heart tests. He did not quicken her pulses; he did not smash down the gates of humdrum life and reveal to her an undreamed heaven beyond. No, his proximity never acted on her as had the proximity of another man who had died in Flanders.

She heard herself speaking, and was surprised to hear in her voice real regret, real honesty. "It can never be, Earle," she said slowly. "I do not love you. I know I never shall love you."

"But don't you understand that my love would awaken yours?" he burst out. "Cannot you see that you could not help but respond to my devotion and catch fire from the flame that burns me up? Oh, Helen! think, just think, what a love like mine would mean in your life. There is no ambition I could not gratify. With you by my side there is no height which we could not reach. I cannot – by heaven! I cannot – go on living without you. I want –"

It seemed to Helen Van Horton that a heavy weight suddenly smashed into her eyes. One moment she was being held fascinated by the almost uncontrolled emotion in the face of Earle Lawrence; the next he had gone, vanished, and with him had vanished the top of the harmonium that had reflected the electric light in a deep yellow sheen, and ruby and emerald points that had winked at her from behind him in the then form of a stalactite. Everything in that quiet yet tempestuous world had gone. She was surrounded, blanketed, with an utter and impenetrable blackness. From a very long distance she heard Lawrence's voice come to her from the void.

"It's all right, Helen; it's all right. The electric power has temporarily failed. We'll soon have it right."

From the outer cavern the grave-like silence appeared to last for an eternity. She heard Lawrence move. There came from him a muttered imprecation. Then a crash that almost made her scream out in terror, for her mind pictured so vividly that garden wherein a monkey had dropped from a tree on her head. She knew the music-stand had fallen, but she smelled, scented as an otter-hound, a sickening musty odour – the monkey smell. Was it real, or the ghost of a loathsome memory?

From out of the blackness came the voice of Fred Bennett: "Hold on a minute. It's only me. Oh, I say! Go easy Ah! Oh, God! It's –"

She thought she heard a slight snap. Terror surged inward from the darkness, was wafted all over her as some dreadful sea. She opened her mouth and could not make a sound. Again she opened her mouth, and then as a flood bursting a dam she screamed and screamed without ceasing.

CHAPTER XXVIII

A WITCH HUNT

WHEN the light went out Raymond Lund was looking at his cards and wondering if he would discard an ace or a seven and trust to luck to buy from the dealer a two or a six to make a straight. Wholly unprepared for the succeeding pitch darkness, at least two seconds passed before he understood the cause.

Each card-player hesitated to strike a match; the simple reason of that hesitation being that in their minds the piles of matches on the table at their sides represented a definite value, almost as though they were ivory chips to be exchanged at the end of the evening for real money.

Lund heard Natalie draw in her breath with surprise.

He heard something move beyond Bennett and Van Horton seated opposite Snell and himself. He waited for someone to produce a flashlight, and the other players also waited for the same reason – reluctance to sacrifice their matches. Then from the other side of the table came Bennett's voice, uttering a protest that ended in an agonized call upon his Maker, a call vibrant with unspeakable horror.

Hands reached for matches. Van Horton was the first to act. Lund saw the phosphorescent glow when match struck box. It failed, for the force the millionaire used broke it. A woman suddenly screamed, so piercingly that his nerves positively felt as though riven by the sound. Scream followed scream, and he wondered what was going on in the small alcove where he had seen Lawrence pleading with an entranced Helen. Was the man killing her?

"Damn it! Strike a light, somebody!" Van Horton actually snarled. He was making a third attempt, and so agitated was he that the third attempt failed. Snell could be heard moving in his chair. The chair rasped along the uneven rock floor. A light sparkled from the match he held above his head.

Lund saw his friend standing against the table, one hand supporting his body, which was leaning over the table, the other hand holding the match high up. The tiny flame flickered. Lund saw Van Horton's pale face, he saw Fred Bennett leaning back in his chair, and he saw Natalie looking directly at him.

Snell's match went out. The scream-shattered silence now was an awful thing to hear. A man – he thought it was Sir Knight – shouted from some point far away. His hands were full of matches, sweeping them into a mound. He would have light if he had to set fire to the place.

Simultaneously he and Van Horton struck matches. At first Lund gave his whole attention to setting fire to the heap of matches he had gathered. So intent was he on his task that he did not look up when the millionaire gave vent to a startled exclamation. With almost studied care he built and coaxed his small fire.

The flame gathered, leaping jerkily from one match to another, and when at last the ruddy glow was mounting to its apex Raymond Lund looked upward at the Princess. It was to see her almost crouched back in her chair, one hand still gripping five bent cards, the other pressed to her mouth as though to stop herself from adding her screams to Helen's. With widened eyes she was looking at Fred Bennett. From her, Lund's eyes moved to the ex-Artillery Major.

Bennett was lying back in his chair. His head sagged back and down from the body as the head of no living man could do. Lund knew that beyond possible doubt Fred Bennett was dead, had died almost without a struggle during the few seconds' interval of darkness between the failure of the electric light and the striking of a match by William Snell. It was a dreadfully sinister fact, pregnant with the freezing horror of nightmare.

As a shrieking tempest suddenly shut out by the closing of felt-lined doors, so fell the silence when Helen Van Horton suddenly ceased her screaming. He could see neither her nor her companion, and the thought occurred that the thing which killed Bennett had just killed her in the blackness of the alcove.

Looking again at Natalie, he found her position unchanged. The awful fascination held her in iron bands, steadied her eyes to unwinking orbs of blackness staring at the dead man. With volcanic suddenness he broke into furious action.

"Van Horton, go to your daughter! Bill – the cave entrance. Let none leave. What's that – that – over there? Look – find out – quick!"

He sprang to his feet, sending his chair over with a crash. Two steps he took to reach the Princess. Without a sign of his intention, without a word, he slipped one arm under her knees, the other around her waist, then lifted her bodily from her seat and strode over to the wall of the cavern against which was set the deep Chesterfield. He put her down in a half-reclining position, her back against the piled cushions at one end, and then – and then he felt her hands brush his neck and become locked behind his head.

"Don't – don't leave me, Raymond, Mistaire Lund. Oh! afraid so am

I. Stay you here, please. It might – it might –"

"Princess, there is nothing in this world which can hurt you now," he said, a strange mixture of grimness and affection vibrant in his voice. "It's all right. They'll have the light on in a moment, and then we'll find this thing."

Very gently he forced her hands apart and stood upright, and was almost turned to the room when she touched one of his hands and gripped it in both hers. Sliding her feet off the couch, she came to be sitting on it close at his side.

The pile of matches on the card-table was burning low, tiny blue flames hovering above it, reflecting the polished surface, and dimly, in a ghostly light, revealing the awful still figure in the chair beyond it.

Farther away, hidden by the blackness, there came to them the voices of Van Horton and Lawrence, the former barking in staccato notes: "What is the matter with Helen?"

"Hysteria," Lawrence snapped. "What happened?"

"Bennett. Neck broken. Killed. Damnation! When are they going to fix the lights? Aren't there any flash-lamps in this accursed place?"

"I don't remember placing any here."

Lund noted that, whereas Mr. Van Horton was completely roused from his habitual calmness, Earle Lawrence remained his calm self, outwardly at least, revealing no effect of the shocks he, with the others, undoubtedly had received.

When the American spoke again, an iron will had recaptured his usual unruffled coldness. "I will remain with my daughter here. Hadn't you better fetch a flash-light, or effect immediate repairs to the electric light?"

"Light is coming," Lawrence stated as calmly as before.

Light was coming. The reflection of a sweeping electric torch shone through the entrance giving to the outer cavern or dining-room. It increased in brilliance, finally to flood a part of the room when its one unwinking eye halted, became motionless in the doorway. At that instant the electric bulbs blazed into living light.

The suddenness of it, coming after a lengthy period of intense darkness, blinded everyone for several seconds. And there the fixed tableaux lay revealed to every actor in it but one.

At the entrance stood Blue Everett. At the edge of the alcove stood Van Horton. Behind him was Earle Lawrence holding in his arms an unconscious woman. Beyond the table near the further wall, with his back to it, was the man Morgan, and, facing him, his head thrust forward between hunched shoulders, William Snell. At the table sat Death.

Simultaneously the actors became alive.

"A fuse at the switchboard burned out," Blue Everett said. "Sir Knight went along to fix it. But – but – what has happened to Bennett?"

Without waiting for a reply he strode to the table and bent down over the dead man. None wished to vouchsafe an explanation; no one spoke until Blue Everett straightened up and turned to those in the alcove. Without a tremor in his voice, he asked: "Who killed him?"

"By Gawd! – is he dead?" Morgan suddenly growled.

Looking at the man, Lund failed to see Lawrence until he reached the Chesterfield with the still unconscious form of Helen Van Horton in his arms. Natalie jumped to her feet and Lawrence laid down his burden. With blazing admiration, Lund realised that Natalie had conquered her terror, and was her usual efficient self.

"Bring to me water," she commanded.

"One moment, Princess!"

Lawrence actually gave her a fleeting smile before walking round the table, and so to Snell and Morgan. Snell stepped back.

Lawrence spoke, cool, icy cool: "What are you doing here, Morgan?"

"I came in to see if I could get a hand at poker," the man replied without hesitation. "Ain't I got no right to be here?"

"Every right in the world, my dear man. Where were you when the light went out?"

"I was at the entrance. Fact I'd one foot only in this room when the glim vanished."

"What did you do then?"

"I took' arf a dozen steps forrard and became kind of bushed," Morgan answered, somewhat defiantly. "I was just wanderin' round when Snell grapped me and pushed me agin this wall. Wot's the idea? I ain't done nothing."

"That is not too certain. Mr. Snell, where you sat enabled you to see across the room. Did you see Morgan at the entrance when or before the light failed?"

"No. Which doesn't prove he wasn't there. I was looking at my cards when the light went out."

"When did you first observe Morgan?"

"I saw him moving about in the shadow. Mr. Lund saw him first and pointed him out. I thought it was the gorilla thing."

It seemed many, many seconds that Lawrence, looking down from his superior height, stared into the upturned eyes of the shorter, coarse, tremendously powerful-looking thug and general scoundrel. His voice sounded then as the crack of a whip.

"Did you kill Bennett?"

"Wot in 'ell did I want to kill 'im for?" answered Morgan, snarling as a beast at bay.

"Did you kill Bennett?"

"Do you think I'm a ruddy fool?"

"Answer me, Morgan. Did you kill Bennett?

"No!" suddenly shouted Morgan, desperation in his voice, indignation showing in his repulsive features. "No, I didn't."

The raised voice penetrated to the conscious mind of Helen Van Horton. Opening her eyes, she first saw the profile of Natalie seated beside her, and memory, horrific memory, flooded her mind. Yet, if her memory held terror, the present moment held less. She tried to sit up, and the movement attracting Natalie's attention – for she was absorbed in the questioning of Morgan – caused the Princess to edge along the settee so that her body intervened between the dead man and Helen's head.

"Let me up, please – please! I'm all right now. Let me up! It was the darkness that frightened me."

She almost forced Natalie from the settee, so determined was she to have her desire. Natalie, unable to prevent the American from sitting up, unable to stop her from rising to her feet, expected a second outburst of hysteria. Her face as pale as that of Bennett, her eyes very brilliant, Helen slowly and unfalteringly moved close to the table, against which, reaching it, she supported herself with her hands pressing the scattered playing-cards, and, for what seemed a very long time, stared down on the corpse.

What passed through her mind no one there was able to understand. They did observe with no little astonishment that whilst she looked down on the dead man she slowly recovered her complete composure. Van Horton's wonder was tinged with gratified pride, for her recent nervous breakdown was to him inexplicable, knowing her calm resourcefulness and undoubted courage in a thousand dramatic and dangerous situations. He never could understand the fear of monkeys created in her mind by the incident in the garden. It was like the fear in the adult of fire when the child has been badly burned.

Julia entered, almost running, to stop petrified at the scene that lay unfolded before her. Coming through the dining-room was Tuttman. They could hear him softly singing inaudible words to the tune of "Now the day is ended". It was when he appeared, still softly singing, that Helen's eyes rose from the dead man to look at him. Her glance appeared to silence the *chef*. He joined the others in watching her cross to the three against the wall. Then, bending down, Helen most efficiently sniffed at Morgan's clothes, sniffed as a terrier will sniff at a rabbit-hole.

"It is not he," she said. "Nor you," on sniffing at Lawrence. "Nor you," when Snell was examined in the same way. Recrossing the room, she stood before Natalie and Lund, and Lund she exonerated in the same fashion. "I smelled the thing. It is not here now. It is gone."

"You are right, lady. It is gone," Tuttman stated from the doorway. They saw him pointing to a patch of white sand lying in a shallow submergence, and, hurrying to it, there they saw distinctly outlined above the impressions of many feet two tracks of an enormous naked foot. Two footprints pointed to the centre of the room; two pointed to the entrance. Evidently the thing had come in and gone out again. Was it possible for it to have crept in, killed Bennett, and gone away again whilst Morgan was wandering about "bushed" in the darkness?

Alfred Tuttman's morbid curiosity impelled him to stalk across to the dead man. He remained silent, his poetical genius temporarily extinguished.

CHAPTER XXIX

VAN HORTON'S LITTLE SCHEMES

LAWRENCE walked over the Nullarbor Plain, revealed by the stars as a circular black cloth whose edge lay just beyond a stone's throw. Outside the surprisingly drawn-in horizon the apparent drop into space stirred the imagination, and a rising star might have deluded the uninitiated into believing that it was a lamp set in a hut window. But the shack inhabited by Dr. Woolworth lay due north, not south of east.

Earle Lawrence was both perturbed by past events and worried by indecision as to the shaping of future events. He felt that early morning as an inventor of an intricate piece of machinery might feel after an assistant had dropped a steel spanner amid the works. His plan, brilliantly conceived and as brilliantly executed, was on the verge of positive results, results that would be chiselled and moulded to create the edifice of his desires. Acting at the beginning in co-partnership with Van Horton, he later had gradually assumed complete control, a position that afforded him infinite gratification. After several years passed in the shadow of Van Horton's tremendous power over the B., D. and C. Pack, his egoism was being fed to the full by the knowledge that Van Horton and his daughter now lived in his shadow.

Across the plain he proceeded, subconsciously avoiding the larger bushes, stepping over the annual salt-bush, his trained sense of direction taking him in a rule-straight line to the oil-bore. His conscious mind was fully occupied by the astounding events of that day, and after a while he began to plan a search underground on a new system, to be inaugurated a few hours later, with the expert assistance of that methodical mind, inspired, equipped, fortified, and bounded by His Majesty's Field Service Regulations – the mind housed in the body of William Bussey.

Bussey and Peter Cuff he found, as expected, at the oil-bore, where they had arrived from Eucla several hours before. As further reinforcement he decided to return with the half-caste, who possessed a full share of his aboriginal father's eyesight and astounding tracking powers. Two hours later the trio were leaving the oil-site on the way to the House of Jewels, the half-caste giving no indication in his silent gliding tread that he had but just returned on a riding camel from Cook, whence he had dispatched a message to a lady in Perth requesting her to send on to him a parcel of clothes, and a second message to a man in the same city.

That night Helen Van Norton slept very soundly. On another bed the maid slept not less soundly, despite the fact that she had been much upset by the tableau presented to her in the drawing-room. Both mistress and maid had been dosed with bromide by the millionaire, who spent that night prowling about the caverns with an ever-ready electric torch in one hand and an equally ready automatic pistol in the other.

Yet, for all the result that accrued from his nocturnal wanderings, Mr. Van Horton might with greater advantage have gone to bed and slept.

Snell slept as the proverbial log, but Raymond sat in the only chair provided them and racked his mind for some possible way of escape. If only Snell or he could discover some secret exit; if only the one known exit was a fraction less efficiently guarded; if only the inner guard were not precisely where he was at the end of a straight passage fourteen yards in length – fourteen yards of brilliantly-lit passage to be traversed before an armed man could be reached and overpowered! His brain wearied itself over the problem, refused longer to wrestle with it, sought and obtained respite by determinedly occupying itself with other affairs, the chief of which was memory of two small hands clasped behind his head and a small, fearful voice crying: "Raymond! Mistaire Lund! Don't leave me!"

She was then dreaming of sitting on a throne in a great cathedral, and though she never saw Raymond Lund she knew he occupied a slightly less resplendent throne on her left hand. An Archbishop was standing in front of her, a glittering crown held before him in his hands. He was about to place the crown on her head, his face utterly void of emotion, a calm, inscrutable face, an ugly face bearing a flat nose with out-turning nostrils, the face of "my so dear Sweet William". She was supported by the magic rosy cloud called Happiness, and in her dreams the hard smooth contact of a small automatic pistol nestling against her cheek was unnoted.

Outside, in the Cavern of the Sword, sat Blue Everett, very much on the alert, armed with pistol and flash-lamp.

Above, the plain was taking on colour, eating up its cloak of black velvet, to stand stark and naked in the dawn, and then, when the sun leapt to the horizon, hurriedly donning garments of green and blue, grey and white. The zephyr that came from the vast Southern Ocean was cool and fragrant with the scents it had caught up on its way from the coast where serrated rocks waged eternal battle with the endless watery hills and ranges.

At ten o'clock Van Horton suggested an immediate conference in his room, to which Earle Lawrence agreed, and ten minutes later there were assembled, with the two principals, Helen Van Horton, Blue Everett, and Bussey. Mr. Bussey's powerful frame was resting on an obviously inadequate Windsor chair, and his small, dark brown eyes, which at times became almost black, were fixed on the face of Earle Lawrence, who was describing the killing of Little and Bennett. Now and then he straightened the points of his moustache with grubby forefinger and thumb. When Lawrence finally stopped talking Bussey made no immediate effort to voice an opinion, although he saw the others looking at him expectantly.

Helen was thinking how unprepossessing the ex-warrant-officer then appeared, but how absolutely glowing with energy! He seemed to be – at least such was the impression he gave her – a volcano gifted with a living intelligence, everlastingly trying to make the foolish inhabitants of the villages scattered at its foot believe that never would it burst into destructive activity. At last Bussey spoke, with his faint Cockney accent. If subdued in volume, it yet was a parade-ground voice. He had to stand, from ingrained, compelling, lifelong discipline, and Helen thought he was going to salute.

"Discipline most poor, sir. When lights failed, flash-lamps should have been in easy reach. Two men should be detailed for duty to patrol all passages. Present guard at gates to be maintained. Suggest that Peter Cuff be given commission – temporary – to act on his own initiative and investigate tracks. He's almost able to pick out fingerprints on a sheet of water. You, sir, and I, must take our turns of duty, as we are under establishment. Cook and batman must also perform guard duty. Mrs. Cuff could be fetched to serve the mess."

"Very good, Bussey. Attend to it. It is in your department."

Bussey swung round on his right heel and left toe, forbore to salute, and left them. His going impressed Helen Van Horton with a sense of relief, not relief from his presence, but a more satisfying feeling of security. Mr. Bussey was the epitome of military efficiency.

"That man will go far – given the chance," prophesied Mr. Van Horton. "With but a thousand like him, I would make myself King of the United States of America."

"I am glad there were not a thousand like him in my late battalion," Lawrence observed unsmilingly. "If ever a raw recruit hated a sergeant-major, I hated that man."

"Well now – to business." The American's voice suddenly assumed the board-room tone. "Did Cuff dispatch the message?"

"Yes. It was handed in at Cook at one-twenty yesterday afternoon.

The woman of whom he requested a parcel of clothes will have dispatched the letter to Captain Black under registered cover. It should be delivered to the captain at Albany this afternoon. He will leave port this evening. At midday to-morrow he will open his sealed orders. On the morning of March 1 he will be twelve miles off Eucla. If the sea is calm that day, or the first day after that date that the sea is calm, he will observe the smoke of a bush fire behind Eucla, steam in to land, and send a boat to the jetty for us."

"So that we shall have to remain here at least six days after to-day?" surmised Helen, her expression peculiarly strained.

"Obviously," assented Lawrence, staring hard at her. Then, turning to Van Horton, he asked: "Have you planned your get-away with the Princess?"

"Yes. Plan cut and dried. If on February 28 the wireless weather forecast predicts fine weather, we'll stage the escape for that night. Mr. Everett here and I have already discussed it."

Mr. Van Horton then went into details of the plan presently to be proposed to the Princess in his character as a fellow captive.

"What do you propose in relation to Lund and his friend Snell?" Everett asked.

"To use the man Snell's simile, they are a foreign product in our petrol system. Obviously they must be removed."

"But cannot they return to civilisation with you and the Princess?" suggested Lawrence, shrinking from the other's sinister implication.

"No, because to do so would to a very great extent put Helen and me in the background as rescuers of the Princess," countered Van Horton crisply. "As I am paying the piper, I do not intend allowing anyone to interfere with my calling the tune. I can imagine the result of their accompanying us. The papers would be full of Mr. Raymond Lund, the famous Australian bushman, explorer, and inventor. And I've a suspicion that the Princess likes Lund more than a princess should like a mere commoner. No, they must go! They must go together. Leave the manner of their going to me. I will act at once."

Everett put forward the question of the payment of himself and the other members of the gang who were to be taken aboard Captain Black's ship.

"Every man will be paid by my Chinese friend when they land at Singapore. Doubtless they will be invited to a house in a convenient quarter for the purpose. They will be paid by open cheque."

And there was a smile on the face of Van Horton.

CHAPTER XXX

THE TEMPTRESS

THE small underground community was affected by the ex-warrant-officer of the Australian Imperial Forces in a hardly lesser degree than rabbits in a burrow by the entry of a ferret. He and Sir Knight inspected the whole system of underground caverns and their linking passages, and at the end of the inspection, on their return to the "guard room", he barked for a sheet of paper and pencils.

Lawrence and Everett found themselves peremptorily invited to a second conference, and at this the four men made a fairly accurate plan of the cavern system.

"You have already searched the place for the animile, or whatever it is, which makes them marks, and is supposed to have killed Little and Bennett," Bussey pointed out, after studying the plan for several minutes. "It is clear that in some way the thing doubled back on you as you searched in a mob. We got to stop that this time. All ranks will assemble here, every man jack of us bar the prisoners. From here we'll start, and we'll look into every crack and crevice as we proceed.

"We'll leave one man on guard, *pro. tem.*, here where the first passage starts. We'll then work the drawing-room, the dining-room, and the kitchen. Another guard will be left at the kitchen entrance of the passage going into the cavern Miss Van Horton calls the Cavern of the Sword. From this cavern a passage leads to the quarters of Lund and Snell, Mr. Van Horton, and you, Mr. Lawrence. Also the rooms of the ladies open on it. We'll leave a man there before we start on all those caves and caverns, leave him in such a position that nothink or nobody can come out of one passage into another, or from one cave to another. Get me?

"You see that we've got the kitchen blocked. When we go on, we'll have that Sword Cavern blocked, too. Nothink can get back to the places we've searched. Right! On we go to the cavern off which lead the passages to the place where the dynamo is, and the cavern where the skeleton is. We'll leave a man there on duty, so that while we search the Skeleton Cavern nothink can't bolt back. I'm thinking where we'll find the thing is that cavern with the skeleton. So we'll search that last of all. Agreed?"

"It is a good plan, Bussey. We will start now," Lawrence assented. "All right. Sound general parade, Blue."

Lund and Sweet William were startled by the sound of a bugle commanding in its clear, crystal notes the assembly. At the time they were engaged in putting down an electric alarm in a sand patch in the passage connecting the kitchen and the Cavern of the Sword. Lawrence had been more than willing and able to supply contact-plates and wiring; and, since Lund was as anxious to track the terror as anyone there, he joined his electrical knowledge to that of Snell without hesitation.

"Getting quite armyfied," Sweet William observed. "Pity you never brought your uniform and Sam Brown. Me, I'd feel good in a tin hat."

"The man Bussey, from London, appears to be a keener go-getter than Van Horton from America, Bill."

"Yes." Snell joined two pieces of copper wire expertly. "I'm glad, mighty glad, he wasn't in my batt."

Sir Knight and Morgan came hurrying along and passed them without speaking. Larsen appeared, scowled, and vanished into the kitchen. Half a minute later there came on them the half-caste, Peter Cuff; but, instead of passing on, he stopped to watch the work with interest expressed on his almost black face, and an inscrutable look in his keen black eyes. Since he did not speak, Snell raised himself to sit back on his heels, and, looking up, saw that Peter Cuff was absorbed in a visual study of the toes of his boots.

"Do they want mending?" inquired Snell with forced politeness.

"No," vouchsafed the half-caste.

"Do you think my boots made the tracks of that monkey thing?"

"No, but your bare feet might."

"You don't say!" Snell appeared to ponder this possibility. Then: "Well, as you don't look like a feller who could worry much and keep out of a madhouse, I'll show one of 'em to you." And, somewhat to Lund's surprise, Sweet William sank back to sit on the passage floor, whereupon he unlaced a boot, pulled it off, removed his sock, and held up the sole of his naked foot with a wicked look in his small eyes.

"What are you acting?" asked Natalie, who had come upon them unseen.

"Foot inspection, Marm," Snell replied, endeavouring to kick the half-caste playfully in the abdomen. "Gent thinks I am an overgrown monkey. Made the mistake by looking at me face."

This was said in tones so utterly respectful, yet so pregnant with genuine complaint, that Natalie, looking into Lund's eyes, broke into a gurgle of laughter. She appeared ravishingly lovely that morning, and Raymond could not keep back the look of admiration. Peter Cuff moved silently away in the wake of Larsen. And when he, too, had vanished into the kitchen, the light of laughter slowly faded from her eyes, replaced by an expression of perplexity, shadowed by fear.

"What are they so doing now?" she asked in the quiet confident manner of one courageous enough to triumph over fear.

"I am not sure, but I believe, Princess, that they are about to carry out another search for the – well, you know."

Their eyes held for a moment. He saw in hers the mental struggle for calmness, the retention of the poise her long line demanded of her, and in that moment he came to realise the horror of big monkeys implanted – who knows why or how? – deeply in every feminine soul.

"You really need suffer no anxiety, Princess," he told her with grave assurance. "There will be a man on guard all night outside your room. In this affair Snell and I are heartily co-operating with our enemies. We are laying down alarms in selected places which everyone of us will know. The thing cannot in future traverse a passage without stepping on one and setting in action a striker on the dinner-gong. You still carry the pistol?"

"Yes, Mistaire Lund. It is here." She pressed a hand against her bosom.

"You will remember not to use it unless absolutely necessary" he reminded her. "It is the only pistol we have among us, and will be invaluable when the chance of escape offers. The chance may occur any moment, as this searching business will distract the gang and possibly reduce the guard at the entrance."

"Remember will I," and the vivid face softened into a smile. "I so afraid am. I am great big girl."

With sock and boot once more on his foot Sweet William was standing just a little behind Raymond Lund, and to see him more clearly Natalie changed her position. He saw her eyes examining him, his feet, his powerful body, each arm, and finally his face. Snell wondered, becoming uncomfortable under the scrutiny. He did not understand that his powerful person and his calm, expressionless face radiated a confident assurance of perfect protection which as an unseen stream flowed about and over Natalie, giving her strength, banishing fear. Able and willing to recognise in Lund restrained power that would become terrible once it was permitted freedom, restrained then by civilised convention and lifelong reliance on legal machinery, she saw, as she had seen from the beginning, that in the body of William Snell dwelt a soul that secretly recognised no conventions, laws, nor customs. Inexperienced though she was, she penetrated Snell's veneer of civilisation and found it extremely thin. Some men, possessing great natural gifts and presented with every advantage of life, are cursed with a mental kink compelling them to do evil. Snell had received no advantages of education and wealth, had no natural gifts other than great strength of body, but he possessed a mental kink compelling goodness.

His small brown eyes gleamed back at her, and over his coarse ugly face spread the very ghost of a smile. What was passing through his mind neither Natalie nor Lund could remotely guess. Lund, in fact, made no attempt at guessing. Snell was always an enigma.

"Have you made the so good friends with Mistaire Tuttman?" asked the Princess at last.

"In a kind of way, Marm. Me and him is good cobbers," replied Sweet William. "He's a bit deep."

Natalie smiled again. "So deep! Well – what you say? – I lower to the deep the weight over the side of the so slow ship. I go to hold audience with the *chef* so poetical. Here his 'Ode to the Future', here the Rolandian translation." She indicated the two rolls she carried. "I plan to throw food to his vanity. *Au revoir*, gentlemen!"

With grave expression, yet with twinkling eyes, she bowed her head in dismissal as from lifelong habit.

The two men stood on one side, stiffened to attention, made suddenly conscious that this vivacious, gracious woman was of Blood Royal.

"Was there ever such a woman before her?" Lund murmured softly when Natalie had passed kitchen-wards. Snell's instant agreement caused him slight consternation, because he had not been conscious of speaking aloud.

Snell said: "She's a rip-snorting corker all right."

On entering the kitchen Natalie discovered Bussey and his "army" on the point of leaving it, the living apartments and the kitchen having been minutely searched without any new discovery of any possible hiding-place. Her entry made Bussey involuntarily come to attention. Almost he barked the command, "Parade – 'Shun!" caught himself in time, bowed stiffly and stalked out with his followers.

Lawrence, who brought up the rear, bowed easily to her, saying: "Is there anything wanting, Your Highness? I am sorry I cannot entertain you just now, but we are all very busy, as you see."

She saw the respect he had for her rank, and saw, or, rather, felt, his sense of power, almost of superiority, over her; yet what gave her a slight shock was the sudden realisation that Earle Lawrence, always so cool and debonair, was mentally disturbed. The emotion was contagious. The lurking fear within her heart which Snell had momentarily banished sprang again to the fore. She knew then, whilst gazing into the light grey prominent eyes, that Lawrence felt fear.

"I am desirous of conversing with the *chef*," she said. "It is permitted?"

"Decidedly, Princess," he answered her lightly. "Tuttman will be on guard duty for a little while, which is why he is now occupying that chair. Pardon me, but I must leave you."

With brows now almost meeting in a frown, Natalie watched him go. Then, surveying the kitchen, she observed Tuttman seated near the entrance in a position allowing him to look along the passage to the first bend, round which worked Lund and Snell. On his knees lay a heavy automatic pistol and a flash-lamp.

"Pardonney mwar, Ma-darm," he said in his best French. "W.O.'s orders – sit tight, eyes front, drop the ghost without questions till return of search-party. Still, we ain't in the army now."

The last statement was made on mature reflection. It was a second thought. With a to-hell-with-orders look on his white, cadaverous features, he rose to his feet, slipped pistol and lamp into the great pocket of his white apron, jerked the chair forward, swept off his white, scrupulously-starched and ironed crown of office, and bowed with real grace.

"I thank you, Mistaire Tuttman," Natalie said gravely, although she wanted to laugh at this man, who so desperately desired to render her homage, even at the expense of his social and political principles. "Your 'Ode to the Future' now translated is. It is that I keep it. I will have it sung in Naagrade at the so grand state concert."

Tuttman swallowed. Looking up at him, she saw the light in his over-large dark eyes, and then she looked down and away, and her own eyes winked with the understanding of the soul of him who so ached to rise to the heights, yet for ever had been chained to mundane sordid things by environment.

"Mistaire Tuttman," she said softly, "Mistaire Tuttman, you a soldier of Mistaire Lawrence are. Why not you serve beneath my flag? Some day may I not be Queen of Rolandia? Follow my so bright rising star now on. You I will make *chef* of the Palace of Naagrade."

Glancing up at him again, she found him looking along the lighted passage with eyes focussed not on it, but on the splendour she created for him. As though she was dissatisfied with the picture, she etched in a finishing touch by saying with the subtlety of her house: "And so the great *chef* of the Palace of Naagrade has of a right a private box at all the so grand state concerts."

Tuttman remained for some further seconds gazing on his visions. Then tiny sweat beads broke out over his alabaster white forehead, and she saw that she had fanned into being the fire of a mental battle. Her power, the almost certainty of her ultimate victory, made with promises she intended to keep, thrilled her. After a while the *chef* stooped so that his face was level with hers.

"Princess, I signed on under Earle Lawrence for the duration," he whispered hoarsely. "I'm not nice to know. I've done horrible things, but I ain't never knifed a man in the back, and I'm not a deserter. What – what were you thinking of asking me to do when you tempted me?"

"Tempted you!" exclaimed Natalie with well-assumed indignation.

"Well, what were you thinking of asking me to do in return for giving me the chance you said?" Tuttman persisted.

Natalie plunged a little recklessly. "I – we desire greatly your help to escape," she said, looking at him direct by suddenly turning her head. She saw the poignant regret spring into his eyes, and heard his statement repeated:

"I signed on for the duration – I signed on for the duration!"

CHAPTER XXXI

NATALIE'S JUDGEMENT

THE utterly negative result of Bussey's well-organised search lay as an invisible black fog over the people who gathered in the drawing-room after a dismal dinner that night. Failure to find the hiding-place of the killer of Little and Bennett made of Bussey a fuming martinet, recalling to Lawrence the days when he was a recruit smarting under the lash of the biting, sarcastic tongue that eventually became famous.

The ex-warrant-officer drew up his guard roster and placed his sentries, two in the entrance cave, one in the Cavern of the Sword, and two on guard over the power plant. These latter were permitted to arrange between them their periods of duty, enabling one to sleep whilst the other kept watch. The guard was mounted from six to six o'clock throughout the night. During the day hours it was thought necessary for only the guards in the entrance cave to remain on duty, but everyone was instructed that when performing duties beyond the Cavern of the Sword, such as bringing water from the one of the two falls which yielded fresh water in the long passage, or attending to the power plant, two men must walk together.

In addition to the system of guards, Lund and Snell had laid down five alarms, whose positions were clearly indicated by small sheets of white cardboard nailed to the wall beside them. Each alarm was buried in a shallow sand-filled hollow, large enough to induce the unwary to step through it and on the contact plates, yet not so large as to prevent the initiated from stepping round them by hugging one of the walls.

Yet, despite these elaborate precautions, gaolers and prisoners lived with nerves on edge. Everybody consciously waited for the next mental shock, much as nervous people during a thunderstorm will wait with taut nerves for the next flash or crash. The thing still existed at large somewhere in hiding, somewhere close to them. When next would it strike? And whom? Through more than one brain the question kept repeating with a hopeless yet sinister disregard for any possible answer.

"Who next? Who next? Who next?"

Suspicion was awake and abroad. Lawrence was wondering at the dawn of the crisis he was creating if Van Horton had strangled Little and broken Bennett's neck. Van Horton was still a powerful man, despite his advanced years. And there was no absolute proof that Little had been strangled with one hand. In Bennett's case, Van Horton had been sitting beside the ex-Major, and it would have been the easiest thing in the world for him to have gripped the man, broken his neck, and resumed his seat at the table during the few seconds of complete darkness.

As for Van Horton, he more than suspected Morgan. Morgan was able to strangle with a single hand-grip, and he was in the room and behind Bennett and himself when the electric light failed.

Snell was suspected by two people. Both Bussey and Peter Cuff thought, although in this they were not in collaboration, that Snell was physically capable of, and had had the opportunity to commit, the two killings.

The women – Princess, American mistress, and French maid – firmly believed that there was at large a monstrous gorilla, or something hardly human, the occupier of the caverns long before Lawrence and the gang had taken possession. Helen Van Horton was positive she had smelled the thing when Bennett was murdered; and this woman, leader of desperate men, and director of desperate criminal coups, was now rapidly losing her superb nerve at the materialisation of a terror that had haunted her for years.

The millionaire was playing the harmonium in the alcove, having seated himself before it when his suggestion that they should dance to the music of the gramophone was not accepted with the usual enthusiasm. Near the wireless set Earle Lawrence was talking to the Princess, and, whilst trying to lighten the load of depression resting on the shoulders of Helen Van Horton, Lund noted that Lawrence was doing the talking, and that Natalie was listening attentively. At the card-table Sweet William was introducing Julia to jackpot poker, and really succeeding not merely in lightening her mental depression, but in taking it away altogether – for that evening at least.

"The Princess accepted the wireless report of the dreadful events in Naagrade very calmly, don't you think?" Helen was saying to Lund. Her manner suggested that she was thinking of other things, but embarked on this topic to make conversation.

"Yes – and no, Miss Van Horton," Lund said, frowning. "The news of King Boris having by a *coup de main* raised his wife to queenship was quite expected by the initiated. The opportunity occurred when the Princess disappeared. The consequent political situation evidently prevented Lawrence's emissaries from pressing their demands for ransom, so that the mass of the people soon thought that the Princess was lost to the country for ever. King Boris, undoubtedly, would see that such rumours were sent out. The most surprising event to the world, knowing the past history of the country, is its sudden overwhelming adoption of communism. Less surprising is the assassination of King Boris, his wife, and his family, because Boris from all accounts has long been asking for something of the sort."

"Yet the Princess will regain the throne," Helen said with more composure of manner. "She was so popular in her own country. She will only have to show herself to the people to be greeted with joy, and King Boris' murderers to be punished."

"I certainly think as you do," Lund agreed. "A carefully arranged *coup d'état* will place her very securely on the throne. Nevertheless, the way the people have dealt with her uncle must distress her very much. The lives lost! The lives of Boris and his family, the lives of his faithful followers, and the lives of the people who died in the street-fighting, can all be laid at the door of the man now talking to her with such outrageous coolness. Lawrence has a great deal to answer for."

"Yes, indeed," Helen said, suddenly faint, for she was recognising that she liked this fine, upstanding, clean-minded man. He was so like the man she had dreamed, the man who would take her from all contact, even from hateful memory, of the B., D. and C. Pack, and place her firmly on the rock of respectability by his side! If he knew! If he knew!

They both saw Natalie abruptly stand up. They saw Lawrence spring up a split-second later. They saw how the Princess, for quite an appreciable time, gazed into the brilliant eyes of the man with a fixity of expression decidedly peculiar. Without speaking, without any relaxation of her expression, Natalie turned away from him, and sauntering to an occasional table there picked up a magazine and idly turned its pages. When she joined Helen and Lund her demeanour was calm, if less buoyant than usual.

When Lund arranged her seat he said gravely: "I hope you will not permit the present conditions in Rolandia to distress you overmuch, Princess. Will you please accept our sincerest condolences?"

"I thank you, Mistaire Lund," she said, and suddenly, most surprisingly, smiled. "The people now merely are suffering from the mob fever which on beholding me will – what you say? – vanish. As for poor His Majesty, well, as say Mistaire Snell, those peoples who stretch their necks receive it in the neck. My uncle was a man of no niceness. No virtue had he, and only one accomplishment. He was of a swordsman superb. Yet he was of the fashion old. Old times, old weapons. Modern times call forth modern weapons. Had His Majesty been so expert with a gat as was he with a rapier, he might have lived."

"A gat!" murmured Raymond.

Natalie smiled wryly. "The Sweet William so names a pistol. Now a gat, now a gun, now a rod, now a – a corpse-producer. Of English I find so hard; Australian, it beats me to hell."

"May I join you, and talk of a purely private matter?" inquired Van Horton, suavely standing before them.

Natalie indicated a vacant chair, and with a bow the millionaire accepted it. He gave one swift glance about the room, saw that Earle Lawrence was at the wireless set, and then, speaking in a low tone, went on: "I have at last been able to prepare a plan of escape." Pausing, he watched the effect of his statement. Natalie's expression did not alter. Helen showed well-acted, suddenly flaring interest. The lids drooped over the deep grey eyes of Raymond Lund.

Then: "I have enlisted on our side the services of Everett. He was, I found, amenable both to reason and the prospect of becoming possessed of a sum of money which properly invested will make him independent for life."

"Oh, Pops, sweetheart!" Helen exclaimed. "How wonderful! Go on, please."

"He is willing to assist in several ways. According to the new-made roster of guards, he and Tuttman will be on duty at the entrance cave from midnight to four o'clock next Friday, the last day of February. Half an hour after he and the *chef* start guard he will overpower Tuttman, secure him expertly, and then from the kitchen make up small bunches of food and fill the several canvas water-bags in readiness.

"At that time the guard in the Cavern of the Sword will be Morgan, who, for a thousand pounds – he accepts my word to pay eventually when he is in hiding – will permit me to bind him, so that he can say he was overwhelmed by us. At one o'clock we join Everett, and then get three hours' start, wearing the sheepskin slip-overs the gang wore during Her Highness' abduction."

"Where do we escape to?" inquired Lund pertinently. "Even if we did secure a car, which is most unlikely, the roads are blocked with the metal spine things, as you remember."

Van Horton smiled with conscious superiority. "One moment! Let me explain everything," he urged. "Everett has it all arranged after we get away. By devious paths he will lead us to a water cache on the Cook-Eucla road. There one of us must walk through to Cook, give the alarm, and return as quickly as possible with some kind of transport. Before that comes to pass, Everett will make his escape to some destination where he will be safe both from the police and his late accomplices. What do you think of that?"

In turn he looked at them, his eyes gleaming with suppressed excitement. Natalie's eyes were veiled by drooping lids. Her small teeth were biting her nether lip. Helen sat with hands clasped and wide, very wide, eyes, in which was unfeigned admiration of her sire. Since Natalie made no remark, Lund observed, in his downright, practical way:

"The distance to Cook is at least seventy miles as the crow flies, and probably more via Everett's water cache. That being on the Cook-Eucla road, from here it must be at least twenty miles. So that the ladies will be obliged to walk twenty miles – it may be nearer thirty – through virgin bush in the heat of summer. Frankly, Van Horton, knowing the conditions, the hardships to which Her Highness, Miss Van Horton and her maid will be exposed, I think the handicap too big."

"There is nothing else for it," Van Horton countered readily. "Everett, who thoroughly knows the country, says that we can reach the water cache in three stages, each stage to be covered at night."

"This water cache, what is it?" the younger man asked, thinking rapidly.

"Everett says that at the time of Her Royal Highness' abduction the gang concealed some twenty-four gallon petrol tins filled with water at a spot which could be reached easily if the plan failed and they were forced to make a hurried get-away."

"Would it not be better, would it not be more certain of success, if you and I, or Snell and I, were to make our way to Cook and return with a relief party large enough to cope with the gang?"

"No relief party would get here without it being known by the gang," the American pointed out. "Being cornered, it is quite likely, too, that they would kill the ladies and dispose of the evidence by throwing it down the blow-hole shaft." Van Horton's voice became reproving. "We must remember, my dear Lund, that we are dealing with a desperate body of men who would surely stop at nothing to secure their own safety."

That, of course, Lund long had recognised. He saw, moreover, that Van Horton's plan was quite feasible, having behind it the cooperation of Blue Everett. He was not satisfied, however, that the presupposed three hours' start, before the next guard relief went on duty, would be sufficient to enable three women unused to walking to get clear away. He thought of a method of increasing the start and explained it, his natural caution well in evidence.

"If we could secure an automatic or a rifle, I could remain behind, and so dominate the entrance from the surface that I could keep the gang bottled up here for at least till the following night. That would enable the ladies to travel more slowly, and with consequently less fatigue."

For a little while Van Horton was silent. "Yes, you could do that," he said slowly. "It would be an exceedingly dangerous thing to do, but emphatically of lasting credit to you. I must see Everett and further the plan. He –"

"You need not to that trouble go."

"I beg Your Highness' pardon?" Van Horton said politely.

"I remark this play you needlessly act, Mistaire Van Horton, of Chicago, bootlegger, drug-smuggler, a – what is it? – a gangster, master criminal, and financier of this my abduction!"

Helen caught a stifled cry, beating it back in her throat with her hands pressed to her mouth. Lund was stiffened with astonishment. He watched Van Horton's face slowly assume the mask of absolute vacuity whilst he gradually rose from his chair.

"Are you – you cannot possibly be referring to me?" he said evenly, the shock having failed to affect his voice as it had failed to alter his facial expression.

"I refer to him who accomplice is of Mistaire Lawrence, to him who paid much money in preparing all this, and who is to pay the criminals beyond. I refer to Mistaire Van Horton, of a pretence a fellow-prisoner to be, he and his daughter criminal, so that affectionate friends will they to me become. You schemed of a great daring, trusting to my friendship to raise you to social heights and world renown. Sometimes the distance is of a greatness between the lips and the cup."

The situation was probably the most dramatic ever experienced by Lund. Also standing, his mind was fogged by these semi-revelations that required so much further explanation to make them clear. He did understand, however, their purport; and if he had required proof, he would have found it in Helen Van Horton's white face and wildly staring grey-green eyes. In them lay guilt starkly gleaming.

Her father spoke again, his control of mind and body hardened to steel. "The news from Rolandia has undoubtedly upset Your Highness."

"Of a littleness, yes. Your low deceit – and yours, too, my once so dear Helen – has upset me much more."

"May I ask who has been relating to you this fairy story?"

"Mistaire Lawrence."

"Ah! I wondered what was the subject of his recent discourse. So you believe the brigand, Princess, without permitting me any defence?"

"Why not? Mistaire Lawrence of a fullness explained to me what I knew three days ago."

"Knew three days ago! How? Who told you?"

"I am not used to answering questions. I them ask. I wish you to withdraw. Go!"

Helen sprang to her feet and stood beside Van Horton. They both met the almost blue-black, blazing eyes of Natalie, eyes that bored into their brains, stripped away the fleshy coverings of their souls, revealing them for every man, woman, and child in the world to gaze on and shudder.

"So you know, do you?" Helen Van Horton was now being aided by her years of training. Her voice was again the slow Virginian drawl of the aristocrat of the Southern States. Her poise was wonderful in the moment of her great defeat. Amidst the ruins of the edifice her dreams had created she stood to outstare a Princess Royal, her beautiful body stilled to marble, her lovely face unmoved by emotion.

Seated in the small leather-backed armchair, her hands lying idly on her lap, her body bolt upright, the Princess Natalie stared with unwinking eyes emitting a gleam of sky-blue ice. Her usually vivid face was now in repose, the calm expressionless repose of a judge. Only in her eyes was expression, the expression of her lovable father, her stern old grandfather, and all her ancestors from the saint to the poisoner.

Watching these two fascinated Lund. They represented the medieval and the modern, despotism and democracy, truth and deceit. Van Horton turned and quietly walked out into the dining-room. Helen Van Horton stood yet, and stared down at the small seated figure that was inexorably sending her deeper and deeper into the hell of her own making.

Helen's eyes at last faltered. Looking up again, she still encountered the unwinking blue-black orbs. Again she looked away. Once more her eyes found those unwinking pools of icy contempt boring into her soul. And then she broke. With a stifled sob she fled out of the room, through the dining-room, and beyond.

CHAPTER XXXII

LAWRENCE'S LOVE AFFAIR

THE cavern occupied by Van Horton was at the end of a short passage leading from the Cavern of the Sword. Midway along the passage a narrow winding corridor of but a few feet in length led to a small apartment occupied by Earle Lawrence.

Van Horton's room was comfortably, even sumptuously, furnished. Besides the plain iron bedstead there were a large table, two easy chairs, and two Windsor chairs, dressing-table, and wardrobe, as well as the knick-knacks usual in what of necessity was a bed-sitting-room. In fact, the furnishing of the living portion of this underground castle was excessively elaborate, considering the temporary nature of its intended occupancy. It indicated that in the Van Hortons and Earle Lawrence there was a desire for bodily comfort amounting almost to a passion, fed by many years of affluence.

With calm deliberation Van Horton removed his dinner-jacket, unstrapped the shoulder pistol holster, and donned a lounge jacket of tweed, to the pocket of which he transferred the automatic. Then from a leather steamer-trunk he produced whisky and soda, drank a stiff nobbler, replaced the bottle and glass, lowered the lid of the trunk, and then seated himself at the table with his face towards the entrance concealed with velvet hangings.

Only then did this American Emperor of Contraband permit himself to think. Even so, the subject-matter demanding thought rested on an unanswered question. The scene in the drawing-room, the revelation made by Natalie that she knew of the duplicity of himself and his daughter, was due to some loose-tongued fool, or deliberate traitor, who had informed her of it three days before. The unanswered question demanding insistently a clear-cut answer was: Why had Lawrence double-crossed him?

Seated there in the brilliantly-lit cavern, smoking a cigar with a deliberation that belied the seething anger, and glaring with a strange fixity of expression at the curtained entrance, the vital question hammered at Van Horton's brain. Why in the name of creation had Lawrence double-crossed him?

What was the fool to gain from such an act? Well, doubtless he would know presently. The explanation could and must wait. The present demanded defined and positive action; and, although he was sixty years old, his body still possessed its strength and his brain its youth.

At various times in his career there had been many who had double-crossed him. Some of the names recurred to him. They were the names of dead men. Of them all, not one man lived to boast of having crossed the Ace of the B., D. and C. Pack. And Earle Lawrence should not live to boast of it either.

From beyond the curtains came a swirl of movement, and his right hand darted to the pocketed pistol and transferred it to his lap, hidden by the table-edge. The action was almost mechanical. It had been completed, and his right hand lay idly on his knee when the curtains were swept apart and between them appeared his daughter.

She was breathing hard, as if she had run a race, and, seeing him seated, she moved slowly across the room, her eyes wide, her face paler than usual, her mouth straight and grim with a grimness that detracted much from her beauty.

"You appear to be in a hurry, my dear Helen," he said coolly.

"I ran here," she admitted.

"Why?" with slightly raised amused brows.

"Candidly, because I am frightened to death. You can have no idea of the horror which floods my mind of monkeys and things."

She shivered as though an icy wind blew through her evening dress of azure *crêpe-de-Chine*. He saw how her hands trembled when she took a cigarette from the box on the table. His were as steady as a rock whilst holding the match. She added, in a sudden burst of feminine indignation: "The brute is here, wandering about. At times I believe I smell it. The idiots search, and they must be blind or tired. It is here all right. How much longer are we to stay?"

"Will you have a drink?"

"I – well!" she sneered. "Well, you are a loving parent, to be sure. I come to you with every nerve throbbing with terror, and you ignore it and coolly ask me if I will have a drink. Yes, I will. Get it me, please."

"A drink is the sovereign remedy for all human troubles," he reminded her. "It steadies the nerves, it releases inspiration, it gives time for reflection." He mixed her a gin and vermouth, and, watching him, she saw that he vigilantly watched the entrance behind her. Realising that she had her back to the curtains, she moved her chair so that she could face both it and her father. When she drank, she did so as a man will when half dead with thirst.

"After many years of collaboration you disappoint me," he told her gently. "I had looked on you as the most resourceful woman, the coolest in a crisis, of any in the world. Now you are disintegrating, falling to pieces."

"So would you be falling to pieces had a monkey fallen on your head, pulled some of your hair out, and clawed and bit before it could be taken away. And the odour – faugh! I can smell it now. If I could see this thing to shoot at, if I knew just where it lurks, it would be different. It is the mystery hiding it, the uncertainty where it will kill next, that haunts me. How much longer are we to stay here?"

"Until the end of the month."

"Seven days?"

"Six, to be precise. On the seventh we embark at Eucla."

"What are we going to do – now?"

"Do you know why Lawrence made the Princess wise?"

"No. Do you?"

"Do you know who told her about us three days ago?"

"No. Do you?"

"I ask questions, my dear Helen, expecting to receive answers," he said in a reproving tone, but his grey eyes now held a green light, and green, not red, was the danger-signal she always recognised.

"No, I don't know. I cannot understand why he did it."

"Nor I. However, the fact is accomplished, and now there remains the final act of his extinction. By the way, what are your feelings towards our friend?"

"Somehow I liked Earle," she admitted with some hesitation. "In many ways he is brilliant. Certainly he is polished. Now I hate him – I hate him!"

Van Horton looked into her eyes, vividly and venomously green now, with the interest of a man who sees his child but seldom. He remarked the now steady light of the most powerful of emotions, saw the resolution burning as the sun, felt satisfaction that Helen was as Helen always had been – alluring when she purred, pitiless when governed by need to act for her own protection.

"You have your pistol?" was his next inquiry. He saw her hands flutter to her dress.

"Yes." The word was as sibilant as a gush of steam.

"Presently you will proceed to the apartment of Her Royal Highness and – ah! – induce her to sleep. She will have to go. I will deal with Lawrence. When he is dead the men can be bought. Inevitably follows the removal of Lund and Snell. The bodies we will have thrown into that most convenient blow-hole. Afterwards the ship will call at Eucla; we will go on board and sail away to Singapore. There we will arrange the play in which we are discovered by a certain friend in a cellar of a house to which he had been directed by a letter received through the post telling him of our plight. To the wondering world we shall describe our sojourn here in caves of vague location. We will tell of our short association with the Princess, of our sudden removal from the Nullarbor Plain, and of our long sea voyage locked in cabins."

Helen was looking at him whilst he talked, her eyes becoming ever more veiled. Without speaking, she selected another cigarette and lit it herself. When he had finished, she said: "Somehow, Pops, there are times when you surprise me. This is one of them."

"Indeed! Please elucidate," he requested politely.

"I can understand," she said in her more accustomed drawl, "your desire to exterminate Lawrence; but to kill the others for no reason, or, rather, without need, is – well, a waste of cartridges."

"Oh! What, then, do you propose?"

"You are growing old, Pops," she murmured, with actually a hint of real affection. "Why not explain to Natalie and the other two our somewhat embarrassing position – that is, after we have settled accounts with Lawrence and taken over the gang? We could issue an ultimatum. If the Princess, Raymond Lund, and his friend will give their words that they never will divulge what that traitor and Lawrence told them about us, and, in addition, will allow us to accompany them back to civilisation as fellow escapees, we shall be pleased to accompany them as friends. The gang can go as arranged on the ship, and be dealt with as arranged with your amiable Chinese friend."

"You have a charming imagination. But what if they decline to accept us as friends?"

"They will not decline when they know that refusal to meet us means death. Have you not seen the glances between the Princess and Lund? Of course, they are in love, although the difference in their social positions makes it impossible. Lund would give his word to save her, and she would not refuse hers to save him."

"Humph!" Van Horton lighted another cigar and pondered. When he spoke he was decided.

"To rely on a person's word, Helen, is to take a chance," he said. "People go to the horse races, and they play poker for money when they cannot afford it. They take chances. I firmly believe that only fools and suckers take chances, especially in business, very especially in our business. I have never taken chances in business, which is why I am a millionaire who has never been in prison. No, although I am getting old, as you just now kindly reminded me, I am not old enough to take a chance on people's words. Personal honour is not so shining a thing as it was a century ago. Ah! Here is Earle. Come in, Earle, and take a chair. Helen and I were discussing personal honour. She firmly believes in it. I maintain that honour, even among thieves, has fallen into disuse. Light a cigar and tell us what is on your mind, for you appear to be a much harassed man."

Van Horton spoke pleasantly enough, but there was on his face no smile of welcome, no expression of any kind. The mental turmoil, seething and boiling, was betrayed only by his eyes; and Lawrence recollected years before seeing that look when the millionaire learned of some defection among his men. The Australian smiled in his easy enigmatic way whilst he pulled a chair to the table and fell to lighting one of his long cheroots. Then, leaning back, he puffed with evident enjoyment and stared first at Van Horton and then at Helen.

"We are waiting for an explanation," she said softly.

"I thought you might be wondering why I decided to acquaint La Reine Natalie of your correct relations with us," Lawrence said with what was to them astounding calmness. "On more than one occasion, the last quite recently, I proposed honourable marriage to you, Helen. If there is but one decent thing in my life, it is my love for you. It is of that high degree of affection which spurs a man to offer marriage. A sordid temporary alliance would be but to insult not only yourself but my love for you."

"You have said something like that before," Helen drawled, and only half-heartedly affected to stifle a yawn.

"I believe I have," Lawrence said calmly. "My various proposals, I admit, have been declined to date. However, I still hope, matters being as they are. Had I permitted them to go on according to your plans I should have felt no hope of your acceptance whatever."

"You interest me. Proceed," barked Van Horton.

"The position now is not very dissimilar to what it has been from the moment the Princess reached this place. She found here a Mr. and Miss Van Horton, two identities very carefully built up from the ashes of Luke Sommers and Mary, his daughter, so well known to the underworld of New York and Chicago. To-night she, as well as Lund and his pal, know you very intimately. They do not yet know that you are just as much prisoners here as they are, and you will not seduce the allegiance of my men, no matter what price you offer them. Do you understand all that?"

"Perfectly, my dear Earle, perfectly," Van Horton murmured, one hand hidden by the table-edge, the other at times taking the cigar from his mouth. "Motive, however, is absent so far. What is your motive?"

"Marriage with Helen."

"What a persistent man it is!" Helen drawled, her features curved into a smile of delighted humour but her green-lit eyes almost hidden by lowered eyelids.

"Yes, aren't I?" acquiesced Lawrence, smiling back with his face and returning her look with a wide, calculating gaze. "You see, Helen – I have to insist on calling you Helen, because it suits you so much better than Mary – you have to marry me. Until you do, I shall always suffer as I have suffered now for years. The men will leave Eucla on the first of next month, and Captain Black will land them at Fremantle. I rather fancy Fremantle in preference to Singapore. There are fewer Chinamen with their accompanying knives. Our men will go ashore as sailors on leave, and I shall be obliged to remain in the engine-room as second engineer, as the chief will wish to visit relations.

"You, too, will be obliged to remain on board – you, Van Horton, securely locked up; you, Helen, to await the arrival of the minister. I shall produce the special licence which I obtained some time ago; we shall be married, and the next day the ship will clear Fremantle on her long run to Durban. There, Van Horton, you may go ashore, and start for any place you please. My wife and I will come back to Australia, where we will settle down in the home of my fathers and contentedly devote ourselves to the production of wool."

"Very simple and well thought out. I like your concise manner, Earle," Van Horton said with suddenly raised brows. "However, what do you propose to do with the – er – other prisoners?"

"They will be induced to remain here twenty-four hours after we have left, when Lund will doubtless arrange for a rescue party to convey the Princess to Cook. I have already sent word to Ah Khan to bring his camels to transport us to Eucla, and also sent word to my ordained friend in Perth to meet us on our arrival there."

"What I am wondering is what makes you so confident that when we reach Perth I shall marry you," Helen remarked almost casually.

"You will, of course, promise to marry me before we leave Eucla," Lawrence pointed out patiently.

"Yes. But supposing I refuse to make any such promise?"

"In that case both of you will be left behind, and Captain Black will steam to some other port so far unnamed. In which case I am quite sure Lund will make affairs with you very unpleasant. Fifteen years, I expect, because when your part is known you will never escape from Australia. In fact, you will never escape from the Nullarbor Plain save in custody."

From the ruins of her dream, the beautiful multicoloured edifice she had erected wherein she was the friend of a reigning Queen, there arose bar by iron bar, behind which she sat year after year to grow old and haggard and broken. How thankful she was that within a cunningly concealed pocket in her gown there lay an automatic! In her heart burned a steadily growing hate.

"Well, Helen, what are your views? Will you consent to marry Earle?" inquired Van Horton blandly.

"No! No, I will not," she replied with sudden shrillness, her eyes wide-open and blazing. And then Van Horton's hidden hand came up over the edge of the table with almost the speed of light, and Earle Lawrence came to gaze down the sinister tube of the automatic.

"You have double-crossed me, my dear Earle," the millionaire said with surprising softness of voice. "No man has ever done that and lived. I am going to kill you and then carry out a little plan Helen and I have arranged. You are a dirty double-crossing dog."

Earle Lawrence's face was slightly white and his eyes were held as those of a snake-charmed mouse. Above the line of the pistol-barrel he saw the twin green lamps of hate.

A second. Another second. Yet another second passed. Then Van Horton pressed the trigger.

No report ensued to shatter the stillness of those tense moments. No sudden darkness quenched the soul of Lawrence with the crashing of a bullet into his brain. He sighed relief, but made no attempt to produce his own pistol. Van Horton savagely pressed the trigger again, but the weapon made no response. And then, dazed with the totally unexpected contretemps, he very slowly released the catch and withdrew from the pistol-butt the clip of nickel-plated bullets set in their brass shells.

The fact that Lawrence continued inactive caused both him and Helen as much surprise as had the failure of the weapon. Now he was regarding them with superciliously raised brows and amused eyes. When he spoke it was in his easy pleasant drawl.

"Try Helen's pistol, Van Horton," he suggested.

Van Horton saw Helen push her weapon along the table towards him, but he knew when he was beaten. Yet even in defeat the millionaire was master of himself. With unshaking hands he struck a match and lit a fresh cigar.

"Some time ago I considered it advisable to substitute cartridges which did not contain any explosive material," Lawrence said when slowly he pushed back his chair preparatory to rising to his feet. "Even so, I took a risk. You might well have discovered the trick and taken steps to replace the dead with the living, so that the living might die." To

Helen he spoke direct: "I will ask for my answer in three days. Good night! Three days, remem –"

The quietude of that room was shattered by the sudden continuous booming of the large bronze dinner-gong.

CHAPTER XXXIII

ALARMS

THE electrically-controlled strikers fitted against the heavy brass Burmese gong beat so rapid a tattoo that the sound of each stroke was merged into one vibrating note that boomed through every corridor to the furthest extremity of the House of Jewels.

The sound of the alarm brought Earle Lawrence to a halt at the entrance to Van Horton's room. It stilled into immobility the hand that carried the cigar to the mouth of Van Horton, and it made Helen shrink back and down into her chair. It awakened Julia. She sprang from her bed in Helen's room to find herself alone, and, in temporary panic, she ran out to the Cavern of the Sword, saw Sir Knight standing at the passage leading to the Cavern of the Skeleton, noted that he held revolver in one hand and torch in the other, and then she dashed in on Natalie sitting up in her bed, her pistol tightly gripped under cover of the bedclothes.

Tortured by the predicament, indignity, and possible physical danger sweeping on the Princess, and tormented by his powerlessness to escape and bring a rescue party, Raymond Lund was lying on the mattress placed for him on the floor, and smoking a cigarette. The swelling roar of the alarm brought him upright to a sitting posture, but failed to awaken Sweet William, who snored softly but persistently.

The very first stroke brought Bussey to his feet. In the guard-room he had just fallen asleep. Blue Everett was with him on the instant. Morgan, who was on guard, stood in the passage leading to the kitchen, his automatic gripped tightly in his right hand, a flash-lamp in his left, his face suddenly drained of its brick-red colour.

Such was the effect of the sudden strident alarm on the nerves of a set of people over whom the terror had fallen – terror of the indefinable unknown agency that had killed two of their number and lurked invisibly to make its next killing.

Men were there afraid of nothing, men by whom the paralysing emotion of fear never had been felt, men willing and prepared to face anything without thought of personal extinction. Now they were white-faced victims of fear, through whom ran the quicksilver of panic. Perhaps the most phlegmatic person there was William Snell, but he was of that unimaginative type that makes the very best soldiers and policemen.

Rubbing the sleep out of his small eyes, he looked at Lund with blank, expressionless face.

"Things happening," he said, in pure statement. "The little old gong makes a row, now doesn't it?"

"Why don't they shut off the confounded thing?"

"Too stonkered with surprise, I'll bet, Captain. Let's do a get to the Cavern of the Sword. Perhaps there'll be a gathering of the clans there. Watch, and if one of us gets a chance to slide off into the kitchen, he may manage to get out and away."

"Come on, then," Lund responded eagerly. "If I manage it, remember the Princess is left in your care, Bill. And if anything happens to her or to you while I'm away, I'll – I'll –"

"Steady, Captain, steady! Everything will come out all right in the end, if this gorilla or ghost thing don't bump us off. I'll bet you a quid I pinch a pistol off one of 'em within the next hour."

"I take you, Snell, because I'll gladly lose a pound to get my hands on a nice comfortable automatic," agreed Lund viciously.

Together they left and hurried along the short twisting passage that debouched into the Cavern of the Sword. They entered it along with the Van Hortons, and met there Lawrence, Natalie, Julia, Bussey and Sir Knight. Lawrence was asking Bussey about the alarm placed in the passage between that cavern and the kitchen.

"Correct, sir," Bussey reported in his clear, precise, military way.

"So is that in the passage leading to my quarters," Lawrence announced. "Sir Knight, remain here. You and I, Bussey, will investigate towards the inner caverns. Perhaps, gentlemen, you would like to accompany us?"

He addressed Lund and Sweet William. Van Horton he ignored, and when Lund said he would remain to keep the ladies company Lawrence flashed a smile before he followed Bussey and Snell into the passage. Van Horton would have followed, but Sir Knight intercepted him.

"No orders to let you pass, Mr. Van Horton," Sir Knight said in his habitual easy and casual manner.

"Don't be stupid. Make way!" commanded the millionaire.

"Better stay put!" drawled the ex-cowboy, and the revolver that had been dangling from a forefinger by its trigger-guard became unswervingly still, the muzzle pointing directly at the centre of Van Horton's forehead. For three seconds, whilst the others watched with bated breath, Van Horton stared at the lounging Sir Knight; then, without further speech, abruptly turned and walked towards his own room.

With his going there fell a significant silence in the Cavern of the

Sword, a silence not without its embarrassment to Raymond Lund. Helen looked at the Princess, and was about to say something when she saw Natalie's violet-blue eyes gazing blankly over her right shoulder. To Natalie, Helen no longer existed.

Lund watched the blood slowly mount into the American woman's face, witnessed the upward surge of anger based on realisation that she was still out of favour. He expected a burst of words, but when Helen did speak it was to say sharply to Julia, standing near the Princess: "Julia! Come with me."

And with this order she turned slowly, walked to the entrance of her room, and disappeared.

The French girl looked pathetically at Natalie, as though she awaited permission to obey her mistress' order. It surprised Lund. He was further surprised when Natalie smiled at Julia and nodded in the direction of Helen's room. Julia curtsied and left them.

It was then that the Princess sighed inaudibly. Lund knew that she sighed with sudden relief at the going of Helen, and saw yet another facet of Natalie's versatile character. Helen had hurt the Rolandian lady in a way that she had never suffered before, and because of this he yearned to take her in his arms and smooth away the hurt with healing kisses. Raymond was swayed by his emotions in those days as never before in his life.

"Shall we steal along to Tuttman and persuade him to make us a cup of his delicious coffee, Princess?" he asked her with a trace of wistfulness in his voice.

"But yes, Mistaire Lund," she agreed instantly. "Remember you not that other night so late we robbed of the pantry in your father's house? We found a cold leg of bacon, eh, my playmate of the long ago? You to the attack went with a table-knife, and I the bread did butter."

"You broke a glass," he accused her.

"Nervous was I. You were gone to the cellar to fetch a bottle of wine. I feared the so terrible *chef* would awake and find me. Dear, dear! Well, to Mistaire Tuttman now we go."

When in the straight passage leading to the kitchen, she impulsively caught at his arm and stopped him. "Julia! You know not the dainty Julia is not of this gang is?" she asked.

"Not a member of the gang?"

"No. Julia in Paris was when in Helen's service she became," Natalie explained in her quaint way. "In Perth they left her when the Van Hortons were kidnapped, bah! by the so terrible Earle Lawrence. Afterwards Helen wrote. Julia was asked to come in special car. She knew not the baseness of Helen and of her father so bad."

"Does she know now?"

"Of a certainty. It is when thieves come to pieces that girls of a goodness learn much."

Lund had to smile, and she saw the twinkle in his eyes. Her expression changed from vivacity to sorrow, and with haste he apologised. "I did not mean to be rude," he explained contritely. "But your mixing of the quotation was so original. You mean: 'When thieves fall out honest men come by their own'?"

"Of a certainty. My English is of a mixture. Alas! it is the language of Australia which confuses me. Yes, like hell."

They both laughed at and with each other, and in that moment Natalie experienced once again the joy she felt when staying with Sir Henry and Lady Lund. Side by side they moved on towards the kitchen.

Again the Princess stopped when they reached the wide patch of sand concealing one of Snell's alarms. A small square of cardboard gave notice of its position. For a second Natalie looked down on the white smoothed grains that bore no track of human foot or boot. From it she looked up into Lund's face, her eyes dancing with quickly fired mischief, as those of a small boy confronted with irresistible temptation. Before he could speak she had swiftly stepped on the concealed contact-plates.

Immediately their ears were assailed by the deep thunder of the gong in the kitchen ahead. It vibrated and rolled from side to side of passage and cavern and cave, beating on them as the wings of a flock of angry gulls.

Blankly Lund regarded his companion facing him, her hands clapped against her ears, her lips parted in laughter drowned by the gong. And then sudden silence.

"The so bad Helen will throw a seven," Natalie said, still laughing.

At her mastery of the Australian language Lund was compelled to laugh. He suspected the teaching of Sweet William, who invariably used the expression in describing the effect of some surprise on a person who went into a fit or suddenly died. Doubtless Snell would explain that with one die no normal person could throw more than six.

Then upon them came Tuttman armed with automatic and torch. Dressed in trousers and shirt, walking with bare feet, the absence of his *chef's* spotless uniform accentuated his leanness, reduced his dignity.

"Oh, Mistaire Tuttman!" Natalie burst out, penitent on the surface only. "The alarm I forgot. With my foot I trod upon it."

"Thank 'eavens! I thought the gorilla was coming. Can I do anything for you, Marm?"

"But yes, my so dear Mistaire Tuttman," Natalie cooed. "I would take of your coffee so delicious."

"Marm, I am your servant. I was making coffee when you trod on that alarm. Come this way, Your Highness."

"In your kitchen we will drink it," decided Natalie.

Tuttman bowed deeply, tried to smile, failed, and led the way to his kingdom.

CHAPTER XXXIV

SEVERAL MYSTERIES

UNTIL he had donned his artistically starched cap, a white linen coat, and a spotless apron, Alfred Tuttman was not comfortable. Arrayed in the regalia of his vocation, he served coffee with far more reverence than the tenth generation butler of a tenth earl would pour out 1680 Chablis.

"Does the *chef* at your palace make coffee like that, Marm?" he asked whilst Natalie was sipping from her cup. As a matter of fact, Tuttman *was* a cook and he *could* brew coffee.

The Princess shook her head, and for a moment there was in her eyes a far-away expression. She was comparing life at the Palace of Naagrade with the days now being spent below the surface of the Nullarbor Plain, and those former days amid pomp and splendour, days of continuous self-repression, did not compare favourably.

"Because he can't, Marm, don't indicate he's a poor cook," the *chef* explained, standing a little back from the table against the electric stoves. "Only them blokes with the artistic temperament can make coffee as it should be made."

He was quite serious, and Lund forbore to smile. The situation there in Tuttman's kitchen was so natural that it did not seem possible that Natalie was a Royal Princess, if not Queen of Rolandia by succession. The unique was becoming commonplace, because she knew intuitively how to adapt herself to circumstances.

"I suppose the others are all away searching for the thing which caused the alarm, Tuttman?" Lund asked, for Natalie seemed lost in a brown study.

"All except Blue Everett and Morgan, who are on guard out there," and Tuttman nodded towards the outer or entrance cave. "Also Sir Knight is in the Cavern of the Sword."

So even in such a crisis Earle Lawrence took no chance of losing his prisoners by relaxing his outer guard. "If you will permit me, Princess, I should like to speak with Mr. Everett," he said. "May I?"

"But certainly," she answered readily.

Lund walked away to the passage leading to the entrance cavern with the intention of testing the real strength of the most important guard. The opportunity had never before been so conveniently presented. Entering the passage, he saw that it was straight for twelve or fourteen yards, and that he could see its full length. At the further end, seated in a chair, was the well-knit figure of Blue Everett. Without haste, he sauntered towards Everett, and had proceeded two yards when he espied the small sheet of cardboard denoting the alarm hidden in the sand-patch immediately below it.

Avoiding the alarm, he went on a further seven or eight yards, when he came to a broad, white-painted mark from wall to wall. He was then fifteen feet from the seated sentry. Several times before, when he, with the others, had gone to the surface for air and natural light, he had crossed the painted mark; and, on questioning Lawrence about it, had been informed that beyond it no unauthorised person was permitted to go.

Here, at the edge of it that night, Blue Everett called sharply: "Halt!"

Lund halted, and smiled in friendly fashion at Blue Everett. The sentry eyed him keenly, the hand holding the automatic resting on his knee.

"Good evening, Everett!" Raymond said civilly, but with sinking heart when he recognised the impossibility of disobeying the order, or the certainty of death if he rushed his man. And behind Everett waited Morgan. "The alarms are active to-night, and I thought I could come along and tell you that the second alarm was caused by the Princess, who inadvertently trod on contact-plates when we came along to Tuttman for a cup of coffee."

"Where are Lawrence and Bussey, and the rest?" Everett asked calmly, but with anxious face.

"They have gone into the farthest caverns, to investigate the cause of the first alarm. It is an extraordinary thing that we can't find the monkey, or whatever it is which leaves those strange tracks. However, as you are unable to be friendly, I'll return to Her Royal Highness. Good night!"

Everett did not reply, and on his way back to the kitchen Lund felt the hard blue eyes beneath the light red brows boring into his back. He reached the kitchen the moment Snell and Lawrence entered.

"Did you find the so strange beast?" Natalie asked with lowered lids.

"No, Highness," replied Lawrence, laughing nervously. "A chunk of rock, loosened by moisture, had fallen from the roof on to the alarm put down in the passage this side of the end cavern where is the power plant. We have had our trouble and our fright for nothing. The second alarm was caused by your stepping on the plate near-by, seemingly. There was your Royal Highness' footmark. Hallo! Bussey not here!"

Snell looked about as though Bussey might have shrunk to the size of a rabbit. "Hanging behind somewhere," he suggested.

"Take coffee," Natalie ordered. "Of a thirst you must be. Yes, the second alarm fault was mine."

"Of us all you seem the least upset, Princess. I admit I am anxious. I do hate mystery."

"My mind drilled is by mystery, Mistaire Lawrence," Natalie said softly, steel in her voice. "For many nights I wonder and wonder why the colour of the hangings is the same as the colour of the dresses of the so clever Helen Van Horton. Then behold! Gone is the mystery, smashed to fragments, when two, three days ago a little birdie in the bush whisper things to my ear. Blue, royal blue, is Helen's colour of favour."

"Well, that is one mystery solved, Highness."

"There are more left."

"Pardon, Princess! What of the beast that has disturbed us so much lately?"

"That is not of a mystery to me."

"Indeed!" Lawrence and Lund were frankly astonished.

"I'd sleep sounder if Your Royal Highness would tell where it is to be found," Snell put in grimly.

"If you know, Princess, tell us," Lawrence urged.

"I am not of those who over the back walls unfold tales of scandal. There is also another mystery which to me a mystery is not."

"Perhaps you will explain this second mystery, then," Lawrence suggested sharply.

"But no. The explanation awaits your seeking. It is of a peculiarity that Mistaire Bussey is unarrived, do not you think?"

Lawrence stiffened where he stood. "Bussey certainly should be here," he said, looking first at Snell and then at Lund. To Snell he added: "He was behind you, wasn't he?"

"Too right, he was. Hard on my heels. He was kind of nervous of being left. I didn't feel none too bright myself."

"Possibly he's gone to talk with Van Horton. If you will excuse me, Princess, I'll make sure."

"You may go. Mistaire Lund, escort me. I would retire." Turning to the *chef*, Natalie said sweetly: "I thank you for the coffee, Mistaire Tuttman. I wish you good night."

Tuttman bowed deeply, and when they had all left the kitchen he started to hum "Now the day is ended". And whilst humming that sweet hymn he methodically and expertly sharpened a long knife on a longer steel. It was as though the act of sharpening a knife fed his imagination.

Arrived at the Cavern of the Sword, Lawrence strode at once to Sir Knight seated with his face towards the passage leading to the innermost caverns. "Did you notice which way Bussey went?" he asked.

"Bussey! Bussey hasn't come back yet," replied Sir Knight.

"Hasn't come back!"

"That's what I said. He never came back with you and Mr. Snell. And he hasn't come back since."

"Suffering cats!"

"What's up?"

"When last did you see Bussey?" Lawrence demanded of Sweet William.

"Somewhere as we passed through the Junction Cavern, as far as I remember. He ain't that handsome that I want to keep looking at him. I told him there he'd better go ahead of me and after you, but you were then so far ahead that he thought, I suppose, I might dong him one. Suspicious gent, Bussey, very."

"You two stay here. I'm going to find him. If I call Sir Knight, come at once."

"You bet!"

Lawrence walked hurriedly away through the twisting, uneven corridor. They watched him as though they never would see him again. Natalie turned wordlessly away and entered her room. Snell leaned against an abutment of rock and filled his pipe. The match had just flared when seemingly far away they heard Lawrence shout. Sir Knight, followed by Lund and Snell, rushed through the passage.

They found Lawrence beyond the blow-hole near to the Junction Cavern. He was leaning against the wall, staring at a sand-patch. There were two distinct impressions of a great naked foot with prehensile toes.

"The thing's here!" he said, impotent anger shaking his voice. "By gad! Back to your post, Sir Knight! Jump to it!"

The lank man bolted. Lawrence addressed Lund.

"Will you two stay here while I go on?"

Lund nodded and began to examine the passage. Lawrence ran on. Snell looked about almost idly, but his gleaming eyes were as magnifying lenses. A few seconds later he drew Lund's attention to fresh bloodstains on the floor of the passage a few feet distant from the blow-hole.

"I reckon Mister Bussey has been called to the Orderly Room," he said expressionlessly.

"By gad, Snell! This is getting over the odds."

"Funniest doings I've ever come across," Snell agreed. He walked to the edge of the blow-hole and there laid himself down with his head over the wide orifice and listened. Not a sound came up from the awful depth; the only sound was the faint hum of the dynamo.

Lawrence came racing back, to stand with them breathing hard, but voiceless. Snell pointed to the rock slab on which were the fresh bloodstains. Stooping, Lawrence looked at them closely. When again he glanced at Snell it was to see him standing at the edge of the blowhole. His right hand was held over it, the fingers closed, the thumb pointing downward as emperors have signified death to the conquered.

CHAPTER XXXV

CHAINED AS A DOG

THE disappearance of Bussey put an end to the circumscribed freedom permitted Raymond Lund and his friend Sweet William. It was apparent that the decision had been reached only after much thought, for it was not until early the next morning that Lawrence, accompanied by Blue Everett and Morgan, entered their cavern, and at the point of automatics ordered them to stand up and not move. Each man was handcuffed by one hand to a length of light steel chain which was padlocked to a stout stalactite forming a complete pillar from roof to floor. In length the chains were some eight feet, so that movement was not wholly restricted.

"Why are you doing this?" Lund asked irritably.

"Because, Lund, I have reached the conclusion that it is probable Snell killed Little, Bennett, and now Bussey," Lawrence answered, with what was the first sign of hostility in his voice. "Snell was sitting at the table with Bennett when he was murdered; he was also in the passage with Bussey when he disappeared. They two were behind, far behind me, because the second alarm caused me to hurry. Suspicion, therefore, is settled on him, and this precaution is taken that you may not aid and abet him."

For several seconds Lund looked at Sweet William, shocked by the suggestion made by Lawrence, faced for the first time by the thought that Snell might be guilty of these killings. That Snell was in any way responsible had never occurred to him. But now ...!

Lawrence spoke again when the automatic was hidden within his coat. He spoke directly to Snell: "If I knew you had committed these murders, if I had positive proof, I would shoot you down this instant. I have been as decent as I could to you – permitted you to move about without a guard. Perhaps I have been a fool."

"You talk like old Major Simmonds, at Yatata prison, when a prisoner was took before him on charge," Snell said, indignation revealed in his gleaming eyes. "As a matter of fact, you have pinched a Princess off a train, as any other bandit might do; your men shot down old Baron Schulz in cold blood, and killed several detectives in doing their duty. Even if I had corpsed the said gents they and you've got no kick coming."

"The detectives were killed in fair fight!" Lawrence said angrily.

"The Baron Schulz was killed as you threaten to kill Snell," Lund pointed out quietly. "I may say that had I been in possession of a pistol and saw the faintest chance of getting out of this place to bring rescue to the Princess, I would have shot sleeping men if I thought they would become a danger when they awoke. When you turned brigand, Lawrence, you put yourself outside all rules of honour and decency."

"I think there I will agree with you. Such being the position, you will not be surprised if I decide some time to shoot you or have you poisoned. Think that over." Lawrence and his two followers then left.

"I wonder if they will send someone with a cup of Tuttman's coffee," remarked Snell after a long silence.

"It may be poisoned," Lund reminded him, once more looking at Snell as though it were the first time they had met.

"Nope. Lawrence is a gunman, not a poisoner. Van Horton, now, is a born poisoner. Morgan is not a poisoner. Poison would not appeal to him as much as a sandbag or an automatic. Larsen kills with anything handy, poison if necessary; but Blue Everett is a clean killer. Guns only with him."

"You appear to be entitled to a chair in Criminology."

"Maybe. I've studied criminals inside and outside of gaols," Snell went on, unabashed by Lund's cutting remark. "You can tell by the shape of blokes' heads what they are inclined to do, even before they do it."

"Oh! And what do you read by the shape of my head?"

Snell grinned broadly. He lit his before-breakfast pipe before he replied. "You are like Blue Everett, Captain. When you get going, anything you can pick up will do as a weapon. To get going you've got to be riled, and once riled, hell won't stop the doings. There isn't many of your sort what sees the inside of quod. Me, now. There is more blokes hanged, and electrocuted, and garrotted and guillotined, with heads like mine than any other sort. We generally use our hands to kill. We like to feel our victims throw a seven."

"You're a bloodthirsty ruffian, Bill," Lund said, with a return to his affectionate manner. "Now, what do you know about the deaths here of these men?"

"If I don't tell you nothing, I don't tell you no lies."

"Then you did kill them? Yes or no! Did you?"

"No."

Yet Lund was not satisfied. Snell was not looking him in the eyes when he said "No". And he said it in a manner that implied the uselessness of persistence.

Breakfast was brought them by the deaf and dumb mess-waiter.

After that the hours dragged away wearily, for there was no interesting method of passing the time. Dinner was brought, and at ten o'clock, since no one came to them, they turned in with the lights switched off.

That first night of captivity was passed in deep slumber, undisturbed by dreams and vague hauntings. Lund awoke when a new day shone on the plain above, easier in his mind now that he half suspected Snell of being the mysterious terror-inspiring monster. If he was, then assuredly Natalie was safe. She had said that the thing was to her a mystery no longer. Had Snell confided in her? Anyway, it was the danger to which she, with everyone else, was exposed, which had worried and frightened him.

The day dragged, timed by the arrival of meals. Lund sent a written request for books, but the request was ignored. He and Snell had discussed the situation of themselves, the probable treatment of the Princess, and the final outcome of the whole affair till exhaustion bade them cease, and they ended where they had begun.

Again they slept, and whilst the third day wore away, towards the third night resentment rose in the heart of Raymond Lund, the peacefully-disposed, law-abiding, hard-to-anger South Australian.

That night he lay awake for hours, listening to the regular snoring of Sweet William, inclined savagely to waken the snorer, annoyed with himself for thinking of matters that defied slumber, slowly becoming inflamed with rage and hate against Lawrence, who had proved himself so magnificent a general, and the men who unswervingly carried out the accepted iron discipline.

His own impotence enraged him most of all. He lashed himself with a whip of a thousand thongs for hesitating to risk his life even in the face of certain annihilation. Chained to the pillar of rock with an unbreakable chain, whilst the woman he loved might well be suffering indignities, might be even then facing death!

That was what he was coming to fear. Why Lawrence had told Natalie of the real part being played by Van Horton, and what the final result of the revelation was to be, were problems then driving him frantic. Throwing himself into the personality of Earle Lawrence, he saw no manner of gain from returning the Princess to civilisation and releasing his other captives. Such a course would always be a danger to him, Earle Lawrence, who doubtless would see sounder logic in the proposition that the dead tell no tales.

The hours passed slowly, unmarked by daylight and starlit nights – one long, brilliantly-lighted period of time divided by meals and sleep.

"It's no use worrying, Captain," Snell said repeatedly.

"How the hell can I help worrying?" Lund fiercely retorted. To which Snell offered soothing advice.

"Try and be like me. Everything comes to the gent who has got the habit of waiting. Our turn'll come, and when it does we'll enjoy ourselves all the more."

And then came the night when Raymond Lund awoke in pitch darkness in the perplexing and annoying state of mind of one who has omitted to remember an important task left undone. For minutes he twisted and turned, his mind drugged with sleep, yet prodded by the pointed iron of the sin of omission.

What was it he had forgotten that he should have remembered? Was it anything Snell had said? Snell, with his criminals and head-shapes and methods of murder. Decent fellow, Bill Snell! Clever, too, in his way. Could find a pin in a dark room. How old Sir Henry had laughed when Snell showed him the way to manipulate a pack of cards! And afterwards Sir Henry had written to the Chief Secretary urging a better handcuff than those used by the police. How easily had Snell broken the locks of those placed around his wrists, using a trick no observer was quick enough to see!

Wide-awake, Lund was sitting up on his mattress. That was it! For days they had been handcuffed to a rock column when Snell could have released them both at any moment he chose. Why had he not remembered that? Why had not Snell spoken of it, reminded him? The imbecile, the fathead! In so desperate a situation they both were justified in rushing the guard, with the faint hope of one escaping to bring a rescue.

"Bill!" he called softly.

Snell made no reply. Lund found, with rising unreasoning anxiety, that he could not hear Sweet William snoring, even his breathing. The silence, added to the intense darkness, pressed in upon him as a weight.

"Snell! Wake up, man! Switch on the light! You know I can't reach the switch, as my chain is a fraction shorter than yours. Damnation! Bill – do you hear me?"

"I hear the so bad swear."

In his yellow silk pyjamas, with a flame-coloured stripe, Lund blinked his dazed eyes when the electric bulbs blazed, and presently he saw, standing by the switch near the entrance, the Princess Natalie. Calmness settled on him as a mantle, the calm of hopeless resignation to a situation utterly beyond him. The voice he heard he barely recognised as his own.

"Will your Royal Highness tell me why you are here?"

"I came the watch to keep."

"To keep watch! Do you know what has become of Snell?"

From her, his eyes went back to his friend's empty bed, and saw on it the glittering opened handcuff, its lock evidently smashed. When his eyes flashed back once more to Natalie he saw that she was standing in an attitude of expectancy, as though she strained her hearing to catch an expected sound. Her eyes were very dark at that instant, whilst the lines about her mouth were straighter than usual, making it appear very grim.

Then she said softly: "Hush, Mistaire Lund! Of a lowness speak. The big great gorilla is beyond, creeping on its prey."

"Then it is Snell?"

"Of a wonder is he. With one hand can he a man strangle; with two a man's neck can he break."

"Natalie!" The name was wrenched from him by the surprise and the horror of her revelation. And to that was added the visible expression of her implacable hatred.

"They pay – the murderers of the so poor Baron Schulz. He so gentle, and to me so good. Pay they do, one by one. I grieve they die so quick and of such silence, Mistaire Lund."

"Why, do you know, did not Snell awake and release me? Why has he hidden his actions from me? Why did he deny responsibility for the thing he had done and now is doing?"

The frozen stare of hate suddenly melted into a dawning smile that caused his pulses to leap. "We talked, the so strong Snell and I, oh, so soft! He it was who heard the Van Horton's plan to rescue me of a make-believe after he and you were of the dead. To me he told it, saying that he had decided to kill one by one, to create the spirit of great monkey so to strike terror into their hearts so black. He told it me when saw he I too feared the gorilla, and then I caused him to promise me to receive my help when wanted.

"You see, Mistaire Lund, though shocked you are, Snell's plan was only the plan to work. Remember you the guard that never slumbers. To fight openly was of a hopelessness. He knew death to you would result. He knew if you knew you would forbid his method. He say with rightness you are too honourable to fight murderers as a murderer. And so to fight was the only way.

"But half of an hour since he came into my chamber and in the darkness awoke me. And I a virgin maid! In the dark I dressed, and as I dressed he told me he had killed Sir Knight on guard beyond my chamber, and planned to creep on the half-caste, and the so beast Morgan. You were of a certainty asleep, and chained still to the rock."

"Why? Why, Princess?"

"For safety," she answered his frenzied exclamation simply. "One by one he kill. In the dark he sees. Of a silence does he move. In his hands they die without complaint, without noise. You free, they hear you, see you, shoot you. Oh! they must not you shoot. I – I – Mistaire Snell grieved would be you die of shots."

"So I am to be kept chained like a dog in case my carcass is punctured!" Raymond almost shouted, his heart over-flowing with the knowledge of her concern for him, his mind frantic from forced inactivity. "Please find me a stone or a hammer or something to smash this chain. Help me to get free – please, please, please!"

She made no effort to accede to his wish, remaining still, calmly waiting with strained hearing for any sound from without. Impotent anger in him became maniacal fury. He wrenched and tugged at the chain with seeming force enough to snap his arm. His brain was clouded with a crimson fog – to be wiped away by the touch of her hands on one of his.

"Wait – wait!" she implored. "Understand not? Mistaire Snell, he will return and chain up himself. Already he kill Sir Knight in the Cavern of the Sword. Now he is in the Cavern of the Wheel. He kill Peter Cuff and Morgan. He come back. In the morning three dead men; many, many tracks on the sand he make by trick with his hands; and he chained up like the dog. Mistaire Lawrence, he see Mistaire Snell. He know nothing. Fearful is he. Next night Mistaire Snell go again. One by one they –"

From a long way off came the sharp roar of an automatic pistol. The sound broke off Natalie's stream of explanation; it stiffened Lund into a stone image. Someone, a man, shouted. In the kitchen the gong was struck, beaten, and thrashed by a madman. Sound! Pandemonium! Death loose and rampaging in company with the grinning monster men call Fear.

Very slowly the electric light went out, down, finally died, leaving Natalie and Lund blanketed in the ensuing unrelieved darkness. Natalie waited, voiceless, motionless, a strange chill running up and down her back. She heard Lund say softly, almost as though physical pain prevented normal tones:

"Bill! They've got Bill Snell! And I – I'm like a dog chained to a rock. For my safety! Ye gods! For my safety! Oh, cannot you get me free? I can't stay here. Don't you understand? I can't stay here now they've got Bill Snell."

He was trembling violently, even whilst his strength gathered for a last supreme onslaught on the chain. He heard Natalie sob, and wondered, in a queer detached way, why she sobbed. He felt her hands clinging to his, knew that her fingers were moving over the handcuff encircling his wrist. There came to his drumming ears a sharp click, and the next moment he was free.

"Go!" Natalie whispered. Then: "No! No! Stay – please to stay. They shoot – they kill. No, you cannot go, you shall not. Yet go! Avenge – avenge! Oh, my so dear Raymond!"

He felt his fingers forcibly opened and as forcibly closed round the butt of a pistol. He felt her hands clinging to him and heard her sobbing whilst she implored him to go and to remain.

"Stay here!" he commanded. "Don't move outside."

Her hands were swept away from his arms and at the breaking of the physical contact her wild emotion subsided. He was gone from the cavern. She knew he was gone. With frantic haste she searched for the entrance, found it, and stumbled along the passage to the Cavern of the Sword.

CHAPTER XXXVI

THE WHEEL

WHEN Lund reached the Cavern of the Sword the red frenzy of impotence, the lurid flickering lights of anger darting through his mind, had dissolved before the ice-cold wind of undeviating purpose. His mind was a small chamber wherein dwelt Raymond Lund, and from this chamber he governed his body as though he sat at the controls of a military tank. And, as the controller of the tank would not suffer personal shock when the machine he drove was struck and battered, so Lund did not feel the impact of rock projections against his body. As in those moments of hand-to-hand fighting during the war, his mind was supreme over his body; he was able to think with extraordinary clarity and amazing rapidity.

The darkness of the Cavern of the Sword was stabbed by sweeping lines of light, revealing sometimes the drab walls, sometimes lighting the stalactite with a thousand lamps of reflections, now and then showing the faces of Lawrence, Larsen, Van Horton, and Helen Van Horton. To Lund they appeared as twittering hens alarmed by a fox. As suddenly as he had started to run, he stopped at the entrance to the cavern.

"Are you sure he's dead?" Van Horton was asking Lawrence in his short, yet deadly calm manner.

"Quite sure. He died like Fred Bennett – neck broken."

"Dere are dose cursed tracks, too," Larsen said, throwing his light on a sand-patch. "It's dat monkey thing loose again. It mus' be, 'cos Snell is chained up."

"Are we sure about that?" Van Horton snapped.

"Who could release him?" argued Lawrence impatiently. "They are self-locking handcuffs with special locks, and, besides, the chains are exceptionally strong. Anyway, we've no time to make sure now. We've got to find out the cause of the shot, and if Snell is loose he's down there through that passage, where we'll find him and fix him."

"If you will be so good as to give me live cartridges and hand me back my automatic, I will lend a hand," Van Horton offered.

"And shoot me in the back?"

"No. I have now other plans which, if adopted, would prove to our mutual benefit."

"There's nothing doing, Van Horton. You'll stay put. And I haven't got your gun."

"Yes, you have. You took it off me the time Bussey disappeared."

Lawrence directed his torch full in the American's face. "You are a liar," he said distinctly.

"I'm not. As it contained the cartridges from which you had extracted the cordite, and therefore was of no use, I had it in my jacket pocket. Someone took it, and that someone was, of course, you, or one of your men acting on your orders."

"By hell! Dat was Snell! 'Member he took my gat. I'm sure he took my gat," Larsen burst out. "He's got Mr. Van Horton's gat with dummy cartridges, so he's de easy guy dat's down de passage."

"Death is all around us, with his hempen ropes –" sang Alfred Tuttman, appearing in the gloom.

"Stop your snivelling!" Lawrence snarled, in a voice so unlike his habitual pleasant drawl that Lund was astonished

"Well, it's a bit thick if a bloke can't sing at his own funeral," growled the newcomer, and from him proceeded the sinister sound of knife-edge hissing along ribbed steel. "I heard a shot, I banged the gong, and I've rushed into the front line, and now you jump on me 'cos I sing my war-song. Anyway, what are we doing here, gathered round a corpse like a lot of crows? Why ain't we up and doing? I'm going to cut somebody's throat before somebody breaks my crimson neck."

"You will stay here on guard, Tuttman," Lawrence said coldly, authority unconsciously revealed in his voice.

"Very good, sir," Tuttman answered, responsive at once to discipline.

"You will stand there, so that you will be able to see along that passage and watch the cavern at the same time. Where is your automatic?"

"In me pocket."

"What use is it to you in your pocket?"

"Oh, it might come in handy after I've got rid of the pig-sticker. I kind of aim straighter with a knife than with a gun."

Lawrence visibly sighed. What was in his mind was never spoken. He was standing with Van Horton, Larsen and Tuttman, close beside the body of Sir Knight, which lay across the entrance of the passage leading to the innermost caverns, when something not unlike a cyclone swirled about them. He heard Helen Van Horton cry out shrilly. A fist crashed against his mouth, sending him down on his back and his head in violent impact with rock. To Tuttman, every light there ran together and jazzed in one terrific pyrotechnic display, before which his stunned mind refused further to function. Van Horton and Larsen met apparently in mid-air, thence to fall to earth in a sitting posture that jarred every nerve in their bodies. A huge figure loomed over the body of Sir Knight. A fallen torch was snatched up and its beam swept from man to man, and beyond and above the unwinking eye of the torch came Lund's voice, gritty with cold hate.

"Now, you swine, I have you," he said slowly. "The first one of you who moves will die quickly. This automatic is not Van Horton's – it has live cartridges in it."

For a second the pistol in his right hand slid into the beam of light. The torch showed Tuttman lying as one dead, Lawrence partly raised on one arm, with his head drooping as though its weight was too heavy for the neck muscles to support, Larsen sitting on the rock floor with his lower jaw hanging loosely, and Van Horton's pale face whilst he crouched as a beast prepared to spring. Against one side of the Cavern of the Sword Helen Van Horton swayed on her feet close beside the shrinking Julia; and on the other side stood Natalie – invisible, as was Helen, in the darkness – one hand pressed over her mouth, the other behind her, supporting her small body against the wall.

Such was the tableau for three interminable seconds. Then with a stunning shock the silence was smashed by the report of an automatic of large calibre. The flash of the discharged cartridge flickered redly, but none saw by its illumination the figure of Blue Everett near the passage leading to the kitchen.

Lund's light went out. The passage of the bullet whipped a press of air against his neck. He was down on hands and knees when Everett fired again, and then the red illumination of the shot showed the passage beyond the body of Sir Knight void of any figure. Doubled up, Raymond was plunging towards the innermost caverns at the risk of dashing out his brains, not daring to press the button of his torch until he judged he had reached the first bend.

Shouts reverberated behind him. They were after him as a pack of hounds – Van Horton, armed with Tuttman's pistol, and Larsen, governed by insensate fury and desire to kill. Their torches lit up brilliantly the passage immediately ahead of them. They were revealed by the beam from a torch held by Blue Everett, following on.

Raymond Lund, knowing that Snell was somewhere in the inky blackness before him, believing him wounded, possibly dead, because the shot heard in the beginning was not fired from the automatic his friend had taken from Van Horton – thereby winning the bet – raced on, now helped by the torch.

He passed the twin water-gushers with flying leaps, jumped across the black yawning orifice of the blow-hole, reached the Junction Cavern. There he dodged the many stalactites, and without hesitation raced into the passage leading to the power-plant.

"Where are you, Bill?" he shouted whilst he ran. And then he strained his hearing to catch the faintest reply. Now he could hear the water falling on the water-wheel with a low hissing roar becoming ever louder as he came nearer.

A minute later his light showed him the wheel. About it was a mass of foaming water. The wheel was revolving at a terrific rate. It was out of gear with the dynamo driving shaft, and its being put out of gear had caused the electric light slowly to expire. The beam from his torch rapidly made an arc. The gear lever on the driving shaft was perpendicular. No sound came from the dynamo, proving that it was not running. There, near the edge of the wide water-pit, lay a man.

It was not Snell. Lund recognised Peter Cuff.

"Snell! Where the devil are you?" he shouted. There was no reply. From the passage behind him came no sound of pursuit. They were creeping upon him.

The beam of his light made a complete circle. He could not see Snell. Horror, anger, grief swept into the chamber of his mind, melting the icy coldness, destroying the calm calculation of the tank-driver. Light! He must have light. He might see Snell deep below in the dreadful water-pit. Fool! Double fool! How could he? He might hear his friend – hear his cries for help.

Springing to the switchboard, he connected the lines with the accumulators. The resultant blaze of light dazzled his eyes so that he stood swaying on his feet, a perfect mark for the creeping gang. The wheel eventually became clearly registered, the spinning water-whitened wheel. It was turning at terrific speed, but not even speed. There was apparently something the matter with the wheel. At a point in every revolution its speed momentarily fell.

There was something fixed to one of the wide cup-shaped paddles, something dark with a blotch of white at one end. Lund stared, fascinated by the wheel, wondering what it was on the paddle that caused its eccentric revolutions. As he had jumped to the switchboard, so now he sprang to the gear lever and pushed it hard towards the dynamo. There followed a grating of metal. The dynamo began to hum, a low musical sound rising rapidly up the scale to a shrill whine. And, as the sound mounted the scale and thinned so the wheel slowed in action, became a thing of labour, chained by power of machinery, pounded by the power of water.

There was a man on the wheel, his arms and legs locked about the iron frame. Even death had not relaxed the muscles. To the very last the mind of the man had governed them from fear of falling into the water-pit.

CHAPTER XXXVII

THE PASSING OF SWEET WILLIAM

TIME no longer was a conscious entity to be assessed and measured. To Raymond Lund, time ceased to be. It was as though he lived outside the government of time. With stupendous detached calmness he gazed on the water-wheel and its dreadful burden, whilst standing at the edge of the fathomless pit. The finer, farther-flung spray fell over him, and in it he saw abstractedly the miniature rainbow made by the electric light.

Was Snell dead? He must be. If he had fallen, or had been thrown, into that pit, the tremendous depth would tear from his body his life. Even so, even had he escaped death miraculously and was down there, swimming in some great pool, there were neither ropes nor any other means of getting him up.

What a man! With his bare hands he had killed six men. Here, in this chamber, had he killed three. The half-caste lay grotesquely, the terrible position of his head indicating how he had died. Morgan on the wheel doubtless had been flung with the ease of a man tossing a ball, and Morgan had clung to the slowly-revolving wheel, being smothered by the pounding water once in every revolution until Snell had thrown the wheel out of gear, when it spun with terrific velocity, and Morgan was drowned.

And Snell had done this thing, had acted alone in order to preserve Lund from – what? That was the question that arose and insistently demanded an answer. Lund could not bring himself to believe his friend had deliberately left him in ignorance of his campaign merely to save him from possible injury. If that was so, what prompted the act?

With lightning quickness Time resumed control of the destinies of mice and men. The proximity of men thirsting to kill leapt into the forefront of present affairs. Lund broke into action after the interval of timelessness, which in reality was a measurable period of a few seconds. It was as though he had been turned into stone at sight of the head of Medusa, and a more powerful god had broken the spell – broken it with a reverberating crack of an automatic pistol.

The report came from some point along the passage. The acoustic properties of the system made the report echo a thousand times, each echo weaker than the last, so that the single shot sounded as the regular tat-tat-tat of a machine-gun mounted on a motor-truck speeding away from the hearer. It informed Lund that someone was continuing the battle opened by Snell, and the only person willing and capable of doing that, other than himself, was Natalie. Natalie might have got another pistol. She had fired that shot, fired it because obviously she was in danger.

Still gripping the torch in his left hand, unconscious that its light no longer was necessary, Raymond Lund raced back the way he had come. He expected to meet members of the gang running to meet him. He met with none – till he arrived at the cavern called the Junction. Into his vision leapt the picture of Snell.

At Lund's feet lay Van Horton. The millionaire's coat – it was his dinner-jacket – was ripped open, the spotless starch-fronted dress shirt was ripped away from his chest, and with extraordinary incuriousness Lund saw that Van Horton's throat was torn almost out. Over against the wall of the cavern lay Larsen. He, too, was dead. Of that there was no doubt, but how he had died was not so clearly indicated.

Beyond Van Horton stood Snell holding at arm's length the thickset form of Everett. Everett's automatic lay close to his feet, and Everett with empty hands was beating on the face of Snell in his last desperate effort to obtain air for his bursting lungs.

Lund suddenly felt nausea. The scene was the acme of brute victory over humanity with all its scientific aids to destruction. Snell was swaying from side to side with pendulum-like steadiness. Everett's movements became ever slower and more feeble, till finally they ceased altogether and the man became limp. No longer did his legs support his weight, and after three seconds Lund was astonished to see both Everett and Snell slowly fall together in the same direction, Everett on his back, Snell on his chest. It seemed that as Sweet William killed Everett, so he himself died.

Walking quite deliberately, Lund stepped over the body of Van Horton and knelt beside that of his friend. He turned Snell over and forced Snell's fingers from Everett's throat, and the act caused Snell to open his closed eyes and smile in his usual dour way. For what seemed an eternity the two looked into each other's eyes. And, when the look was broken, Lund's eyes travelled slowly over the great hairy chest revealed by the torn pyjama jacket, his gaze finally to stop at a point four inches below the heart, whence slowly oozed thick bubble-filled blood.

"I've got mine," Snell said clearly. "But I didn't do so bad, did I, Captain?"

Lund made no comment.

Snell spoke again. "In a way I'm sorry I had to kill Everett and

Bennett and Little. Larsen asked for it a dozen times, and there's less stink in the world now Van Horton's left for parts unknown."

"You ass, Bill! Why didn't you let me in on this game?"

"The Princess became the General just before I corpsed Bussey. I was only the private. Reach me that pistol Everett dropped. Everett's bullet has shorn me of my strength as Samson's hair-cut made him come a thud."

Into the cavern stepped Natalie, followed closely by Julia. The maid looked back nervously, and evidently she was on the verge of panic. Her pretty face was strained, whilst almost automatically she accompanied the Princess to where Lund was kneeling beside his friend. The dead man failed to arouse her interest, so intent was she on something or someone in the passage she had just left. When Natalie fell on her knees beside Lund, Julia stood still, nervously looking back.

When Natalie's deep violet eyes rested on Sweet William, he weakly took the handkerchief from Lund's fingers and tried to hide the wound. He struggled upward, only to sink back on the rocky floor exhausted. Lund removed his coat, and made of it a pillow mechanically, his mind unable to grasp the obvious and positive fact that Snell was near his end.

"Sorry, Marm," Snell said in a whisper. "Sorry! Ought to stand in presence of Royalty. Losing my manners and my grip."

"Mistaire Snell, you so wounded be?"

"Bit of a scratch, Marm. Morgan winged me, but Everett got me good and proper. My fault. I'm getting slow and old."

Gently Natalie moved the great hand away and, lifting the handkerchief, looked at the wound. The bleeding had almost stopped, but all round the wound the flesh was becoming hideously discoloured. Very slowly her fingers relaxed and the handkerchief fell back. For several seconds she looked at Sweet William intently, and in that strange silent communion of those two widely-separated human beings no other ever knew what passed.

"I'm going out, Marm," Snell said quietly to her, as though neither Lund nor Julia was present.

"Yes, Mistaire Snell, I know. Still, we must move you to a couch of more ease. And water we want, Mistaire –"

"I want nothing. There is nothing you can do. His nibs will be along directly. Captain, keep your eyes skinned for Lawrence. There ... I told you. Behind ..."

Raymond Lund looked round preparatory to springing to his feet – looked round to find the muzzle of an automatic within six inches of his head, and beyond it the white, cadaverous features of Alfred Tuttman. At an oblique angle to his vision he saw Earle Lawrence securing and pocketing Everett's fallen pistol.

"Don't move!" Tuttman ordered.

Lawrence stood beside him. His eyes were bloodshot and his face white and drawn. Yet, in spite of his appearance, he was, as always, serenely polite.

"Thank you!" he said, pocketing also the pistol Lund had set down on the floor when he knelt beside Snell. "Now, will you please stand up? You may live if you obey without demur."

Lund was ordered then to walk six paces forward. Whilst he did so, Tuttman backed the same distance. Next Lund was told to turn round, and, doing so, faced where Snell was lying, with Natalie still kneeling beside him and Julia standing near her. Behind Lund was Tuttman. Slowly Lawrence approached, and, standing over Sweet William, gazed down on him.

"So it was you who killed Little and Bennett and Bussey, and Sir Knight and Peter Cuff and Morgan, and Van Horton and Larsen and Everett! Quite a respectable tally."

It was an effort for Snell to speak. There was blood at the corners of his mouth. When he did speak, his voice was very low. "I spared you, Lawrence. I could have got you seven times."

"Tush! You would have got me if the chance had occurred. But it didn't," Lawrence almost sneered. "Now you are trying to persuade me not to shoot you."

Weakly Snell shook his head. "I knew it was no use trying to get you."

"Precisely. I was always ready."

"As I told you before, Lawrence, you were not born to be shot. You were born to be hanged – and hanged you'll be."

"You are very clever, Mister Warder. I don't think I'll be hanged. But if I am, it will be for killing you. Why? Because, whilst I had no objection to your killing the others, I intend to avenge Everett, who was my pal. You look quite done up, Snell, but I am going to make sure of you."

Lawrence was standing facing Lund, on the further side of William Snell. The automatic he held became pointed at Snell's heart. The sudden overwhelming horror of this totally unexpected and callous intent paralysed Raymond Lund, and seemed to turn Natalie to stone. Snell's eyes were calmly centred on the pistol. And then with a shrill cry Julia sprang past the Princess, and, throwing herself on Snell, covered his body with hers. Turning her head, she looked up at Lawrence, screaming:

"No, no! *Mon Dieu! Mon Dieu!* Mine this man is! He is my Beel – my Beel! *Mon Dieu!* Oh, *Mon Dieu! Mon Dieu!*"

Lund saw Snell's right hand rise slowly and begin to stroke Julia's dark shingled hair. The thick fingers were slowly, laboriously combing the strands, showing white among the gleaming strands.

"Get away, you little fool!" snapped Lawrence. "If you don't, I'll fix you too."

"Keel, keel, keel! But not my Beel, not my Beel! *Mon Dieu!* Oh, *Mon Dieu!*" shrieked Julia.

Lund was watching Snell's fingers slowly moving through the Frenchwoman's hair, gently, caressingly, lovingly. He was confounded by the knowledge, the utterly astonishing fact that Julia loved his friend, loved his dear, atrociously ugly, faithful friend. His muscles became taut to permit the spring that would carry him in one bound to the furious devil about to shoot. And then his breathing stopped, caught, held in abeyance by the vision of Snell's slowly moving hand, which abruptly fell to the ground to become still, still as in death. Julia swiftly turned her face from Lawrence to Snell. They could see her looking into her man's face, they heard her wail when she caught his head to hers and broke into a torrent of heartbroken sobs.

With a cry of hate and rage, Raymond Lund crouched to spring. Through a bloodshot veil he saw the man he desired overwhelmingly to kill as Snell had killed. And then a great glaring light shot across his brain. The light went out, followed by the blank darkness of oblivion.

CHAPTER XXXVIII

NATALIE'S ORDEAL

THE terrific blow on the back of the head which Tuttman gave with the butt of his pistol sent Lund pitching forward on his face. Lawrence, uttering an oath, stooped and flung Julia away from William Snell, only to glare into the serene dead face till, with a scream almost animal, Julia sprang back to shield the body with her own.

When again Lawrence stood upright Tuttman was feeling for the beat of Lund's heart, and when Lawrence stepped round Snell and Julia and approached him Tuttman rose to his feet and in his mournful placid manner said: "He's corpsed."

"You saved a cartridge, Tuttman," Lawrence sneered. To Natalie, walking regally towards them, her face as stone, her eyes as the void beyond the stars, he added: "It seems that Your Royal Highness has lost a – er – friend."

She made no reply to his gibe, nor did the fixed, frozen expression of her face alter. Not a glance did she give then to Raymond Lund, nor did she give any indication that to her Alfred Tuttman existed. Coming to stand near the big Australian, she looked up into his face with eyes that seemed to penetrate right through him. When she spoke, her voice was as the tinkle of breaking icicles:

"The Iron Youth! Insult you the youth of Germany, of all the Allies, the so glorious youth who died, when say you were one of them. Of the sewer are you – a rat, a rat of the spirit, a conceit of the buffoon, a thing I would not employ to feed my hounds. A soldier – you! Nay, a rat to feed on rats. A – a man! Nay, a thing, an – oh! what is it? – an abortion!

"In my eyes look. Dare not you? Of the bravery you are void. Dying men you can shoot with courage. An honest woman you cannot look in the eyes; you dare not meet in my eyes the contempt you raise. A man! You dare not shoot me. You dog – no, cur, for a dog's courage have you none. Of a whiteness is your liver. In my eyes you dare not look. No, no! Look not at my ears so small. No – not at my bosom so still. Into my eyes look, you beast, you offspring of hell. Behind me nothing of interest lies, only men dead, men dead, but clean and brave. Look at me, a woman, a woman of littleness, a woman your master, one who stares you out because a cur you are. Go!"

"You are coming on in your English, Princess," jeered Lawrence, his face deathly white with consuming anger.

"Go! Do you me hear? Go!"

Lawrence looked at the awestricken Tuttman. He looked at Natalie, he looked at the scene of death about them, but never even for a second did his eyes meet the eyes of Natalie. As a whipped hound, so he began spiritually to cower before the straight slim figure confronting him. His self-confidence oozed from him as water from a sponge. He felt his stature shrinking even as those terrific unmeetable eyes stripped him of his clothes, revealed him in stark nakedness of soul, showed him to himself as a human abnormality. Then on his burning ears fell the ice-cold blows:

"Did you me hear, beast? Go!"

One supreme effort he made to look into her eyes, managed to focus his vision on the bridge of her nose. That was as near to her eyes as he got. As she had repeatedly informed him, he dared not meet them with his own.

She had him whipped as a mongrel dog, and he knew it. He knew he was a human mongrel, and the knowledge burned him, seared him, tortured him as no torturer of the Inquisition could have done. He felt Tuttman's hand on his sleeve. He made one other – his last-supreme effort to prove his manhood – and failed. With Tuttman he walked out of the Cavern of the Dead.

The Princess heard their retreating footsteps whilst she stood still as a statue, not a tremor in her body, gazing with flaming eyes at the point lately occupied by the face of Earle Lawrence. His and Tuttman's steps finally died away. From the distant cavern came the whine of the dynamo; from close beside her came the heart-tearing sobs of Julia.

Presently Natalie looked down on Raymond Lund. He lay on his chest, his head turned, his face towards the body of Van Horton. One arm was stretched beyond his head; the other was doubled under him. How long she stood looking down on the playmate of – it seemed – years ago, on the man whose open sunny nature had captivated and held her heart, she was not conscious. Every incident of her stay with Sir Henry and Lady Lund, every word of her conversation with Raymond Lund, both at his home and in these caverns, she recalled to mind with an ease that astounded her.

There was blood flowing gently from the ghastly wound on his head. That she thought was strange, for somehow she understood dead men did not bleed. She felt she must do something to stop the bleeding. Her maternal instinct demanded it, commanded her to fall on her knees. The ice about her heart was melting, and panic reared its head. To conquer that she sought for something with which to staunch the bleeding, and with sudden wild abandon, caused not by reason, she ran along the corridor to the twin water-gushers, there partly to rip away a linen petticoat, drench it with water, and fly back to the Cavern of the Dead.

Again kneeling, she sponged the wound in Raymond's head with a portion of the wet linen. With the remainder she made a compress, and this she bound to the wound with strips from another garment.

She wanted to laugh at the futility of her actions. She wanted to let loose the pent-up grief in sobs as wild and as uncontrollable as those of Julia. If only she could! But first she must make her dead comfortable. She robbed Van Horton and Everett of their coats, rolling them into neat pads, which she placed beside Lund's head. Then very gently, as though he had been alive, she turned him over on his back, and slipped the coats beneath his head.

Now as an image of Buddha she sat and watched the calm boyish face; watched motionless, dry-eyed, her mind numb, almost blank. The electric light flared down on him, was reflected by the ivory buttons of his pyjama coat. They twinkled, those buttons – slowly, regularly – and after a little she began to wonder in a detached way why they moved like that. She looked up at the light bulbs, expecting to see them a-swing in the draught. They were fixed and still. It was peculiar, the way those buttons gleamed at intervals.

And then with one swift movement she bent over Lund and slipped her hand inside the jacket. The movement of his beating heart was an electric shock rushing up her arm, surrounding and tingling every nerve in her body. Slowly she withdrew her hand and brushed back the hair from his forehead. His eyes were closed. Perhaps if she kissed the lids they would open.

It was then Natalie cried, but with a sound different from Julia's crying. As Natalie cried it felt as though the ice of a thousand years was melting into water flowing away through her eyes. And, as it flowed, so the warmth of life crept back into her dead heart, reawakened and revived it. Still she cried, and presently Julia knelt beside her, and after a little while Julia touched Natalie on the arm, and Natalie, becoming aware of her, impulsively took Julia in her arms and, comforting her, comforted herself.

Hours passed, eight of them measured by Natalie's watch. Lawrence did not come, nor did he send the deaf and dumb mess-waiter. Tuttman made no appearance, nor did he strike the gong. Helen Van Horton – where was she? At last Natalie induced the maid to stay with Lund whilst she went along to Tuttman and asked for food and drink. Helen's room she found empty. There was no one in the dining-cavern or the kitchen. The electric stoves were cold. She called out for Tuttman, but received no reply. She called for Mrs. Cuff, whom Bussey had added to the kitchen staff, but again there was no reply. Then she wanted to run, but mastered the impulse. It had become clear to her that she and Julia, with the unconscious Lund, had been abandoned.

On the kitchen table stood a coffee-pot full of coffee. Natalie secured two cups and, carrying the pot as well, made her way back through the deserted passages to the Cavern of the Dead. Julia lay asleep beside the form of Raymond Lund.

It was quite a task to waken the maid, but when she had done so Natalie made her drink a cup of the coffee. Then between them they dragged Lund to the Cavern of the Sword and into Helen Van Horton's room, and managed to get him on the American's comfortable bed. Julia was bidden to lie down on her own. Natalie dozed, lying on a settee.

By Natalie's watch forty-eight hours passed. She spent them watching Raymond, and in helping Julia to forage for food and drink. For an hour she listened in at the wireless, when she heard the news of the day given from an Adelaide station, and was undecided whether to be angry or not when nothing was said of her abduction and possible fate. There was a report, however, that the President of the Republic of Rolandia was negotiating a loan of many millions with a group of financiers. Natalie wondered if her ransom was one of the items to be covered by that loan.

Lund regained consciousness when Natalie was asleep and Julia on duty over him. At sight of the light of intelligence in his wide eyes, she rushed to the sleeping Princess and awoke her, to the accompaniment of a torrent of voluble French. Natalie, her face drawn by the hours of watching and fatigue, sank on her knees beside the bed and thrust her hands over the coverlet towards him.

And he said: "I have been ill? I remember. Tuttman felled me. If Your Royal Highness will kindly withdraw, I will get up and dress. I am quite all right now."

He saw with growing amazement her tear-filled eyes, and then gazed at the two small hands and the fingers of them as if in search of him. He heard her sob, and the words she spoke between her sobs vibrated with yearning:

"The – Princess – now – to – the devil – is, Mistaire Lund. Rolandia a President has. Vive le President! Natalie – Miss Natalie – kneels here. Is – is she – always to be – Miss Natalie – Mistaire Lund?"

"Natalie!" he whispered faintly. "Natalie! Oh, Natalie!"

YET Lund's recovery was not so rapid as he had thought and as Natalie had hoped. There followed long hours when he lay in a strange lethargic state staring at the cavern roof with wide expressionless eyes and when Natalie's soft pleadings failed to penetrate his consciousness. With the passing of unnoted hours her strength, both mental and physical, was expended lavishly, and the drain on her small body was revealed in her eyes and in the corners of her mouth.

She came to lean heavily on Julia, finding the maid's experience in this phase of life's rawness much wider than her own. Together they tried to manipulate the electric stoves, and together failed. The necessity for hot water and heated food became a problem of immense magnitude, until Natalie suddenly thought of the likelihood of there being dead bush lying on the plain above.

Princess and maid gathered dead roots and twigs and, taking them below to the kitchen, made a small fire and managed to boil water with which to make soup of meat extract for Lund, and tea for themselves. Abandoned by the gang, helpless because of Lund's helplessness, the Princess leaned on the efficient Julia in the task of nursing Lund and preparing food for themselves, whilst the French girl grew to love the Imperial woman who was so extraordinarily sympathetic, resourceful, and brave.

Sometimes Julia cried almost noiselessly, whereupon Natalie sat with her on the bed or the divan, and with her arm about the maid's waist comforted her in her grief. Julia, at these times, told how she came to love Sweet William during the moments he obeyed Natalie's command to thrash Larsen. Snell became the girl's hero from that hour, and afterwards, when he taught her to play poker and became her friend and protector, they both realised that love united them.

Julia lay sleeping one morning, having sat up beside Lund all night, and Natalie was occupying her chair placed at the foot of his bed – which had been Helen's – so that she could watch his pale face, whilst fervently hoping that the next period of consciousness would be permanent. On the further side of the bed was set the dressing-table with its gold-plated appointments and oval, bevelled mirror. In the mirror Natalie could see the velvet plush curtains concealing the entrance.

Now and then her eyes lifted from the filled pages of Helen Van Horton's extraordinary diary to look idly at the curtains in the mirror. Always she had looked at them with eyes focussed on the pictures in her mind created by the American's experiences up to the time she fled with Lawrence; but now when she gazed into the mirror her eyes froze into a stare, and her skin began to goose-flesh. She saw that the curtains were very narrowly parted by two long white fingers, and above the fingers was a solitary eye, black and glittering.

The shock made her want to scream. She thought first of the prowling gorilla which had been Snell. Then into her mind flashed remembrance of Sir Knight, who lay outside hidden by a blanket. Reason, rushing to her aid, banished the foolish idea of ghosts; yet, when she sprang up and faced about to the curtains, they were, as always, hanging close together and motionless.

For many seconds she stood quite still, her heart beating frantically. She expected – she hardly knew what. Then from some distance away came the sound of something falling with a light metallic crash. It was one of the few occasions in her life that Natalie was frightened, really frightened, and she knew that the longer she remained inactive the more fearful she would become. Snatching up an automatic, which had been found near one of the corpses and for some time had lain neglected on a small table, she passed silently into the Cavern of the Sword, there to stand looking about and listening. Unmistakably there was someone or something in the kitchen. She was creeping along the passage leading thither when she was halted by a mournful voice raised in song:

> "Down among the dead men!
> What care I to-day?
> I'm alive and kicking;
> They've had their little say."

Tuttman! Tuttman had returned. Why? Why? Why?

Tuttman she found bending over a heated stove. "Well?"

Turning round, he found himself faced by the round orifice of an automatic pistol held steadily at a distance from him of six feet.

"Good morning, Your Royal Highness!" he said, calmly deferential.

"What do you here?" Natalie demanded.

"Reported for duty, Marm, an hour ago. Took my discharge from Earle Lawrence two days ago; but, though I got back to the oil-bore all right, it's taken me a long time to find the entrance to these caves. You see, Marm, Mr. Lawrence and party has done a bunk, and when opportunity came I faded away, as all good soldiers do. Here I am. I knew you would require my services. Breakfast is almost ready. The coffee is made."

"You dare here to come after Mistaire Lund you struck down?"

"That couldn't be helped, Marm," Tuttman said earnestly. "Lawrence was going to kill him. Told me so before we entered the Junction Cave to find Mr. Snell and the stiff 'uns. When the chance came I outed Mr. Lund and swore he was dead. Now, didn't I?"

"You struck him to save him?"

"Too right, Marm. Lawrence was seeing red even before he found his friend of years very dead. I did the best I could in the circumstances. I put Mr. Lund comfortably asleep and then escorted Mr. Lawrence and his promised bride off the premises. I would have left the dummy waiter behind, but they wanted him to carry their stuff. Mrs. Cuff, too, they took as companion for Miss Van."

"What do you now?" Natalie whispered, so great was her surprise.

"I'm heating tinned vegetables and meat extract soup for Mr. Lund, Marm. He'll come to, presently, but he wants nourishment. As I said, I've made good coffee, and, as I found Van Horton's liquor store, might I advise the plus of a little brandy?"

"Was it you looking in between the curtains?"

"Yes, Marm."

Natalie fell silent. The pistol was lowered and Tuttman sighed vastly. Then: "To where go the gang?"

"To an unknown destination, Marm, what's left of 'em. Why worry? Mr. Lawrence says to Miss Van Horton: 'Will you marry me, or will you be left behind for the Princess to deal with and hand you over to the police – if she ever gets back to civilisation?' And she says quickly: 'I'll marry you.' I says under my breath: 'Heaven help you, Lawrence, for she'll cut your throat, or poison your beer, and you'll want all the help possible.'"

"So they marry?"

"Yes, Marm."

"Which way – how did they go away?"

"I don't remember, Marm. I've forgotten."

"You tell the lie, eh?"

"Well, Marm, it won't kinda do for me to remember," explained Tuttman patiently. "You see, when I go to bring assistance to get you all back to Cook, I'll be asked quite a lot of questions, and as I was conscripted to cook for the gang and was a prisoner, just as you was, it won't do for me to remember too much."

"Go you for help?"

"Certainly, Marm. We can't stop here for ever." On the pale cadaverous features was a look of surprise at Natalie's doubt.

"But you – of a certainty you will be caught and in prison be placed?"

"Caught! Why, Marm? What for?"

"Of the gang were you."

"Me! Really, Your Royal Highness is mistook. You must have been dreaming. I was, as I said, conscripted. Don't you remember you took pity on a poor kidnapped *chef* and offered him a job in the Palace at Naagrade? You even translated his 'Ode to the Future' into Rolandian. In gratitude for that, in hopes that you let me cook for Your Royal Highness, no matter if you return to Rolandia or remain in Australia, I sneaked away from Lawrence, forfeited my thousand pounds, and go soon enough to bring assistance and a doctor to Mr. Lund."

For almost a minute Natalie gazed at him without speech. He was the most extraordinary man she had ever known. He had, as he said, lost a thousand pounds. He had come back – broken from the gang – and now was willing to serve her and bring help. Well, somehow she had liked him from the first.

"When will you go the help to bring?"

"I'll be ready to leave in a couple of hours," he answered. "I must show the French tart how to work these stoves. Then I must shift Sir Knight further out of the road. You see, it'll take me three days to reach the railway, and then it will be another day, perhaps two, before I can get back. You were dreaming, weren't you, Marm, when you thought I was one of the gang?"

Natalie decided. "Yes, Mistaire Tuttman. Bad did I dream of you. My *chef* you shall become. Prepare breakfast. I starve. Of the cooking Julia is the dud. Give me the soup for Mistaire Lund."

When Tuttman had instructed Julia, when he had filled the larder with baking powder bread and carried many buckets of fresh water from the gusher to the kitchen, when he had removed the body of Sir Knight and prepared food and rations for his long tramp to Cook, it was past noon. Natalie accompanied him to the surface of the vast plain.

"Of time you will lose none, Mistaire Tuttman?" she said.

"I'll have a rescue party and police, doctors, and aeroplanes here in five days at the longest, Marm."

"It is good. Bon voyage!"

"I wish Your Royal Highness *au revoir!*" he said, bowing gallantly. He walked away for a dozen yards, then suddenly turned and came back, and in an appealing voice said: "You'll give me my chance, Marm, won't you?"

Natalie's eyes became soft and shining as sunlight through a veil of rain. "Of a certainty will I," she confirmed. "I will replace the money you surrendered. Of you I will make famous. Your 'Ode to the Future' shall be sung over all the world. It is my word."

Once more Tuttman removed his hat and bowed. There were tears in his eyes, but he was actually smiling. Without further speech he turned and strode rapidly away to the oil-bore.

Watching him beneath her hands, which were shading her eyes from the glare, she felt a delicious lightness of heart. At long last she was free – free of Lawrence and Van Horton, free of the chains of Royalty. For she knew what she was going to do. And whilst she stood there, a dainty figure in a blue dress, with the soft wind playing with her hair, she heard Tuttman singing his own crude doggerel to a lilting, an astoundingly joyous tune. She held her breath to listen:

> "Over the Nullarbor Plain so bright,
> I'm so happy, I might be tight;
> He loves her and she loves him,
> And I'm so gay and full of vim."

His tall swinging figure was half its height when she ran down the steps with eyes like stars, and flew along the passages to Helen's room, there to find Raymond Lund clear-eyed and waiting.

THE END

www.ingramcontent.com/pod-product-compliance
Lightning Source LLC
Chambersburg PA
CBHW030412020726
47493CB00003B/1044